MW00914971

WAR AND SOLACE

A TALE FROM NORVEGR

EDALE LANE

PAST AND PROLOGUE PRESS

CONTENTS

War and Solace: A Tale from Norvegr

By Edale Lane

Published by Past and Prologue Press

Edited by Melodie Romeo

Cover art by Enggar Adirasa

First Edition September 2023

Printed in the United States of America

Created with Vellum

❧ Created with Vellum

ACKNOWLEDGEMENTS

Creating, editing, and publishing a novel is a grand endeavor best not attempted alone. Being an Indie author, I depend on volunteers and paid professionals to assist me in producing the best possible book for you, my readers. I wish to thank my beta reader team of D.K. Griffin, Marguerite Schaffron, Dawn McIntyre, K. ter Horst, and proofreader, Dione Benson, for lending their contributions to the final version of this novel. My loving partner, Johanna White, was with me every step of the way as a sounding board and second set of eyes. Also, I greatly appreciate J. Scott Coatsworth and Stephen Zimmer for their expertise and connections.

CHAPTER 1

Norvegr, along the border of Raumsdal and Firdafylke, spring 643

Tyrdis fought shoulder to shoulder with her brother Erik, fortifying their mighty blue shield wall to repel the enemy's advance. Her leg muscles strained as she lunged her *rönd* against the red and black buckler of some unseen enemy hulk intent on crushing her beneath his weight. She jabbed her spear beneath the row of defenses, hoping to graze his knee or calf with its sharp iron tip while attempting to avoid incurring the same injury herself. Her view was limited to feet grinding into mud and the inside of her shield. Without a helmet, she dared not raise her head in search of a target lest she lose an eye or worse. The shieldmaiden's powerful frame, toughened by over ten years of battle experience, held fast against the onslaught.

Grunts and curses joined the blunt thud of wood against wood and the clinking ring of metal striking metal. Tyrdis and Erik surged forward an inch, digging in and bracing themselves against the onslaught. The man to her other side fell, and blood splashed onto her boots and greaves. Quickly, another shieldmaiden rushed in to fill his spot, reinforcing the wall so it wouldn't break.

"Curse Garold, that useless *dunga!*" Erik muttered under his breath. "He could sooner guide a herd of swine up his own arse than lead warriors to victory."

"Hold the line, Erik," Tyrdis returned. "Blame is irrelevant. We are in the serpent's jaw now."

She knew she was right. Once a battle had begun, the goal became survival, and hopefully, triumph over one's foes.

But Tyrdis had to admit her brother's words also rang true. The first warrior of their band, Garold, was Jarl Raknar's cousin who gained his appointment through nepotism rather than merit. Their king had called for all the jarls to send contingencies to fight in his war against Firdafylke. Being career soldiers in Raknar's hall, Tyrdis and her brother had acted out of honor, duty, and valor to answer the call to face their kingdom's enemy and protect their homeland; however, she had hoped for a more competent leader.

"Even the gods look away," Erik griped. Overhead, clouds blotted out the sun while the dark waters of the fjord slapped impatiently at the rocky shore. The heath on which they battled lay at the terminus of the long, narrow inlet and sloped upward toward a line of trees. Being nestled between steep mountains on three sides, the expansive valley was a prime spot for farming or building a town. Both kings contended over this stretch of land, but politics were as irrelevant to the shieldmaiden as the sheep and goats that probably grazed here yesterday. She was steadfast in her dedication to service, just as her father had trained her to be.

A roar of battle cries and clamor of stampeding troops arose from behind. Tyrdis's long, blonde braids whipped around her head as she spun to glance over her shoulder. A second wave of enemy warriors had emerged from the trees and rushed toward their exposed rear.

"Circle up!" she shouted to their outnumbered band. Her stony glare found Garold, slack-jawed and pale, shuffling toward the center of the ring.

"Tortoise formation!" Garold called out in the high pitch of a screaming mare. Their ranks closed in around the back, but Tyrdis could easily deduce the slim odds they had of turning the tide.

However, there was a chance. If they formed a spear tip aimed at the weakest arc of Firdafylke's circle, they could punch through and shift to individual combat as they executed an orderly retreat up the slope. Once they commanded the high ground, a runner could race to the nearby town of Sæladalr. Jarl Niklaus Ivarson would surely send reinforcements.

Prideful arrogance on Garold's part was the only reason Niklaus's warriors hadn't joined them—that and the fact Garold hadn't properly scouted the enemy to determine their numbers. She could imagine his faulty thought process: *'Oh, look—red and black shields! Let's go bash them into oblivion and then head to the mead hall for cheers, beers, and women.'* Tyrdis made a mental note to inform Jarl Raknar how poorly his cousin had performed—if she got out of this battle in one piece.

She took a step back and lifted her head to survey the battlefield and size up the situation. Firdafylke outnumbered them two to one, though both had suffered casualties. Identifying the weak link, she weaved her way through the second row of warriors to the midpoint, where Garold stood, sweating in shock and dismay.

"There," Tyrdis pointed. "We pierce their line and free ourselves from this trap. Give Erik and I ten warriors to cover our retreat while you and the others carry our wounded to safety in the hills. Then we can send for Jarl Niklaus to bring his army, and we will crush them together."

"You wish me to crawl on my belly to Niklaus for help?" he sneered. "Go back to your spot. I have the situation under control."

Even as Garold defied her common sense, a volley of arrows from enemy archers rained into their midst. Shields popped up for cover but not before two of their number were injured and a third fell from a shot to the chest. When a second volley sent arrows near Garold's feet, he barked the command, "Point, here!" He aimed the tip of his sword at the weak place in the line Tyrdis had indicated. "Charge!"

And they were off, hacking, pushing, and piercing their way to safety, punching a hole in the enemy line. As they pealed through, an open field beckoning them to safety, Tyrdis, Erik, and a dozen other stalwart fighters turned to engage the pursuing forces.

At once, Tyrdis was face to face with a barrel-chested, bearded fellow with a spear in one hand and a sword in the other. She blocked his lance with her rönd and thrust her spear into the belly of a second red shield who attacked her flank. Tyrdis didn't own an expensive sword, but on her belt were a battleaxe and a seax, a type of long knife; she grabbed the axe. The two exchanged a few blows while Tyrdis positioned herself uphill from her taller opponent. When his wooden shield shattered under the onslaught of her weapon, she pressed her advantage and buried its iron head in his chest.

Almost immediately, another attacker was upon her. Using superior footwork and well-rehearsed tactics, she made short order of him as well. She retreated a few yards, scanned for her fellow Raumsdalers, and spotted her brother fending off two challengers. Then a wiry young fellow with a scant beard and mustache matching his medium brown braid hopped in front of her. The man was no larger than she and held his weapon out with the inexperience of a gawky youth presenting flowers to a girl instead of that of a seasoned warrior sizing up their foe. She batted away his first attempt at an attack and pinned him with a stern stare.

"Be gone," she commanded. "You are an inferior fighter and pose no challenge. Do not make your mother cry."

"Shieldmaiden!" he retorted in anger. "Your arrogance surpasses that of a king." He threw another swing with his axe, putting himself off balance with the over extension. Tyrdis sidestepped it and blocked a second warrior's strike with her shield, then sliced the new foe with a swipe of her axe.

When she glanced back at the youth, his seax was in mid-swing. Following through with her weapon, she inflicted a grave wound that drove him to his knees in disbelief. "Now stay down."

Tyrdis spun to face a warrior and shieldmaiden who attacked her at once. The bulky soldier's hammer shattered her shield, sending harsh vibrations through her arm while she held off the woman's blow with her battleaxe. Dropping the bits of shield, she backstepped and drew her short-bladed seax, facing her foes with a weapon in each hand.

Around her roared the din of battle, even as fire rushed through her veins flooding her with strength. Tyrdis was not distracted by war cries or wails of anguish, or those who rushed past or fell to the ground. The battle was a blur and her vision narrowed to the two enemies who stood between her and another sunrise. Her reflexes were second nature as if her body inherently knew what to do. Each action and reaction were as easy as strolling through town or pulling on her clothing. She could do it in the pitch of night or when half asleep. Only now, the shieldmaiden was alert and cunning, unwavering in her purpose and unyielding in her determination. She dispatched the pair in moments, leaving their bodies a bloody warning to the next who may try to defeat her.

"Fall back!" Garold yelled. She glanced over her shoulder at what remained of their fighting band fleeing in a disorderly free-for-all, leaving their fallen comrades behind. And many yards ahead of the others ran Garold without so much as a weapon in his hands. Her heart hardened against the dishonorable first warrior as if he was a snake from Firdafylke. Oh, she would tell the jarl about this.

Hearing a moan, Tyrdis spun to her left to spy her countryman Thorgil struggling to rise, his hand pressed to a gaping wound issuing blood.

"Thorgil, make haste," she called and started toward him to lend aid.

Suddenly, Tyrdis was struck from behind, a powerful blow that propelled her forward, and she hit the ground face first, dirt and grass filling her mouth as she gasped to catch her breath. The pain was far worse than she had known before, and she was no stranger to injuries. She felt sick and light-headed and completely unnatural. She tried pushing up from the ground, but her body was like lead. Rolling onto her left side, the warrior woman glanced toward the source of her pain. The blood-soaked tip of a spear poked through her abdomen to the right of center, alerting her to the shocking revelation she had been impaled.

Tyrdis blinked and reached a hand to the wound, wondering what to do about it. She was in no condition to run. The shaft was too thick to break, and she knew the spear would be the length of a man's height or more. She took in the surreal sight of her lifeblood pouring from the puncture, pooling on the ground beneath her. Was this how it would end? Would Valhalla's gates be the next sight she beheld? No. The Valkyries would come for her and place her on one of their winged horses to deliver her safely to Odin's hall.

Maybe it will be Brunhilde herself, flying on Aragorn's back, carrying her enchanted spear, Dragonfang. Would she favor me? she wondered.

Tyrdis had never known love; she had been too busy perfecting the art of warfare, hammering her body into supremacy, and proving herself worthy. And, besides, who would she have loved? Men were acceptable, but she did not feel the lust of attraction for their rugged bodies or careless ways. Women were the fairer sex, yet none had cast a wishful eye in her direction. Tyrdis had determined love was a commodity she could live without, one that would surely prove to be a weakness, and it was her goal to be the strongest, most honorable, fearless warrior in all Raumsdal.

And yet, as she considered she may not see the next sunrise, all she could think about was missing out on love—knowing a woman's touch, enjoying the ecstasy she had heard others speak about. It was silly. There were more important things, like ... *where is Erik?*

Without warning, a heavy boot stomped onto Tyrdis's back, planting her face into the soil again. She cried out in shock as he tugged the spear through her body, leaving a gaping tunnel in its wake.

"Mangy Raumsdal cur!" he spat in ire. To add insult to injury, he snatched up her axe and seax, leaving her without a weapon to grasp. "I hope you rot." The crunch of his boots marched away.

Weak, cold, and engulfed in sorrow, Tyrdis closed her eyes and prayed. *Odin, Allfather, chief of the gods: my enemy left me no weapon, but you saw them in my hands. Freya, will you choose me for Folkvang instead? While I revel in the thought of seeing* Ásgarðr, *I'll not release this life so easily. My country needs protection. Let me live to see this war won. I know the gods take no sides in the affairs of men, but I believe there is more for me to accomplish in this world before moving to the next. Grant me your favor, and I shall not disappoint you.*

Everything seemed as if it lay far in the distance behind a veil of mist. Clouds still dimmed the springtime sky, only now her vision appeared as dark as twilight. The world sounded as if her head was underwater, and her powerful body hadn't the strength to move. Tyrdis followed her breathing, listening to her heartbeat, and realized she still clung to *Miðgarðr,* but for how long she couldn't say.

CHAPTER 2

Sæladalr, Raumsdal town near the Firdafylke border, shortly after the battle

"*H*ere, Svanhild," Adelle said as she placed a lathed wooden cup of steaming liquid in her little girl's hands. "Take this tea to Gyda and don't spill any; it's hot."

"I won't spill, Mama." Svanhild carefully conveyed the tea from the stone hearth across the longhouse to the bed where Gyda lay propped up by down-stuffed pillows on soft furs.

Adelle's kind, brown eyes followed her daughter with loving pride. Though she was only seven years old, Svanhild had started assisting in her work as the village *grædari*, one who uses herbs, medicines, and traditional methods to treat the sick. If someone broke their arm or leg, Adelle set it for them. If they contracted a fever, needed aid with childbirth, or were injured in an accident, she treated them until they were better. And most importantly to the community, she tended to warriors' wounds, repairing damaged bodies so they could return to battle and hack off someone else's limbs, until at last the patient would be beyond saving. It was a cultural ritual she loathed.

Joren, a young man both gentle and smart, was Adelle's official apprentice and could already assess a patient and apply the appropriate remedy without her constant supervision, but he was busy changing the blankets on the empty beds. With her sixteen-year-old son, Runar, following Jarl Niklaus Ivarson around trying to prove himself as a warrior—stupidity he inherited from his father—Svanhild had become the center of Adelle's world. The babe Adelle had borne between them had died suddenly as an infant for no apparent reason, fueling her commitment to become the most effectual healer in all Raumsdal.

Love flooding her heart for the little girl with honey hair and a generous spirit, Adelle took a glance around the hospice where she and Svanhild lived and cared for their patients. The lodgepole structure with plank siding wasn't as massive as the jarl's longhouse but more than twice the size of an average home. It consisted of a single rectangular room with a central fireplace and beds perpendicular to the long walls rather than the typical benches running alongside them. This was to give the healer free access to both sides of the patient.

A wide door opened across from the fireplace, and the wall opposite it housed rows of shelves containing jars of dried herbs, salves, ointments, candles, and sundry medicines. Beneath the shelves stood a table bearing rolls of bandages, tools, and implements Adelle used in her practice. Cooking pots hung from hooks, clothing was stowed away in chests, and dolls and toys littered Svanhild's bed beside her own. High on the A-frame ends, she had installed air vents, which many houses did without. Adelle understood the vital properties of fresh air contrasted with the poisonous nature of foul air.

Behind the hospice, which had been erected close enough to town to see it yet far enough away to protect citizens from the spread of disease, were a yardhouse and a covered extension adjacent to the back wall shielding wash tubs from rain and snow. Adelle had been taught cleanliness was essential to the healing process, with which the spiritual leaders agreed. Sæladalr didn't have a hot spring, but the town still boasted a bathhouse that saw frequent use as the Norse people enjoyed a warm bath in fragrant water. She used these tubs mainly to wash wound dressings, blankets, and clothes while she and Joren would sponge-bathe the patients.

"Thank you, child," Gyda said as she took the cup. The old woman blew on the tea before daring a sip.

"You must finish the cup," Adelle ordered. "If you do as I say, you'll be back home spoiling your grandchildren in no time."

Gyda's smile may have been missing a tooth but not its shine.

"The beds are all ready for new patients," Joren declared as he sauntered over to a chair at the table where he sat and stretched. Sandy hair fell around an oval face adorned by a wispy beard. His eyes were the blue common to the Norse people, though he was smaller than most young men his age.

"Don't be trying to pretend your back hurts," Adelle chided with a disapproving look. "I was the one up all night with Grith, listening to him whine like a scolded pup with his gout." She had treated his swollen foot and knobby ankle with an extract made from crocus corms. It was a highly effective treatment—if the ornery blacksmith would consent to take it regularly rather than wait for a full-blown flare. *Men!*

"Yes, but I was up early this morning chopping wood for the fire to boil the water to wash the blankets," he retorted, pointing a playful finger in her direction. As she passed nearby, he reached out to point at the colorful beads dangling below her throat. "Where'd you get those? They're new."

"Helga gave them to me as payment for setting her son's broken leg." Stopping, Adelle brushed the gift with delicate fingertips, glancing down at it. Her light brown hair was tied in a casual knot, befitting her efficient nature. Because of frequent bloodstains, to be practical she wore simple and inexpensive clothing. Today that meant a blue apron pinned with two bronze broaches over a fog gray underdress, its sleeves rolled to her elbows.

"It's pretty," he commented, "but a couple of chickens would have been more valuable."

"People trade what they can, Joren," she explained in the manner of a mentor. "Potters give me clay jars; sheepherders, wool; fishermen, fish— you get the idea. Warriors are the worst," she groaned, rolling a sour gaze to the open-framed rafters. "They'll ask, 'Who do you want killed?' Although one did actually present me with a fabulous bearskin which I keep on my bed. The point is, what we do is a higher calling, not a means to gain wealth. You must make peace with that or find another profession."

"No, I understand," he answered. "I do feel called."

When Joren met her gaze, she wondered if his slight build, short stature, or weak eyesight provided the stimulus for his calling more so than a vision or word from the gods. In a society that valued physical strength above all else, such a man must turn to the gods, either as a *gothi*, musician, skald, or healer. Some brewers of ale and fermenters of mead were not brawny men, but to perform the labor of a farmer, command a fishing boat on rough seas, or take up arms as a fighter required attributes her apprentice lacked. In Adelle's eyes, Joren's only shortcoming was his low self-esteem.

"I like Mama's pretty necklace." Adelle beamed down at Svanhild, who had rejoined them after setting the empty teacup on a hearthstone. "It will last longer than a chicken, and one day when I'm grown up maybe I can wear it."

"See?" Adelle raised a brow and the corner of her mouth to Joren. "Value lies in the beholder's eyes."

Sounds from outside caught her attention, and Adelle hurried to the open door, Joren following on her heels.

"Grædari!" a lanky youth cried out as he rushed toward the hospice. "Wounded from the battle."

"Another battle?" she muttered half to herself. "Bring them in quickly."

Men and women from the village carried three litters while two more of the injured soldiers walked beside them under their own power. A tall, red-haired man with a wild, wiry beard leaned on a staff, hopping on one foot, while the shorter, dark-haired fellow with a bloody cloth wrapped around his head cradled a misshapen arm that dripped a trail of blood behind him.

"We were routed," the ginger warrior grumbled in disgust.

Suddenly, Adelle's heart leaped into her throat as she thought of Runar. "Jarl Niklaus's forces?" She waited breathlessly for his reply.

"No," he answered as they filed into the shelter of her abode. "We are Jarl Raknar's men from the north. Our first warrior in charge ran off and left us behind. Repair my leg so I can chop off one of his."

How typical! she thought as she scowled at him.

"Sit over there, you two," Adelle instructed, pointing to the far end of the room. "Put those more seriously injured on these beds."

The folks carrying the litters did as Adelle asked, leaving the pallets along with the patients on the beds. "They look bad," a stout woman commented with dismay. She exchanged a look of concern with the healer. "I'm glad they aren't our brothers and sister." Bowing her head, she and the others exited the house.

Seeing the volume of blood and gaping flesh, Adelle turned to Svanhild and took her by the shoulders. "Go to the mead hall and tell them the grædari needs the strongest drink they have and bring me two jugs of it."

With the gravity of the situation reflected in her somber eyes, the little girl sped out the door behind the others. Adelle turned her attention to the victims of war.

With a quick assessment, the experienced healer determined all three had suffered serious damage, but the gaping hole in the woman's side was the most immediately life-threatening. "Joren, see to those two," she commanded. "Address the older warrior's wounds first, then the younger one. You know what to do."

His expression betrayed his doubt, and he hesitated before moving.

"Clean the affected areas, apply a compress; if necessary, cauterize. Then be liberal with the wound salve. I'll double-check your work if you like, but I must tend to her immediately. Do it, now!" Her tone carried the weight of a troop commander on the battlefield, and he hastened to obey.

Adelle focused her attention on the shieldmaiden bleeding out before her. First, she unfastened her belt and dropped it to the floor. Then she cut away the flimsy, gray wool gambeson which had failed to protect the combatant, baring the crimson-soaked skin beneath it. She had never seen a woman with such well-defined abdominal muscles, which surely had helped keep her alive. As she wiped a damp cloth around her torn flesh, the woman moaned and tried to push herself up.

"Lie still," Adelle ordered. She shifted her gaze to the warrior woman's face, which was twisted in pain. Sweat beaded across a forehead framed with blonde braids. When she blinked open her blue-green eyes, Adelle sucked in a breath at how singularly stunning they were to behold, even in their dazed state.

"Erik." The woman spoke the name and glanced around toward the other wounded. A veil of uncertainty clouded her expression as her breathing came more rapidly. "Where's my brother?"

"I don't know," Adelle answered, placing a firm hand on the woman's shoulder to return her to a reclining position. "We'll find him later. Right now, I must treat you or you'll die. Then you won't find him until he joins you in Valhalla."

Her words seemed to comfort her patient, and she relaxed, her lids falling shut.

"My daughter has gone for more alcohol, but, for now, I'll need you to bite on this leather strap," she said. "You've been run through with a spear."

"Indeed," the woman concurred impatiently.

Adelle pressed the folded cloth over the anterior end of the chasm in her side. "Hold this as firmly as you can."

The shieldmaiden's hands clamped over hers with more strength than Adelle had expected, and she wiggled hers free. She nudged through a barrel of collected dowels, rods, and metal bars until she found a thick, iron blank and thrust it into the fire. When she returned to her patient, she found her with the bloody cloth still tight to her side.

"I must cauterize your wound to stop the bleeding," she explained, "and not on the surface alone. My inspection concludes no major organs were pierced and your muscles have held their shape quite well, but the internal vessels must be cut off also, or you will continue to bleed on the inside and die anyway. I'll be thrusting the hot iron through the channel dug by the spear, and it will be extremely painful."

The woman raised her lids and caught her in an unyielding gaze. Through gritted teeth, she declared, "Pain is irrelevant."

The statement threw Adelle off guard. "Pain is very relevant," she corrected. "It is an important indicator to tell us something is wrong with our bodies, and we must give it our attention. To ignore it would be detrimental to our wellbeing."

"Giving in to pain is a sign of weakness and can get one killed in combat. Do what you must and do not be concerned with my discomfort."

Adelle wasn't certain whether this woman was to be admired for her courage or dismissed as having lost her sanity. With a confused shake of her head, she went to retrieve the hot iron from the firepit. She returned, holding it with two padded mitts sewn from a dead warrior's gambeson.

"My name is Adelle," she said, drawing her patient's attention. "And you are?"

"Tyrdis Vignirdottir, from Heilagrfjord."

Adelle touched Tyrdis's hands, wet with warm blood, and eased them aside, tossing the saturated rag into a bucket. "Bite on the leather strip now."

Without moving her gaze, Tyrdis clamped her teeth over the strap and Adelle plunged the rod through her wound. The smell of burning flesh singed her nostrils. Tyrdis strained against the pain, her fists tugging on the poles of her litter. Then her body went limp as she passed out again.

Adelle had treated countless agonizing injuries caused by carelessness, ill-fate, or the darker nature of man in her years as a healer. Few men, much less a woman, had ever displayed such stoic behavior when being inflicted with tremendous torture. Yet Adelle understood a great truth long scoffed at by the menfolk: women's bodies were designed to endure more pain and still keep going.

She pulled the rod out and retrieved a second iron from the fire, this one with a flat, square end. Adelle used it to burn the top entrance of the wound. She carefully rolled Tyrdis on her side and branded the back of the hole, sealing it from further bleeding. If fate was kind, the warrior would be left with a horrendous scar and tale of valor to go with it. If not, and Tyrdis had already lost too much blood, she had little time left for this world.

Adelle applied a healing balm to both sides of the trauma and then wrapped a bandage around Tyrdis's abdomen. She would have to wake her soon to ensure she received as many liquids as possible to aid her body in producing more blood. Her patient would be weak for a long time, but preventing infection was her acute concern. Many an injured person seemed to be improving, only to succumb to raging fever days or weeks later.

Called to medicine from a deep-set desire to heal and provide solace to the afflicted, Adelle always prayed to Eir for those under her care to live. She understood the gift of healing came from the gods, but sometimes a person was fated to die, and no amount of expertise on her part could save them. Something about Tyrdis felt different. She represented everything Adelle opposed, yet there was something extraordinary in the perfection of her physical form, her defiant attitude, and her exceptional eyes.

Eir, healer to the gods, hear my prayer. Send your restorative energy to our realm. Touch Tyrdis with your seidr. Please, let her live.

13

CHAPTER 3

"*H*ey, I'm in real pain over here," called the dark-haired warrior who cradled his hurt arm.

Adelle turned away from Tyrdis to her other patients. There was nothing more to be done right now, and the woman needed rest.

Svanhild caught Adelle's attention as she returned lugging two large jugs which she set down just inside the doorway. "These are so heavy!"

"Thank you, honey." She took a few steps and stroked her daughter's hair with an approving smile. "And you were strong enough to bring them all the way from town." She followed Svanhild's worried gaze around the room where the coppery odor of blood hung thick. "Now, fill the kettle and hang it over the fire. We need to brew more medicinal tea for our patients to drink."

"Yes, Mama," she replied obediently and went to it.

"You need to check what I've done for these two men," Joren said from where he stood tentatively between their pallets.

"I'll be right there," she assured him. "First, strong drink for these fellows' pain, and I need to assess their wounds."

"Praise Thor!" the big man with the red beard cheered. "It's about bloody time."

"Patience is a necessary virtue in this world, my friend," Adelle answered as she brought a jug and two wooden cups to the men.

"My arm looks bad, and I can't feel my hand at all," the smaller ambulatory patient stated with a fearful expression.

Adelle handed them their drinks and pulled back the shredded sleeve of his tunic. A sick sensation of anguish washed through her at the sight of his mangled limb. Muscles and sinews were lacerated to the broken bones that splintered beneath them. The tourniquet tied above his elbow had kept the blood flow to a minimum, but she had dealt with this kind of injury far too often.

She laid a hand on his shoulder and stared him square in his searching eyes. "What is your name, soldier?"

"Myrbrandr."

"Are you a brave and resilient warrior?" she asked in a timbre of kindness.

He swallowed and raised his chin. "On Thor's hammer, I am."

Adelle nodded. "Myrbrandr, your arm cannot be repaired; the damage is too great. If you want to live, I will have to amputate it."

Horror consumed his visage as his jaw fell limp. "But surely you can do something," he uttered, clinging to a thread of hope.

"It is practically severed in three places," she explained. "Not only will it be entirely useless and cause you nothing but pain, but puss will set in and turn to gangrene. The flesh-killing menace will spread into the healthy parts of your body, and you will die. The only cure, your only choice other than death, is to remove what's left of your arm with a clean chop of a red-hot blade. I'm sorry, Myrbrandr. You think about it while I see to your friend."

Leaving the man to grieve and come to terms with the consequences of war, she pivoted to the tall, red-haired fellow and examined his leg.

"What is your name?"

Adelle couldn't remember the name of every patient who moved through her hospice, but she wanted to personalize each one, to give them the feeling she cared about them, which she did. She only actually knew people from her village and a few in Skeggen, the central town where King Gustav Ironside had his fortress. Having relatives there, she usually visited once a year. She may well have forgotten these warriors' names by winter, but she would know them while they remained under her care.

"Roar the Red," he replied, "and you better not have the same news for me as you did for Myrbrandr."

"The gods have smiled on you, Roar," she said. "I believe I can save your leg. As for your temperament, that is up to your wife."

He howled with laughter and slapped Adelle on the shoulder. "Believe me, healer—she has tried!"

Adelle cleaned his leg, set the simple fracture, and stitched up the long gash. Then she applied a poultice and wrapped it in a bandage.

"What about these men?" Joren reminded her he was waiting.

"The water is hot for tea," Svanhild called and looked at her expectantly.

"Thank you, precious. Get down the blue and white striped jar and put a measure into each of two cups, then pour in the water for it to steep."

Adelle made her way over to her apprentice to examine his work. "This gash requires stitching," she said as she pointed at the younger man's side.

"I was waiting for your approval," he answered nervously. "I didn't want to have to pull them out if I missed something."

She pulled back the folds of skin and muscle, then leaned in to sniff the area. Resuming her posture, she pointed. "Smell the cut." Joren followed her instruction, then gave her a questioning look. "Do you smell bile?"

"No," he answered. "Only blood and sweat."

"Then once you have cleaned the gash to ensure no dirt remain lodged inside, it is ready to sew the skin back together. If you smell bile, however, it must be drained first, and an elixir dropped in to hopefully counteract the harmful issue. Once I even reached a needle and thread into the body cavity to stitch together a sliced piece of viscera before moving on to the external damage. A man can live with one good lung or kidney, but a leaking bowel will poison him to death in a matter of days."

Adelle often would feed a patient with a gut wound onion or leek soup, then sniff for the pungent odor, but it would take time for the liquid to pass through his system. She feared this man may bleed to death before such a method rendered its result.

Joren listened intently and nodded. "Shall I sew up his side now?"

"Yes, but tell me about the other man's trauma first," she said, shifting her attention to the second patient.

"I treated his deep cuts with the honey ointment and bandaged them, but he has two that required more attention." Joren pulled back a sliced portion of the man's gambeson to reveal a reed-sized hole in his shoulder, the surrounding flesh already an angry red. "It looks like an arrow wound, which he must have pulled out himself. His breathing sounds clear, so I don't believe it hit his lung. And over here."

Adelle inspected his shoulder, noting it was not pierced all the way through, while her apprentice positioned himself on the other side of the bed. She agreed with his conclusion. "The bleeding has slowed, and I don't think cauterizing will be necessary here. A few stitches and a poultice will heal faster."

Joren nodded. "This side of his chest has been sliced and ribs grazed, but, once again, his breathing is clear," he reported. "I am more concerned about his head wound. It is swelling, and I have applied pressure and a tight bandage, but it continues to bleed."

"Svanhild?" Adelle called and instantly the little girl was by her side.

"Yes, Mama?"

"Gather the pillows from the empty beds and bring them here," she instructed, and Svanhild hurried to comply.

"First, we need to elevate his head to slow the bleeding by having it above the level of his heart," Adelle instructed. "I have found that applying snow to swollen body parts reduces the inflammation and discomfort to the patient."

"But spring is well underway," Joren responded. "Where will we get snow?"

"Short of sending someone up the mountain, there is a snowmelt stream that flows into the fjord not far from here."

"I know where it is," Svanhild announced as she returned with the pillows. Joren helped Adelle place them under the warrior's head and shoulders.

"I do not want you going alone," Adelle said to her in an authoritative tone. "There could still be Firdafylke soldiers in the area."

"The cold numbs the pain, right?" asked a voice from behind.

Adelle glanced over her shoulder at Myrbrandr who stood from the bed where he had been sitting. "Yes."

"The water in that stream will be almost freezing still," he said. "If you'll wrap my arm in a sling, I'll go with the girl and bring back a bucketful. It may help me as well."

"Very true," she answered. But Adelle hesitated. Was this one-armed casualty capable of protecting Svanhild? She thought not.

"Thank you, Myrbrandr, but I'll find someone else. You need to rest and drink the tea Svanhild brewed. Have you thought about what I said?"

"Yes." He plopped back onto the bed, wincing at the jarring landing, and dropped his gaze to the floor. "We could try to clean and bandage my arm ... wait and see if the gangrene comes first, couldn't we?"

"We could," she concurred, "but there is little I can do for your pain besides giving you mead and willow bark tea."

He nodded. "It's very painful, and I can't move it, but I'd like to try to save my arm."

"I'll go for the icy water," Joren volunteered, "if you'll do these men's stitching. Svanhild doesn't need to show me; I know where it is."

Adelle was about to go herself, but, as unimposing as Joren was, he would possess more strength than she did to bring back full pails. She agreed with a nod. "Watch out for stray warriors who may be lurking about."

Joren set off with two empty buckets, and Adelle gathered her needle and thread. The man with the abdominal wound woke up while she made the stitches, and he moved, causing her needlessly to prick him with her needle.

"Lie still," Adelle commanded, drawing his attention to her.

"Where am I?" The stranger's voice rang with alarm as his wide eyes searched the house.

"I am Adelle, the grædari of Sæladalr, and you are in my hospice," she answered cordially. "You suffered a severe injury in battle, and I am tending to it. If you do not lie still, you could hurt yourself more."

"I'm in Raumsdal?" His hands fisted and released at his sides and his breathing raced.

"Yes," she answered in a calm tone. "Do not fear. This is a house under the protection of Eir, and no harm will come to you." Adelle had suspected by his clothing he was not a member of the other warriors' troop.

Her patient raised his head to look down at what she was doing.

"Hey, you aren't one of our group," Roar barked with disapproval in his manner.

The wounded man peered across the room at Roar, who, being older and burlier than he, could have crushed him with ease, despite having a broken leg.

"What is your name?" Adelle asked, drawing his attention back to her. She read the uncertainty in his wide eyes.

"Birger," he answered.

"Birger, you say?" Roar retorted. "You needn't worry about me. I don't bother with insects. I only challenge real men."

"Leave him alone, Roar," Myrbrandr muttered. "We have bigger things to worry about than a gut-cut Firdafylker who'll probably die all on his own."

Birger swallowed and fixed Adelle with a pleading gaze. "Is it true? Am I going to die?"

"Not if you'll lie still and do what I tell you." This time there was a sharp irritation in Adelle's tone. Her next words were directed at the two warriors across the room. "You two tend to your own problems. There is no war inside my hospice, no taking of sides, no taunts or jeers. I have taken the oath of a healer but Odin himself could not save you if you cause trouble here. Is that clear?"

"As a mountain stream," Roar answered.

Once Adelle had finished stitching both men's gashes, cleansing the affected areas with a wash of wine, leeks, and garlic, rubbing on a soothing, honey balm infused with crushed cannabis seeds, and bandaging them, she paused to take a breath. Noticing Svanhild sitting beside Tyrdis's bed, she walked over and wrapped her arms around her daughter.

"You were a good helper today," she said, realizing how tired she suddenly felt.

Svanhild stared at the shieldmaiden with an expression too grave to mar the face of a child. "Is she going to die?"

Adelle gazed at Tyrdis as she slept, the raw, twisted look of agony in her aspect as her muscles twitched and tensed of their own accord in restlessness. The chiseled cheekbones, robust jawline, broad forehead, and straight nose of her symmetrical face gave it a pleasing appearance, and her full lips, though tinted with dried blood, allowed Adelle to imagine how she would look on a good day. Then she recalled peering into the depths of her singular eyes and had to turn away.

With a kiss to the top of Svanhild's head, she answered, "I hope not, honeybee. She's young and strong; she may pull through."

"She looks strong," her daughter agreed. "Mama, I thought all the warriors were men, like Papa was. Why was she in the battle?"

With a worn-out sigh, Adelle hugged Svanhild closer, daring to glance back at Tyrdis. "Some women are also warriors. They're called shield-maidens, and while most stay back to support the men who are on the front lines, I suspect this one led the charge. It just goes to show, Svanhild —it's not only men who possess more aggression than compassion, or more muscle than common sense. Women can be misguided too."

CHAPTER 4

*V*ague awareness of her surroundings teased Tyrdis—the smells of sweat, blood, herbs, and the sweet smoke from the fire, along with old timber and wet wool. The muffled sounds of people's voices, footsteps, the tap of a wooden cup on a tabletop, and a door creaking came to life in her ears. Her fingertips awoke to smooth linen and soft fur beneath them. Then, with the powerful thrust of one being knocked from a horse, the pain struck her side. It was tremendous and deep, burning and aching, throbbing her into full consciousness.

For an instant, the battle replayed itself in her mind, and she recalled the shock of the spear from behind, piercing her back to pin her to the ground, and her foe yanking it from her body as she lay in agony. *Pain is irrelevant,* she reminded herself. Another voice—an unfamiliar, kind voice—rattled around in her fuzzy memory. *"Pain is very relevant."*

Prying open her lids, Tyrdis beheld a child's sweet face besieged with freckles. "Mama, she's waking up!" the girl called excitedly, setting her honey-colored hair bouncing about her shoulders and her bright, brown eyes dancing with delight.

Tyrdis realized at once how dry her mouth was as she tried to speak. "Grædari," was all she could muster.

The attractive woman who had tended her upon her arrival appeared at her side with a cup of tea. "Here, sip this."

She slid a hand behind Tyrdis's neck and lifted her head, touching the smooth rim of the wooden cup to her lips. It was warm, not too hot, and, while pungent with herbs, indeed came as a welcome blessing. She drank, letting the liquid soothe her throat and infuse her with vitality.

Tyrdis fixed her gaze on the healer and tried speaking again. "Where ...?"

"You're in my hospice." She sat on the side of the bed and pressed a comforting hand on Tyrdis's forehead, probably checking her for a fever. "I'm Adelle and this is my daughter, Svanhild. You are Tyrdis from Heilagrfjord, Jarl Raknar's army, correct?"

A vague recollection of the name snaked through the foggy swirls of Tyrdis's mind. She nodded and sipped more tea. Her weak hand dropped from the side of the cup, leaving it in the healer's grasp alone.

"Adelle," she addressed. The name had a pleasant sound on her tongue and in her ears, and she was grateful to the woman for her aid, but Tyrdis had a more pressing matter to resolve. She swallowed and summoned what strength she could. "Where is Erik, my brother?"

"No other injured were brought in from the battlefield," she replied and set the cup aside on an upended crate serving as a small table by the bed. "Only those here and Roar, who has moved out to recover in the village. His leg is healing nicely, and he doesn't require constant care."

Her response kindled a fresh concern to wrinkle Tyrdis's brow. "How long have I lain here?"

"Three days." Adelle rose from her side and pulled back the blanket.

"Three days!" Tyrdis exclaimed, the shock bolstering the strength of her voice. "I must find Erik." When she tried to sit up, a stabbing pain crippled her, awakening her wrath at the injury and the cowardly enemy who hadn't the courage to fight her face to face. Clamping her teeth together, she sunk back into her bed, refraining from the moan of anguish that struggled to escape her lips.

"Be still!" Adelle scolded with the look an angry mother gives a misbehaving child. The chastisement prompted Tyrdis to scowl at her beneath discontented brows. "I need to change the dressing on your wound and apply a fresh poultice to combat the redness. You will require much more than three days' rest before you can get up and walk; do you understand me?"

Adelle might be a pleasure to behold and display a kind nature, but she certainly possessed a bossy streak as well. Tyrdis was only accustomed to taking orders from her jarl or first warrior—never from another woman.

She scowled rather than give in to the temptation to dispute her benefactor.

A masculine voice sounded from the open doorway. "And how are our comrades from Jarl Raknar's band coming along?"

Tyrdis lifted her head and twisted her gaze toward a robust young man wearing a blue wool mantle trimmed in fur and a bittersweet smile. A silky mane the color of oats hung to his broad shoulders and a trim beard a shade darker framed his chiseled jaw and firm chin. Recognition lit her eyes at the sight of his friendly face.

"Sweyn Niklausson," she breathed and relaxed onto her pillow.

"I haven't forgotten the lessons you taught me in last summer's games, Tyrdis," he recalled with humor as he crossed the room to stand on the opposite side of her bed from the healer. "You gave me no quarter, and I ate mud because of it. I did not enjoy my siblings' teasing laughter, but I respected you for treating me as a competitor instead of as a jarl's son. In a kingdom ruled by politics and intrigue, I admire the genuine spirit of a warrior."

Seeing Sweyn brought Tyrdis a measure of contentment, and she almost smiled. Adelle took the distraction of the visitor as an opportunity to perform her duties as a healer, fussing with Tyrdis's wound and applying the medicine and clean wrappings.

"Have you word of my son, Runar?" Adelle asked with both concern and irritation in her tone.

"He is well," Sweyn answered respectfully. "My father sent him and other youth to Skeggen for training and to serve with the king's guard until they are ready for battle. He should be safe there all summer."

Adelle nodded and returned her attention to Tyrdis, who appreciated it, but could only spare thoughts and emotions for her brother. "Erik?" She was almost afraid to ask, but she had to know.

Sweyn sat on the foot of her cot and shook his head. "He feasts in Valhalla with Odin, Thor, and our ancestors. Your companions reported how he died valiantly wielding an ax, having defeated many enemies. You should be proud."

Though the news wasn't completely unexpected, it still hit Tyrdis with a more powerful blow than the spear which had almost killed her. Both Erik and she understood the possibility this would happen to one, if not both, of them, and they had made a pact to accept the will of the gods.

Still, he had been all she had—her last living family member. Now she was alone.

Summoning the fortitude befitting her station, Tyrdis steeled her jaw and nodded to him without tears or a weak display of emotion. She kept her eyes on the youthful man who had, on past occasions, looked to her as a mentor to train him harder than the men of his father's longhouse dared. Young Sweyn would make an excellent jarl when he matured, and she was glad it was he who had brought her the devastating account; still, he was not her brother. Erik was gone from this mortal plane and would not rally at her side again until the day the Valkyries came for her.

"Tyrdis, I'm sorry for the loss of your brother." Adelle's tone was sincere and empathetic. Her healing hands and gentle fingertips sent energy back into Tyrdis's numb skin as she worked her craft. Her mere presence was like a fragrant balm.

"I lost a husband to war four years ago," Adelle recounted, "and even now I occasionally wake to reach for him, only to find an empty place where he used to lie. Sweyn, I pray to the gods when you become jarl, you'll be quick to negotiate and slow to send our defenders to die."

He smiled at her and inclined his head. "Adelle, we need more voices like yours to strike a balance in public opinion, although you know a kingdom-wide Thing was held in Skeggen over the winter. All freemen had an opportunity to vote, and the majority agreed King Gustav Ironside's summons to war was justified. In the midst of the dark, snowy season, assassins from Firdafylke attacked Gustav's sons, killing Jarivald, his heir, and wounding Ivar before he could drive them away. The jarls and the freemen decided such treachery could not go unpunished, and that once spring arrived, we, as a united kingdom, would retaliate."

Adelle pulled the blanket back over Tyrdis and crossed her arms with a stern expression. "I'm sure the plan sounded splendid over a barrel of mead in the comfort of the king's hall," she growled. "But if a hundred or two hundred, or a thousand warriors were to slay each other, would it bring Jarivald back? What has been accomplished beyond adding to the kingdom's mourning and distress?"

"Firdafylke knows we will not lie down like defeated dogs and accept their malicious attacks," Tyrdis replied, her voice strengthened by devoted resolve. "Do not even more of their women and children weep than ours?"

"My father's warriors and I should have stood with you in the fray," Sweyn said with regret.

"Sweyn, our defeat was foolish Garold's fault, not yours. I advised him to send out scouts and to enlist the aid of your army, even if held in reserve. But he was arrogant and his tactics erratic and flawed. Someone must tell Jarl Raknar. Garold does not deserve to lead."

"I am soon to travel to Skeggen on my father's business," Sweyn replied. "If Jarl Raknar isn't there, I'll send a trusted messenger to speak to him about the matter. Why were you not chosen as first warrior?"

After her outburst, Tyrdis's energy waned, and fatigue overcame her. She sighed and said, "Because Garold is Raknar's cousin, and he asked to be put in command."

Tyrdis passed her gaze around the room, relieved to spot Thorgil and Myrbrandr alive, but heated fury raced through her blood as she recognized someone else from the battle. Raising a shaky left arm, she pointed at the lean fellow with the brown braid lying beside Thorgil and spat out her accusation.

"That man is one of our enemies! I dealt him that wound myself."

Adelle shifted a hand to her hip and stared at Tyrdis with irritation. "Then explain to me why he is not already dead if you are such a fierce and skilled killer?"

Tyrdis narrowed her gaze on Adelle, her frown deepening. "He is a novice, an unworthy opponent. He does not deserve to dine in Odin's hall with my brother."

The smirk on Adelle's face infuriated Tyrdis. It was as if the woman supposed she had granted her foe mercy. Maybe she had, but she wasn't about to admit to such.

"All are welcome in a house of healing, Tyrdis," she replied. "I have sworn to practice my art on anyone in need, regardless of who they are or where they're from."

"You should let him die," Tyrdis hissed between clenched teeth. She caught a breath before presenting a sound explanation. "It is an inefficient waste of your time, energy, and resources to treat a man who would knife you in your sleep. You only patch him up today to be executed by King Gustav's order tomorrow. Sweyn, tell her not to offer solace to the enemy."

Sweyn swung his gaze from the injured foe to Adelle, and then to Tyrdis. He rubbed the back of his neck and shook his head. "You are angry and in pain, mighty shieldmaiden. My father said King Tortryggr of Firdafylke engages in prisoner exchanges. I wish Adelle to ensure his recovery so we may trade him for one of our captured warriors. Would this not be the right course of action?"

Well, if that little upstart isn't a cunning young man after all! Tyrdis could hardly argue with his logic. "Acceptable," she relinquished. "Excuse my outburst. Sweyn is correct. Besides, the swine might possess valuable information—if we can loosen his tongue."

"There'll be no torture in my hospice," Adelle forcefully declared, then added with a grin and a wink, "unless I'm performing it to ensure the proper restoration of my patients."

The infuriating woman spun on her heel and marched across the room to check on the injured men, leaving Tyrdis as irritated with herself as she was with Adelle. She prided herself on complete control over her emotions, and yet she had lashed out like an undisciplined child. Sure, she believed every word she had spouted; still, Sweyn's argument held merit. So did Adelle's dedication to her calling.

Though uncertain why, Tyrdis wished for Adelle to like her—or at least admire her qualities as a defender of the realm—however, the healer seemed to be opposed to everything about her. *She just doesn't understand. She is disgruntled because fighting cost her a husband and she hasn't been able to find another. I concede it is a challenging task, considering how many more women fill the population than men, but she is attractive, attentive, and effective in her skill. She even trains an apprentice. I consider her to be quite desirable as a mate ... for someone who wanted one, that is.*

Her thoughts were interrupted when Svanhild returned, carrying a steaming bowl in both hands. A flavorful aroma reawakened Tyrdis's senses despite her exhaustion, and her mouth watered for a taste.

The little girl set the dish on the crate table and sat on the stool beside the bed. "Mama said to feed you this bone broth to make you strong again. Then you have to go to sleep some more."

Tyrdis was inexplicably drawn to the child, although she had scarcely engaged with youngsters even when she had been one. Rosy cheeks highlighted the girl's heart-shaped face, which bore a button nose above strawberry lips. She peered compassionately at Tyrdis through her mother's acorn eyes.

"I will comply," Tyrdis responded.

Svanhild giggled. "You talk funny."

Tyrdis's expression relayed her bafflement as she speculated as to what the child meant. Her dialect was no different from Sweyn's and Adelle's and she hadn't said anything amusing. "I speak like a warrior."

The little girl laughed and beamed at her.

Sweyn interrupted her confusion. "Tyrdis, I'll check on the others and be back to see you before I go. I can see you are in excellent hands."

"Thank you, Sweyn." She meant it. It struck Tyrdis that she cared about the jarl's son and considered it her duty to regain her strength to ensure his safety. He could not take the place of her younger brother—he was a jarl's son, after all—but she would look out for him all the same.

"Let me put an extra pillow under your head and I'll spoon the soup into your mouth," Svanhild instructed in imitation of Adelle. For the first time since she could recall, Tyrdis smiled.

"Are you training to be a grædari as well?" She lifted her head for the girl to slide the pillow in.

Svanhild pursed her lips in consideration. "I haven't decided what I'll be yet, but it never hurts to know medicine."

"I suppose it doesn't."

Though Tyrdis couldn't understand why, she felt more at ease with this girl than she had with anyone besides her brother—a brother she would never laugh or sing or fight beside in this lifetime. The smile faded away.

Svanhild brought the spoon to Tyrdis's mouth, and she partook of the nutritious broth.

"It's not too hot, is it?" Svanhild asked with a look of concern. "I could blow on it for you."

"No, thank you. It is acceptable."

Tyrdis drank the broth with affection growing for Svanhild even as grief for Erik swirled inwardly like a storm. Was this all by the design of the gods, or did they even care about the affairs of mortal men? All Tyrdis had ever known was duty and diligence, victory and valor. Yet, in her moment of weakness, her reality spun on its head at a little girl's compassion.

CHAPTER 5

"*I*'m sorry, Myrbrandr," Adelle said after examining his mangled arm. "It's hot and filled with disease. I know you're suffering, though I have given you every medicine I dare without poisoning you. You can live a long and fulfilling life with one arm."

He rocked in anguish, his face a guise of desperation. Beads of sweat lined his forehead, and she wiped a cool, damp cloth over his fevered skin. "All right, then," he consented. "I don't wish to die."

"Have you a wife to return to?" Sweyn asked as he joined Adelle and Myrbrandr.

He nodded.

"She would rather have you return maimed than not at all," Adelle testified.

"What other trade do you have?" Sweyn inquired. Adelle was glad for his visit. He was good for morale.

"We have a farm," Myrbrandr said and lowered his chin. "My oldest son is smaller than Svanhild, but my wife is sturdy. He will grow quickly and there are two children behind him. Somehow, we'll manage."

Sweyn laid a hand on his shoulder. "You are a credit to your family, loyal to Raumsdal and your king. I'll commend you to Jarl Raknar. When we win the conflict, perhaps he will award you a captured slave for the sacrifice of your arm. Then your farm can continue to thrive."

"I appreciate your support, Sweyn Niklausson." Myrbrandr lifted haunted eyes to Adelle. "When?"

28

"The sooner, the better. I hate to impose," she said, glancing at Sweyn. "Could you assist?"

He granted her a solemn nod. "I've done it before."

Sweyn withdrew his sharp, gleaming sword from the scabbard on his belt and walked a few steps to lay it on the hot coals glowing in the hearth. Adelle moved to her table and shelves to gather the necessary supplies.

Sparing a peek in Tyrdis's direction, her heart clenched with concern. Svanhild smiled, laughed, and chattered as she spooned broth into the shieldmaiden's mouth, and Tyrdis appeared to look at her daughter fondly. *I don't want her to become attached to that warrior woman,* she considered. Unease tightened her gut. *If she doesn't die, she'll leave as soon as she's able, probably return to the battlefield before she's ready, and get herself killed anyway. I wish to shield Svanhild from more loss and nights of weeping. I'll ask Joren to tend to Tyrdis from now on.*

Adelle placed her needle and thread, bandages, salve, and poultice herbs in a basket. Then she filled a large cup with strong drink and took it to Myrbrandr. "Drink this quickly," she instructed. "Then lie down."

As he drank, she carried over a broad bucket and a wooden plank, her mind troubled with thoughts of Tyrdis. *She could be a bad influence on Svanhild. What if my little girl were to start admiring her? Suppose she doesn't die and is hailed as a war hero; will Svanhild latch onto some wild notion of wanting to emulate her? It's bad enough Runar chose a warrior's path.* The more she stewed over it, the stronger her resolve that Svanhild and Tyrdis should have nothing to do with each other. It was for the best.

After securing the wooden plank between Myrbrandr's cot and the empty one to its left, she slid the bucket underneath to catch most of the blood. There wouldn't be much, as Sweyn would use a flame-hot blade to perform the chop.

"I'm going to move your arm onto the plank," she said with tender consideration. He winced as she positioned the wasted limb on the sturdy board. "Try to leave some skin on the bottom that I can pull over and stitch cleanly around the stump," she instructed Sweyn. The young man joined her with his glowing steel.

"It will hurt," Myrbrandr presumed with a touch of fear in his glistening eyes.

Adelle whisked around to the right side of his bed, giving Sweyn room to execute his role. "No more than it already does," she said. "You may sense your arm for days afterward, but soon you'll have no pain at all. You'll feel some pressure when Sweyn strikes the blow, but it will be over in a flash. Now, bite down on this." She inserted a leather strip between his teeth as she had done for Tyrdis. Though he fought to be brave, Adelle could tell by his expression he didn't possess the discipline and fortitude the shieldmaiden had displayed. Few did. But she could understand well his sentiments, for who wished to go through life missing an arm? At least it was his left one, and he could still walk and see and enjoy most regular activities.

Holding his gaze, Adelle instructed, "Look at me. Recall how Tyr sacrificed his hand to save the world from Fenrir, the wolf. Tyr is more than a god of war; only he was brave and true enough to take the risk required to ensure Fenrir was bound forever, even until the day of *Ragnarök.*"

While she held his attention, Sweyn made a true strike, landing in exactly the right spot to sever the broken portion of his arm while leaving a functional stump above his elbow. Myrbrandr cried out and turned a horror-stricken stare to what remained of his arm. Sweyn brushed the dead, mangled remains into the bucket.

"That went quite well, Myrbrandr," the jarl's son declared with a pleased look. "Tyr must be smiling at you this very moment." He carried the bucket away, leaving Adelle to sew the flap of skin around the scorched stump. Myrbrandr's eyes rolled back, and he passed out. It was for the best.

BY THE TIME Adelle had finished her work on Myrbrandr, Joren had returned and Sweyn had gone. Tyrdis and Thorgil slept while the Firdafylker, Birger, sat propped up in his bed, watching. When he noticed her staring at him, he said, "Myrbrandr was brave. I would not want to lose a limb like that. Is it true Sweyn's father plans to trade me for one of your warriors my king holds hostage?"

"That's what I've heard," Adelle answered. She recalled Tyrdis's claim the enemy would just as soon slit their throats if he had the chance. He didn't appear to be a violent man, and he displayed empathy rather than enmity toward Myrbrandr. However, he was also a prisoner in her hospice who wished to garner her favor and protection as long as he was weak. Though she wished him no ill will, it would be wise not to trust him.

Svanhild washed the bowl she had served Tyrdis from in a basin set on the stone wall surrounding the firepit. "I wouldn't want to have my arm cut off either," she commented. "But better than a leg, I think. Do you miss your home?" she directed to the foreigner.

"Yes," he replied, most likely in honesty. "But you all have been kind to me, and I praise the gods for it."

"It's like I said," Adelle confirmed in a detached tone. "I'm sworn to apply my talents to heal anyone who suffers pain or affliction. Svanhild, will you help me outside?"

"Yes, Mama."

Her precious daughter dutifully followed her out to the back lean-to. Adelle sat on a bench, weary from many weights upon her heart, and Svanhild scooted in beside her, peering up at her with questioning brown eyes.

"Do you remember the black cat that came around before we adopted Freida?" she began conversationally.

Svanhild tilted her head. "I remember Midnight. I found him. He had been trampled and we nursed him back to health."

"We did," she agreed. "But Midnight was a wild cat, not a house cat like Freida." As if by divine providence, the gray-striped tabby with black-tipped ears padded around the corner to rub against Svanhild's leg. The little girl greeted her with a delighted smile and picked up the cat, sat her in her lap, and stroked her fur.

"Here you are, Freida." She grinned as the cat purred at her affection. "I'll bet you were hunting. Freida keeps the mice away." It was the rationale Adelle had stated many times for why they kept the cat, but really it was because Svanhild adored her. "She's a tame cat."

"She is." Adelle reached over, sunk her fingers into lush fur, and scratched behind Freida's ears. "But remember how as soon as Midnight was all better, he ran away? You were so sad and cried when he left. Our house wasn't his home."

"I know," Svanhild admitted. "But it was his home while we were taking care of him. He just missed his family in the forest and wanted to go back. It's not because he didn't like us too."

"That's right." Adelle was hoping this memory would serve its purpose as she shifted to what she wanted to say. "I don't want you to get too attached to Tyrdis, honeybee. Once she's all better, she'll leave us and probably never come back. And if she doesn't get better, she'll leave us for one of the afterlife worlds. I don't want you to be sad and cry."

Svanhild moved her attention from the tabby to her mother. "But Tyrdis isn't like Midnight. What if she doesn't have a family to go home to? And she won't die; I know it. She's strong and you're the best healer in all the world. I like her, Mama, and she likes me. I can tell. Only you and Amma have ever looked at me like she does. Even Runar ignores me—when he isn't away pretending to be a warrior. I made her smile, and she never smiles." There was pride in her tone when she said it, adding to Adelle's distress. "Tyrdis says I can be whatever I want to when I grow up because I have potential." She grinned, displaying two front teeth larger than the others.

Adelle wrapped an arm around her daughter. "You do have potential, Svanhild, and don't you forget it. You're smart, kind, and a big help to me in the hospice. But I thought you wanted to train to be a grædari like me."

"I do," she answered. "But I could do other things, too. Tyrdis says the world is my longboat, but I'm not sure what that means. The world is a lot bigger than a longboat."

She placed a kiss on the top of Svanhild's head. Adelle knew exactly what Tyrdis meant—that Svanhild could go wherever and do whatever she desired. It's what Tyrdis had done, she suspected. "I know, sweetheart. The world is big, but maybe you'll find a nice man right here in Sæladalr, fall in love, and raise a family. That's an admirable ambition, even without another calling. But you would make a fine healer, too."

"Is that what you did, Mama—fall in love and raise a family?" Svanhild blinked as she awaited her mother's reply.

She didn't think about it often. To be honest, Adelle wouldn't know what falling in love felt like. She had married Sunevar because everyone expected her to. Their parents were close, and she and Sunevar had been friends since childhood. He was familiar, a decent, honest man who treated her with respect. She could offer no reason not to wed him, especially when he encouraged her to complete her training and open her own hospice. He had supported her with compassion after losing their infant when other men might have blamed her.

Did it matter that her loins never burned with passion for his body to join hers? They hardly fought, and, when they did, they made up. If he strayed from their marriage bed seeking more tantalizing pleasures than she could provide, he did so discretely so none—including her—had been the wiser, while other men would flaunt their affairs like a badge of honor. He had been a loving father to their children, though Svanhild had been only a toddler when he took up his spear and followed Jarl Niklaus into battle.

It wasn't Niklaus's fault, and she never blamed him. Skalds sang songs and recounted tales praising the glory of warriors feasting in Odin's Hall, which reflected the values of her people: strength, courage, pride, and honor. But what good were those qualities to the children who were left without fathers? Had she married for love? Maybe not, but she had loved Sunevar in her own way. Her children and her work as a healer filled her life with passion and purpose. She hadn't looked for anyone else after her husband was killed; Adelle had all she needed right here.

"That's right, Svanhild," she responded with a smile. "Your father was a strong, kind man with a good sense of humor. He respected and loved me and you and Runar. But he was foolishly led astray by the lure of battle and died at the end of an enemy's sword."

"And now he dines with Odin in his great hall," she completed in a resigned sorrow that always pricked Adelle's heart to hear. Svanhild didn't actually remember her father, only the stories that were told about him. "Maybe Tyrdis's brother can be friends with him in Valhalla now. I wish I could go see him there."

"Only we can't." Adelle smoothed her daughter's hair with one hand while hugging her tight with the other. "A vast chasm separates *Ásgarðr* from our realm and it can only be reached by crossing *Bifrost*. Only the gods know where to find it, so sometimes Odin or Freya or Thor might come down in disguise and walk among us, seeing who they can trust or who is showing proper hospitality. Then they reward those whose lives are pure. But we can only travel to their land when we die."

"I didn't want Papa to die." Svanhild nestled closer and hugged her mother.

"Neither did I, honey; neither did I."

CHAPTER 6

Skeggen, two days later

Sweyn Niklausson hopped out of his longboat onto the pier upon arriving in Raumsdal's central town of Skeggen with an envoy of two merchants, four armed guards, a traveling storyteller, and two passengers coming for a relative's wedding. The crew of four sailors who manned the low-draft vessel stayed behind while Sweyn and the others walked the short distance from the edge of the vast fjord toward a bustling market square along a path squishy with mud from the recent spring rains.

Glistening snow still capped the peaks which rose above and around the low-lying bowl, majestically stretching skyward in ancient dominance of the surrounding landscape. Firs and pines formed a blue-green skirt spreading about the lower halves of the mountains, giving way to mixed forests and more varied vegetation where the slopes gentled into hills, ending in the narrow crescent of near level land along the shoreline.

Little more than a ribbon lay between the steep rises of indomitable rock and icy, deep waters, making Skeggen a poor area for farming, whereas Sweyn's border town of Sæladalr boasted the most arable land in the kingdom. However, its central location, easy access by boat, rich timber, plentiful game, and defensible position made the capital ideal for trade. In addition to the safe harbor provided by the fjord, a nearby pass made for reasonable summer treks to and from mountain outposts and the land of the Swedes to the east.

"We should stop by the market when your business with the king has concluded," commented Edan, one of the burly warriors Jarl Niklaus had sent to guard Sweyn.

It's not that Sweyn resented his father for insisting on sending security with him every time he traveled; he understood Niklaus was only concerned for his safety. But *helsike*, he was a grown man, had seen twenty-one summers, and had spent six years training in warfare. If there was a better swordsman around, Sweyn would like to meet him. Still, the country was at war, and it had already been proven that assassins could turn up anywhere. It was important for his father, as the commander of the king's forces, to stay where the fighting was and send him, someone knowledgeable and trustworthy, to relay messages to and from King Gustav.

"We shall, Edan," Sweyn replied amiably. "Perhaps you can find something pretty to woo Gislaug with."

The two men exchanged grins. Edan was ten years Sweyn's elder and ready to settle on a wife, only the flirtatious, younger Gislaug had been playing hard to get.

"There's so much here; how will I decide?"

Sweyn looked around as they entered the boisterous marketplace. The enticing aromas of roasting meat, flavorful soups, and fresh-baked bread filled his senses as vendors prepared fresh foods over open fires or in outdoor clay ovens. Sheepherders sold raw wool while weavers hocked dyed cloth. Laughing children scampered about to the tap, tap of the smith's hammer down the lane.

"Silk scarves from the Amber Road for your women!" called a twiggy merchant, robed in colorful garb.

"Belts and boots!" shouted another.

Open-air tents and wooden carts filled a grassy space just outside the palisade town walls, and Sweyn and his companions marveled at the variety of merchandise as they passed.

"This is making me hungry," admitted Karvir, another of the bodyguard crew. He was even more seasoned than Edan, and Sweyn couldn't help but think they would serve the kingdom better by defending the border than by escorting him through a perfectly safe town ... or was it?

He studied Skeggen as they passed through the open gate. The dwellings were round, square, or rectangular plank houses like the ones in his village, many sprouting grass from the sod insulating their roofs. Their wood-framed doorways lay under pitched eaves, some adorned with carved designs or covered porches. Larger houses with yard space were enclosed with wooden or rock fences to keep small livestock in or a neighbor's out. Craft shops stood beside residences where potters, brewers, tanners, and smiths worked. Almost every home had a spinning wheel and a loom where the women would make cloth to sell or fashion into clothing for their families. Chickens roamed freely, pecking at the ground amid a hush of subdued clucks, while cats and dogs lazed about paying them no mind. Down a side street lay a patchwork of garden squares and, in the other direction, a stable. But the most prominent building at the center crossroads ahead was the alehouse. That, too, would have to wait until after Sweyn's meeting with the king.

Out the back gate and up the hill stood the massive great hall of King Gustav Ironside, also protected by a wall of mixed earthworks, stone, and timber. It commanded a view of the entire eastern end of the fjord where his scouts could easily spy any ships or land forces hours before they would arrive—plenty of time to mount a defense.

The way to the king's citadel passed an orchard with runestones marking the path to a sacrificial grove. Sweyn had been there before and had seen the carved totems to the gods—not nearly as large and elaborate as the statues at Uppsala, which he had only heard about—yet, nonetheless, impressive to his eyes.

With the others having strolled off at the market or in town, Sweyn and his quartet of warriors entered the great hall.

"Sweyn Niklausson and his escort, my lord," announced a well-dressed servant Sweyn had met before.

"Come in, come in!" King Gustav rose and waved to them with exuberance. He was a big man, with a muscled chest, a long, brown beard, and streaks of gray in his unkempt hair bound by a silver circlet he sported as a crown. Sweyn considered it a bold choice for him to sit at court in an orange tunic, as the bright color combined with his rotund body gave him the appearance of a ripe gourd. Several pudgy fingers bore rings of gold or silver crafted with an inlaid design or colorful gemstone.

The musicians stopped playing, and a wench scurried forward to offer them a bowl of mead to dip their horns in.

"Thank you for your hospitality, King Gustav Ironside," Sweyn replied in a courtly manner. Pulling the travel horn from this belt, he dipped it in the bowl, followed by his attendants. While the king's hall would surely have cups to spare, most travelers carried their own so they could drink from barrels on a ship or streams along a path. A good drinking horn was as much a piece of a Norseman's equipment as was his belt, boots, cloak, or ax.

"Come, sit at my table," he offered. "It isn't mealtime, but I'll have Elida bring you bread and cheese." He glanced at a woman in a gray apron and signaled with a flick of his hand. She scurried into the pantry and returned with a platter while Sweyn and the others settled onto benches near the king.

To Gustav's right sat his son, Ivar, a lanky young man with dirty-blond hair and a disinterested expression. The thin line of his lips and defensive posture, along with a residual glare in his beady eyes, suggested Sweyn may have interrupted an argument, but that was none of his concern. On the king's left, Kerstav, his younger son, a beardless youth, glowered in kind.

"Your generosity is appreciated after our journey," Sweyn responded, ignoring the feuding brothers. "I'll be sure to praise your welcome to my father, who faithfully serves you on the front lines."

"I am grateful for his service. To Jarl Niklaus." Gustav raised his silver chalice, and the men raised their horns. "Skol!"

"Skol!" they repeated—including the king's sons, who were slow to join the toast.

A finely dressed woman, whom Sweyn knew was not Gustav's wife since she had died a few winters ago, also sat at the table with two warrior advisors and the king's favorite gothi. He had met these men before but couldn't recall their names.

"Now, Sweyn, tell me how the war goes." Gustav set down his cup and fixed Sweyn with a serious expression.

Sweyn swallowed the bite he was chewing and shook his head. "Not as well as we had hoped. We capture a piece of ground, and they take it back. We raid their supply line, and they attack our farms. Casualties are too high. My father commands your troops along with his, but Jarl Raknar sent his warriors with a brash fool to lead them. They were routed a week ago near Sæladalr, and I haven't seen Garold, Raknar's cousin, since he and what remained of his followers fled, leaving their dead and wounded behind."

The corners of the king's mouth turned down, and he narrowed his eyes at Sweyn. "Why weren't your warriors with them? A larger force would not have been defeated."

"Because we were neither consulted nor informed," Sweyn grumbled in irritation. "I suspect Garold wished to make a name for himself and ran headlong into an enemy trap. My friend Tyrdis—a warrior at his side—believes this as well. It's a miracle from the gods she still breathes after a Firdafylker's spear pierced her."

"Ah, yes, the shieldmaiden of Heilagrfjord," he mused, as if in remembrance.

"Give me a band of my own, Father, and I will show them tenacity and cunning the southlanders have never witnessed!" Ivar demanded. "I have more motivation and resolve than any here."

"Admirable, my son, but no," Gustav replied in a patronizing tone. He held up a hand and lifted his chin, turning his gaze away from Ivar to Sweyn. "Hot blood does not win battles, isn't that so, Sweyn?"

Sweyn glanced at Ivar, who was perhaps a year younger than he. They had competed in the games before and he knew the prince to possess skill and strength, though he didn't always show good judgment.

"My lord, Ivar wishes to avenge his brother's murder, and the attack on himself," he stated evenly. "It is understandable. Yet I must agree with you that only cooler heads will prevail. This brings me to a proposition Jarl Niklaus has sent."

Gustav straightened, lifting considerable weight with the squaring of his shoulders, and the two princes leaned forward bearing curious expressions. "What does your father propose?" the king inquired.

Sweyn summoned his most mature, sage manner, and launched into what he came here to relay. "Our spies in Gimelfjord, the enemy's capital, have informed us King Tortryggr is receiving supplies and reinforcements from Svithjod, their southern neighbors. That is why we are always outnumbered. Such news forces us to reevaluate our plans going forward. My father suggests we call a truce to negotiate with Tortryggr, who is a reasonable man. If he will agree to launch an internal investigation and deliver those responsible for Jarivald's death to you, so they may be publicly and painfully executed, the war need not continue."

The king's eyes darted first to one son, then to the other, before he fixed them on Sweyn. "And how do we know King Tortryggr didn't send the assassins himself? He could deliver his own political enemies to us to carry out his dirty work while allowing the true murderers to go free. This plan cannot be trusted!" His fist pounded the table as his voice rose. Leaning forward, he pointed at Sweyn. "What would Jarl Niklaus demand if it had been you slain instead of my son?"

"With all respect and humility, my lord, he would not wish hundreds to die in a vain endeavor."

"Vain endeavor?" Gustav bellowed. His jaw hardened as a deep furrow rose between his brows. "We have long laid claim to Firdafylke's northern land—the fertile fields and green pastures that were once ruled by our ancestors. We will spill every drop of our foes' blood to regain them and then demand Tortryggr turn over the assassins. This betrayal cannot go unpunished. I must be compensated for the life of my oldest son!"

"Land is no compensation for my brother's life," the king's youngest son grumbled, as he dared to flash a glare at Gustav.

Gustav's glower forced Kerstav to look away and lower his chin in repentance. Sweyn had a feeling the tension between the brothers and their father had been high since Jarivald had been killed.

"Father, let me go to Heilagrfjord and petition Jarl Raknar for more fighters," Ivar proposed. "I can inform him of Garold's failure. I know I would make a better leader."

"One day, Ivar," the king confirmed. "Not yet. I need you here. There are traitors among us, and whom can I trust save those who share my table now? Sweyn, I know the brunt of the conflict has fallen in your father's lap, but we mustn't shrink from the cry of justice. I'll send envoys to Jarls Raknar and Bjarke to provide more supplies and soldiers. Do not lose heart, lad—we shall prevail. Odin, Tyr, and Thor will pat our backs and shake our hands. We'll drink and feast together soon, and how glorious it will be! Now, eat and drink until you are ready to return to your ship. I must take my leave." Gustav pushed up from the table and held out a hand to the finely clad woman at his side. "Audfrey?"

The woman—older than Sweyn and younger than the king—took his hand with a demure smile and gracefully exited at his side.

Ivar glared at his father's back as the two departed. Turning to Sweyn, he said, "He should know how deadly, how capable I am, and yet he holds me back."

"He is a father who has lost a son," Sweyn explained in a gentle tone. "He doesn't wish to lose another. That's all. We all know how skilled you are."

"If you will excuse me." Kerstav rose and headed out the back door of the longhouse.

The musicians struck up their instruments, and the warriors engaged in casual conversation, but Sweyn was troubled by the king's obstinance. *It's as if he cares more about taking the land than finding justice for Jarivald, and he doesn't care how many lives he sacrifices.*

A SHORT WHILE LATER, Sweyn and his warriors bade their farewells to Ivar and headed back through town toward the docks. There was still plenty of daylight to begin their trip, and he didn't want to waste time.

"Edan, do you still intend to buy your girl a gift at the market?" Sweyn asked as they strolled along.

"Yes, and you should get one too," Edan recommended. "That way, when you finally find a woman who thinks you more than a half-wit, you'll have something to favor her with."

Sweyn laughed and slapped his comrade on the shoulder. He was about to make a clever reply when something ahead caught his attention. The thunder of horse hooves approached from outside the gate, accompanied by irritated shouts. A little girl with a basket of flowers was crossing the mucky, rutted road at the same time the rider barrelled through.

Seized by impulse, Sweyn dashed ahead and pulled her out of the way just as the galloping steed and rider careened through the gate frame. She sucked in a gasp and peered up at him with soulful robin's egg eyes, now wide with fear. In an instant, she dropped the basket and threw her arms around his neck.

Sweyn hoisted the child to his hip and yelled at the rider. "Watch where you're going, fool! There's no call for speeding through here."

Pulling his mount to a skidding halt, the rider twisted over his saddle to glare at Sweyn. "Who are you calling fool? That careless urchin shouldn't have been in my way."

Studying the brute on horseback, Sweyn pieced it together: *late thirties, blond hair, reddish beard, thinks more highly of himself than others ...*

"Garold the Spineless," Sweyn sneered as he gathered the girl close to his chest. "I've already spoken to King Gustav and, if you have any sense, you'll avoid his displeasure and keep riding north to beg forgiveness of Jarl Raknar."

Garold returned a scornful look and spat in Sweyn's direction. "You'll be finished when I'm done with you."

Sweyn set the girl's feet on the ground and stepped in front of her. "Come down from your horse and let's do this here and now, in the presence of many witnesses." He laid a hand on the hilt of his sword. "You left Tyrdis and other brave warriors to die while you fled like a helpless, frightened woman. I would have fought at your side had you but informed me of your attack."

"I don't need you," he growled. "And I haven't time for a duel today, but just wait, Sweyn Niklausson. You can't insult me without retribution." With a slap of the reins, he kicked his pony and trotted on to the alehouse.

Sweyn shook his head.

"Bleeding coward!" Karvir spat in the mud in disgust. "Come on, Edan. Mayhap the market will temper my anger toward that arse." The two men moved on, leaving Sweyn with the frightened girl.

"I'll catch up," Sweyn called after them. Turning back to the little girl, he smiled. "What's your name?"

"Hallfrid," she answered in a small voice, diverting her gaze. Sweyn decided she was older than Svanhild, but not yet showing the signs of womanhood, so maybe about ten years of age.

"That's a pretty name." He picked up her flower basket, scooping some of the spilled ones back inside. "Were you going to sell these at the market?"

She nodded, still not daring to look at him.

"Where are your parents?"

Hallfrid shook her head. "I don't have any parents."

Compassion flickered in Sweyn's chest. "Where do you live then?"

She shrugged. "Here and there. Sometimes people let me sleep in their barns or sheds when I do work for them, like mucking stalls or feeding pigs. I picked these flowers in the meadow this morning. It's almost May Day and everyone will want flowers. The merchants in the market will trade me food for them."

Sweyn wished there was something he could do for her. Orphans were common everywhere in times of war, and it seemed it was always a time of war. Adelle's ideas were radical, but they were also practical. How could their society prosper amid continual destruction? He wished he could have made the king see reason, but Gustav was set on revenge.

Reaching into his pocket, Sweyn withdrew a silver coin. "Do you have a safe place where you can hide this so you will have it when winter comes?"

The girl's eyes lit like stars at the sight of the shiny coin, and a dreamy look flooded her smudged, gaunt face. Her chestnut hair was unbrushed and her dress was too short, but she had a pair of shoes laced on her feet that seemed to be in good repair. She nodded and stretched out a timid hand as she bit her bottom lip.

"Don't be afraid, Hallfrid," he instructed and placed the coin in her grimy hand.

Hallfrid slipped the silver piece into an ankle-high leather shoe and wiggled her foot to make sure it was secure. Then she beamed at Sweyn as if he was Baldr, the beloved of all the gods.

"I know who you are," she said. "I wish you would be king one day. You see everyone—even me." Though people passed on the muddy street or haggled nearby, none seemed to pay them any attention.

"I may be jarl one day, like my father, but I do not pretend I'll be king. It's enough to be a good man, just as soon you will be a good woman. May fortune shine on you, Hallfrid." He smiled and patted her head, but, when he moved to walk on, she caught his hand.

Tossing a glance at her, Hallfrid peered unwaveringly into his eyes. "I know things. No one even notices me. I'm like a shrub or a wandering lamb, just a piece of the scenery, but I see and hear what goes on."

Granting her his full attention, Sweyn turned back. "Hallfrid, what do you know? What have you seen and heard?"

A flash of horror crossed her visage, and she looked away. "I can't tell. Besides, no one would believe me. I'm no better than a thrall."

"I would believe you." Sweyn waited, wondering what the girl would reveal. Something he could use against Garold, he hoped. Ire burned in his gut every time he thought about the reckless coward.

She lowered her chin and shook her head. "Maybe one day I'll tell you, but nobody else, and not yet." She reduced her voice to a whisper and peered at him intensely. "It's too dangerous. I can't let them kill you because you should be king instead of the fat one."

Sweyn relaxed. It was probably nothing of consequence, anyway … some sexual indiscretion by the king or one of his sons … unless it had been with a child. Her, perhaps? He shook the disgusting thoughts from his mind.

"Very well, Hallfrid," he consented. "I'm sure I'll be back. Maybe you'll feel comfortable telling me then."

She gazed at him admiringly once more and smiled. "Thank you, Sweyn Niklausson, for everything—saving me from Garold's horse, the coin, but mostly for seeing me. I might tell you if things get desperate. Safe travels to your home."

Sweyn rejoined his escort in the market and soon they set off in the longboat toward Sæladalr. Though they were going home, many things troubled him—Gustav's refusal to consider his father's proposal, Garold galloping through the town, and what mysterious knowledge an orphan girl possessed.

CHAPTER 7

Sælådalr, two weeks after the battle

Tyrdis lay in her bed, propped up by pillows, watching and listening but saying nothing. A vein throbbed in her temple and the consuming ache in her side never relented, yet she wouldn't complain. Most of all, she despised being helpless. She hadn't been able to sit up for the first week to use a chamber pot, and Adelle had to change her bedding regularly. It was more than embarrassing—it was humiliating. At least now she could take care of her own waste and didn't have to be tended to like an infant.

Joren had taken over feeding her and she had transitioned from broth to porridge, and then to boiled meat, vegetables, and bread. She adhered to her regimen of medicinal tea, wound cleaning, and poultice applications, and had to admit Adelle was more than competent at her job. Toward the end of her first week, Tyrdis had suffered from a mild fever and night sweats, and some puss and redness persisted along her burned portion of flesh, but she had steadily improved. When she thought back about the spear being rammed straight through her entire body and out the other side, then being left to die, she considered it nothing less than miraculous she had survived.

Svanhild visited her briefly each morning, but her mother kept her busy doing other things, leaving them little time together. As Tyrdis thought about it, Adelle had maintained her distance as well, almost as if she was avoiding her. Perhaps she was, which was entirely understandable. *Why would she, or anyone, wish to make friends with someone like me? Besides, I'll be back with my band soon enough and, after the war, return north to continue serving Jarl Raknar ... as long as Garold is no longer giving the orders.*

Tyrdis had taken her first steps three days ago; she admitted only to herself what a struggle it was, as she displayed a neutral appearance despite the agonizing pain. Each day, she walked a little more. Being thoroughly weary of lying about doing nothing, she carefully got to her feet now and took a slow stroll around the hospice.

A gray-striped cat stared suspiciously at her from a high perch on a shelf. Tyrdis wondered how it managed to climb up and down from there without disturbing Adelle's herb jars. She got the feeling the cat would be more contented once the strange woman was gone.

Myrbrandr had left to join Roar as they recuperated in Niklaus's hall while a farmer who had almost chopped his foot off and a woman who appeared to be in shock from some sort of beating had taken their places. Tyrdis had tried to talk to the woman, but she had only stared at her through fearful eyes and curled into a ball. *Did I come across as that intimidating? I did not intend to frighten her more.* She walked quietly past the woman's bed, around to where her fellow soldier, Thorgil, rested on his cot near the man she had wounded in the battle.

"Thorgil, it is good to see you alert," Tyrdis declared as she stood erect at his feet, displaying perfect posture despite how excruciating it was to do so. Pain may be many things, but she would never allow it to be her master. "That was quite the blow to the head you sustained. We were not certain if you would wake again."

"It is good to have returned from the veil of shadows, Tyrdis. The last thing I recall was seeing your face as you stopped to help me on the battlefield; then I woke up here this morning. They tell me it's been two weeks."

"Indeed. However, Adelle is a most capable healer to whom we both owe our lives."

"As do I," Birger added. He pushed himself up with one hand while he pressed his other to his bandaged side. "And also to you, Tyrdis, for not chopping off my head when you easily could have. I apologize for underestimating you. It was a foolish mistake I'll not repeat."

Tyrdis stared at him disapprovingly. "You should be a fisherman, craftsman, or trader—not a warrior. Have they not sufficient farms in Firdafylke?"

To her surprise, Birger laughed, as if he was among friends, and shook his head. "I am a carpenter and a carver. I specialize in carving figures and designs of ivory, stone, bone, and antlers, and I build things too. But Jarl Stefnir ordered every able-bodied man between ages eighteen and forty to join in the defense against the invaders. So, here I am."

"Invaders?" Tyrdis scowled. She started to cross her arms over her chest, but the motion proved too painful, and she settled for clasping her hands in front of her at the spot her belt should be. Wearing this borrowed tunic with no gear or weapons made her feel practically naked. "What about the assassins you sent to kill our king's heirs?"

Birger sighed, offering her an apologetic expression. "I know nothing about assassins, and neither does Jarl Stefnir. Whoever killed your prince, my town of Oskholm had nothing to do with it."

"Do you know every man and woman in Firdafylke as personally as your own mother?" she interrogated, releasing her hands to fall to her sides again. Agitated, and uncertain how to proceed in these strange surroundings with their unreasonable rules, she shifted her left hand to rest above her hip. "I'm certain the murderer would not announce what he had done for all to hear. One may kill a man in a fair fight in front of witnesses and be praised for his prowess, but to sneak into a neighbor's barn and attack his sons behind a hooded cloak in deception is a crime before men and the gods."

Defensively, he fired back. "And what is punishing innocent people for other's crimes? Gustav Ironside should have met with King Tortryggr and presented his grievances rather than invade our borders, his warriors slaughtering men in their fields and carrying off their women for slaves. His actions are brutal and barbaric."

"Our king is grieving the loss of his firstborn son and heir," Tyrdis countered with less venom.

"And how many more fathers, mothers, sisters, brothers, wives, and children now grieve because of it?" Birger's words hung in the air, a question Tyrdis did not wish to consider. Her place was not to question the king or her jarl but to obey their orders.

Thorgil answered in her stead. "Such decisions are not ours to make. Who can fathom the mind of a king? Tyrdis and I go where we are told and attack when we are commanded to," he explained, though no explanation was necessary. Even a craftsman should understand such things. "The only decision she made was to wound rather than kill you. Your countryman dealt her a killing blow, and yet she stubbornly refused to die. We scrape and battle, risk our lives while taking others, because the fire burns within us. It was passed to us from our ancestors, patterned for us by the gods. After death, we rush to Odin's battlefield to spend our energy in contests of might and courage, so we may earn the right to feast at the Allfather's table. What are the affairs of kings compared to such glory?"

"Something I'll never understand." At the sound of Adelle's voice, Tyrdis glanced over her shoulder. "Feeling stronger I see, Tyrdis. Good, but don't overexert yourself."

Holding her gaze for a few seconds, Tyrdis wondered if the healer truly cared for her well-being or if it was her job to offer sound advice. She searched Adelle's expressionless face for a clue. *It is foolish to wish for such things,* she told herself. *I don't need her approval or Svanhild's attention or anyone to coddle me. I am a warrior.*

She responded with a curt nod. "As you wish, grædari." She lowered her chin in deference to the lady of the house and returned to sit on the side of her bed. To be honest, she was tired after her wee bit of walking and standing. *I despise weakness with a passion!*

Thorgil and Birger exchanged tales from their childhoods while Adelle checked on the other patients. After a few minutes, Thorgil said, "Tyrdis, give us a story."

"I do not engage in idle conversations," she quipped. "What purpose is there for you to become friends today when you might have to shed each other's blood tomorrow?"

"Warriors!" Adelle formed the word as a curse under her breath, dragging Tyrdis's frown deeper.

What did I say but an honest fact? Why is she angry with me?

Summoning internal courage, Tyrdis changed the subject. "Where is Svanhild?"

"I sent her out to collect berries from the patch on the hill behind the house," she answered evenly. "I noticed they were ripening, and berries not only taste good but possess healing properties as well. A diet rich in them keeps people healthy."

Tyrdis nodded. She liked berries in a bowl with thick cream. She remembered her mother preparing them for her when she was a small child. There had been no berries and cream since her mother died. An unnecessary indulgence. *"Food is fuel to grow a powerful body, not a source of pleasure,"* her father had proclaimed. Yet, even now, imagining a dish of fresh-picked berries smothered in cool, rich cream sent a lightness through her, which threatened to break out in a smile.

Suddenly, Joren rushed through the door with a panic-stricken look, gripping his floppy cap in a fist. "Raiders!"

Tyrdis snapped to attention in an instant and was on her feet, locked into battle mode.

"Raiders?" Adelle froze as she seemingly tried to register the words. "Where?"

"In town," her apprentice huffed out. "I don't know if I was followed." He straightened from where he had leaned over to catch his breath and peered out the doorway behind him. "I don't see anybody."

Then a distant scream sounded, followed by a donkey's loud bray, shouts, and the clanging of steel.

"Svanhild." The name fell from Tyrdis's lips like a prayer. Before anyone else moved or spoke a word, she rushed out the back door and scanned the hillside beyond the herb garden for the little girl. Movement, a squeal, menacing laughter … two dirty men without colors or shields. One lifted Svanhild off her feet with his hand clamped over her mouth. With her focus leveled on him and a solid purpose charged with adrenaline, Tyrdis bolted toward them.

She had no weapons, no shoes, no strength, and yet her resolve was all she required.

"Ow!" The grubby man let out, shaking fingers no longer pressed to her mouth. "Little hellion bit me!" The other raider laughed as he reached out to grab the thrashing, kicking child.

"Let me have her first," he demanded.

As they bickered over their prize, the thugs didn't notice Tyrdis until it was too late. The first man stared incredulously at a half-dressed woman in an oversized man's tunic reaching for him with bare hands.

The skilled warrior grabbed him by the chin with one hand, stretched the other behind his head, and snapped his neck. He crumpled into a berry bush, limp hands releasing Svanhild, who landed on her feet.

Tyrdis spun without hesitation to confront the second attacker, whose mouth gaped at her beneath saucer-sized eyes. Realizing she couldn't produce sufficient power from her right side, she drew back her left arm, stepped with her right foot, then lunged forward with her left. She swung her hip with her shoulder and elbow, whipping the heel of her hand into his nose as her force pushed the fragile bone into the man's brain. He fell at her feet, an eternal look of horrified astonishment seared onto his face. From experience, she knew he would never rise after such a blow.

"Svanhild, are you harmed?" Tyrdis knelt before the girl, honestly frightened for her safety.

Svanhild threw her arms around Tyrdis's neck and hugged her with shaky limbs. "They didn't have time to hurt me. You came and saved me."

Tyrdis embraced the precious child and pressed her cheek to hers. She wasn't certain if the dampness she sensed was her own tears or Svanhild's, but it didn't matter. Adelle's daughter was free from danger.

She glanced around at the overturned basket, the berries spilled in a pile, the trampled bushes, and the body of the man whose neck she had broken. "You are safe now. I will never allow anyone to harm you."

"I know, Tyrdis. I just love you."

The honest affections of the child were almost enough to undo decades of discipline and reduce Tyrdis to a blubbering, sentimental heap of mush. Approaching footsteps yanked her out of the unfamiliar sentiment.

"Svanhild, Tyrdis!" Adelle called as she and Joren, burdened by anxious looks, rushed to them.

"It's all right, Mama," Svanhild responded as she released her hold. "Tyrdis saved me from the bad men."

Adelle scooped Svanhild into her arms and held her against her breast in a tight embrace, rocking her as tears streamed down her face, while Joren's shocked gaze took in the carnage.

"Oh, my dearest honeybee!" Adelle cooed in relief. "I would have never sent you out here if I'd known raiders were coming. We must hurry back inside and bar the doors in case there are others. Joren, help Tyrdis."

With the imminent threat past, Tyrdis felt suddenly weak in the knees. She was breathing hard, her energy spent, and it seemed as if someone pounded on the hole in her side with a blacksmith's hammer.

"Thank you," she said in a formal tone, "but I do not require assistance. It is a short walk to the hospice."

"Nonsense," Adelle chided. "You're bleeding." Tyrdis glanced down at the widening red spot on her tunic and sensed pain-induced nausea stirring in her belly.

She snorted in frustration. "Very well. I will comply." She wrapped an arm around Joren's shoulders, and he caught her about the waist to assist her back inside.

With the doors bolted and Joren keeping vigil through a sliver between the wall planks, Tyrdis relaxed onto the bed, floating on a cloud of satisfaction as she watched Adelle and Svanhild rejoice in the moment. Presently, Adelle walked over and sat on the stool beside her bed, her expression unreadable.

"You killed those men," she stated. It sounded to Tyrdis like an accusation, and she stiffened.

"Was not the child's safety paramount?" she returned with rigidity, raising an incredulous brow.

Adelle's countenance softened, and she let out an anxious breath. "Svanhild's safety is most assuredly paramount. You've left me at a loss for words, except to say how very, very grateful I am to you ... and amazed."

The knot in Tyrdis's stomach eased, and the tension melted off her shoulders. She relaxed deeper into her pillows and ventured a rare smile. "Then it was an acceptable course of action. Svanhild is unharmed; all else is irrelevant."

"Your recovery isn't irrelevant," Adelle replied with the endearing quality she had used with Tyrdis the first few days she had spent under her care. "I fear you've set your progress back at least a week. If you keep doing things like that, you'll lose your fitness to be an effective shieldmaiden."

"If I have incurred a permanent weakness, I shall adapt. Knowledge is more effectual than physical strength, anyway." Adelle's smile lit her lush, brown eyes, and something beyond satisfaction stirred in Tyrdis's soul.

"Here, let me check on the wound you've pulled open."

As Tyrdis closed her eyes, the healer touched her with gentle kindness, and equal parts bliss and lassitude settled over her, lulling her to sleep.

CHAPTER 8

*A*delle was shaken by the incident and stirred by the woman who pushed beyond expected physical limits to rescue her child from molestation, abduction, or worse. They could have killed Svanhild, and, because they dared touch her, their bodies now lay motionless on the hillside. Adelle opposed violence with every fiber of her being, and yet she could only feel relief and appreciation for Tyrdis's actions. She watched in disbelief when the shieldmaiden dispatched two healthy men with her bare hands in the blink of an eye. When she finally reached them, realizing her daughter was unharmed, she had felt a fierce desire to catch Tyrdis in an embrace and kiss her.

Of course, she didn't. Tyrdis was a woman, which didn't matter to most people; only Adelle had never kissed a woman before. She hadn't even thought about kissing anyone since her husband's death. It had simply been an impulse brought about by an extreme circumstance. Man or woman, Adelle wanted nothing to do with warriors. They were crude and brutal, often dumb as a post, with no regard for anything of beauty, and yet it was as clear as a snowmelt stream that Tyrdis adored Svanhild —the finest jewel, most fragrant flower, dearest being in all Miðgarðr.

The woman was blunt and arrogant, traits common in professional fighters, and yet she had treated Adelle and her daughter with admirable respect. Tyrdis was a paradox, one who forced Adelle to reexamine her most firmly-held beliefs. *Could there be value in one who exercises martial abilities? Can a warrior ever do good?*

Adelle glanced down at Tyrdis's sleeping face, her fingertips lingering on her skin. She had tended the wound and rebandaged it; she should pull down her patient's tunic and cover her with the sheet—and she would. *Tyrdis tossed aside her own best interests and put her life in jeopardy; why? A sense of responsibility? A desire to be a hero? Could she truly care more for a stranger's child than herself? Will my Runar grow to be like her instead of the ruffians who use any excuse to bash each other?*

"Mama, is Tyrdis all right?"

She jumped at Svanhild's voice over her shoulder and quickly yanked down the hem of Tyrdis's tunic. "Yes, sweetie. She's just sleeping."

"It hurt her to run out and fight the men," Svanhild stated with a worried expression.

Straightening, Adelle wrapped an arm around her daughter. "No, honey. Just a little. She'll continue her recovery and be well before long."

"Can I help take care of her again?" Svanhild bit her lip, her searching eyes packed with consternation as she peered at Adelle.

Adelle's gaze passed from Svanhild to Tyrdis and back as she grappled with her own implacable values. *Maybe there is a time and place for a warrior's skills,* she allowed, *such as when they are defending the helpless.* She still worried about Svanhild's grief when the heroic woman would leave, but she couldn't shield her child from every hard thing.

"Yes, Svanhild," she answered. "It would be a good way to show Tyrdis your appreciation."

Her little girl hugged her and kissed her cheek, then beamed at her. "Thank you, Mama."

A knock at the door jolted fresh alarm through Adelle, and she hopped to her feet, anxious about who it might be. Instinctively, she pushed Svanhild behind her.

"Adelle, it's me, Sweyn." Relief washed over her like a gentle shower.

"Joren, let him in," she instructed.

Her apprentice unbarred the entry and the jarl's son swept in, sporting his noble warrior garb. "Is everyone here all right?"

"Yes," Joren answered, "thanks to Tyrdis."

"Tyrdis?" He pivoted in astonishment to the shieldmaiden who lay passed out on her cot.

Adelle walked toward him as she explained. "Two of the raiders ... well, Svanhild was out picking berries, and ..." She glanced back at Tyrdis before meeting Sweyn's gaze. "Their bodies lie behind the hospice."

An admiring smile accompanied Sweyn's dancing eyes as delight radiated from him at the news. "I tell you the truth, Adelle; as long as Tyrdis stays in this house, you are in good hands."

With a nod, she agreed. "I believe you are right."

"Who attacked us?" Thorgil asked. He sat up in his bed, leaning his shoulders against the wall with a pillow behind his head swathed in bandages.

Birger shrank back as his nervous eyes darted to Sweyn. It seemed to Adelle he wished to disappear altogether.

Sweyn rubbed a hand to the back of his neck, offering a frustrated expression. "Father isn't sure. We also killed a couple fighting in town while the others ran away. If any were wounded, the strong ones carried them off, and we didn't capture anyone alive. The obvious answer would be a band from Firdafylke, only they had no red and black shields, none wore armor, and they didn't have an obvious leader. I'm prone to suspect they were a gang of common criminals or mayhap some of those thieving malcontent outsiders who live up in the mountains."

He glanced at Birger. "We could bring the bodies down from the hill and ask him if he recognizes them."

"Excellent idea," Thorgil proclaimed.

"I'll get a litter," Joren said and hurried out the back door.

Birger shrugged. "I don't know every man in the king's service, but I'll answer truthfully if I recognize them or not. It's shameful to attack children, and I pray these are not my countrymen."

"They probably came here to pilfer medicines," Adelle suggested. "People have done it before. But then they saw Svanhild ..." She pulled her daughter to her side.

Sweyn and Joren hauled the corpses in through the back door and set them on an empty bed. Birger walked over and peered at their faces, studying their clothing and simple gear. "Neither had a spear or rönd?"

"I didn't see any on the ground," Sweyn replied, "nor did those we killed in town. Only common axes and knives."

Birger looked Sweyn in the eyes. They were around the same age, yet so different in size and station. Sweyn appeared like the nobleman he was with fine clothing, lean muscles, clean, and confident, whereas Birger was twiggy and raggedy with fine fingers adept at crafting, not wielding a weapon. Adelle sensed honesty in his words.

"I swear by Thor's hammer, I've never seen these two men before.

They did not serve in my unit and do not live in my hometown. I cannot swear they aren't from Firdafylke, but they aren't dressed like warriors. Where are their gambesons, their greaves or bracers? Not everyone is equipped with chainmail or scale armor, and even fewer possess a sword or helmet, but every soldier I've ever seen was equipped better than these."

Sweyn lay a hand on his shoulder. "I suspected as much. And wouldn't even a raiding party make better plans? Why not strike at night or in a more organized manner? I believe a group of outcasts and rogues thought to take advantage of our conflict with Firdafylke by stealing whatever they could get their hands on. They may have thought all the men would be off fighting, not realizing we must protect our border town. Don't worry … Birger, is it?"

Birger looked up with hope into Sweyn's face. "Yes."

Sweyn patted his shoulder and removed his hand. "No one will blame you."

The foreigner exhaled with relief, and a smile returned to his face. "You are a wise and reasonable man, and I thank you. I know you wish to keep me as a prisoner until the day of the exchange, but I am feeling better, and my wound no longer oozes blood. If Adelle needs my bed for another patient, I am fit enough to be moved to a prison cell."

Sweyn stepped back and inspected him with an assessing look. Then amusement lit his eyes. "If you are so fit, stay here and help Adelle. I fear there will be more wounded arriving any minute from the skirmish with the raiders." Then his expression turned stern, and his tone hardened. "But if I hear you tried to run away or caused trouble, my father will have no prisoner to exchange, for I would execute you for being an ingrate."

Birger paled. "I would not bite the hand that feeds me, my lord. Even a dog knows better."

"Good," he decreed and inclined his head in final assessment.

As PREDICTED, two men and a woman from town soon arrived with deep cuts and cracked heads to treat, which kept Adelle and Joren busy for the rest of the day.

Adelle was glad her mother had come to help. She had been worried after the trouble in town and ventured up the hill to check on the hospice. When she had heard of the incident with the men and Svanhild, Adelle thought she would have to sedate her. Bruna was also a widow and had six grandchildren altogether, but only Svanhild lived nearby. Adelle's sisters had moved to other towns when they married and, with Runar in Skeggen serving in the king's guard, that left only Svanhild for her to spoil.

"Here, Svanhild, pass out these bowls of stew to the patients," directed Bruna.

"Yes, Amma." Svanhild skipped and twirled across the floor to collect the first wooden bowl and spoon.

"Now slow down and don't spill it," Bruna chastised with a wince. She pushed back a strand of ash-brushed ginger hair that had come loose from her braid before spooning a portion into the next bowl.

Bruna had inherited a sturdy house and sold cloth she weaved and dyed in the Skeggen market once a moon, but she frequently made time to come visit and had watched Svanhild when she was younger while Adelle worked. Although they had endured some strained times in the past, Adelle and her mother now enjoyed a comfortable relationship.

When the meals had been distributed, Svanhild carried her bowl and settled beside Tyrdis. Adelle sat with Bruna at her worktable near the hearth yet couldn't seem to tear her attention away from her daughter and the powerful shieldmaiden.

"This tastes wonderful, Mother," she commented. "You always were a good cook, and I detect the herbs I asked you to include."

"Thank you, dear," she replied with a smile. "Do you remember Karl, the mead hall keeper?"

"Of course; I know Karl." Adelle didn't visit the mead hall often, though she purchased alcohol for its anesthetic qualities for her patients.

Her mother smiled at her over the rim of her bowl and savored a slow bite, leaving Adelle to wonder about far too many things. Bruna swallowed and said, "His son recently returned from a long voyage, and Karl says he's looking for a wife."

Adelle smirked. "Let him look then." Her gaze drifted back to Tyrdis. "I'm not interested in another husband."

"Even if it was that fine Sweyn Niklausson?" Bruna raised a brow with the question, giving her daughter a teasing look.

"Mother! He's too young for me and far above my station. No. I am happy with my life the way it is. No more husbands for me."

"Then what about for me?"

Adelle whipped a shocked expression to her mother. "Karl's son? Mother, he's my age!"

She laughed, probably thoroughly amused by the look on Adelle's face. "No, silly—Karl. His wife died two years ago, and he threw himself into his work. Now, he has confided in me he's getting lonely. We may have been spending some time together, and it's not outside the realm of possibility. Even people our age need companionship. I'd think you would too." Bruna's face softened from laughter to affection, even concern.

"Really, Mother," Adelle returned, resting a hand on her arm. "I'm not lonely. I have Svanhild and Joren and all my patients. My work is so rewarding, and I meet interesting people."

"Interesting people like her?" Bruna motioned toward Tyrdis. She was engaged in some sort of eating game with Svanhild, who hooted and giggled as she teased Tyrdis with a spoonful of food she held an inch from her mouth. "I must meet her and thank her for protecting our honeybee."

Adelle thought about Tyrdis; she found it difficult to think of much else since that morning. "She is interesting … bold, selfless, and Svanhild has really taken to her, but she's a warrior all the way from Heilagrfjord. Once she's healed, she'll be on her way, and I likely won't see her again."

Bruna cocked her head, studying her with an intent gaze. "And if she wasn't a warrior from Heilagrfjord? If she was a farmer or a craft maker living right here in Sæladalr?"

With a deep scowl, Adelle asked, "What are you implying?" She stiffened and diverted her eyes from both Tyrdis's bed and her mother.

"Sweetheart, I'm not accusing you of anything. You say you don't wish to marry, and I know you've always been independent, never one to wait for a man to do for you. I only thought you mayhap should consider a companion of some sort—even if it's not a husband. You haven't taken your eyes off her since I arrived. Did you think I wouldn't notice?"

"She saved Svanhild's life, at the peril of her own," Adelle snapped back in a hush. "But she's a warrior, and I know what that means."

Bruna nodded and took a few bites in silence. Then she shrugged. "Ingmar's husband was a merchant. One would think it a safe occupation for a gentle, intelligent man, and yet he was killed while on an ordinary trading venture when a sudden storm blew upon the sea, sinking his boat, and sending all aboard to *Ran*."

"That's different," Adelle spoke with a quiet resolution. "You know I oppose violence. I have nothing in common with her."

Bruna lifted her gaze to spy Svanhild beaming at Tyrdis as she bounced on the stool by her bed, finally landing a spoonful in the shield-maiden's mouth. "Ah, yes, I see how you have nothing in common with her whatsoever."

CHAPTER 9

Sæladalr, the morning after the raid

Sweyn, accompanied by trusted warriors Edan and Karvir and his Uncle Horik, sat on his father's right at a long pine table in the jarl's great hall. His mother, Lynnea, a delicate woman whose frailty belied her age of only forty years, occupied the seat at the other end, swirling honey into her porridge with the flair of an artist. On the opposite side of the dining table, his four younger siblings were lined up like ducklings in a row from tallest to smallest, attacking their breakfasts with gusto.

"I wish King Gustav had given more consideration to my advice," Niklaus grumbled in annoyance. The lines etched into his brow revealed more anxiety than age, as did the dark circles under his gray-blue eyes. He wore his long, ash-blond hair braided down his back with a full beard of a similar hue skirting his rugged face. A brawny man, accustomed to defeats and victories alike, Niklaus's skill at warfare was only surpassed by his temperate wisdom. Sweyn understood years ago how much he could learn from such a noble father and sought to emulate his style of leadership.

"I agree with Gustav," Horik declared and bit off a bite of pheasant from the bone in his hand. His hair was darker, his stature taller, but he bore the same sturdy build as his older brother. "We need to stop trading blow for blow, insult for insult, and crush them. We could mount an attack on their capital from the sea, row at night, and surprise them at first light."

Niklaus shot him a sardonic glare. "Soon there will be no dark as the time of the midnight sun approaches. Do you propose we can organize such an assault in a fortnight? Besides, if we attack their capital, they will do the same to ours."

"Not if we soundly defeat them first." Horik gulped a drink from his cup to wash down the meat. "You can negotiate all you want once we have them on their knees. Then we will get the favorable end of the bargain. They sent men into our town, attacked our women and children, brother. One of my friends was injured."

"We don't believe the raiders were Firdafylke warriors," Sweyn stated in disagreement with his uncle. "We uncovered no evidence they were any more than a band of outlaws bent on thievery and general mischief, though we were fortunate none of our citizens were killed. My father's proposition was reasonable and demonstrated understanding, not weakness."

"The point is moot." Niklaus dropped his spoon into his empty bowl beside his cleaned plate. Leaning forward on his elbows, he glanced across the table at Lynnea. "The children need to prepare for their lessons now."

She nodded and rose to herd them out, despite leaving most of her porridge in the bowl.

"Father!" Njal, the next son in line after Sweyn, protested. "I should be allowed to take part in important discussions. What if your darling Sweyn is killed or behaves dishonorably and you need to name me heir? I should know what is going on."

"You, Njal," Niklaus addressed, pointing a stern finger at him, "must learn to discipline *yourself* before you can be placed in charge of others."

Njal scowled at him. "I don't know what that means," he grumbled.

"Precisely." Niklaus reached over and patted the seventeen-year-old on the shoulder. He had a ruddier look than Sweyn and wasn't as tall but had always displayed a highly competitive nature. Sweyn could admit his brother possessed both skill and prowess with weapons and could handle a horse and a small boat; however, he agreed with his father that Njal lacked the maturity to be involved in key decision-making.

"Son, I love you and Sweyn and all my children equally. You know that. But now is the time for you to master not only a bow, spear, ax, and sword, but your emotions and your tongue as well. You are to be on the practice range with the other young warriors soon; they are expecting you, so don't let them down. You'll have plenty of time for politics when you're older."

"Yes, sir," he uttered in resignation and left the table with his mother, brothers, and baby sister.

Niklaus returned his attention to the four men remaining. "I have arranged a prisoner exchange to take place in Oskholm the day after tomorrow when the sun is straight overhead. We will meet with Jarl Stefnir of the northern fylke under a banner of truce."

"A perfect time to plan an attack!" Horik proclaimed eagerly. His brother glared at him in impatient disapproval.

"We chose the spot because there is nowhere to hide a waiting army for just such a scheme. If a man's word is no good, then there is nothing good in him, Horik. You know our father taught us that."

Horik leaned back, crossed his arms, and sulked.

"Sweyn, I want you, Edan, and Karvir to collect our prisoners and get them ready to go. We should leave before the sun is too high so we will not tire ourselves on a rushed journey. We'll bring the bodies of the dead raiders and ask Jarl Stefnir if he recognizes them. Horik, can I trust you to be in charge for two days?"

He snorted and retorted with a sneer, "Certainly you can. Since when have I become so untrustworthy? Didn't I support you sliding into leadership after Father died? Have I ever raised a force against you or tried to undermine your authority?"

"No, Horik, you are loyal, even though we're not of the same mind on many matters. I am confident if trouble was to arise while Sweyn and I are gone, you are the strongest warrior to lead a defense of the town."

Horik nodded, the perturbed expression waning from his face while Niklaus paused to take a drink.

"Now, for other matters. As you know, I would prefer diplomacy to war any day," Niklaus said. "Unfortunately, King Gustav wants to punish Firdafylke and maybe take some of their arable lands for Raumsdal as compensation. We could always use more fertile fields, but peaceful neighbors are of equal value." He let out a long exhale and glanced at Sweyn, who approved of his father's perspective. "If the king is set on fighting, the best thing we can do is to devise a plan to ensure a quick victory. The longer hostilities drag on, the more loss both sides will suffer. So, Horik, Sweyn, be thinking about it. After the prisoner exchange, we will meet to formulate our strategy."

With all in agreement, Sweyn and his men-at-arms set out to collect Birger from the hospice and bring him to the barn where a few others were being kept.

* * *

"BIRGER, I LOVE IT!" Svanhild exclaimed. She beamed at him, then rushed over to where Tyrdis lay, recuperating from her previous day's exertion. "Look, Tyrdis—a bunny!"

The girl thrust a carved wooden object about the size of a small drinking cup into the shieldmaiden's hands for her inspection. It bore a remarkable likeness to a friendly, curious rabbit, sitting up on its haunches with one ear erect and the other bent over. Tyrdis stroked the smooth surface of the white wood.

"I carved it from a piece of aspen that Joren brought in with the kindling," Birger explained. "I thought such a nice specimen shouldn't be wasted in the fire, and Svanhild brings so much joy to everyone, I wanted to make a gift for her."

"Don't you think it's just so special?" Svanhild exuded excitement as she asked Tyrdis for her opinion.

"Above average craftsmanship and a subject your mother would approve of," Tyrdis decreed. "I find it acceptable indeed." Tyrdis supposed the peace-loving healer wouldn't have been pleased with a wolf, bear, or other fearsome creatures, but a gentle lamb or bunny would be fine for her daughter to play with. She handed the figure back to Svanhild, trying to hide her smile at the girl's joy. Who would have thought the mighty shieldmaiden, who had faced the deadliest villains, grappled with vicious beasts and ferocious storms, and overcome winters harsh enough to subdue a jötunn, would ever have fallen under the spell of a child?

In an instant, her warm heart chilled to ice at the unexpected and unwelcome sight of that swine Garold marching through the open door with two towering, musclebound thugs on his heels. "I have come for the Firdafylke prisoner," he announced. "By order of King Gustav, all captive enemies are to be executed forthwith."

Tyrdis stared at him in disbelief, processing the fact that the brash "leader" who had ordered them into a trap, then left her and her comrades to die, had the audacity to waltz back in here, issuing commands.

Adelle raced across the room in a rage, shouting, "You'll do no such thing! How dare you intrude into my hospice? Don't you know this place is sacred to Eir, goddess of healing and companion of Frigg? If you incur her wrath, you risk dying of infection from the next scratch inflicted on you or coming down with a fever or plague. Surely, even a warrior is not so foolish as to anger the gods."

Svanhild grabbed Tyrdis's hand, fear jolting through her so powerfully the shieldmaiden could sense it. The child stared at the strangers with wide, brown eyes, and Tyrdis gave her hand a comforting squeeze. Then she released it and pushed herself out of bed while Garold made his reply.

"Look, woman," he began in a patronizing tone that set Tyrdis's teeth on edge. "It's not my intent to disrespect the gods; however, they live far away in Ásgarðr while the king lives only a day's journey from here. Eir may or may not take offense at my intrusion, but Gustav will be angered if I disobey his orders. Now, step aside."

Adelle raised her chin boldly with her hands on her hips, blocking his way. "You do not have permission or the authority to remove any of my patients."

Immense pride in Adelle's actions arose in Tyrdis. *So, she does have it in her to fight when she deems it necessary,* she thought. *She may not strike her foe a physical blow, but she has the strength and courage to stand up to him all the same.*

Joren fell in on Adelle's right side, though with more uncertainty, while Tyrdis stepped up to her left, forming a human wall between Garold and his goons and Birger.

Tyrdis's expression was like granite as she narrowed her eyes on a man about her height who would not be her equal on a good day; unfortunately, this was not a good day for the injured shieldmaiden. "I am surprised to see you, Garold. I would have thought Raknar's chastisement for your failure would have you licking your wounds back in Heilagrfjord."

He shifted an astonished gaze to her and took a step back. "Tyrdis." She supposed he was surprised to see her alive. "It is fortunate you are recovering so quickly. I received mixed reports about whether you survived or died in the battle. My cousin will be pleased to have retained so skilled a warrior. But, no." Now his demeanor switched from polite to defensive. "I didn't return to see Raknar; I only gathered more soldiers to replace the ones we lost. I am needed here, at the front, not up north in Heilagrfjord far from the fighting."

"And you honestly spoke to the king, and he ordered you to execute prisoners from a battle that occurred over two weeks ago?" She fixed him with a penetrating stare.

Garold shuffled his feet, and his eyes darted away; when he returned them, they were hard and his jaw unyielding. "I have a job to do, Tyrdis. You won't stand in my way."

"You will not remove a soul from this hospice." Tyrdis seethed with restrained fury. "Jarl Niklaus is arranging a prisoner exchange. He cannot get our warriors returned with none of theirs to offer in trade. If you are so eager to shed Firdafylke blood, why did you flee the field of combat, leaving Thorgil," she said, motioning to where he lay with a bandaged head, "me, and others behind? Spilling the blood of unarmed hostages is only further evidence of your cowardice. Be gone or I will kill you myself."

Garold had the audacity to laugh at her, and Tyrdis tightened every muscle at his insult.

"Tyrdis, thank you for defending me to this ..." Adelle waved a dismissive hand at Garold. "Person," she arrived upon. "But I'll no more have you killing him than him killing my patient. I don't tolerate violence."

"And how will you stop me from carrying out my duty, grædari?" the weasel sneered. "Now, out of my way, before my assistants carry you out."

Tyrdis slid in front of Adelle with determination. "There are ways I could stop you short of ending your miserable life."

Before he could answer, Sweyn and his two attendants entered behind them. "What's this?" Sweyn asked. He bore an irritated expression as he stared daggers at Garold. Tyrdis relaxed, confident her friend would straighten things out.

Garold spun to the younger but more impressive man behind him. "Oh, Sweyn." He offered a fake smile as he tried to persuade the jarl's son to humor his wishes. "These women won't step aside so I may carry out the king's command."

"Which is?" Sweyn crossed muscular arms over a brawny chest and peered past his straight nose at the boot-licking little dung ball.

"To collect and execute the Firdafylke prisoners," Garold answered innocently, as if he wasn't a snake in the grass.

Sweyn shook his head in disapproval. "I can't allow you to do that. King Gustav sent no such directive to my father, so how is it you are here speaking on his behalf? Don't you serve your brother, Raknar, and doesn't he vie with my father for the king's favor? How do I know you were even given such an order?"

Garold stiffened, and his look of decorum morphed into a snarl. "How dare you question my honor? What cause would I have to lie?"

What cause indeed? Tyrdis wondered. She responded with confident protectiveness as Svanhild slid her little hand into hers and gripped it, peering up at her with a fearful gaze. The room was stagnant with tension, and she could have heard a fly land in the moment of silence.

Sweyn cocked his head pensively at the unwelcome guest. "True or false, I cannot accommodate you, Garold. You'll return to Gustav with no Firdafylkers—dead or otherwise. My father has already arranged a prisoner exchange with Jarl Stefnir for the day after tomorrow, and I'll be taking charge of Birger to see that he and the others make it there on time and in sound condition. Remember, this is Jarl Niklaus's fylke, and he gives the orders here."

Garold glared at Sweyn, flexing his hands into fists at his side. Then he raised a finger, jabbing it into the blond warrior's chest. "You'll hear about this, Sweyn Niklausson. I'll inform the king of your treason, and then we'll see."

Tyrdis had endured enough of Garold's insolence. "If there is a traitor in this room, it is you, Garold, and I demand satisfaction. I hereby challenge you, outside, here and now. You are not fit to clean Sweyn's boots, and yet in your ignorance, you spout threats."

Garold slapped a hand to the hilt of the sword at his side. "I ought to take you up on it, Tyrdis, but I would be laughed at for fighting a half-dead woman."

"I suspect this half-dead woman is more than a match for the likes of you," Adelle interjected with assurance, drawing Garold's humiliated glower.

"I won't allow such a duel," Sweyn declared with authority. "We can't go about killing each other when there is an enemy to fight. Take out your frustrations on the Firdafylkers—only not that one." He pointed at Birger. "Birger, come with us. You're going home."

Sweyn's guards elbowed Garold and his hulks aside to escort Birger to the door.

"Thank you, Adelle, Joren, all of you," Birger said in a tone infused with relief. "May Odin grant you wisdom, Thor, strength, and Tyr, courage. I pray to Freya for a quick end to this war. Sweyn Niklausson?" He raised questioning eyes to the jarl's son. "Did your father consider Loki could be behind all this? I mean, mayhap a trick was employed. I'm only a carver, so what do I know? I just thank you all for treating me as a human being rather than blindly blaming me for deeds not my own."

"Goodbye, Birger," Svanhild said as she peeked around Tyrdis. "Thank you for my bunny. Now I'll *always* remember you."

He smiled at her. "I don't need a token to remember you, child." He lifted his eyes until they met the shieldmaiden's. "Tyrdis, thank you for not killing me."

"It would have been an inefficient waste of my energy," she replied in an even tone before glaring at Garold. "You, however ..."

"Tyrdis, I mean it," Sweyn rebuked her. "Garold, you and your men should leave the hospice now and allow Adelle and Joren to return to their responsibilities. I pray you are of a more reasonable mind when next we meet."

"Reasonable," he grumbled and bared his teeth. "Let's get out of this stinking hole." He purposely bumped into Sweyn on his way out, his dutiful lackeys trailing after him.

"Don't worry, Adelle," Sweyn assured her. "I'm asking Edan to stay here and keep a watch on the door until my father and I return. You'll keep the lady safe, won't you Edan?"

His friend grinned. "As safe as a clam in its shell. I'd enjoy an excuse to give that one a thrashing."

"Wouldn't we all," Sweyn muttered and rolled his eyes. "Tyrdis, no more challenges, all right? I need you to lie in that bed and follow Adelle's directions completely, so maybe in a few weeks, you can fight at my side. Understood?"

"Understood," she confirmed with a serious nod. "Safe travels and watch for traps."

He grinned at her. "I was taught by the best."

"Thank you, Sweyn," Adelle said as she saw him out. "And Birger, I suggest you leave your fighting days behind." He offered her an appreciative look and a wink, then left with Sweyn and his man, the other posting himself outside the door.

CHAPTER 10

"*I* didn't like the scary man, Mama." Svanhild nestled between Adelle and Tyrdis and wrapped her arms around her mother's waist.

Resting a comforting hand on her daughter, Adelle answered, "I didn't like him either, but he didn't hurt anyone, so all is well."

She glanced at Tyrdis, who watched them intently. Two weeks ago, she was ready to execute Birger herself, yet today she stood up for him. Had her beliefs about killing changed, or simply altered for the prisoner exchange? Mayhap spending time with Birger, getting to know him, and the shared experience of overcoming grave wounds tilted the scales on the side of mercy. Or maybe she disliked Garold so much that whatever he proposed, she argued for its opposite. Regardless of her motives, Tyrdis's action was to support Adelle against a bloodthirsty, and possibly deceitful, man. Without a thought to her own weakened state and physical well-being, she issued a challenge when Garold tried to force Adelle aside.

Warriors, she contemplated. *Are they sometimes necessary? Sweyn is a nobleman, but he's a warrior too—Tyrdis's student, in fact. Without them to stop Garold and his soldiers, what would have happened today? How would it have affected Svanhild?*

Lowering her gaze to her daughter, Adelle said, "Everything is all right, honeybee. Run down to Amma's house now and show her your new bunny carving. You can tell her what happened."

Her face brightened, and Svanhild released her grip. "Yes, I need to show Amma." She scampered to Tyrdis's cot, retrieved her toy, and skipped back. "I can't wait to tell her everything!"

Adelle smiled after her, resisting the urge to issue redundant warnings to be careful along the way. Murmurs sounded around the house and Thorgil spoke out in a robust voice, "What a horse's ass, that one. I'm glad Sweyn showed up when he did, though. It wouldn't do for Tyrdis to open that hole in her side again by fighting him."

"I agree," Adelle stated. "Joren, check on the patients and get their tea while I march this implacable shieldmaiden back to her bed."

"I would sacrifice more than a few drops of blood in defense of your hospice, Adelle," Tyrdis confessed as they walked the short span to her cot. "It is my duty to protect."

"Right now, it's your duty to rest and recover from your wound." Adelle helped her into the bed and covered her with a blanket. "I'll get you some tea."

"You are kind, Adelle," Tyrdis said as she settled into her pillows. "You are worth protecting."

Struck by her words and the way she delivered them, Adelle sat on the stool rather than rush off to fetch tea. She was absorbed by the look in Tyrdis's exotic blue-green eyes compelling her to remain in her company. This wasn't what Adelle had wanted—not at all—and yet she couldn't help herself. She wished to understand this woman who had saved her child and now stood up for her and an enemy, of all people.

"What made you change your mind?" she asked curiously. "Why defend Birger when you wished him dead before?"

Her reply was casual, with a neutral expression revealing nothing. "I was angry and in pain when I first arrived, worried about my brother, but Sweyn's proposal for a prisoner exchange was reasonable. Birger wishes me no ill will, and he crafted a gift for Svanhild. He has behaved appropriately in your hospice and caused no trouble; therefore, he deserves to live."

"But not Garold?" Adelle searched Tyrdis's stunning eyes for clues of what resided inside the capable woman.

Tyrdis's features hardened. "He is not worthy and wastes the air that others enjoy breathing."

"So, you would have killed him," Adelle concluded sorrowfully.

Tyrdis fixed her with a confused look. "In a fair fight, not the way he intended to slay Birger. He threatened you, Adelle. He led our troop into a disaster, then fled like a coward. You stood up to him. I saw the fire in you and was proud. Sometimes I am called upon to do what needs to be done, things others cannot or are too timid to execute. Mark my truth—I would not have allowed him to harm you or defile your hospice dedicated to Eir. I respect the gods, even when I don't understand them."

"I believe you, Tyrdis." Adelle had a sudden urge to reach over and take her hand. It was nice to have a protector, for she had been long without one. However, it weighed heavily on her heart to realize she needed one. The callouses on the shieldmaiden's palms were softening, her nails trimmed, and her skin inviting and warm. They were strong hands … and dirty ones. Adelle wrinkled her nose as she noticed the body odor and the state of her hair. "Let me get your tea."

When Adelle returned, she handed the cup to Tyrdis. "Drink this." When she obeyed without question, Adelle collected sheets and hung them from the rafters around the bed.

"What are you doing?" Tyrdis asked.

"It's time you were properly bathed. I don't have a tub or hot spring out here, but there's a well in the back. I'll bring a wash basin, soap, and a cloth to give you an overdue cleaning." *And I will not think about how magnificent your body is, because I already know it will be. This is part of my duties as a healer—nothing more.*

"I concur with your course of action," Tyrdis stated formally. "Adelle, I may be a warrior, but I am not a bloodthirsty brute bent on destruction. When you cut off Myrbrandr's arm, your intent was not to torture him with pain but to save his life by removing the rotten part. It was a horrendous act, yet you performed it for the greater good. Sometimes we must do things that seem cruel when they are truly necessary for the benefit of all. I hold you in esteem and do not wish you to think me an uncaring killer."

Adelle's heart caught in her throat at Tyrdis's confession. Indeed, many would see the amputation as cruel, turning a brave fighting man into a cripple. And didn't she regularly engage in battles against infections and diseases to protect the person they had attacked? Is that how Tyrdis viewed her role in society? From a certain perspective, her argument made sense. *I can't become connected to another warrior,* she reminded herself. *But she holds me in esteem and cares what I think of her. I think she is the bravest human I've ever met.*

Sliding her hands away, Adelle said, "I don't think you are anything like Garold. I see how you care for Svanhild and Sweyn ... and me—all of us. I respect you too. Now, if you will kindly undress, I'll bring the bathing water." Adelle stood and walked away, hoping she could maintain her professionalism when she returned.

* * *

TYRDIS TUGGED the tunic over her head behind the privacy curtain Adelle had strung up. Doing so pulled her injured side, and she winced. It was all right; no one was there to see her expression of pain.

She respects me! The knowledge filled the warrior with a tingly giddiness that was so unlike her. It gave her a thrill like when she hit a center mark with a bow and arrow or the first time she'd caught a fish as a child. She felt as if she had just been named the winner of the Winter Solstice games. It was foolish, she knew; still, Tyrdis would take what joy she could because who knew what tomorrow would bring?

But Adelle was coming back to bathe her. Maybe she should just take the bucket of water and soap, shoo the healer away, and do it herself. How could she remain detached with Adelle's hands all over her body? *It will be a test of my resolve,* she determined.

Tyrdis was sitting nude on the edge of the bed, examining her wound when Adelle returned with heated water, soap, and several clean cloths. Tyrdis straightened to her standard, perfect posture as she met Adelle's gaze. She could have sworn the woman reacted to the sight of her body, but neither of them said anything.

"I removed the bandages, presuming they needed to be changed," Tyrdis explained and glanced down at her side. She was suddenly self-conscious for no apparent reason. Having never been taught modesty, she had no problem changing clothes or bathing in the presence of others. Yet, under Adelle's stare, she felt completely vulnerable. Her mouth went dry, and her palms began to sweat, though she couldn't fathom why.

Adelle looked away, awkwardly fumbling to set the washbasin on the small table by the cot. "Yes, you're perfect ... I mean, you're perfectly correct. After you've been washed, I'll put new ones on." When she sat on the stool, their knees brushed against each other, sending an unexpected shiver up Tyrdis's spine. This was like sitting on a rock during a dry lightning display.

The healer focused her attention on the disgusting burn mark on Tyrdis's midriff. "It's oozing a little today, but we'll get it cleaned up. Now, I'll wash your hair and scrub your back. Do you think you can manage the other parts?"

Tyrdis gave her question serious consideration. "It will be difficult to bend over to wash my feet, but I can manage if—"

"Certainly," Adelle broke in. "I'll wash your feet before I turn the rest over to you."

A wicked, lustful, selfish part of Tyrdis wished Adelle would bathe all of her, yet she understood how she might think it inappropriate. They hadn't known each other long. Still, Tyrdis couldn't help but wonder if Adelle was experiencing the same attraction. Even if she was, Tyrdis hadn't a clue how to behave in such a situation. She had no familiarity with courting rituals, seduction, or any interpersonal relationships, for that matter. What was acceptable and what wasn't? What if she was wrong and Adelle was simply doing her job?

She thinks highly of me now, Tyrdis reminded herself. *I do not want to do something to negate her respect.*

Adelle's fingers massaging her scalp and weaving through her wet hair were like a touch from a goddess, blissful beyond her imagining. Then Adelle held the wide bowl up close to her face.

"Dip your hair and head in to rinse," she said. Tyrdis followed the instruction and Adelle wrapped an absorbent cloth around her head to keep her long, golden strands from dripping on the bed.

After scouring her neck, shoulders, and back, Adelle lowered the basin to the floor. "Put your feet in. I'll bring clean, hot water for you to finish with. Nice warrior tattoos," she observed. "What do they mean?"

Tyrdis sank her feet into the water, now tepid, and wiggled her toes. It pleased her that Adelle had noticed and asked about them rather than frowning at the reminder of her profession. "This one," she pointed to a geometric design on her upper arm, "is the symbol of Raumsdal, and the one under it is Jarl Raknar's emblem. Over here," she pointed to her other arm, "is the sign of Tyr, the god for whom I was named. These bands mark my fidelity to my fellow warriors."

After examining each one, Adelle dropped her gaze to Tyrdis's feet and scrubbed them with a small cloth. "It's good to know what they mean. I noticed you also have many scars."

Tyrdis lifted her chin with pride and glanced down at Adelle over her nose. "Thank you. They prove my value."

"Wouldn't it be a greater sign of your prowess if you remained unscarred?"

"Some may think so," Tyrdis answered. "Receiving the wounds is not a prize but enduring them without growing faint is. Many shrink from battle after being cut or stabbed, choosing to leave the fighting behind in favor of a less risky endeavor. Anyone who stands his or her ground with weapons in hand will eventually be struck a blow, regardless of how skilled they are. Those who return to their posts to continue in their service with steadfast devotion are worthy of Odin's Hall."

Adelle smirked, exhaling a dry laugh. "Yeah, die with a sword in your hand and all that foolishness."

"It is not foolishness!" Tyrdis's bubble of bliss was burst by Adelle's dismissal of one of her core beliefs. How could she mock such a vital principle? "Do I call your devotion to Eir and performing the healing arts foolish? Do I dismiss your commitment to nonviolence, even though it makes no sense?"

"Well, you just did, didn't you?" Adelle blasted back. She snatched the bowl from under Tyrdis's feet. "I am grateful to you, Tyrdis, and I can comprehend that sometimes fighting, even to the death, is necessary, such as to save more lives as you have demonstrated. But our people's persistence in constant wars and conquests hinders our progress. Don't you see that?"

Tyrdis frowned, a deep furrow forming between her brows. "The powerful rule; it is the way the world operates. Steel sharpens steel; it strengthens us. No, we should not constantly be at war. Yes, I support diplomacy, but you implied that the desire to spend the afterlife in Valhalla is a foolish one. A warrior cannot charge confidently into battle without the assurance the prize he will receive if he should perish is greater than that he will gain if he lives. I dare say all people would be better off if they did not fear death. Don't you aspire for your soul to enjoy paradise when you leave your body behind?"

Adelle exhaled a breath and slumped her shoulders as she carefully placed the vessel of dirty water on the bedside stand. "I guess I have a different vision of paradise. Tyrdis, I didn't mean to insult your beliefs. We all share them. I only meant there is also virtue in a life of peace, one lived long with the goal of gaining wisdom and understanding, such as Odin pursued. My son is only sixteen; what value will he have added to the world if he rushes blindly into the point of an enemy's spear and dies? Or if he takes the life of another young man who has no children to leave behind? There are other paths to greatness than by the sword alone. That's all I'm saying."

Lowering her head, Tyrdis folded her hands in her lap, essentially covering any glimpse between her thighs. "I apologize for my outburst. It was a gut reaction and not carefully thought through. I pray for a long life and many children for your son." She lifted her gaze to catch Adelle's. "Just be understanding of his rite of passage into manhood. It is not wrong to aspire to a noble cause, and should he fall—which I am sure he won't while serving in the safety of the king's guard—believe in the reward that has been promised him. If I have offended you or caused you grief, I am sincerely sorry."

Tyrdis had a sudden urge to envelop Adelle in her arms, to grant her comfort and protection from any pain, to feel her body pressed tight. Wouldn't it be divine? Holding her close, Tyrdis could feel the smoothness of her skin, inhale her fragrance, meld their energies together like two metals in a furnace being forged into an alloy stronger than either was alone. What would it be like to touch another intimately, to express the emotions she always kept locked away in a safe chest buried deep within, hidden behind the buttresses of a stone stronghold?

Am I afraid? That's silly. I fear nothing—not death or life or pain or suffering, not wild animals or storms, not the crucible of battle, not even being alone. But if I reach for her and she pulls away ... it would break my heart. No. Better to go through life alone than to care so deeply and be rejected.

"There's no harm done," Adelle responded in a gentle tone. "I used the wrong words. If you weren't so damn distracting sitting there with your perfect body on display, I might keep my wits about me. I'll bring clean water for you to complete your bath. Let me know when you're dressed, and I'll come to apply a fresh treatment and bandages to your wound. The most important thing now is for that hole in your side to heal."

Before Tyrdis could compose a reply, Adelle was gone. Relief trickled in and Tyrdis allowed herself to smile. *She does not hate me, and she likes the way I look. It does not mean she shares the attraction I have for her, though. She may simply aspire to such fitness herself, though I find her body most desirable just as it is. I wonder how long it will take me to recover? And then what?*

CHAPTER 11

Oskholm, northern Firdafylke, two days later

Sweyn and Jarl Niklaus rode through the gates of Oskholm, Jarl Stefnir's town, ahead of a cart driven by salty Karvir whose bushy brows and lined forehead signaled his age. Edan and a more youthful warrior brought up the rear, the butts of their spears resting against their boots in their stirrups. A large, white banner flapped in the breeze from Niklaus's spear as he led the way, and the prisoners walked unbound alongside the cart of raiders' corpses.

A contingent of six guards wearing distinctive red armbands fell in to escort them through a town of curious and fearful onlookers. Mothers held their children tight and backed into doorways while angry men glared or spat on the ground as they passed. Sweyn hoped they weren't riding into a trap, but the Firdafylke warriors maintained a neutral manner.

The town looked like theirs, except for the red flag embossed with a black serpent flying from a mast at the entrance to Jarl Stefnir's domain. An average-sized man with a bald head and bushy, brown beard blocked the path with his arms akimbo. He wore a silver circlet, a chainmail shirt over a red tunic, and a fur-trimmed mantle around his shoulders. A sword hung in its scabbard at his trim waist. Although it would appear he didn't possess the powerful sword arm Niklaus did, Sweyn understood looks could be deceiving. One didn't become jarl through ineffectual weakness.

"Jarl Niklaus," he stated and jutted up his square chin.

Niklaus inclined his head and pulled his pony to a halt. "Jarl Stefnir, thank you for agreeing to this truce."

Remaining stiff-backed and unmoving, he replied, "It was King Tortryggr's idea. Have you also returned our dead?"

Niklaus glanced back at the cart before returning an accommodating look to his counterpart. "I was hoping you could tell me. Do you recognize any of them?"

Stefnir signaled to an aide, who checked the faces of the bodies in the wagon. When the man shrugged and shook his head, the jarl frowned and clipped over to examine them himself. "They are not mine," he concluded. "But these three are." He motioned to Birger and the others. "Arnulf!" he called. "Bring them."

"Your town and hall remain in good repair, I see," Sweyn offered, attempting to melt the ice he sensed between their peoples.

Turning a perturbed expression from Niklaus to Sweyn, the Firdafylke jarl snorted. "Niklaus's son, Sweyn, is it? You have grown since last I saw you. Understand, young man—we are not your friends. Your flattering words will not spare you from our axes and spears. You have invaded our land, killed our brothers and sons, all for your king's vanity."

The bitterness of Stefnir's words pierced Sweyn's heart as he recalled happy visits to this town, and Karyna, the jarl's daughter. A rush of memories and repressed emotions washed over him at the thought of her. Was she here? Was she well? He wanted to ask about her, but—

"Your people started this conflict, Stefnir—make no mistake about that," Niklaus snapped. "Do not rebuke my son for being cordial. Even enemies can admire each other; isn't it so?"

Stefnir's frown deepened, and he rubbed a hand over the skin of his head as he ambled up to where Niklaus sat on his small bay horse. "Yes," he grumbled. "But a reasonable king doesn't declare war over the death of one man."

"Even if the one man was his oldest son and heir?" Niklaus raised a brow with the question, staring inquisitively into Stefnir's eyes. "It was not my decision, nor was it my son who was assassinated. I admire your King Tortryggr and his skill at diplomacy, but I do not rule in Raumsdal, nor do I comprehend a father's grief over the loss of a son."

"How do you think this will end?" Stefnir inquired. "Will the murderers suddenly feel remorse and confess? And if they do, will it satisfy King Gustav, or will he insist their confessions are false? He desires power and will not rest until he has conquered our kingdom and added it to his own. I do comprehend the grief of a father who has lost a son, yet I would not take out my wrath on those who weren't responsible."

"Here, my lord!" Stefnir's guard called as he strode toward them with three Raumsdal warriors, looking a little thin in Sweyn's estimation.

"Here," Stefnir declared in a gruff, formal tone. "Let us conclude our business and you can be on your way. You have one day's safe passage to cross into your kingdom unharmed. Then the truce is over."

Birger gave Sweyn a questioning look; he responded with a smile and a nod. Then Birger and the others walked toward Arnulf while Raumsdal's men passed them to join Niklaus's party.

"Don't worry, Stefnir," Niklaus returned just as coolly. "We'll be gone. I wish neither you nor your people personal malice. One day we may enjoy a drink together in Odin's Hall."

For an instant, Sweyn pictured Valhalla—a splendid palace adorned in silver, a warrior's paradise with walls of spears roofed with shields, where the valiant feasted on freshly-roasted boar and drank mead to their bellies' content. The valiant whom Valkyries whisked up to Ásgarðr on their winged horses would sing songs, exchange stories, battle each other to the death, then rise to feast again until the end of the age. Here all were allies and fighting was for sport alone until the fateful day of Ragnarök, when Norse, Jutes, and Swedes would march together under Odin's banner to battle the jötnar and all the enemies of the gods.

With a curt nod, Stefnir replied, "Until that day, Niklaus. May both we and our sons act with honor and courage so that Odin finds us worthy."

When they arrived back at the great hall in Sæladalr, the ex-prisoners were overjoyed to greet their family members and friends. Jarl Niklaus proclaimed a minor feast in their honor, filling his banquet hall with musicians and merrymakers.

After enjoying their own roasted boar, leek soup, bread, and early peas, Sweyn, his father, and his uncle left his mother, Lynnea, and the rest of the family for a small, secluded table in the corner. Horik lit a lamp and

Niklaus rolled out a piece of parchment, laying a charcoal-tipped stick beside it.

"The summer solstice is coming," Niklaus said with a sense of urgency. "We must act soon, or we'll have to wait for a whole moon to have the shadow of darkness again. I want this war to end, even if the king is content to drag it on all summer. Therefore, I propose we strike the important port of Griðlundr." He drew a jagged coastline and marked an 'X' in an inlet.

"Why not their capital of Gimelfjord?" Horik asked. "If we capture King Tortryggr, we can force them to capitulate."

Niklaus shook his head. "Gimelfjord is too far away and will be heavily fortified. Besides, I don't want to risk King Tortryggr being killed."

"Why not?" Horik exhaled incredulously. "Wouldn't that signal a clear victory for us?"

"Not necessarily," Sweyn answered. "It could fuel our enemies' fury and draw Svithjod to declare war on us in retaliation. As it is, they are only aiding their neighbor, but, if they were to send their entire army, we would be crushed between the two forces."

Horik ran fingers through his medium-brown hair and let them linger to scratch an itch. "I suppose," he grumbled. Sweyn's father gave him an approving nod.

"Griðlundr is the primary launching point and destination of their whaling and trade expeditions. It's far enough down the coast they may not suspect an attack, yet not so far away that they'll have time to prepare if their scouts see us coming. If we capture Firdafylke's most vital port, King Tortryggr must consider trading it for the fertile land along our southern border that King Gustav desires. Otherwise, we could confiscate or destroy the resources they're counting on for the coming winter, even if Tortryggr sends his main army to retake the town."

"And how do you propose we capture Griðlundr?" Horik asked impatiently. "If it's so important, they won't leave it unprotected."

"No, they won't." Niklaus's eyes gleamed with inspiration, and he took a sip of his drink, keeping his brother waiting. Sweyn had to wonder if Njal or any of his younger brothers would challenge his every decision once he became jarl. It was smart to have varying counsel rather than surround oneself with only yeasayers. A wise leader considers many points of view before locking into a course of action. He just hoped none would engage in violence or trickery to steal his seat of power. Sweyn had always been fair and friendly with his brothers, but he knew such disloyalty often occurred between siblings. Njal was already displaying signs of jealousy at being excluded from decision-making. Sweyn made a mental note to discuss it further with his father in private.

Placing the charcoal end of the twig on the parchment, Niklaus drew an arrow in the water off the coast, pointing down at the X. "I will lead five longboats filled with warriors to attack by sea. See this point where the mountains jut out?" He tapped with the clean end of the stick. "We'll set up here and wait for the sun to pass beyond the horizon, then speed around and enter the harbor before dawn arrives. Most people will be sleeping.

"At the same time, Horik," he calculated, drawing a new arrow across the land area of the map, "you and Sweyn will lead the other half of our fighters through this pass and down to attack the town from the rear. Their scouts will see our ships and sound an alarm. If they don't, all the better," he threw out with a shrug. "Their warriors will rush to engage us in the harbor while you cut them down from behind. They'll be forced to divide their attention, allowing our longboats to land."

"It's a good plan, Father," Sweyn agreed with excitement. "I think it will work. We should take care to avoid killing women and children, so King Tortryggr cannot accuse us of a massacre. Besides, the more hostages we hold, the more eager he will be to meet our demands."

"Do you hear the wise words coming from my son's lips, Horik?" Niklaus pinned him with a commanding expression. "Ensure that you instruct and discipline the warriors under your command," Niklaus charged his brother. "I have no tolerance for raping and ravaging. This mission depends on a swift, coordinated attack. Once the port has been secured, let your fighters enjoy themselves with camp women. That goes for you too."

Horik leaned back in his chair and smirked dismissively. "Do you think I can't control my warriors or my own lust? Why do you hold such a poor opinion of me?"

"Past experience," Niklaus muttered.

Bolting forward in fury, Horik's fist pounded the table. "In case you haven't noticed, I'm not a youth anymore. Even you sewed your wild oats before taking on the responsibilities that have twisted you into this." He waved a hand at Niklaus in disdain. "And you've turned poor Sweyn into a trained lapdog."

Offended at his uncle's comment, Sweyn rounded on him. "I choose my own path, Uncle Horik; don't be offended if it isn't the one you follow. I like women who like me, and plenty of them do. It's not a weakness to think before acting or to employ reason rather than brawn at every turn. You are a more experienced warrior but don't think I'm not your equal with a sword. Great Odin's beard! Why can't the two of you work together?"

"Settle down, Sweyn," his father chided softly. "Brothers will be brothers, as you know. Horik, are you on board with the plan?"

"We'll need more soldiers than are camped outside now," he responded in a reasonable voice.

"I agree. Sweyn, tomorrow take a vessel to Skeggen and inform King Gustav of our plan. Ask him for fifty fighting men and to secure the cooperation of Jarl Raknar. Horik, ride east to our neighbor Jarl Bjarke in Austrihóll and gain his backing. Tell him I have a longboat for him should he wish to come to lead his troops."

Horik let out a sigh. "If we gain fifty men from the king and the other two jarls to combine with ours, they should suffice. I admit, the plan is sound, but what about Sæladalr? You can't possibly think it is safe to leave our town unprotected with the enemy so near."

"Put Tyrdis in charge of the town's defenses," Sweyn suggested. "She hasn't recovered enough to join us in the attack, but she has the knowledge and experience required to coordinate a defense. We can ask for volunteers to stay so she'll at least have a dozen skilled fighters to support the townspeople if necessary."

"A woman?" Horik's eyes widened.

"Is she strong enough for the task?" Niklaus asked with concern rather than derision.

Sweyn laughed, a twinkle lighting his eyes. "She had only started taking steps around the hospice when the raiders came, and she dashed outside to slay two with her bare hands. It might be the death of her to ride all the way to Griðlundr and take part in a full-on battle, but she can protect Sæladalr."

With a nod, Niklaus agreed. "Stop by and talk with Tyrdis about it before you leave in the morning. However, if we don't secure the extra warriors, we'll have to scrap this plan and go back to engaging in endless border skirmishes. Make sure the king understands we need the resources for a strategic win if he is serious about annexing Oskholm. It's clear Jarl Stefnir suspects such is his intent, thus our chilly reception, but I'd rather deal with his wrath than Gustav's. This plan must be carried out within a week's time or there'll be no dark left to hide our approach. Now, everyone, get a good night's sleep."

"If this is all just Gustav making noise, and he isn't willing to commit his warriors, I'll be seriously pissed," Horik protested as he pushed up from the table. "I'll get Bjarke's support; he owes us a favor."

"Father, if the king hesitates, should I continue on to Heilagrfjord and consult Jarl Raknar directly?" Sweyn asked.

Niklaus's gaze bore into Sweyn's. "If King Gustav hesitates, inform him I will make peace with Firdafylke and no longer support his war effort. Let him go challenge Tortryggr to a duel if he likes. I've lost enough men and resources over his vengeance."

CHAPTER 12

Two days later, three weeks after the battle

*T*yrdis reclined in her bed, watching the gray-striped tabby stalk a mouse along the back wall of the hospice. Although she had never kept a pet, she could appreciate the value of having a huntress like Freida around. Rodents were a nuisance, and someone needed to keep them away from food and medicines. While snakes could perform the same function, they weren't as reliable, tended to frighten people, and would make poor companions for Svanhild.

The feline bided her time, creeping slowly and silently toward her unsuspecting prey. The mouse scurried a few inches, then stopped at a morsel of grain lying under Adelle's worktable. While it was distracted and had its hands full with the kernel, Freida pounced. Tyrdis felt inward pride in the cat's skill, deciding she must reward her for her service … cheese, perhaps?

Svanhild skipped to Tyrdis with a cheerful smile and a bowl of porridge spotted with fresh berries. The shieldmaiden, who sat propped up in her bed, pinned the girl with a speculative expression. "I can feed myself, thank you."

"I know," Svanhild chirped as she settled on the stool beside her. "But feeding you gives me an excuse to come visit. Are you feeling stronger today?"

"Much stronger," Tyrdis replied, hiding an amused grin. "Strong enough to lift that spoon to my mouth." Svanhild slumped, casting down a disappointed look, and stretched the bowl toward her. "However, I still require your aid."

Her words perked up Svanhild as intended. "What do you need me to do?"

"My foot itches, and I can't reach down to scratch it without pulling against my side." Tyrdis spooned in a mouthful of the hot, inviting food, further warmed by the girl's enthusiasm.

"I'll scratch it for you! Which one?" Svanhild pulled back the cover from Tyrdis's feet and peered at them.

Tyrdis wiggled the toes of her right foot. "This one." Little fingers scratched at her arch and her foot twitched. "Tickling is not allowed," she ordered in a pseudo-hard tone.

Svanhild giggled. "Sorry." Tyrdis couldn't pull her gaze from the delightful child as she ate, but her thoughts wandered to Adelle. She hadn't avoided her since the bath—not the way she had for a while—but she had been avoiding making eye contact. Was she embarrassed? Why should she be? She hadn't been the naked one.

She must have sensed what I was thinking, Tyrdis considered with dire concern. *Can she read minds? Was I giving off vibrations or a scent that Adelle construed as desirous? She couldn't have realized what I was feeling ... could she?*

Tyrdis shouldn't have been emitting any emotions. She was a rugged soldier, not the kind of woman prone to even having feelings, much less allowing them to be known. She could get away with it with Svanhild; people expected everyone to fawn over such a precious child, but not the town's grædari. Besides, Adelle wouldn't be interested in her the same way. She clearly preferred men, having married one and borne him children. And she certainly had no love for warriors of either gender. Had Tyrdis offended her without realizing it?

The tingling sensation she had experienced at Adelle's touch returned, shooting through her body with tantalizing realness, and she clenched a fist to ward it off.

"What's wrong?" Svanhild moved her fingers away from Tyrdis's foot. "Am I tickling again? I didn't mean to. Did I get the itchy spot?"

Smiling at Svanhild, she replied, "Your scratching was precise and effective. Thank you. I was wondering if there is tea to accompany this porridge?"

Svanhild leaped up. "Yes! I'll get it right away." Wagging a finger at

Tyrdis, she added with a serious expression, "No gulping. Mama says you must eat slowly."

Tyrdis raised a brow. "I *never* gulp."

With a snicker, Svanhild scampered to the hearth. A few moments later, it was Adelle who arrived with her tea. "My honeybee says you are feeling stronger this morning." She set the cup on the little upended crate and sat on the stool beside Tyrdis.

"I am, thank you." Setting her empty bowl aside, Tyrdis took her tea. "How fare your other patients?"

Adelle took a glance around the room before returning her attention to Tyrdis. "I believe they will all live, thank you. If you keep up your progress, you'll be ready to return to your family in a few weeks. I know they will be glad to see you."

Tyrdis expelled a heavy sigh. "I have no family to return to."

Regret shot through Adelle's expression. "I'm sorry. I knew your brother had died, I didn't—"

"Do not be troubled, Adelle," Tyrdis bade her. "You did not know. I could conclude Jarl Raknar might be pleased to regain my services, though he will not like what I have to say about his cousin."

"Tell me about them," Adelle requested, "about you. Why did you become a warrior?"

Glad the lovely healer was showing any interest in her at all beyond getting her well and moving out of her hospice, Tyrdis allowed herself to relax. "My father, Vignir, was a mountain man. My mother was part of a group crossing over the Fille Fiell when they were trapped in a late snow-storm. Her father died in the blizzard, but Vignir rescued her and some others, so she agreed to marry him. When she became pregnant with me, she grew fearful and uncomfortable, so my father packed them up and moved them down the mountain to the village of Heilagrfjord.

"When the jarl—Raknar's father—saw how strong and bold he was, he offered Vignir a place in his service. I was born, then Erik, but Mother had an even more difficult time with her third child. I was six and Erik four when both Mother and the babe perished during the birthing."

"I am so sorry," Adelle responded with a consoling expression. "It must have been hard for your father."

"It was," Tyrdis recalled. "He was a quiet, solitary man, strict and formal. She must have had a soothing, humanizing effect on him because he hardened after she died. He knew nothing about daughters, so he raised Erik and me the same way—to value duty, honor, and military prowess. I was never a soft girl prone to displays of emotion; that does not mean I harbor indifference. Shows of affection have not been part of my experience as Father considered them an unnecessary sentiment, but I can prove my devotion to others by protecting them from danger, which is indeed of greater value."

"I can see that," Adelle said with a contemplative nod. Then she cocked her head. "And Svanhild?"

Tyrdis snorted out a half laugh. "Whether a gift from Freya or a trick played by Loki, the girl has a singular effect on me. I am not accustomed to children, and they typically avoid me. Svanhild is an enigma."

"Would it surprise you to learn she doesn't take so fondly to everyone?"

Tyrdis met Adelle's gaze with a questioning one of her own. "Indeed?"

Adelle allowed a smile to cross her lips before glancing back to where Svanhild assisted Joren with Thorgil. It was clear she was eager to help, but she wasn't spooning food into his mouth or tickling his feet.

"Even before you rescued her from the raiders, it was all I could do to keep her away from you."

Tyrdis frowned, peering at Adelle with disappointment. She was about to ask why she felt the need to keep her child away from her when Sweyn stepped through the open doorway.

"Joren, Adelle," he greeted and headed straight toward Tyrdis.

"Good morning, Sweyn." Adelle rose to meet him at the foot of the bed.

"How is our shieldmaiden?" he asked.

"Better," came Tyrdis's confident reply.

Sweyn was dressed for traveling and Tyrdis noticed other warriors outside. Sensing this was more than a social call, she swung her feet over the side of the bed and walked to stand beside him and Adelle.

"Did all go well at the prisoner exchange?" Tyrdis asked. Though she hadn't her trousers and boots, she was at least wearing a proper tunic. She was glad to be clean, her hair brushed and braided, and assumed a proper posture with her feet shoulder-width apart and her hands clasped behind her hips.

"Yes," he replied. "Birger sends his best wishes and our men are happy to be home. But, unfortunately, the truce was short-lived. Jarl Stefnir has every intention of defending his border no matter what methods he must employ, as we would expect. Tyrdis, how fit are you?"

"She is in no condition to fight, if that is what you mean," Adelle interjected in a commanding voice. "It will take time for her insides to heal and her muscles to knit themselves back together. If you have any regard for her well-being—"

Sweyn lifted his palms to calm her. "Adelle, I am not suggesting we send her into the fray just yet."

"I haven't a weapon to practice with," Tyrdis replied. While she appreciated Adelle's defense, she was eager to do something besides lie about feeling weak and useless. "But I have been up walking and engaged in stretching exercises. I concur with Adelle's assessment that I would be ineffective in battle at present, but I could return to light training."

"You certainly cannot." Adelle rounded on her with an icy stare. "If you tear your side open again, it may never heal properly. If you ever hope to wield a weapon with power in the future, you will heed my instructions."

Staring into Adelle's eyes, she recognized the fire she had shown when she stood against Garold and his thugs. More than a mere challenge, Adelle displayed an iron will equal to a king's as she radiated the authority invested in her by Eir herself. Tyrdis had to respect her; however, she couldn't surrender to her feelings of affection and misplaced desire. Adelle hadn't even wanted Svanhild near her, after all. She may as well act the part of the callous shieldmaiden Adelle had supposed her to be.

Tyrdis switched her focus to Sweyn. "What do you require of me?"

Adelle exhaled a muffled curse and crossed her arms. Svanhild must have felt the shift of mood in the room because she appeared between them, grabbing both women's arms in her little hands.

"My father has devised an attack plan to bring this war to a swift end," he explained, "or at least force King Tortryggr into negotiations. I'm on my way to present it to King Gustav. The plan will require leadership roles from me, my father, and my uncle, and, though he will protest and possibly throw a tantrum, we know my brother Njal is not ready to be put in charge of the town defenses while we are away. Niklaus agrees you are the best choice for command. It would only be for a week at most, and it's possible nothing would happen at all. However, we have suffered raids, and Jarl Stefnir's troops are too close for comfort. He did not respond favorably to us yesterday, and I can't say when he may choose to attack. We'll leave a dozen trained warriors—more if possible—with you, and all the men and women of Sæladalr will be instructed to follow your orders to the letter. You won't have to lift a weapon, only coordinate a defense should it be necessary. Njal can swing a sword; he just doesn't have the experience to lead. People know your reputation, Tyrdis. They'll obey you."

"I would be honored to accept this responsibility," Tyrdis declared.

"You can't command the town defenses from out here in the hospice," Adelle objected, "and you haven't healed enough to leave."

"Adelle, I am up to the task," Tyrdis answered with strength. "Your jarl has honored me with his request and puts his trust in me. Sweyn, tell your father I will not disappoint him."

"I forbid it!" Adelle lifted her chin and shifted her fists to her hips.

"You cannot forbid me," Tyrdis countered in irritated disbelief.

"Very well, kill yourself for all I care," she shouted back.

Tyrdis felt a tug on her arm and glanced down into Svanhild's worried face, eyes welling with tears. "Stop arguing, you two."

Adelle pulled Svanhild to her side. "I know what is best, and this tiresome woman will not listen."

"But if Tyrdis doesn't protect the town, who will? Who will keep Amma safe?"

"Amma can come out here and stay with us," Adelle replied.

Svanhild pulled away from her mother, passing her gaze between the women. "Then who will protect us?"

"I will," Tyrdis vowed. She pinned Svanhild with a serious expression. "I will allow no one to harm you, ever. I swear it on Tyr's severed hand, Svanhild. Your mother is only concerned for my well-being, but I am more concerned for hers—and yours. I don't have to leave here until the others go to battle. Then when I am in charge, I will post guards at the hospice and lookouts in Jarl Niklaus's tower to watch for danger."

"No, Svanhild," Adelle contradicted with a glare at Tyrdis. "She's hardheaded and an impossible patient. She cares more about garnering Jarl Niklaus's favor than protecting us. If that was her only aim, she would stay here as I instructed her."

"Look," Sweyn interrupted. "I don't want to cause strife between you all."

"This is not your fault, Sweyn," Tyrdis snapped. She bent over and reached under her cot to retrieve her trousers and boots, though it caused a terrible pain in her side to so do. "Adelle, I appreciate all you have done for me. When I have the means, I vow to repay you. But I shan't trouble you further with my disagreeable presence in your house. I shall move into Jarl Niklaus's hall and familiarize myself with his preferred way of doing things."

"Good!" Adelle barked. "I think it's for the best."

"Mama!" Svanhild tugged on her arm, big tears rolling down her freckled cheeks. The sight broke Tyrdis's heart, and she wished more than anything to fall to her knees and wrap the girl in a loving embrace. But she was Adelle's daughter, and she had the right to control whom she allowed close to her. Besides, she didn't want to come between two people she cared about.

Tyrdis didn't truly understand what she felt for Adelle; she only knew this tension made her hurt inside even more than her enemy's spear had. She regretted the argument and the position it had thrust Svanhild into, but, great Odin's beard! Why couldn't Adelle understand she had a responsibility to answer Jarl Niklaus's call?

"Honor and obey your mother, Svanhild," she said with a last glance at the distraught child. "It is acceptable for a dutiful daughter to do so, and you are an ideal daughter. Adults quarrel sometimes; no one is angry with you."

As Tyrdis turned to join Sweyn, Svanhild's voice rang in her ears. "Be careful, Tyrdis, and don't hurt yourself more. We love you." Choking back her own tears, she nodded to Sweyn and exited with him, wondering exactly who "we" meant.

CHAPTER 13

A pale sensation of regret wormed its way through Adelle's righteous anger as Tyrdis, Sweyn, and the two burly warriors disappeared from her view. Svanhild, who still gripped her hand, sniffed and wiped small fingers under her nose. "She left us," her daughter stated in disbelief.

"I told you she would," Adelle replied empathetically, hoping Svanhild didn't realize her outburst was the reason. She only was thinking of what was best for Tyrdis and her recovery. Didn't she understand? Why was she being so obstinate? She needed more rest, more time for her body to heal. She had almost died, for Freya's sake. Tyrdis was going to stay longer, and then ...

"I guess Jarl Niklaus needs her more," lamented Svanhild. "But she promised to protect us if the bad people come back. Will she keep her promise, Mama?"

Big, tear-filled eyes peered up at her, and Adelle wrapped her arms around her daughter. "I'm certain Tyrdis is a woman of her word, honeybee—as sure as summer and winter."

Adelle glanced around to see the onlookers in the room had returned to minding their own business now that the emotion-packed scene had played out and the warriors were gone. She suddenly felt drained and disappointed, as much with herself as with Tyrdis and Sweyn. *Why did I get so angry? Why did I say things I didn't truly mean? I know she cares nothing for status or politics, and she obviously cares for Svanhild and me.*

Then her daughter's last words to Tyrdis dawned on her. She had said "We *love you.*" Who was "we?" Was Svanhild's declaration meant to include her? Maybe she loved Tyrdis in the way she loved her countrymen in general. She couldn't even claim her as a friend, for they hardly knew each other. Besides, she didn't think of women that way ... at least she hadn't in the past.

Heat flashed through Adelle at the memory of seeing Tyrdis's body when she had bathed her and the unexplainable reaction it had spawned. Her legs were so long and sleek, her abdomen toned and trim, and her firm, pert breasts were just hand-sized, beckoning to Adelle in a way that made her avert her gaze. *And she saved Svanhild's life. I could love her for that reason alone.*

Yet, becoming close to Tyrdis was impossible. Maybe she didn't have a family to return to, but she fought for Jarl Raknar and wore his symbol on her body ... although she was free to stay and serve Jarl Niklaus if she wished. She seemed friendly with Sweyn, and he openly admired her. Even so, Tyrdis was a warrior with all the misguided values and brief lifespan that accompanied the job. Adelle simply had no future with someone like her, even as a friend. It was better that Tyrdis left now rather than give herself and Svanhild another week to become more involved with the woman. A clean break would be best for them all.

* * *

Skeggen, *the next day*

Sweyn arrived at King Gustav Ironside's great hall for the second time in less than a fortnight. Edan and Karvir accompanied him on the longboat journey again, as it was faster by sea. The highlight of the trip had been spotting a whale breach. Its massive body crashing down onto the choppy waves rocked the small craft, but his father's oarsmen had kept them upright.

The king was in the middle of a court proceeding when the three slipped quietly through the open door to stand behind a group of spectators.

"Emil is a snake!" thundered the beefy man with a wild red mane and beard encircling his tight features. Jabbing a finger at the scowling acorn-haired fellow with beam-sized arms crossed over his chest, he continued. "He insulted my sister's honor by accosting her in secret, kissing her without her consent, and then he tried to coerce her to sleep with him. He's as dishonorable as his lying, cowardly father."

The accused lunged at the angry, ruddy man with his fists and jaw clenched. "Your sister is a tart who'd lie with anyone who breathed. She wanted me sure as there's a sun in the sky, and how dare you insult my father, who is not here to defend himself!"

"Olga, tell King Gustav what that *niðingr* did." He thrust a frightened-looking young woman to the fore, and she curtseyed before the king.

"My lord," she began tentatively and glanced over her shoulder at her big brother.

"Don't be afraid, Olga," Gustav said. "Just tell us what happened."

"I—I was walking alone after enjoying a drink with some friends at the alehouse when Emil ..." She hesitated and bit her lower lip, whipping her head back to the burly red-haired man. "Skelk, I ..."

"Oh, for Hel's sake, woman," he rebuked in a growl. "I saw the whole thing."

"How could you have seen anything when you claim I committed this indecency in secret?" bellowed Emil. He threw up his hands and faced the king. "He's obviously lying."

"Why, you *sorðinn* heap of manure!"

A guard had to hold Skelk back from attacking Emil right there in the king's hall.

Gustav leaned forward, piercing him with an intense stare. "You will control yourself, Skelkollr." He turned and waved to a distinguished-looking, mature man in fine, colorful silk clothing. "Lawspeaker." The slender man with a long, braided beard stepped onto the platform to stand beside the king's chair and offered him a slight bow of respect.

"My lord," he responded with a tongue as silver as his hair.

"You all know Snorri, our lawspeaker," Gustav announced. "Tell us, what does the law say on this matter?"

Snorri straightened, clasped his hands behind his back, and faced the assembly, accuser, and accused. "A man must not touch a free woman in a sexual manner without her explicit consent. To do so is shameful and a misuse of his superior physical strength. If the woman has taken offense by his action, he must pay her compensation. However, if the accusation against him is false, his accuser must pay him compensation for damaging his character before the community."

"Thank you, Snorri," Gustav said with a nod, and the lawspeaker stepped back. "So, which is it? You can't both be telling the truth."

"I have brought three character witnesses." Emil raised his hand, and two men and a woman made their way to the front. "They will testify I never insult women in the manner this *skitr* head has alleged."

"Well, I have three brothers and five cousins to back me up," retorted Skelkollr. He flexed his biceps and eight men of varying sizes squeezed through to form a wall behind him. Skelkollr sneered at his adversary and rested his fists on his hips with a satisfied smirk. Olga's shoulders slumped, and she shrank behind the row of relatives.

"Look at mighty Skelkollr." Emil motioned toward him and laughed. "He is so puny and cowardly he needs eight powerful men to help him fight his battle."

Fire flew from Skelkollr's eyes as he yanked an axe from his belt. "I'll kill you for your insult—both to my sister and to me, you níðingr !"

"Your slur has earned you a death sentence!" Emil's friends held him back as he tried to charge forward. "I demand a *holmgang*!"

King Gustav rose to his feet and held up his hands to still the murmuring crowd. "You two have been quarreling for years, and I've had enough of it. But we are at war, and I cannot have two of my best fighters killing each other. Skelkollr, you have charged Emil with a serious offense, and you have both hurled vile insults at each other which cannot be ignored. Therefore, I will agree to this duel to take place in the public square this midafternoon before many witnesses; however, it shall not be to the death. If you must kill someone, let it be the Firdafylkers. The first to draw blood will be considered truthful in the eyes of the gods. But, if one of you kills the other, that man will be seen as guilty and cast out of Raumsdal forever. Do you agree to the rules of combat?"

Both men nodded and voiced their approval, easing the tension in the room. It seemed to Sweyn that Skelkollr had invented an excuse to shame someone he was feuding with, and his sister was a reluctant participant. However, that didn't mean Emil had done nothing in the past to warrant the big man's wrath. They had indeed exchanged vile insults a Norseman would kill over. All things considered, Sweyn was impressed with Gustav's decision on the matter and committed it to memory. As Jarl, settling local disputes would become part of his responsibilities one day.

"If that is all," Gustav said, "court is dismissed for today."

The spectators began excitedly making plans to watch the duel as they filtered out and the two feuding parties kept their distance from each other. Sweyn made his way to the king.

"That was a wise ruling," he complimented with a smile. "May I have a moment of your time, my lord? My father has sent me to relay his new plan of attack against our enemies. He believes it will drive King Tortryggr to make concessions."

"Yes, yes." Gustav stepped down from the dais and walked with Sweyn and his companions to his lengthy feast table. "You recall my sons, Ivar and Kerstav?"

The two young men sat slumped in their seats, which seemed to have been purposefully pushed apart from each other. Ivar appeared disinterested and his younger brother, Kerstav, irritated.

"Well, are you going to watch the holmgang or not?" Kerstav demanded.

"What for?" Ivar snarled. "Who gives a fig about those fools? They can kill each other for all I care."

"Nay, Ivar," his father corrected. "We don't want our people killing each other when we have enemies for them to slay. Don't you listen to anything I say?"

"Sorry, I'm not as perfect as Jarivald was!" Ivar bolted up, sending his chair toppling over to hit the plank floor with a sound that alerted the hall's Cú to lope off and find a safer place to lie. Sweyn noted the huge, wiry wolfhound and thought he might like to keep a pair in his great hall, but that would be a long time in the future. His father thought they were too big, and their short lifespans saddened his mother. He also offered silent gratitude to Freya that his brothers were not so moody as Ivar and Kerstav.

Gustav yanked Ivar's arm, spinning him around, and glared at him with a look bordering on hatred. "You mind your temper, young man, or it will be the death of you too. We have a guest, and you behave like *this*?"

Paling like a widow in the dark of winter, Ivar flicked an apologetic glance at Sweyn. "Sorry, Sweyn. Kerstav is too eager to watch a fight while I'm still disturbed over seeing my brother murdered. Can any of you imagine how I feel knowing I was there and couldn't prevent his death?" He lowered his gaze to his father's boots.

"Couldn't prevent it," the king muttered in disgust. "What's done is done. Now, set that chair right, sit down, and let's hear what Sweyn has come to report. Can you do that?"

"Yes, sir." Ivar shuffled over to find Kerstav had already reset his chair. They exchanged a troubled look, and the prince settled into his seat. "Thank you."

"I didn't mean to—" Kerstav began.

"Forget it." Ivar shook his head and turned his attention to Sweyn as he and the king took their seats.

"You see how the problems never end for one in authority," Gustav said in a light tone. With a laugh, he added, "Are you sure you wish to become jarl one day?"

"By that time, I hope to have learned to handle them with the ease you employ, my lord," Sweyn replied. He nodded to Edan and Karvir, who joined them at the expansive table.

"Did your prisoner exchange go well?" the king asked, then frowned into an empty goblet. "Elida!" he bellowed. "Drinks and food for everyone," he ordered his maidservant. She bowed and scurried off to obey.

"It did, no thanks to Garold," Sweyn reported. He cocked his head and raised a brow at Gustav. "Did you order him to execute our prisoners?"

The king erupted with a belly laugh and shook his head while his face turned red. "I told him I didn't think he was capable of besting one of our foes, even if the man was bound and beaten. I suppose he could have construed the comment as a challenge." He shrugged as if it was of no consequence. "He has been loath to return to Heilagrfjord and face his cousin's reprimand. But seriously ..." Gustav bore his gaze into Sweyn, all hints of amusement swept away. "How goes the war?"

"That is why I have come," Sweyn stated, catching Ivar's and Kerstav's notice as well. "My father has devised a most excellent plan to win the conflict; however, we need additional support from you and Jarl Raknar to carry it out."

King Gustav listened with rapt attention, asked a few questions, made a few suggestions, and, in the end, agreed to the strategy. Ivar volunteered to travel and demand Jarl Raknar send more fighting men to support the kingdom, and this time his father approved. "But do not embarrass him by mentioning Garold's shortcomings," Gustav insisted. "They are close kin, and Raknar will take offense."

WITH ALL AGREED upon and a meal shared to seal it, Sweyn bade the king and his sons farewell to get started back home.

"I want to stop at the market again," Edan said as they strolled down the main street of town. "Gislaug was very appreciative of the silk scarf I bought for her." He grinned and wiggled his eyebrows. "I wish to get her a necklace or pendant this time."

"For the love of the gods, man!" Karvir swore. "Does she think you're made of money? Do *you* think you're made of money? How can you afford all these gifts?"

"Can I help that I'm lucky at dice?" Edan's grin grew wider. "You already have a wife, so you don't have to worry about wooing one with presents."

"Ha!" The older man let out a sarcastic laugh, causing Sweyn to snicker. "It gets far worse once you marry them. 'Honey, the roof is leaking, the table needs mending, I need a new dress' ... oh, and the worst one of all: 'Do you still think I'm pretty? Why don't you spend more time with me?'" He tossed his head back and pulled at his shoulder-length hair while Edan gaped at him in horror and Sweyn doubled over with laughter.

"Spend as much time as you need in the market—both of you," Sweyn said when he had caught his breath. "I'll meet you at the ship."

Sweyn wasn't sure what he would do about finding a wife. His father wanted him to marry a noblewoman, but Raknar's daughter was only ten and he had never met Jarl Bjarke's children. *Does he even have a daughter?* He wistfully recalled Jarl Stefnir's daughter, though it had been years since the celebration when he first met Karyna. Even as a lad, she had caught his eye. Her hair had been the color of a fawn's and as fine as spider silk, yet it was her mischievous spirit that had drawn him in. She was daring, with a wicked sense of humor and a hint of superior attitude. They had occasions to see each other since that childhood summer, and, though Sweyn didn't know what kind of woman she had grown into or if she'd already been promised to someone else, he had never forgotten her. Oh, he'd had a few romps in the hay and even fell in love once—or so he had thought—with one of the *völva's* acolytes a few years ago. Sometimes he still had dreams about her, even though he knew she was off limits.

Too bad we're at war with Firdafylke, he sighed to himself. He had looked for Karyna when they went down for the prisoner exchange but hadn't seen her.

A sudden clanging sound brought Sweyn back to the present, and he glanced around to see a woman had dropped her tin pails on her way to the corner well. Feeling benevolent, he rushed over to help her.

"Thank you, young man," she replied with a smile as he handed them back to the older woman. "You're not from around here."

"No. I'm from Sæladalr. Do you need help?" he offered.

"No," she answered, trying to hide a smile. "I've been collecting water from the well since before you were born."

Sweyn strolled through town, half daydreaming and half looking for Hallfrid. He was curious about how she was doing and still wondered about the secret she had mentioned earlier. He spotted her coming out of a yardhouse with two brass chamber pots.

"There you are, Hallfrid!" he called cheerfully in greeting. "Industrious as ever, I see."

"Estrid, the butcher's wife, is weaving me a new dress for me doing her cleaning," the little girl answered with a big smile. "I need a new dress because this one is tattered and getting too small."

"That's a fair trade," Sweyn agreed, "but I think you're lovely no matter what you're wearing."

Hallfrid blushed and swished her too-short skirt around her calves. "That's because you're too nice to be a jarl's son."

"Now, what makes you say that?" Sweyn's tone was playful, but her opinion was troubling to him.

"Because." She lowered her gaze and began walking, presumably back to the butcher's house with the pots.

"You were going to tell me a secret last time we talked," Sweyn reminded her.

Hallfrid froze in her tracks and slowly peered up at him with a fearful expression. "Shhh," she warned, and whispered, "it's too dangerous."

Sweyn bent down so his head was level with hers and searched her wary eyes. "I can protect you. If it's a matter of genuine concern, someone with authority should know. And if you're afraid to stay here, I could take you with us this afternoon on a longboat to Sæladalr and you can work in Jarl Niklaus's household."

Her lips scrunched up in a pout and her brows pulled down. "You aren't one of those men who likes little girls, are you?"

Sweyn's mouth fell agape, and his eyes flew wide. "Good Odin, no!" He wanted to reach out to her but felt she might misconstrue such a move at the moment. Lowering his voice to a hush, he asked, "Is that what happened? Did a man touch you inappropriately?"

Hallfrid shook her head with convincing denial.

"It's all a lie," she whispered. The little orphan glanced around nervously and then caught his gaze. "I like you, Sweyn, and I don't want you to die for a lie."

"What do you mean it's a lie?" Sweyn's heart pounded in his chest, his airways constricted, and his mouth was suddenly dry. "You must tell me what you know."

CHAPTER 14

Sweyn's imagination was on overdrive as his every honed instinct screamed at him to pay attention while Hallfrid's troubled gaze peered around the area. A couple of men tramped by complaining loudly about prices and a woman with a covered basket herded her children back from the market. A goat with a little bell tinkling from a rope around its neck trotted up, sniffed at a vine that had sprouted near the smelly yardhouse, then opened its velvety lips, exposing impressive teeth that tore into it with gusto.

Still in a crouch, Sweyn laid a reassuring hand on Hallfrid's arm. "Let's see you back to Estrid and return her pots," he suggested and stretched up to his full height. "Then mayhap you and I could go for a little walk to look for wildflowers."

A measure of relief budded on her gaunt face, and the little girl nodded. "I know where to find the prettiest flowers."

When Sweyn spoke to Estrid, the butcher's wife, who was engrossed in her weaving, she barely acknowledged him. "I am Sweyn, Jarl Niklaus's son, visiting from Sæladalr, and Hallfrid has offered to show me around. I shan't keep her long."

The pinch-faced woman spared him a disapproving glance. "See that you don't," she replied and returned her focus to her craft.

They exited through the gate in the town's palisade, past the raucous market where a man's pet bear was creating a sensation, and out into a gently-sloping meadow between the foothills behind Skeggen and the expansive fjord before it. A shepherd steered his shorn flock up a slope to their left, but he paid them no attention.

Surrounded by lush green shoots and a sea of purple heather, Hallfrid smoothed her frayed skirt and sat on the ground. Sweyn dropped beside her, picked a flower, and handed it to the girl. "Now, about that lie. Hallfrid, I can't even fathom what it has been like for you growing up without a proper home and parents to care for you, how frightened you must be that someone will turn you into a thrall. You clearly heard or saw something significant that has to do with the war. You haven't known me long, but you can trust me with the information, and, by Odin's beard, I swear to protect you, no matter what."

Hallfrid inhaled a deep breath and huffed it out. She glanced around one more time, just to be sure, and then her eyes met Sweyn's. "I had been pitching hay in the king's stable. Sometimes Jarivald would allow me to sleep in the hay if I fed and watered the ponies. Often, I would brush them down and pick their hooves. I'm not really strong enough to muck stalls properly, but Jarivald would feel sorry for me in the winter and let me sleep in the warm barn in exchange for light work."

When her gaze fell to the grass, he prompted her, saying, "You were in the stable the night Jarivald was killed?"

She nodded. When she raised her chin, sorrow, fear, and distress grappled for prominence on her face.

"Just tell me what you saw." Sweyn's tone was honest and sensitive, with no hint of demand.

"Jarivald and Ivar came in arguing and their loud voices woke me," she began in a fragile manner. "They were yelling and exchanging curses, but I don't know what the fight was about. I tried not to listen because it wasn't my business. Then I heard the clinking of metal, and they were shouting, 'I'll kill you,' and 'You can try.' So I peeked out of the hay because I was frightened."

"Is that when you saw their attackers?"

Hallfrid shook her head, and tears welled in her hooded eyes. "The princes were fighting each other with their swords. They were angry and Jarivald cut Ivar. Then Ivar jabbed his sword into Jarivald's chest. It made a horrid sound, and I was so scared I had to hold both hands over my mouth to stay quiet. He made wheezing sounds and fell down bleeding. They both looked shocked; none of us could believe it. Ivar stood there breathing hard and then Kerstav ran in."

Sweyn wiped a hand down his face. Blood rushed through his veins as rapidly as thoughts flashed through his mind. *Ivar killed his older brother?*

"Kerstav shouted, 'Ivar, what have you done?' and Ivar said, 'He started the fight; see, he cut me.' Ivar was bleeding too. Then he said, 'I didn't mean to kill him,' and Kerstav said, 'We must tell Father what happened.' But Ivar didn't want to tell, and they started arguing. That's when King Gustav walked in."

"The king knew what happened?" Sweyn was stunned with disbelief. Had he been afraid people would say he couldn't manage his own household? Or would they cast accusing glares at Ivar for killing his brother? Jarivald had been popular throughout Raumsdal. But it wasn't that uncommon for brothers to fight, especially when power or property was at stake. If it had been a fair contest like Hallfrid testified, Ivar wouldn't be punished.

Hallfrid gave a resolute nod and sniffed, swiping a hand under her eye to catch a tear. "At first, he was angry with Ivar, then he fell to his knees, cradled Jarivald and grieved. I was terrified and didn't dare move—I could hardly breathe. Ivar said he was sorry but insisted Jarivald started the fight. Kerstav cried, and hollered, 'What will we do?' That's when Ivar straightened like a real man, returned his sword to its sheath, and said, 'I will stand before the Thing and give an account to all the kingdom of what happened here tonight. Jarivald was arrogant, thinking he could not be beaten, and he drew the first blood. I defended myself and proved I had more daring and skill than my brother. I deserve to be named heir.'"

Sweyn nodded. "People would have understood."

"That's what Kerstav said, but the king wouldn't have it," Hallfrid testified. "He said it would be putting a target on Ivar's back because Jarivald had many friends. Gustav said without any witnesses, people may not believe Ivar's story and spread rumors that he cheated or outright murdered his brother. He said the whole incident would reflect badly on their family and one of the jarls might get a notion to seize his throne. Then the king said, 'We'll tell everyone assassins from Firdafylke snuck in by night while the two of you were grooming your horses and fell upon you like vicious wolves. That will give us the excuse we need to take the fertile land along the border I desire. If we can add to the size and wealth of the kingdom, then Jarivald's death will not have been in vain.' When Ivar and Kerstav protested, the king got mad. He insisted no one but the three of them could ever know what really happened, and he made them swear a blood oath. He said if they ever told the truth, they would die a hideous death and be dragged down to Helheim forever and ever. It was so scary, and all the while, Jarivald was lying there dead."

"The war ..." Sweyn swallowed and attempted to rein in his emotions. This was not the time to act like an impetuous youth. *You are a man—a jarl's son,* he reminded himself. *You must rule with your mind, not your passions.* Every muscle tightened as his hands flexed into fists. "The war is based on a lie." *Greedy Gustav just wanted an excuse to invade Firdafylke and take more land for himself. He has coerced my father into spearheading this effort and our casualties have been the greatest. Still, widows and mothers across Raumsdal grieve because the king lied and manipulated us all to do his bidding. He is not an absolute monarch. Without the support of the jarls, he is nothing. What a foul act of deceit! Loki could take lessons from that mongrel.*

"I was scared and left the next morning to find others willing to let me work for them and sleep in their barns. It was a cold winter, and I couldn't stay outside, but I didn't want to die a hideous death and be dragged down to Helheim, and I knew that's what would happen if I told." Hallfrid sniffed and hugged herself while a tear rolled down her cheek. "I kept having nightmares about it, but when you were so true and brave and helped me, I thought, 'Maybe he's the one.' So I started thinking about telling you because you would know what to do."

Sweyn took a cleansing breath and stretched out his hands to check if they were steady. They still shook a bit, so he clenched them back into balls. Steeling his jaw, he fixed Hallfrid with a forceful gaze. "First, we will tell your mistress I am taking you to Sæladalr to serve in Jarl Niklaus's hall. Then you will ride on the longboat with me and my friends."

"I've never ridden in a longboat before." Her tears dried, and she seemed a little less frightened.

With a tender smile, Sweyn replied, "It will be an adventure for you. When we get to my father's longhouse, you and I will speak to him alone and convey all you have told me. He will know what to do. Hallfrid, you were wise to keep quiet about what you saw, and even wiser to share it with me. What's done in the open is honorable, but what is done in secret is shameful. A king may employ trickery against an enemy, but never his own people."

Sweyn pushed to his feet, resolve giving stability to legs that were shaky a moment ago. He reached down and helped Hallfrid up. "Come with me, and all will be well."

CHAPTER 15

Sæladalr, the next day

*A*delle strode into the alehouse with purpose at midday and marched right up to Karl's bar. Sitting on a stool in front of the aging man, who clearly had never been a warrior, was her mother, hanging on his every word in spellbound delight. Adelle barely stifled a groan as she rolled her eyes. There were hardly any patrons in at this time of day, though a couple of older fellows tossed their bone dice on a tabletop in a game of *taflkast.* When Bruna and Karl didn't notice her, she tapped on the far end of the bar.

"Adelle, darling!" Bruna swiveled toward her with a cheerful grin. "Karl was just telling me about the time when he defeated twelve brawny warriors."

That was completely unbelievable. What was wrong with her mother? Was this the man she was considering marrying?

Responding to her skeptical expression, the narrow-shouldered Karl, with two braids in his gray beard and a poor attempt at a comb-over on top, broke into laughter. "It's true!" he declared. "The game was to guess which of three cups a coin was under. I showed them the coin, mixed up the cups, and they all guessed wrong."

"Because it's a trick," Adelle said. "Everyone's heard of it."

"Only it wasn't!" Karl slid a finger along the side of his nose and winked at Bruna. "I gave them each a chance to fool me and I found the coin every time."

"Fascinating." Adelle's tone begged to differ as she gave him a droll look. "I need strong ale for my patients' pain." *And I wouldn't mind a jar of mead for myself,* she thought.

Adelle had tossed and turned all night after she argued with Tyrdis and watched her leave with Sweyn. She wondered if the woman had been out training with Niklaus's guard this morning, or if she had torn open her wound again. She didn't take any medicines with her and must be in pain without them. The tender burned flesh from her cauterization could become infected if not cleaned and treated properly. *Maybe I should send Svanhild with a care package,* she considered, before shaking the thought away with renewed irritation. *She shouldn't have stomped off like that—aggravating woman!*

"Coming right up." Karl beamed as he lifted a heavy jug from under the bar and set it before Adelle. "Oh, just in time!"

Following his gaze over her shoulder, Adelle spotted a rugged man of average size and build with his light brown hair pulled back in a band, so none of it hid his symmetrically pleasing face. His beard was trim, his eyes playful, and the teeth he flashed with his smile in good repair.

"In time for what?" he asked, halting just behind Adelle.

"Bjornolf, my big, strong son, back from his adventures," Karl praised, motioning toward the man her age. "Adelle needs you to carry this jug of medicinal ale out to her hospice."

"I don't, really," she began and wrapped her fingers around the vessel's handle.

"Adelle, have you had a chance to visit with Bjornolf since he arrived home?" Karl asked.

"I don't believe she has," her meddling mother replied, raising a brow at Adelle.

"Let me carry it for you," Bjornolf said and plucked it out of her hands with ease. "Don't worry, Papa; I'll be back before the crowds arrive." Turning a charming smile to Adelle, he added, "He thinks he'll make a barkeep out of me, but I'm just helping for a few days. I heard Jarl Niklaus is planning a splendid attack on our enemies and I can't be left out of it."

"It would appear nobody can," she muttered. She shot Bruna an annoyed glare and fell in beside Bjornolf.

"What?" he asked, clearly puzzled by her comment.

"Nothing." Adelle just wanted to change the subject. "I'd rather hear about your voyage of exploration."

"It was legendary!" The man glowed with excitement as he related details of the two-year trip, some of which seemed incredible, but most believable enough. Adelle enjoyed being distracted from her aggravation over Tyrdis and invited him to stay for a small midday meal.

As she sat eating with Bjornolf, listening to his nonstop stories, her mind soon started comparing him to the taciturn shieldmaiden. He was attractive; she was amazing. Bjornolf was sanguine verbose, while Tyrdis was a serious woman of few words. She could tell by his physique that he must possess a powerful arm, but she knew firsthand the shieldmaiden's strength and skill. This fellow talked about a grand adventure, but Tyrdis displayed courage he could only dream of. *And they both can't wait to raise weapons in a foolish war.*

The longer she sat observing and assessing Bjornolf, the more she considered she should be attracted to him. He was pleasing to look at, had a resonant voice, and a cheerful disposition. The man was clean and even smelled good, but not the alluring scent Tyrdis emitted. His eyes should have lured her in with their animation, yet they seemed flat compared to the exquisite hue of shallow seawater sparkling in sunlight that graced the shieldmaiden.

Adelle glanced around the room to spy Svanhild sitting on the bed Tyrdis had occupied, playing with her carved rabbit, and talking to herself. Why wasn't she over here visiting with Bjornolf? She may enjoy his stories. Did she miss that tall, powerful specimen of a woman too? *Come to think of it, Svanhild spent much more time with her than I did.*

"Adelle?" Joren interrupted Bjornolf's story, which came as a relief to Adelle as she had lost track of the action long ago.

"Yes?" She rose and glanced back at her guest. "Pardon me, Bjornolf. What is it, Joren?"

"I want you to look at his puss and tell me if it's normal or the diseased kind that requires leeches to clean."

She moved to join him and Bjornolf called, "So good to catch up with you, Adelle. I know you have patients to care for, but maybe you'll come to town tomorrow evening. Papa has musicians coming in to play for a dance in the mead hall, and there will be games and storytelling."

Adelle hardly ever participated in social events in town. She secluded herself out here most of the time with her cat, daughter, apprentice, and patients for company. Even when there were no sick or injured to care for, she threw herself into gardening or cleaning or teaching. Maybe she should go. Would Tyrdis be there? *Probably not. She's less sociable than I am.*

"Mama, I want to go dance." Svanhild had moved to her side and peered up at her with an entreating gaze.

Adelle stroked a hand over her daughter's hair and smiled. "If we can get away, we'll be there."

Cheer gleamed from Bjornolf's face as he stepped through the open door. Adelle shook her head with a little laugh and turned her attention to the patient's wound.

No sooner than she finished assessing it, half a dozen men in armor brandishing weapons burst in and surrounded her. She didn't recognize any of them; however, she identified the red and black colors they bore. Pulling Svanhild behind her, she lifted her chin in defiance while terror screamed through her blood, causing her capable limbs to quiver.

"This is a house of healing dedicated to Eir and under her protection," she stated with as much authority as she could muster. Joren turned as white as a sheet, and she knew he would be no help. *Oh, Freya! If only Tyrdis was here.*

"We know," one barked, his stare piercing her soul.

* * *

"KEEP your shields up and be mindful of your stances." Tyrdis barked out instructions to the recruits whom Niklaus had placed under her tutelage —three farmers, a baker's son, a hardy milkmaid who showed great promise as a shieldmaiden, and Trygve, the jarl's middle son of fourteen years. Niklaus had informed them both he would reserve judgment on whether Trygve could join the war party based on his proficiency in a week hence. The lad was respectful, attentive, and eager—much like Sweyn had been at his age—and he had an impressive skill set from participating in all the games since he was ten. However, he lacked the size and strength required to stand in the shield wall. Tyrdis suspected he would be assigned to stay behind with her and help guard the city.

All she had done for the past two hours was call instructions and point from the bench in the practice yard Niklaus had ordered her to sit upon, and already fatigue assailed her. She had gotten up twice to adjust her students' grips and foot placements and was disgusted by the weakness on her right side. *Adelle said it would take time to heal and I could incur greater damage if I overexert myself. I don't want to reopen the wound or slow its progress, but I can't just lie about doing nothing either. I can sit on the bench and instruct the fresh enlisters without causing further harm and certainly oversee posted sentinels and lookouts while Niklaus and the others are gone. She should understand how irrelevant and useless I feel confined to a bed. I must contribute in the most effective way I am able.*

Tyrdis had divided the novices into three pairs to spar after going through the fundamentals. "Use your peripheral vision, Helga. Be aware of what is coming from the sides as well as the front." The young woman nodded, keeping her keen focus on the wiry farmer she was paired with. Tyrdis matched Trygve with the baker's son, who was closest to his size, while the two older and larger farmers served as training partners. She wished she could get in there to mix it up with them and properly demonstrate the moves she was teaching but admitted it would be a huge mistake. Using words instead of her body was only one of many ways Tyrdis must adapt for the next several months until she regained her full strength.

They trained with dull weapons and were supposed to aim for their partner's shield, not their bodies, until they gained more precision to avoid injuries. Clinks, thuds, and the shuffle of feet echoed off the palisade wall as they practiced. Noticing how lethargic and uncoordinated their movements were becoming, Tyrdis called out, "Halt! Time for a different activity. Set down your weapons and take a drink. Then we will run this obstacle course for a while to let your arms rest. Iron weapons and wooden rönds get heavy. We will build your strength and stamina."

Sighs of relief and accompanying smiles emerged from the recruits as they set down the axes, swords, and shields. *Tomorrow we will work with spears and pushing exercises to simulate fighting in the shield wall,* Tyrdis planned. *More fundamentals, balance, and strength-building for today.*

The new soldiers had to keep their balance while running across a log, hop to another doing the same, then weave around large stones, jump over barricades, swing by a rope around an old, thick tree, and then race back through the course, hopefully with speed and accuracy. Helga was on her second run when the loud clanging of metal on a hollow brass pipe sounded and Tyrdis instinctively shot to her feet.

"Arm yourselves!" she shouted to her students. Glancing around, she snatched up a spear from the practice weapons rack, then shifted it from her right to left hand.

A warrior sped around the end of Niklaus's longhouse with an axe in one hand and a seax in the other. "A small raiding party is striking the docks," he reported.

"We'll follow you," Tyrdis stated with determination. Turning to the recruits, she instructed, "Stay together and behind Grolier and me. Shout war cries and bang your weapons on your shields. Scaring them off is always the best, easiest solution to a situation such as this. Do *not* try to be a hero." With that, she spun and trotted after Grolier.

With her blood pumping and adrenaline flowing, Tyrdis barely registered the pain jarring through her wound site with each impact of her boots on the hard ground. They wove through tight-knit houses, craft shops, and gardens along the dirt road toward the fjord, while alarmed citizens rushed into their houses. Chickens squawked and goats bleated as they scurried out of the way. A few protective dogs barked loudly toward the invaders.

The small band of defenders rounded a fishing hut to spot a dozen men wearing Firdafylke colors shoving their longboat out into the water. "They took off with half of the whale blubber and meat we've been carving from our kill!" shouted an angry fisher in disbelief.

"Was anyone hurt?" Tyrdis glanced about, seeking any injured townspeople.

"They hit Sten in the head when he tried to stop them." The irate fisher motioned toward a man sitting on the dock, holding his bleeding head.

"I'm all right," Sten replied in a disgusted tone. "Firdafylke skitr!" He spat on the planks to emphasize his curse.

"Let's go after them!" Grolier yelled and dashed toward the nearest boat.

"No," boomed an authoritative voice behind them. Tyrdis pivoted to see Jarl Niklaus pacing toward them. "It could be a ruse to draw us away from protecting the town, a mere distraction. Let's take up positions around Sæladalr in anticipation of the actual attack."

"But my meat and blubber," protested the whaler.

Niklaus gave him a reprimanding look. "Is your life worth a trifle? Plenty remains for you to carve from the bones, and you'll kill another before summer's end. We must remain focused. Grolier, check the road going north in case their ships landed above us and their primary force approaches from that way. Helga, can you still climb like you did as a child?"

Tyrdis considered the lanky, young woman under her charge as she nodded. "Yes, my lord—better."

Niklaus pointed to a tall pine tree graced with an abundance of branches. "Shimmy up as high as you can and spy out all directions, then come down and report." As she dashed off, he said to the rest, "With me."

While Tyrdis remained vigilant, the immediate threat was gone, and she noticed the throbbing in her side. The pain reminded her of Adelle's healing hands and kind eyes, and she was immediately struck with a renewed urgency.

"The hospice, Jarl Niklaus." She fought to conceal any sound of panic from her tone. "We must protect Adelle and the others who are outside of town."

"Even our enemies should respect the gods enough to leave her alone," he replied as they marched up the small rise toward his fortress. "Nevertheless, I concur."

Tyrdis's heart pounded louder in her chest with each step as a feeling of dread shrouded her senses. She couldn't think until she knew Adelle and Svanhild were safe. They had just reached the jarl's gate when Joren and Svanhild came frantically rushing down the path.

"They've taken Adelle!" Joren cried out as they continued to run toward the group.

"You have to save Mama!" Svanhild added in anxious distress. She threw her arms around Tyrdis's waist, and the shieldmaiden dropped her spear to embrace the girl. Tears streamed down her cheeks, and she gasped for air through her terrified sobs.

"Was she or anyone hurt?" Niklaus asked with concern.

"No," Joren answered. "They said no harm would come to her, that their grædari died and they need a healer, but how can we trust them?"

"We can't," Niklaus growled, disgust permeating his words.

Tyrdis supposed the others were as worried and resolved as she was, but she maintained her focus on the little girl who had run away with her heart. "We will get her back to you, Svanhild," she swore with iron fortitude. "*I* will get her back."

CHAPTER 16

yrdis pushed to her feet and took Svanhild's hand as she pinned Niklaus with an impermeable expression. "We mustn't waste time."

"What happened?" A robust-looking man with light brown hair and a trim beard jogged up as others from town and the jarl's compound gathered around.

"Bjornolf, if only you had stayed longer at the hospice," Joren bemoaned. "They kidnapped Adelle."

The fierce determination the news etched into Bjornolf's features mirrored Tyrdis's, and she was grateful to have an ally in her mission. He stiffened, his hands balling into fists at his side.

"Wait," Niklaus cautioned. "My sons Sweyn and Njal are due back any time now. I cannot go with you until at least one of them has returned, and most of our warriors are away with the main army. I have sent for reinforcements and feel sure they will arrive soon."

"I shall lead the rescue mission," Tyrdis volunteered. "If we make haste, we can intercept them before they reach the enemy camp."

While the stalwart shieldmaiden maintained a professional exterior, inwardly she seethed with fury. *This is my fault!* Her mind perceived it wasn't logical, but it couldn't restrain the flood of guilt and remorse that enveloped her. *If only we hadn't quarreled. I should have stayed with her until Niklaus was ready to depart for his attack. Since when have I allowed emotions to sway me so? Such an extreme action was unacceptable for one as level-headed as I. If I had only been there!* Tyrdis's nails dug into her palms and her teeth ground together under the pressure of her clenched jaw.

She must have squeezed Svanhild's hand too tightly as well, for the girl gazed up at her with understanding through her own grief. "It's all right, Tyrdis. It wasn't your fault, or yours, Bjornolf. There were a lot of soldiers and neither of you could have stopped them by yourselves."

"Svanhild's right," Joren concurred as he flicked a glance between the two steadfast protectors. "Tyrdis, you would have undone all Adelle's work trying to fight them off, and without your strength they would have prevailed. And Bjornolf, they may have killed you had you tried to resist. I know you both mean well, but we must listen to Niklaus and employ a strategy."

Tyrdis's muscles strained even more under the truth of his words. She despised being in a weakened condition. It wasn't natural. Wounded or not, she had to retrieve Adelle unharmed. Mayhap Firdafylke's army was without a healer, and obtaining one was their only motivation. But what would happen when Adelle's skills were no longer required? What if an important patient died under her care?

"Come into my hall and we will set forth an expedient plan," Niklaus commanded. "Tyrdis, don't think I will abandon Adelle, but this is poor timing indeed. We must strike Firdafylke's port as soon as possible, before the solstice of the midnight sun."

Reluctantly, she followed the others inside, never letting go of Svanhild's hand.

"Will they truly not hurt Mama?" Doe eyes peered up at Tyrdis, tugging the tendrils of her heart and fraying her calm control. Despite logic, she continued to kick herself for leaving the hospice defenseless. Although it was an unwritten rule during warfare that buildings dedicated to the gods, such as temples or healing houses, were not to be attacked, these places were still vulnerable and needed to be safeguarded.

"Our foes wish for their people to be healed just as we do," Tyrdis explained. "Your mother cannot help them if they cause her harm. She should be safe." *For now,* she added bitterly to herself.

As they sat around the jarl's table discussing options, Grolier and Helga returned from scouting to report no further sign of their enemies.

"Then the attack on the port was just a distraction, as Father said," Trygve surmised, "while capturing our grædari was their chief objective."

Tyrdis allowed for an instant of pride in the lad as he stepped up in the absence of his older brothers. His wavy hair looked like spun gold and his smooth face was almost as fair as Sweyn's. She didn't know the in-between brother, Njal, well, but he—like Trygve—seemed eager enough to prove himself. Niklaus had mentioned how excited the young man was to represent him to Jarl Bjarke in Austrihóll.

"Indeed," Niklaus agreed. Svanhild had wandered over to a bench with Solfrig, the jarl's youngest child and only daughter. The darker-haired girl about Svanhild's size had given her a doll to comfort, which in doing so allowed Svanhild to comfort herself. Lynnea sat nearby pulling a needle and thread through fabric bound by a wooden hoop, and Tyrdis couldn't for the life of her comprehend why the jarl's wife engaged in such a point-less activity at a critical time like this.

"Trygve, do you know where to find Gunnvaldr?" Niklaus asked.

"The old hunter who lives in the woods?" His son's expression lit.

"Yes. Go get him and bring him here," the jarl instructed. "He is the best tracker I know. He will be able to lead a small party to the place they took Adelle."

"Only a small party?" Bjornolf frowned. "What if we meet the resis-tance of a hundred men?"

"Then you will not engage them," Niklaus commanded. "The first necessity is to gain information. Where did they take her? Is she well and unharmed, as they claimed? How many guard her? What is their routine? If an uninformed, undisciplined gang of marauders rush the camp to liberate our healer, they would likely get her killed. Besides, as dear and important as Adelle is to all of Sæladalr, she is still but one soul. Following our plan and capturing Griðlundr is essential to ending the war, thus restoring peace and saving more lives. I am confident Adelle would agree."

She would, Tyrdis had to admit. Gloom hung over her like an icy cloud, obscuring any cheerful thought. She didn't have time now to contemplate why Adelle meant so much to her, or why she couldn't rest until she knew the healer was safe. It was simply a fact of life. Adelle's well-being mattered. She glanced at Svanhild again. *At least she's safe.*

"We needn't wait for Sweyn's return," Tyrdis suggested. "I can command the scouting party. You know I am disciplined and possess keen intuition."

"Yes, Tyrdis, and I would not deny you the right to join the expedi-tion," Niklaus responded. "However, you have not regained your strength and my men do not know you as well as I do. How would you rebuff a challenge?"

"But my lord," she protested, inwardly damning her weakness.

Niklaus raised a palm and smiled. "I also see how loyal you have become to the woman who tended your wounds. Yes, your reputation is for duty first, duty always, but you are only human."

"I could lead the party," Bjornolf proposed, lifting his hand to volunteer. "I am fresh from adventures abroad and in the prime of my life."

With a snort, the jarl shook his head. "I've heard the talk around the mead hall, how you seek a wife and have moved Adelle to the top of your list of prospects. I recall how you, Sunevar, and Adelle kept close company in your youth, and he mustered the courage to ask her to marry him first. With him gone and you back home, you think to pick up where you left off years ago. You are too emotionally invested to remain disciplined. We shall wait for Sweyn."

So that's his game. Tyrdis scrutinized Bjornolf more closely, looking for something to find fault with. Unfortunately, he seemed sincere and hadn't demonstrated any obvious flaws. She scowled, sinking further into darkness. Why did his interest in Adelle make her feel so uncomfortable? It was none of her business if the adventurer wished to court her. *She will see him as a warrior and be displeased,* Tyrdis considered. *Bjornolf will fail to win her heart.* The thought gave her a slight measure of satisfaction; however, the same could be said of herself.

* * *

Sweyn noticed the anxious energy radiating through his hometown as soon as he and his companions stepped off their longboat. It was dinnertime, though the sun still floated in the sky like a huge, orange ball. He helped Hallfrid onto the pier and tied a rope around the mooring.

"Sæladalr is bigger than I thought it would be," the girl commented. She raked fingers through her windblown hair and smoothed her skirt, trying to make herself appear more presentable.

Sweyn would have smiled and complimented her had it not been for the unease he sensed. The distinct odor of whale oil filled the air, and he spied the bones laid out on the bank a few paces down from the wharf. A fisher exited a fish hut and met them with a solemn regard.

"What happened?" Sweyn asked while his crew finished securing the craft.

"Filthy Firdafylkers attacked us, is what," he grumbled. "They took off with our healer, Adelle."

"What?" Alarm raced through Sweyn's veins, and he took Hallfrid by the hand. "We have to hurry," he instructed her.

"Truly?" questioned Edan. Karvir stepped beside Sweyn with revenge in his deep-set eyes. His rough hand moved to his axe handle.

"Let's go see my father and find out about this treachery." Setting a brisk pace, Sweyn led the way to the great hall on the hill at the far end of town.

Jarl Niklaus and the family were eating when Sweyn, Hallfrid, Edan, and Karvir entered. Sweyn recognized Tyrdis sitting with Svanhild and Bjornolf across from them at the table but didn't see Njal. *He must not be back yet.* The mood was somber. No musicians played, voices were hushed, and Lynnea kept his little sister close to her side. Hallfrid was older than Solfrig, but the fearful mood washed over her too.

"So, they have taken off with Adelle," he stated, determined to free her.

Niklaus raised a brow at Sweyn. "Have you adopted a new child I am unaware of?"

"This is Hallfrid, from Skeggen, and she is under my protection," Sweyn declared. "We'll talk about why she is here in private and as soon as possible. But first—"

"But first, tell me of King Gustav's decision," his father insisted.

Sweyn and his followers approached the table.

"Sit, son," his mother invited. "You and your friends need to eat. Hallfrid, come meet Solfrig and Svanhild."

Hallfrid gave her an appreciative look and glanced up at Sweyn for a nod before rounding the table. It was kind of his mother. She could have insisted the urchin bathe and change into proper clothing before joining them, but Lynnea was a kind woman who was recognized for her exceeding hospitality throughout the kingdom. If he hadn't been so deeply troubled, Sweyn would have smiled. A vast ocean churned within his gut, turbulent enough to steal his appetite. Nonetheless, he took his seat, and his companions eagerly dove into the meal.

"Yes, Father," Sweyn disclosed. "King Gustav approved the plan and will be sending fifty additional warriors to join us within a few days. He understands the importance of the timing and has sent orders to Jarl

Raknar to contribute as many. If Jarl Bjarke joins in, we will have sufficient force to prevail, but there is an urgent matter I must discuss with you—only you."

Their eyes met. Recognizing the significance of the issue, his father nodded. "Eat, and then we'll retire to my chamber."

"Sweyn, the jarl wishes you to lead a scouting mission to assess what happened to Adelle," Tyrdis said. "If we leave early in the morning, we should have an answer before the day is done. Gunnvaldr, here, will read their trail and take us straight to where she is being held."

Sweyn glanced at the wiry old man with arms like weathered vines and whiskers white as winter. Gunnvaldr flashed a toothless grin at Sweyn as if to say, *"Aye, that's me, the best tracker in Raumsdal."*

"I'll come with you," Bjornolf stated.

"Me too," echoed Karvir and Edan.

"I want to go," added Trygve with a hopeful look. "We aren't planning to actually fight, and I can learn much. Tyrdis can take charge of me, Sweyn, so you won't be bothered."

"Not me," Braggi piped up. Sweyn's youngest brother of ten years had displayed no interest in games or practice combat at all. Instead, he followed the skalds and musicians around and had already learned to play tunes on the flute. "I like Adelle, but someone has to stay behind to watch over Mother and Solfrig."

"That's a good job for you," Niklaus agreed with a wink at his artistically inclined son.

"You are not a bother, Trygve," Sweyn responded. "It's true you can learn much from Tyrdis, but I need you to stay out of harm's way. There are too many variables for me to be concerned about without you being one of them."

Trygve nodded as an eager expression lit his face.

"I will supervise the boy," Tyrdis confirmed. "However, my top priority is ensuring Adelle's safety." The intense look in her eyes informed Sweyn the shieldmaiden was hellbent on rescuing Adelle at any cost.

Curious.

"As it is mine," Bjornolf seconded with bravado.

Though a cog clicked in Sweyn's brain, he hadn't the time nor inclination to speculate about anyone's feelings or intentions but his own. *Our king is a liar. What will Father do about it?*

CHAPTER 17

After the meal and completing the plans for tomorrow morning, Sweyn brought Hallfrid to his parents' room behind a partition at one end of the longhouse. Because she looked nervous, he kept a comforting hand on her shoulder. Niklaus sat on the edge of a sturdy bed and motioned to the smaller one across from him. Sweyn settled the girl down first, then joined her.

"Now, what is all of this about?" He pursed his lips at Sweyn and leaned his elbows on his knees.

"Hallfrid is an orphan girl of Skeggen who spent the winter working in King Gustav's stables." Unease wriggled through Sweyn's gut as if it was filled with worms. "She witnessed what happened the night Prince Jarivald was killed. Hallfrid, tell my father what you told me."

Fearful eyes glanced at him before staring at her folded hands. Her thin shoulders were hunched, and Sweyn sensed her racing breath. "It's all right, little flower. My father is an honorable man."

She nodded. "I know. I'm not afraid of him," she said, daring to peek at Niklaus. "It's King Gustav who frightens me."

"Why?" Niklaus asked in a confused manner. "What did he do to frighten you?"

After a steadying breath, Hallfrid recounted the tale of Ivar and Jarivald fighting, Kerstav discovering what happened, and then the king's arrival on the scene and all that followed.

"Gustav saw an opportunity rather than an embarrassment and

113

concocted a story about assassins from Firdafylke attacking them and killing Jarivald," Niklaus responded in astonishment. "His son and heir is lying dead on the ground and he's plotting how to spin it to his advantage."

"He made Ivar and Kerstav swear to never tell, or demons would drag them down to Helheim," Hallfrid added with a shudder.

"Her story rings true to me," Sweyn testified. "Each time I have seen the king's sons recently, they have been arguing and on edge, broody, angry, and not the way I remember them from the past. And Gustav refused your suggestion of a meeting with King Tortryggr about discovering the identity of the supposed assassins. Was it because he knew they would find none?"

"More likely, because he covets the fertile land south of our current border," his father answered in subdued disapproval. "He has always been an ambitious man. Ambition is not a bad thing and is even desirable if it drives one in the right direction. Yet there is nothing but dishonor in what he has done if this is true."

"Why would Hallfrid make it up?" Sweyn locked gazes with his father.

"To gain your sympathy perhaps?" Niklaus suggested. "To improve her own situation. Serving in our household is a sight better than a stable. Mayhap one of the king's sons was making advances toward her and she wished a way out."

"No," Hallfrid pleaded. "I didn't make it up. Jarivald was nice, like Sweyn, and I would want whoever killed him to be punished, except it was a fair fight. Everyone would have understood, and Ivar wouldn't be in trouble. But now, people are going to war, killing and dying to protect a lie. Please, Jarl Niklaus, give me a trial so that I may prove I speak the truth. I'll put my hand in the fire and ask Freya to burn it if I lie and keep it safe if I don't." Sincerity radiated from her lean face and shone in her honest eyes.

Niklaus shook his head and waved his hand at her.

"We don't believe in such barbaric trials," Sweyn said. "Everyone's hand gets burned, truthful or not. It's the law of fire, not a test of integrity."

"The fact you stand behind your story with such devotion, however, is convincing," Niklaus confirmed. "There is a bathhouse in town. Go tell Lynnea I asked her to take you there and to get you clothing suitable for serving in our household. And Hallfrid." She froze, giving him her undivided attention. "Tell no one what we spoke of—not even my wife."

"Yes, my lord. Thank you, my lord. Wild beasts couldn't drag it from me." She slid off the bed and turned an adoring gaze to Sweyn. "Thank you both."

When she had left them alone, Sweyn asked, "What are we going to do about it?"

"Do about it?" Niklaus studied him in curiosity. "Gustav is king."

"Only because the jarls support him," Sweyn answered with conviction. "Did you know he demanded a third of the spoils brought back by Bjornolf and his fellow adventurers when they returned? Yet he contributed nothing to finance their voyage. Forget about the times he placed his own interests above those of the kingdom in the past; this is inexcusable. You are risking your life for what—his greed? Our fylke lies on the border with Firdafylke, and your warriors are bearing the brunt of it. Our town gets raided, and our healer kidnapped, while he sits in safety to the north. You, Raknar, and Bjarke should confront him over his lie. We must call a halt to this unfounded war and make peace with King Tortryggr."

"And what about Gustav? Do we allow him to remain king, disgraced and humiliated as he will be, or do we banish him? And if he is no longer king, who will be? A young prince who just killed his own brother or one of the jarls? Which one of us?"

"We can call a kingdom-wide Thing and let the people vote," Sweyn suggested. "Any of you would be a better leader than a man despicable enough to blame innocent people for killing his son."

"And what if the other jarls don't believe this version of events?" Niklaus eyed him with speculation.

For that question, Sweyn had no answer. He exhaled a sigh and his shoulders slumped. He was suddenly aware of how tense they had been and how tired he was.

"Don't get me wrong, son," his father said. "I agree with you on the principle of the matter. Who do you think taught you to value honor above all else? But there are many facets to consider. We have no proof, and it would come down to the king's word against a little orphan girl's. And once Gustav knows she witnessed the fight, I doubt we could protect her anymore. It would be like giving her a death sentence."

"What if Ivar or Kerstav were to speak up and tell what really happened?" A seed of hope sprang into Sweyn's heart at the thought.

"And break a blood oath to their father and king?" Niklaus appeared unconvinced. "I need to consult the völva and make a personal *blót* to Odin. Much wisdom is required—more than you or I alone possess. For now, we will act as though the planned attack will go forward. Lead the scouting mission tomorrow and use your best judgment. If you can get into the camp without violence to ensure Adelle is being respected, then do so. Otherwise, simply assess the situation and return unnoticed. Tell no one. This is a most delicate matter."

* * *

TYRDIS HAD LEFT the table and erected herself near the doorway to watch everyone who came and went from the hall. For a fleeting moment, she had been curious about what Sweyn wanted to discuss with Jarl Niklaus before she resumed brooding over her failure to protect Adelle. Svanhild sat across the chamber in a circle of other children, rolling a ball back and forth between them. Tyrdis couldn't even recall playing childhood games that didn't involve teaching a skill needed for combat.

Though there was still no music or storytelling in the longhouse, there was conversation, and two men engaged in a game of Hnefatafl. Several others tossed dice, while a small covey of women sat around a loom, chatting and laughing as they wove wool into fabric. Almost all women, regardless of their station, spent time weaving, yet she never had. *I could learn if it was expedient to do so,* she told herself. *How difficult could it be?*

With her back against the wall, she shifted a look at Bjornolf, who was huddled with Edan and Karvir over horns of mead. Tyrdis drank beer, ale, mead, or wine, as they were provided to her because they were the customary beverages, but she never overindulged. For her senses to be dulled even one bit was completely unacceptable.

Tyrdis didn't realize what a sour expression she wore until Bruna snuck up on her while she was busy studying Bjornolf. "What's wrong?" she asked.

Lifting her chin, Tyrdis reapplied her neutral expression and turned her attention to Adelle's mother. "I'm sure you have been told."

"About Adelle? Yes, I'm worried too." Bruna motioned to an empty spot on a bench along the near wall. "Will you sit with me for a while?"

The invitation surprised Tyrdis. Bruna had visited the hospice several times while Tyrdis was there, yet they hadn't interacted often—just a few words now and then. Mostly, she had observed Bruna with Adelle and Svanhild and tried to recall her own mother.

With an official nod, Tyrdis accompanied Bruna to the bench and took a seat beside her. "Do not be troubled, Bruna; no harm will come to Adelle while I breathe. Sweyn is taking us on a mission tomorrow to evaluate her situation and I will share whatever details I can when we return. She saved my life, and I am honor-bound to save hers in return."

Bruna's frosted red braids were coiled around an ivory face that hinted Adelle would still be attractive twenty years from now. She gave Tyrdis what could pass as an amused expression. "I'm sure that's the reason."

Tyrdis responded with a confused frown. "Didn't Adelle tell you I am dedicated to my duty?"

"She did, and I don't doubt it." Bruna glanced across the room to the table where Bjornolf sat with the other men. "Bjornolf's father Karl and I have decided to wed at the harvest festival. There is still plenty of life left in both of us and no reason we should grow old alone. I may not feel the same intense passion for him as I did Adelle's father, but we are of an age where companionship matters more. He is quite anxious over the situation, and we have both brought our prayers before the gods. Tyrdis, do you believe the Norns decide our fates as some stories imply and many gothis teach?"

Sinking into deep contemplation, Tyrdis tilted her head at Bruna. "I have been too busy securing my own future to give the question its due attention. I suppose what I believe is less important than what I do."

"On the contrary," Bruna chided softly. "One must believe before he or she can do. No, I think you presume you hold the keys to your destiny, no matter how comforting it would be to conclude all questions of life and death are out of your hands."

"How do you mean?"

"You could have died—should have died—on that battlefield with your brother," Bruna stated. "Did you survive because mystic beings called the Norn decreed it, or because you willed it?"

"I am alive because of Adelle," Tyrdis answered. "Because she is a talented healer who carries the favor of both the gods and mortals. Is this why you are not more anxious? Because you know she is favored by the gods, and they will protect her?"

"I am anxious, Tyrdis," Bruna admitted. "And I also have faith. Isn't doubt a steppingstone to trust? I know she has faith in you."

For the second time in minutes, Bruna's words caught Tyrdis off guard. She closed her mouth the instant she realized it had fallen agape. "I fear I let her down."

"Your argument?"

"So, she told you how stubbornly and ungratefully I behaved." Tyrdis lowered her chin in humiliation and busied her fingers rubbing the hem of her tunic.

"Hardly!" Bruna laughed. "She said it was all her fault, that she shouldn't have gotten angry. Tyrdis, if you had been there this morning, you couldn't have stopped them. You must realize that."

"I would have tried." Tyrdis stared blankly at a spot on the floor in front of her, drained of all her emotions, save regret.

"I know, dear," Bruna said and placed a hand on her arm. "Svanhild bubbles over with excitement every time she talks about you—which is often—and Adelle admires you as well. I fear she married Sunevar to please everyone … to please me. Now she swears she'll never marry again, despite dashing Bjornolf's attention."

Dashing? Does she think he is dashing? His physical appearance is adequate and his personality acceptable, but dashing? Wait—am I missing the point? She said Adelle doesn't want to marry him, or any man.

Tyrdis turned a questioning look to Bruna. "Oh, I'm just running my mouth because I'm trying to hide my fear. If I'm going to have faith, I must cast aside worry. But we know so little about you. Have you ever had a husband?"

"No." Tyrdis didn't know how to respond to Bruna's line of inquiry or where it was leading. It made her feel uneasy. She didn't like to talk about herself. What was there to say? "I am a dedicated warrior. I have no time for relationships."

Bruna responded with a soft smile. "Even the Valkyrie Hildr made time for a husband. But maybe you are like Sigrid Olafsdottir of Svithjod or Eldrid, the woman blacksmith who lives in the village on the coast. Neither is said to lie with a man, but only with other women."

What personal questions! Tyrdis snorted and crossed her arms. "I do not frolic about with men or women. I focus my attention on gaining perfection in my craft and performing my duty with honor."

"Ah," Bruna smirked. "Just as I thought. There *is* something you fear."

Her accusation shot a red-hot arrow screaming through Tyrdis and it was all she could do to control her reaction. With teeth clenched, she uttered, "I do not acknowledge fear."

"No, sweetie, but it's still there. Don't be upset," Bruna consoled. "If you feared nothing, you wouldn't be human, and, despite your extreme efforts to hide it, you are indeed human. You feel, you care, and to hear Svanhild tell it, you even smile on the rare occasion. Caring for another is not a sign of weakness, Tyrdis. On the contrary, it is a measure of greatest strength. Go find my daughter tomorrow—not because you feel obligated, but because you care for her."

Bruna stood, patted her shoulder, and strolled deeper into the hall to join some of the other women. Tyrdis remained on the bench, mulling over the strange conversation and the uncanny way Bruna saw through her façade.

CHAPTER 18

The next day

Tyrdis rode single-file behind Sweyn as their party snaked along a switchback trail leading into the highlands. On the other side of the ridge, they would descend into Firdafylke territory. Towering conifers lined the rocky path as they left most of the leafy, deciduous trees behind in the valley. An eagle gliding high above them was a good omen. From up here, the town below was but a tiny dot and its inhabitants were as minuscule as fleas. She welcomed the green boughs as they provided shade from the heat of the summer sun.

Ahead, the twiggy old tracker Gunnvaldr stopped at a fork in the trail. He squatted and touched the dirt, raising a handful to his nostrils to sniff. He stretched up to examine the tree branches and needles before taking a few steps in one direction, then doing the same in the other. Turning, he gave Sweyn a confident nod and pointed.

"This way."

Bjornolf assisted the rickety elder back onto his pony, and the procession continued with Trygve riding behind Tyrdis, while Edan and Karvir brought up the rear.

She had supposed she could tolerate the travel since they would be on horseback rather than hiking the distance, yet the dull throb of pain had become her constant companion. She decided it was no better than she deserved for leaving Adelle unprotected and she welcomed the awful scourge.

A hundred scenarios played through her mind as Tyrdis tried to think of something other than her failure: what would happen when they caught up to the enemies, what to do if they had reached their camp, and what action to take if they had not ... what to do if they had hurt Adelle. No. She couldn't entertain that possibility.

Last night, Svanhild had come and lay on the bench beside her in Jarl Niklaus's great hall, cuddled under her light blanket as a comfort to them both. Tyrdis had swallowed a lump in her throat, unable to say anything to the little girl, and had merely wrapped an arm around her. Svanhild offered prayers to Freya, Eir, Tyr, Odin, and even Thor in hopes one god was listening. Then she had fallen asleep. Tyrdis had lain riding the ebb and flow of Svanhild's breath for a long while, playing through the odd conversation she had with Bruna.

Now, as she rode along in silence, having devised a plan for any eventuality they may run into, Tyrdis's thoughts turned inward. When she had lain dying on the battlefield, she recalled her greatest regret in life had been not knowing love, yet Bruna had touched on a truth the mighty shieldmaiden did not wish to face. *Am I afraid of getting too close, of sharing something meaningful with another?*

The few people she had loved had died: her grandmother, her mother, her brother, and Jorie, a childhood friend. When Tyrdis had been twelve, a winter plague visited Heilagrfjord, claiming her grandmother and Jorie. Of course, her mother had been gone many years by then. She and Erik had both been adults before their father was killed in a duel. A man he had clashed with from his mountain days arrived in town three years ago. He insulted Vignir, who then challenged him. Both died of the wounds they inflicted on each other that day. Tyrdis found it hard to stir up the sentiment of love for her strict, distant father, but she had respected him and noticed his absence with sorrow.

It is unreasonable to invest such deep emotion into another as to cause inconsolable heartache when they are no longer present. And yet, she felt it was already too late for her—especially where Svanhild was concerned. Why? How had another woman's child entwined herself around Tyrdis's heart like a rope around a mooring post? And what about Adelle? It was admirable that she was skilled at her craft, and she was attractive and kind with seiðr in her touch ... and bossy and stubborn. Beyond that, all

Tyrdis knew was she had been married to a man, borne his children, and would likely not be interested in her in any way that involved intimacy.

Intimacy. Is that my reservation? Many of the warriors would engage in sharing physical pleasures after a heated battle, affirming they were still alive, expending their vigor, and enjoying sexual release. Tyrdis never joined them. She had told herself it was frivolous and unproductive; her time and energy could be better spent training. But had she been afraid? Of what? *What if I allowed myself to care for someone else, only she didn't want me?* The thought of such a turn of emotional events was beyond consideration. It would be better to avoid entanglements altogether than to suffer rejection.

I am vulnerable because I lost my brother and have no one else in my life, she concluded. *That is why I have latched on to the first people to show me kindness —Adelle and Svanhild. These feelings will fade when I return to Heilagrfjord, and they will forget about me.* Even thinking about it made her feel raw and dismal inside.

Feelings are irrelevant. Tyrdis raised her chin to scan the surrounding forest. A woodpecker hammered into a tree trunk, and a trio of songbirds chirped away. Other than that, there was the clomp of their pony's hooves and Edan and Karvir's muted conversation. She spotted no smoke from fires or other obvious signs of their foes.

Only actions matter. My actions led to Adelle being abducted; therefore, my actions must lead to her release. Her safety is paramount, and I will see it done.

Descending the slope was trickier. Tyrdis had to lean back to balance on her mount, which stretched the skin and sinews of her wounded side to a more excruciating level than coming uphill had. Gritting her teeth, she bore the discomfort without complaint. At the bottom of the ridge, the terrain leveled out to gently rolling, and a broad meadow unfolded before them.

"This must be part of the land King Gustav wants," Sweyn said in a bitter tone. Tyrdis had noticed how quiet he had been while they rode, which she found odd.

"It would be marvelous for grazing," Trygve commented. "Look—I see some cattle now."

"Stay to the treeline," Sweyn instructed.

Gunnvaldr twisted around to talk over his pony's brown rump. "The trail leads through the meadow."

"Yes, but herders may spot us," Sweyn replied. "We'll pick up the trail on the other side."

The meadow gave way to vast fields of grain and then, past an orchard, Tyrdis spied ringlets of smoke rising from campfires.

Sweyn held up a hand to halt the procession. "Everyone take a break while Gunnvaldr and I scout out the camp."

"Here, let me help you." Trygve was at Tyrdis's side to help glide her down from her horse before she noticed him. She couldn't hide the grimace of pain when she dismounted and, despite some embarrassment, was glad to have him there to steady her.

"Thank you, Trygve." She laid a stabilizing hand on his shoulder and acknowledged him further with a nod. "I am all right."

The youth shook his head with a disbelieving half-smile. "I don't know how you made that ride over the mountain. It was hard enough on my backside, and I wasn't injured. One day, I aspire to be as tough and tenacious as you."

"I can testify you are well on your way. Now, I'm off to find the woman's bush while you fellows relieve yourselves at yours."

Trygve laughed and Tyrdis would have joined him if she didn't hurt so much. When she returned, the group was refreshing themselves with traveling biscuits and drinks.

"Here." Edan handed rations to her. "Better replenish your strength; we don't know what we'll be doing next."

"Thank you." Tyrdis took her share, ate, and drank. They were close now, and her nerves tingled.

They had just finished when Sweyn and the guide returned.

"It's a large camp, maybe a hundred warriors with retainers, slaves, and women besides," he reported. "We observed a large tent with two guards posted from which important-looking people came and went. It may be where they are holding Adelle."

"Could we sneak in under the cover of darkness?" Tyrdis asked. "If there are only two guards—"

"We would have to pass too many tents to reach it," Sweyn answered in disappointment. "I recognized Jarl Stefnir, whom I've met before. He was none too friendly at the prisoner exchange, yet not totally unreasonable. Perhaps I could enter the camp under a white flag and ask to see her."

"That's too dangerous," Bjornolf countered. "They would just capture you and hold you for ransom. Then what will we tell your father?"

Sweyn shook his head. "They could have captured or killed both of us when we rode into Oskholm a week ago, but they didn't. I believe they will respect my station and, even if they detain me, will not go so far as to murder me—not while my father commands a large army only a day's ride away."

"I will ride in with you," Tyrdis said, not as a request, but as a statement of fact. "They will not view me as a threat, and it is better to have a witness present."

"Shouldn't we do what Father directed?" Trygve asked. "Assess their strength and bring him the information."

"But we don't know for certain if Adelle is in the camp," Bjornolf replied. "They could have brought her here yesterday and taken her elsewhere this morning."

"I agree. We need to get a look inside to be certain," Sweyn concurred. "But if we all go marching up there, the soldiers may get nervous and attack us. Tyrdis and I will ride in alone, unarmed, under a white flag."

"I want to come too," declared Bjornolf. "My father has made plans to wed Adelle's mother. That will make her my sister if nothing else, and I have a stake in her welfare."

"Yes, but the fame of your exploits precedes you," Tyrdis countered. "Jarl Stefnir will likely recognize you and be suspicious of your plans." It was an unlikely scenario, but Tyrdis didn't want this over-eager, presumptuous adventurer making a blunder that could cause their mission to fail. Sweyn understood diplomacy, and she knew him well, whereas Bjornolf was an unknown factor.

Sweyn laid a hand on his shoulder. "She's right. People have heard of your voyage and the spoils you brought back. If something goes wrong and we don't return in a timely manner, I'm counting on you to get everyone else back home safely."

Frustrated disappointment played over his face, but Bjornolf nodded his agreement.

"Ready?" Sweyn caught Tyrdis's gaze.

"Ready."

Trygve helped Tyrdis back into her saddle. She wouldn't have allowed it except she was saving her one gut-wrenching hoist for in front of their foes. Appearing older than his twenty-one years, Sweyn looked as if he carried the weight of the world on his shoulders. They trod along in silence side by side with Sweyn holding a long pole with a white banner tied around it. A patrol of armed guards met them a few hundred yards before the camp, the captain of which recognized Sweyn.

"Sweyn Niklausson," he barked from atop his dun horse. "What brings you here?"

"You have taken our town's grædari, Adelle, against her will and without my father's leave," he answered.

"State your intentions," Tyrdis demanded of her enemy.

Sweyn gave her a reprimanding look and added, "We wish to speak to whoever is in charge concerning her treatment and well-being."

"Jarl Stefnir is in the camp," the guard stated. "I will take you to him." He glanced at the treeline with alert suspicion and ordered the rest of the patrol to spread out and watch for signs of trouble.

"This is not a trick or a trap," Sweyn volunteered. "We are only here to assess the condition of our healer."

"She is unharmed and well cared for," the Firdafylke patrol leader answered. "Healers are in short supply, and we require her professional services—nothing else."

Following him into a camp of foes staring at them in apprehension and with hatred etched on their expressions, Tyrdis prayed he spoke for everyone.

CHAPTER 19

"Here, keep his leg elevated," Adelle instructed a young woman only a few years older than her son, Runar. Working with Karyna had drawn concern for Runar's welfare near the surface, and she treated each patient as she hoped he would be cared for if wounded.

Karyna had told Adelle how, in assuming the responsibility that accompanied being a jarl's daughter, she began assisting their grædari, an old man with decades of experience, when the war broke out. Then last week, a contagious illness of unknown origin spread through the camp. Many others recovered, but the aged healer succumbed and died, leaving Karyna in a vital role she wasn't prepared to fill.

Adelle shoved a pillow under the warrior's leg, which had been sliced to the bone by some horrendous piece of sharpened iron or steel wielded by one of her countrymen, no doubt. He lay on a rickety cot stretched over a dirt floor under a canvas canopy held high on spear-width poles. It was a wonder a brisk wind didn't topple it.

"It needs to be cleaned and stitched with a needle and thread. Have you done that before?"

"I assisted Freyvoldr," Karyna answered nervously, biting her lower lip. "I'm adept at sewing cloth. Is it much different?"

The young woman's eyes were the pale blue of forget-me-nots and her long, yellowish-tan tresses hung loose down her back. Karyna hadn't once seemed squeamish at the blood and gore oozing from the patients' wounds, nor intimidated by their protests and cursing. Adelle had to give her credit for being a strong woman in that regard.

"Normally, no," Adelle replied. She pulled back a ragged piece of the warrior's trousers to reveal the extent of the injury. "But see how deep this laceration goes? Through muscle and vessels. It will require both of us—one to pinch the two halves of the calf together, and the other to perform the stitches."

"I want the real healer sewing up my leg!" the man growled with an anguished expression. "Let the other one practice on somebody else."

Karyna met Adelle's gaze. "I'll assist."

"If it will set his mind at ease," responded Adelle. "Thank you." Then she spoke to the patient. "I am certain Karyna could do just as well. The part you should be concerned about is the ointment and poultice recipe that will draw out any infection and ensure you keep a healthy limb."

"Will you do that too?" he pleaded.

Adelle threaded her needle and eyed him with authority. "I'll teach Karyna to make it and she will apply it when we are done. Then your leg must stay wrapped, and you," she pointed at him with a commander's stance, "must remain in bed long enough for it to heal."

"I hope the chest has all the ingredients you need," Karyna said. "This is only a tent with no herb garden like back at Oskholm's hospice."

"If not, we'll gather them from the forest and meadow."

Karyna gripped the man's leg on both sides of the gash and pushed them together while Adelle made tight stitches to close it. He gritted his teeth and grumbled but held still as he was expected to do. This was not their only patient; the tent was full. A few were still recovering from the mysterious disease, but half a dozen bore battle injuries.

"Your warriors gave us quite the fight yesterday over by the river," he commented, to take his mind off the procedure. "The contest ended up a draw as far as I could tell."

"I can't take credit for their actions," Adelle returned somberly, "nor do I bear their responsibility. If it were up to me, there would be no wars. Obviously, I wasn't consulted on the matter. There," she concluded, tying off the last thread.

Rifling through a wooden chest, Adelle sniffed various leather pouches tied with different colored strings. There was no standardized formula for marking medicinal herbs, and practitioners each used their own systems, passing them down to their apprentices. She removed five pouches, a jar of honey, and another of a prepared salve.

She handed Karyna a pouch. "Take a heaping spoonful of these hemp seeds and grind them into a fine powder. Then separate it in two—half for a pain-relieving tea brewed with willow bark and the other half will go into the ointment with the yarrow, garlic, and honey."

The young woman nodded and spooned the seeds into a stone mortar and pestle. "Which pouch is the yarrow?"

"The one with the yellow tie." Adelle held it up to show her.

"I've heard of the benefits of eating garlic," her student mentioned as she ground the hemp seeds, "but not of using it in an ointment."

"Eir, in her bounty and wisdom, has blessed Miðgarðr with an abundance of herbs that are useful for many purposes." Switching into teaching mode helped Adelle stay present and focused, not dwelling on circumstances she could do nothing about. "In a balm, it keeps insects away, reduces swelling, and can aid ear and toothaches. Consumed, its odor also dissuades insects, can reduce headaches, combat coughs, dropsy, jaundice, and constipation. It can even counteract some poisons if consumed quickly enough and in a sufficient quantity."

Karyna's jaw slacked, and she shook her head. "And most people think it only flavors soups and stews. Here. Is this powder fine enough?"

Adelle glanced over her shoulder into the stone bowl. "Yes. Do you know the broadleaf plantain called groblad?"

"I believe so," she answered in a tone that let Adelle know the young woman was eager to learn. "My mother used the immature, tender leaves in salads."

"Go gather a basket full of the leaves, any size," Adelle directed. "I need them for his poultice. I'll show you how to brew the tea and enhance the ointment later. We must get his leg finished and wrapped up, then check on the other patients."

"I'll get them right away." Karyna turned and froze, a startled expression on her face.

Wondering what was wrong, Adelle pivoted toward the open tent flap to see Jarl Stefnir stride in, flanked by Sweyn and Tyrdis.

"See?" The bald jarl, who seemed smaller than she recalled as he stood between strapping Sweyn and tall, athletic Tyrdis, waved a hand in her direction. "Safe as a clam in its shell. We aren't barbarians, you know. No one can be without a grædari, especially in a time of war, but I respect the gods, boy. Did you think I would just turn her over to the warriors for their pleasure?"

Adelle was afraid to take her eyes off Sweyn lest the sight of Tyrdis rushing to her rescue might turn her brain to mush. She watched relief pour through him at the sight of her. Then his attention swiftly shifted to Karyna, his expression morphing into hopeful curiosity.

"I am well, Sweyn," Adelle confirmed. "It is as Jarl Stefnir says, and he promised to send me back when I have completed Karyna's training."

Karyna had become very still, and Adelle felt a flurry of emotional energy radiating from her. Stiffening, she raised her chin. "I must go collect groblad leaves. If you will all excuse me."

She gave the trio a wide berth and flitted out of the opening behind Sweyn.

"Karyna, wait," he called and followed her out.

Jarl Stefnir scowled and wiggled a finger through his wiry, brown beard to scratch his chin. "Damnable war," he swore. Shaking his head, he wandered after them at a slower pace … which left Tyrdis.

Adelle took a deep breath before daring to gaze into her alluring eyes. She was suddenly struck by the fact Tyrdis had traveled many hours and crossed a small mountain to get here. Without her medicines and making such a demanding ride, she must be using all her fortitude just to stand without crying out in pain. Compassion and regret swept through her, and her mouth gaped.

"I should not have left you," Tyrdis stated. She hid her pain well, but the weariness showed … and something else Adelle couldn't quite pinpoint.

"I shouldn't have accused you of seeking fame and glory," Adelle replied. "How are Svanhild and Mother?"

"Worried about you, but otherwise in good order." Tyrdis stood like she was at attention in a row of troops being inspected by the king.

Adelle crossed to stand in front of her. "You shouldn't have come," she breathed softly.

Tyrdis raised a brow and spoke in an offended tone. "Would you have preferred Bjornolf?"

Taken aback, Adelle responded in surprise. "Certainly not. Why would you suggest such a thing?"

"He fancies you," Tyrdis replied without sentiment. "He waits nearby with Trygve and the others."

Adelle let out a dry laugh. "He can fancy me all he wants for the good it will do him. I made clear I'm not seeking a husband."

"He claims you will soon be his sister and he must watch out for you."

Raising a fist to her hip, Adelle narrowed her eyes. "Oh, does he? And what about you? While I am very glad to see you, the trip will set your recovery back. You must be aching tremendously."

"Ensuring your safety is the only thing that matters to me, Adelle." Though she refrained from any hint of emotion, the honest intensity in her voice was enough to make Adelle believe. "I would have come without Sweyn or Jarl Niklaus's consent if I had to. It's my fault—"

"No." Adelle moved in a step and met Tyrdis's gaze with authority. "It is not your fault, nor mine. These people need my help. Joren can take care of our hospice without me for a little while, but Karyna requires a teacher. She has a sharp mind and isn't afraid to get her hands dirty. It honestly surprised me to discover she's the jarl's daughter."

"But our kingdom is at war with theirs." This time, a plea sounded in Tyrdis's tone. "The situation can spin like a coin, and promises and assurances become meaningless. Once Karyna knows enough to work on her own and they don't need your skill anymore—"

"Shhh." Adelle took Tyrdis's hands and gave them a little squeeze. Her calluses had softened from weeks of not holding weapons, but her long fingers remained strong and warm as they twined through hers. A dizzy feeling swept over Adelle in a moment that felt far too intimate, and she could sense her pulse racing. The patients on their cots faded away until there was only the two of them. "Would you give your word and break it?"

"Never."

"I have to believe Jarl Stefnir is also honorable. You serve the king, the jarl, whoever sits in authority over you," Adelle explained. "I serve the goddess Eir and the oath I took as a healer. Boundaries and kingdoms are meaningless. We are all members of the same race, the same family of mankind. Their people love and hate, laugh and cry the same as ours. We honor the same gods, tell the same stories, sing the same songs. I want to come home. I miss Svanhild, Mother, Joren, everyone ... you. But being a healer isn't just something I do; it's who I am."

"Providing protection is not merely my job, Adelle; it is who I am. I failed to protect you."

"I'm not harmed." A compulsion beyond her will drew Adelle's hand to cup Tyrdis's cheek. And there was that desire to kiss her again, gnawing away at her control. She recognized a deep longing in her soul to break through all the barriers and connect to such a unique individual. No—to connect specifically to *this* individual, this woman. Some women engaged in such liaisons. It wasn't even really frowned upon, especially given the fact she was a widow with children. But did Tyrdis feel the same way?

"For now," she whispered. Tyrdis's free hand came around the small of Adelle's back.

I think that's a yes. But not here and now.

Adelle caught Tyrdis in a warm hug, pressing her cheek to hers, and feeling the pounding of the shieldmaiden's heart upon her breast. Tyrdis relaxed her stiff muscles and melted into the embrace. Hearing a patient's cough reminded her they weren't alone, and Adelle backed away, but she couldn't wipe the longing from her expression as she tried to look past Tyrdis's tough exterior.

"I'd like to think we are friends," Adelle said, "except we don't really know each other."

"I wish to know you," Tyrdis admitted. "You are a most admirable woman."

A smile swept over Adelle that shone in her eyes. "You realize that means you'll have to lower your defenses and allow me to see you. Are you brave enough for that?" she teased.

With a gleam lighting her face, Tyrdis almost smiled. "I have already allowed you to see all of me, if you recall."

"Smart ass." Adelle emitted a laugh before pressing her lips closed, delight dancing on her countenance.

"Tyrdis, it's time to go," Sweyn called from the tent door.

Adelle's demeanor turned serious, and she caught Tyrdis's tunic sleeve. "Look after Svanhild and Mother for me, will you?"

For an instant, she perceived a hint of desire radiating from the shield-maiden. She inclined her head and replied in a manner as dependable as steel. "Be assured, as I breathe, no harm will befall either of them. Be expedient in training your apprentice and come home to us."

"Adelle, be of strong courage," Sweyn charged. "My father will not abandon you, and Jarl Stefnir has given me his word. We will have you home before winter."

"Tell Niklaus I am filled with gratitude for his faithfulness and that I'm well. My best to your mother."

When Adelle's gaze shifted back to Tyrdis, she had already turned and was walking out to meet Sweyn. Regret tugged at her heart to see her leave—again. But she had been right. They didn't really know each other beyond the roles they had been born to ... roles that conflicted at their very cores. Or did they?

She views herself not as a warrior at heart, but as a protector. A protector and healer could walk hand-in-hand, couldn't they? Only time would tell.

CHAPTER 20

Outside the healing tent, coinciding with the previous conversation

"*K*aryna, wait!" Sweyn called as he trotted after her. He was met by two guards crossing spears in front of him.

"Won't you even talk to me?" he asked with a plea in his voice. He hadn't realized seeing her would affect him so strongly, but he hadn't been expecting to—and now she was training to be a healer. What's worse, she was even more attractive than the last time he'd seen her, which was when? Three years ago? He had questions. Uppermost in his mind, *Is she married?*

Sweyn stood breathless as he waited behind the barrier of spears, hoping against hope she would turn around and dismiss them. Maybe she would reject him instead. All around him, warriors bustled through the camp, passing between them, blocking his view of Karyna. The smell of smoke from small fires filled the air and Sweyn could sense tense, distrustful eyes glaring at him. With long, swift strides, she marched between the last two tents before reaching the meadow, then spun around.

Karyna held a basket in one hand and her other she propped on her hip while she scowled at him with an angry appraisal. "Oh, let him pass," at last she snapped, then headed onto the meadow.

Relief mingled with trepidation when the soldiers unblocked his path. "Touch her and die," one snarled, but the multitude of enemies was not what caused him to shake. When he caught up to Karyna, her attention was focused on the ground.

"I wasn't expecting to see you here," he said. "I hope you are faring well." When she continued to ignore him, Sweyn added, "And you're training to be a grædari. How admirable! Have you heard Eir's call?"

She plucked some broad leaves from a weed-looking plant, stuffed them in the basket, and whirled toward him, her beautiful face a mask of rage. "I heard the call of my suffering countrymen, you bastard!" She jabbed an accusing finger into his chest. "You attacked us for no reason, and now my friend Rurik is dead."

A wave of guilt rippled through Sweyn as he paled beneath her charge. He had thought there had been a reason, only now he knew the disturbing truth and could tell no one. He recalled Rurik—a beanpole of a fellow who relished playing pranks, drinking, dancing, and laughing. Sweyn reckoned he'd become an entertainer one day. What had he been doing among the warriors? Had he grown serious as he matured, or did his father expect it of him?

"I'm sorry to hear of it, Karyna, but I didn't start this war. King Gustav called my father to mobilize his troops after the last snowmelt as retribution for the murder of Prince Jarivald," he explained, seething with inward fury as he repeated the lie. "*I* did not attack *you*." *I could never.*

"You can't just march in here and pretend we're still friends, Sweyn," she retorted. "It's been what—three years since your last visit? And I haven't heard a word from you since. Now Raumsdal has declared war on us and that makes you my enemy."

"I am not your enemy, Karyna, and my father doesn't view Jarl Stefnir as his enemy."

"Well, the abundance of attacks you've led against us begs to differ," she barked, glowering at him with stormy eyes. She had filled out into a grown woman, much as his muscles had increased with his maturity. Karyna had been like a nymph or sprite; now she was a force of nature. Something tightened in Sweyn's gut, and he clenched his jaw, grappling to maintain control of his rising emotions.

Swallowing his desire to spill everything, he responded in a tender, calm fashion, "We are dealing with difficult circumstances. I never wanted to hurt you or Rurik or anybody." With her back to him, she continued to collect the leaves for her basket. "Talk to Adelle about me. She knows me well and can testify we are only doing what we are told."

"And if your king ordered you to do something repulsive, like slaughter children or shove your mother off a cliff, would you obey?" Straightening, she returned her intense gaze to him, awaiting an answer.

"You are a jarl's daughter. Surely you understand the chain of command. You know I wouldn't obey such a preposterous order, but this is different. It's not personal. The war isn't between you and me."

"Maybe not," she admitted with a little less venom. "But we're caught up in it and you can't expect me to act as if things are normal. Besides, I figured you had forgotten me."

"I didn't avoid coming to visit," Sweyn explained. "Things kept coming up. Besides, the last time I saw you at the Solstice celebration a couple of winters back, you couldn't stop looking at Rollo. Your father was enthusiastic about making a match for the two of you, and I thought ..."

He glanced up at her with a shy, questioning look, and shifted his weight from one foot to the other.

Karyna smirked and returned to picking leaves. "Rollo, Jarl Torsten's son, might have been handsome, elegant, and refined, but perhaps too much so. Let's just say, such an arrangement would never have been satisfactory for me, and I told my father exactly that after I discovered ... Rollo's true nature."

Sweyn smiled, both at the knowledge she hadn't married the man and at the humor he detected in her voice. The moment she stopped exhibiting anger toward him, he felt overjoyed. "I haven't found a suitable partner yet either," he responded.

Her basket filled, Karyna stretched back to her full height and slowly turned to him. "I know you are a good man. No one could change so much in such a short time, but we can't even entertain such thoughts— not now. I'm still angry with you for forgetting about me and I realize the war isn't your fault. It is what it is, but you belong with them, and I belong here, doing the best I can to help my people."

Staring intently into her baby-blue eyes, Sweyn declared, "I did not forget about you. You are the most unforgettable woman I've ever met. To be honest, I thought you had lost interest in me, and I didn't want to be bothersome."

Karyna let out a heavy sigh and lowered her chin, giving her head a gentle shake. Then she waved a dismissive hand in his direction. "Go on, now. Go lead warriors into battle so I can try to patch ours up when you're done maiming them. I don't know, Sweyn. How did things get so messed up?"

She glanced up, catching his gaze, and Sweyn wanted to rush to her, to gather her in his arms and tell her everything would be all right, except that was something he couldn't promise. He trembled inside, knowing the reason for their present situation, and hatred for a greedy, lying king sprang to life within him.

Swallowing, he diverted his eyes and mumbled, "I don't know. But it should be over soon. I'm sorry, Karyna. I'm sorry for everything."

It was with a heavy heart Sweyn turned and walked back to the camp, while Firdafylke guards—never far away—continued watching him like hungry hawks.

* * *

TYRDIS RODE in silence as their procession made its way back over the ridge toward Sæladalr, replaying every nuance in her mind. She was relieved to find Adelle safe, disappointed they couldn't secure her release, and trying hard to understand the healer's point of view. *We are at war with them, and she rushes to their aid without a care that she was captured or her life may be in danger. Is that foolish or praiseworthy? I understand she has a calling and prefers peace to war, but ...* She shook her head as if it could bring her clarity.

Shifting topics, a tiny thrill danced along her senses when she recalled Adelle taking her hands, holding them, lacing her talented fingers through hers, and then the embrace. Tyrdis could have remained in her arms all day—longer—and never wish to let go. Adelle had projected affection, and Tyrdis could have sworn she discerned longing in her gaze, even if it was for but a moment. Was it possible? Did she stand a chance of building a relationship with her, despite the odds?

A familiar, terrifying thought trickled through her hopeful mood. *What if you open your heart, bare your soul, really let her in, be vulnerable, be a woman to her, and she rejects you? Or maybe she realizes she truly prefers men? Or she is only toying with you; what would a warrior be like? Why do you even entertain such rubbish? Duty, honor, strength. You are iron, you are steel, molded from the blood of your ancestors, sharpened in the crucible of battle. What use are love and affection to one such as you? Are you not above such sentiments?*

She frowned at the reminder that she had never allowed herself to explore such pleasurable possibilities and at her myriad of rationaliza-tions. *Then Bruna was right, and I am afraid. What if I choose courage? What if I say, Hel take it all—I want the experience, even if I get hurt? Great Odin, I almost died. What could be worse than that? And what if it is wonderful? Either way, the next time I lay skewered in the mud, my lifeblood flowing away, I won't have the regret anymore.*

Now she had to focus on safeguarding Bruna and Svanhild and preparing to defend the town when the army strikes out for their attack. She studied Sweyn's back as he plodded along ahead of her. His shoulders were slumped, and he hadn't said a word. *He recognized Adelle's new student, the jarl's daughter. She didn't seem pleased to see him, and he chased after her when she left. But he seemed distant and distracted even before. It is none of my affair. Then again, Sweyn is my friend. Friends should offer consolation and words of counsel. They should also be willing to listen.*

She clicked her tongue and squeezed her knees into her pony's sides, prompting him to pick up his pace until she rode beside Sweyn. "You are troubled," she stated with a furrow between her pinched brows.

He sighed, rearranging his hands on the reins, glanced at her, then back at the path. "Oh, it's Karyna," he let out in frustration. "We used to be friends, only now she sees me as the enemy."

"Our kingdom attacked hers," Tyrdis replied, as if giving a lecture. "In essence, we are her enemies."

"In the eyes of men, perhaps, but not in truth," Sweyn contradicted. "Whatever happened to truth? Does it not even matter anymore? You respect people, believe they are strong and honorable, follow their direc-tives, and then they turn out to be false pretenders. Is integrity a thing of the past, or did it never exist at all?"

Tyrdis perceived he was no longer speaking about Karyna, though she suspected he thought of her as more than a friend, hence how her lack of a greeting affected him. But there was more to his rant. The young woman had never been in authority over him.

"I do not know how to lie," Tyrdis replied. Hide her feelings, yes; bear false witness, no. "Please, if you think me false—"

"Not you," he muttered and rolled his shoulders as if they were stiff from aching.

"You have been uncharacteristically taciturn since we left early this morning," she noted. "Something else troubles you."

"It does, but I can't talk about it."

Tyrdis rode at his side, not speaking, merely waiting for him to be ready to say more. After a while, he did.

"The war is wrong." The deep, bone-weary frown he wore made Sweyn look ten years older.

"Because it separates you and someone you care about," Tyrdis suggested. "It puts you and Karyna at odds."

"Yes." He glanced at her, and she met his eyes for an instant. "But that isn't all."

"Adelle believes all wars are wrong, but such a perception is flawed. When a king is corrupt, when he deceives his neighbors and covets what is theirs, then sends young men and women to die for his pleasure, we are bound by honor to stand up against him. When one murders the children of another, retribution is in order. When the innocent and helpless are victimized, a swift sword is often the only rescue for them. Honorable warriors defend their communities and their kingdoms from those who would steal, abuse, brutalize, usurp, and kill for no reason. The evil may reign for a while, but I must trust righteous warriors will bring them to their knees one day."

"It is but a wish and a dream to envision a world without war," Sweyn concurred. "A war fought for a just cause is worth the sacrifices, on that we agree. But what happens if you discover everything you thought was right and just and true isn't? What if we're the wrongdoers?"

"I concur. Going to war is extreme to avenge the murder of a single man, but Jarivald was our prince and heir." Tyrdis was confused and anxious over Sweyn's line of conversation. "It is not outside the history of the Norse to do so, and can be justified, especially if the opposing king was indeed responsible for the assassination."

Sweyn said nothing but looked at Tyrdis with a pained, mournful expression, as if he was a dam about to bust. Shaking his head, he turned back to the trail, spurred on his horse, and left her behind. That's when the truth struck Tyrdis with the impact of a battering ram: Jarivald hadn't been murdered by Firdafylke assassins at all. King Gustav lied.

CHAPTER 21

"Y ou won't stand for it." Horik's words rang with a subdued edge. He, Njal, and Jarl Niklaus glanced at the door as Sweyn entered the otherwise empty hall. Bone tired and in a bad mood, he trudged over to sit with them.

"Where is everybody?" Sweyn asked as he crashed into the seat beside his father.

"At the dance at the mead hall," Njal answered. "Except for Mother, Braggi, and Solfrig. They've gone to bed."

"What is the situation with Adelle?" Niklaus asked.

Sweyn dragged his horn through the bowl of ale resting on the table and downed a gulp. "They let Tyrdis and I see her." A few minutes ago, he had delivered Tyrdis to the hospice where Bruna was staying with Svanhild and sent the others from his party to their homes. He wanted her to do nothing but rest after the trying day. Although the stubborn shield-maiden had insisted she was ready for service, he knew better. Besides, he needed to check in with Joren to make sure the apprentice healer was doing satisfactory work. Before the abduction, his father had suggested bringing Joren along for their assault to treat the wounded immediately in the field, but now the idea was moot. He must remain to oversee the hospice. Bruna and Svanhild were good at helping, but neither could perform a diagnosis or carry out surgery.

"She's in the field camp of a large army caring for their wounded, as we suspected. Njal, Horik," he inquired, "is Jarl Bjarke sending support?"

"Aye," his uncle replied and refilled his cup from the bowl. "Not only that, but he's coming himself to lead his warriors. Bjarke was exceedingly enthusiastic about the plan."

"I think he intends to help himself to some of the trade products stored in warehouses at the port," Njal added sourly. "But what's this you heard about ..." Sweyn's younger brother glanced around warily at the empty hall and lowered his voice. "Ivar killing Jarivald," he whispered.

Sweyn shifted in his chair and shot a glance at his father.

"I was just telling them about my visit to the völva," Niklaus confessed. "I know I told you to keep the story secret, but Revna the Wise—and she's got to be a hundred years old—was not surprised to hear it. She claims Jarivald's ghost visited her in a dream."

Horik made a face and waved his hand. "I don't believe in such things," he declared. "Old woman has probably eaten too many of the wrong kinds of mushrooms over the years. Still, I find it much more likely King Gustav Ironside would lie for his own benefit than some little orphan girl who has nothing to gain. Did Niklaus ever tell you how Gustav manipulated his way to the throne? He wasn't born a prince, you know. It could have been Raknar or your father who rules in Raumsdal now just as easily and, believe me—Raknar hasn't forgotten."

"Father?" Njal turned a questioning gaze to Niklaus and leaned closer. "Is that true?"

"Do you think your Uncle Horik a scoundrel and a liar, boy?" sounded Horik's incredulous rebuff.

"You never told us that," Sweyn commented, his curiosity piqued.

Niklaus's mouth twisted into a grimace, and he rubbed the back of his neck. Then, shaking his head, he responded, "Ancient history, which has no bearing on the dilemma at hand. I am far less concerned with the luck of the draw twenty years ago than I am with the rot in the kingdom today. Power corrupts, even when it is not absolute. Every negotiation must benefit Gustav, and every venture return with a percentage for him. Sure, much of those resources go to weapons and supporting an army, but I know for a fact the king keeps just as much for himself. It is not evil to wish to live well in comfort or even luxury if such is earned and deserved. But now good men and women are dying because of Gustav's lie, and Horik is right—I won't let it stand. I'm just uncertain how we should proceed."

"Besides confirming the story is true, what did Revna say?" Sweyn asked. "Did she have a prophecy for you?"

Horik blew air through his lips, making a sound like a horse, while he rolled his eyes and dropped an open palm to slap the table. "Prophecy! Bah! You don't see Thor sitting around a table with his advisors debating. He takes action—rights the wrong with his mighty hammer, Mjölnir. Here's what I think we should do." He caught Njal and Sweyn's eyes before turning his attention to Niklaus, pointing at him with knitted brows.

"We should go through with the attack on Griðlundr, seize the port, then negotiate a treaty with King Tortryggr of Firdafylke—don't even bother including Gustav. If he won't come and fight for his own spoils, why should he have a say?"

Sweyn supposed his uncle had a point.

"Then we take the entire army, with Raknar and Bjarke, and march to Skeggen and confront Gustav over his lie. We can bribe Ivar and Kerstav, and, if not, they can be exiled along with their dishonorable father."

"Then who would replace him?" Niklaus interrupted. "And I doubt he will capitulate. Gustav would command all the warriors loyal to him to fight us."

"And they would lose," Njal pointed out. "Three jarls with their fighting forces would outnumber them many times over."

"I said before," Sweyn reminded him, "we should call a kingdom-wide Thing and let the free men vote between Ivar, Raknar, Bjarke, and you, whom they wish to be the next king."

Niklaus leaned forward on his elbows and steepled his fingers. Resting his chin atop them, he stared at a spot on the wall. "Revna's prediction declared the man who should be king, would be king, but he would not wish to pay the price. She didn't say which of us it would be, but my biggest concern is the contending jarls turning on each other, unwilling to abide by a vote by the people. Bjarke is young, enthusiastic, and a mighty warrior akin to a bear, while Raknar, the more cunning fox, has long bided his time, seeking an opening to grab the crown for himself. I'm the only one content to stay as I am."

"Which is why you should rule the kingdom," Horik stated. "I know, I am always pushing you, disagreeing with you, discounting your slow, steady, discerning ways, but that's because a little brother's lot in life is to annoy his older brother. The fact you don't aspire to rule, coupled with your proven ability to do so, renders you the perfect man for the job."

"Not if it costs me you," Niklaus countered. "Or Sweyn or Njal. You all, the family I love, are the price I would be unwilling to pay. I'd rather be a meager sheep herder in a tent in the meadow with you safe around my table than rule all Norvegr without you."

"Father," Sweyn entreated. "You taught me that right words and right actions stand above all our wishes and desires. Truth and honor must endure, regardless of the cost. I would rather die fighting for such than live in safety, knowing I had abandoned our values. I don't even think we should attack Griðlundr as planned. We will still lose fighters we need to confront King Gustav, and it poisons my soul to think of continuing this sham of a war knowing the truth. How can I raise my weapon to kill our neighbors when we support a false cause?"

"Think of the end goal, nephew," Horik cajoled. "We'll capture vast resources we'll need to secure the throne and put everything in the kingdom right. Once you are prince, you can propose all the diplomatic treaties you desire and oversee an era of peace if it pleases you."

"I don't know." Njal raked his fingers through his burnished locks and caught Sweyn's gaze for an instant before turning it on their uncle. "Though it doesn't happen often, I agree with Sweyn. It's not right to rush into battle, to kill unsuspecting people conducting trade in a port town when we know the supposed reason doesn't exist. It would be different if we were conducting a raid in the east or on an island of Britannia where the people are not of our culture and religion, where they speak a foreign language, and our survival doesn't depend upon cordial relations with our neighbors."

"You have all made good points," Niklaus confirmed. He sat back with a heavy sigh. "Jarl Bjarke and his army should arrive, when?" He glanced at Njal.

"He said four days," Njal answered, "so they would have a day to rest before we launch the attack."

"And Raknar?" The jarl shifted his attention to Sweyn.

"Ivar was riding up to collect them. My best guess would be they should arrive around the same time, if not a day sooner."

"Will Ivar lead the king's contingent?" A hint of concern tainted Niklaus's visage.

Sweyn shook his head. "I don't believe so. King Gustav hasn't allowed him to leave Skeggen until he consented for the journey to Heilagrfjord. Ivar has been most disgruntled about it, but I don't think the king trusts him to let him out from under his thumb."

Niklaus nodded. "This conversation does not leave this room," he demanded. "Whatever we decide, Raknar and Bjarke must be in agreement, or we'll find ourselves in a civil war."

They each granted a solemn nod, and Niklaus pushed up from the table.

"Is there anything to eat?" Sweyn asked. His stomach, tied in knots as it had been, still protested a missed meal.

"We left a few morsels of lamb and some cabbage," Horik answered with a mischievous grin. He also stood to leave the table. "You'll find it in the pot on the hearth. Now, I'll get to the mead hall at just the right time— when all the pretty women have become loose from their drinking!" He gave Sweyn a wink and headed out.

Njal stayed with Sweyn while he ate. "I'm glad Father let me go with Horik to Austrihóll," he said. "It was my first time there and my first time to be a part of something important. Sure, I do a lot of training and have fought in a few skirmishes, and I had a part in the blessing of the ships this spring, but ..." He shrugged. "Mostly only you get to do meaningful things."

"Well, I didn't have many opportunities until I was around your age." Sweyn washed down his lamb with a swig of ale.

"You were sixteen when you led your first expedition—I remember!" Njal pointed an accusatory finger at him. "And you went to Oskholm in Firdafylke several times, like for the Solstice celebration. And didn't you like that girl for a while? What was her name?" he puzzled.

"Karyna." The name dropped from his lips as if it were made of iron, prompting his little brother to probe further.

"You saw her!" he exclaimed. "You saw her today, didn't you?"

Swallowing another mouthful, Sweyn slumped in his seat and stared blankly ahead at a fly hopping about the table. It had a big, ugly, black body, with tiny, delicate wings, and he wondered for just an instant how they kept it in the air. He wanted to swat it, to flatten it into a sticky spot just for annoying him, but there was nothing handy to strike it with. *Lucky fly.*

At once, Njal's manner softened to that of a concerned friend rather than a pesky burr under his saddle. "You still care about her. I take it she isn't happy about the war."

"No," he muttered. "She isn't. But at least she isn't married yet. Njal, she was more beautiful than I remember, and she was just a little angry I hadn't come to see her again, which must be a good sign, right? I mean, she must have wanted me to if my absence upset her. But then that rat bastard Gustav had to start a war with them and she and her father want nothing to do with me—like it's my fault. I don't know."

"It'll be all right, Sweyn," Njal consoled. "The war should be over soon enough. And just think—if Father becomes king and we're princes, Karyna and her father will look much more favorably at you."

"Jarl Stefnir, perhaps, but Karyna doesn't care about position and status. I only hope she still cares about me."

"Hey, beautiful women in Raumsdal are as easy to find as stars in a clear night sky," Njal said merrily as he stood. "And I know some younger ones just right for me will be at the mead hall, like Uncle Horik said. You'll have your pick of them, brother—just don't choose the same one I do, you hear? We wouldn't want fratricide to become too popular." He laughed, giving Sweyn a slap on the shoulder as he passed. "You should come."

"No, thank you, and no joking about wanting to kill me, please," Sweyn replied with as much humor as he could muster. "I'm too tired and melancholy for a party tonight. Besides, why would I covet the kind of trollop you'd set your heart on?"

"Those are fighting words, brother!" Njal tossed back lightly. "I'll have you know I have excellent taste in the ladies." In parting, he used a more sensitive tone and an honest expression. "Don't lie in our room and brood all night. I'll know if you do."

"I'll do my best," Sweyn said, "but no promises. Have a good time."

With a grin and a wink, Njal answered, "Oh, I will."

His plate cleared of food, Sweyn downed the last of his ale, scooped another horn full, and drank it too. Many nights he would sleep in the hall with the other single warriors, but tonight he preferred to be alone in the room he shared with his brothers. His youngest brother, Braggi, was asleep facing the wall, his steady breathing a comfort to Sweyn. Trygve had met up with his friends when they arrived in town and hadn't returned yet, and he wasn't certain Njal would return at all. Faint streaks of light seeped in through thread-like cracks in the wall planks, allowing him to see to find his bed and reminding him how near to the summer solstice it was.

I really don't want to attack the Firdafylke port, he bemoaned to himself as he sat on the edge of his bed. He pulled off his boots, thinking, *It would be one more reason for Karyna to hate me. Why her, Odin?* He tossed empty hands in the air and gazed at the rafters. *Why can't a local girl make me feel the way she does? What spell does she cast to ensnare me?* But he knew she had done nothing other than be herself, and he couldn't help being entranced. Sweyn had gotten over loving the völva's acolyte; he would get over Karyna if he had to.

CHAPTER 22

*W*hen Tyrdis opened her eyes the next morning, a freckle-faced blonde girl hovered over her. "Amma, she's awake!" she called out.

Drifting into consciousness, Tyrdis recognized where she was—in Adelle's hospice, back lying on the bed she had occupied for weeks, with Svanhild standing vigil. But Adelle wasn't here; she had been kidnapped, and ... "How late is it?"

"Not yet midday," Bruna answered from across the room as she strolled in her direction.

"You were very tired and hurting when you got here last night," Svanhild said. "I rubbed the ointment on your wound and Amma poured tea in your mouth. Then you fell fast asleep. Did you see Mama? Is she all right? When is she coming home?"

"Give Tyrdis a moment to wake up," Bruna chided as she eased Svanhild out of the way and took the stool beside the bed.

Svanhild clasped her little hands under her chin, her face openly displaying her anxiety, while Bruna laid the back of her hand on Tyrdis's forehead.

"I am not sick." Tyrdis pushed up in bed with a frown. *How could I have slept until midday?* "Yes, Svanhild, I saw your mother, and she is in satisfactory condition. I am sorry, but I do not know when she is coming home. She asked me to watch over you and your grandmother until she does, which is precisely what I shall do."

"Adelle would say you pushed yourself too hard yesterday," Bruna commented as she lifted her hand, sliding it around to press to Tyrdis's cheek with affection. The same kindness she had first recognized in Adelle's eyes shone through her mother's. "But you don't break easily. Let's agree to watch over each other until she returns, shall we?"

Without awaiting an answer, Bruna rose and swanned over to the hearth with graceful movements. "That is acceptable," Tyrdis agreed aloud.

Svanhild beamed and bounced back onto the stool. "You need to eat now and get strong again."

"I am exceedingly strong, little honeybee," Tyrdis replied with a straight face, "and do not doubt it. However, I am hungry if you have food prepared."

Svanhild giggled and Bruna called, "I'm dishing it up now."

"Do you believe they will treat Adelle well and allow her to come home soon?" Joren asked. He left the other patients to walk over and peer at Tyrdis with concern on his youthful face.

"She is training one of their women in the art of healing," Tyrdis expounded. "The jarl's daughter, Karyna. She appears to be your age or a little older, and Adelle finds her a suitable apprentice."

"That's good, right?" Bruna's expression lit with optimism as she walked back, carrying a steaming bowl. Svanhild took it from her so she could engage in her favorite feeding ritual. Tyrdis supposed she could consent to be fed if it put such a glow on the child's face.

"I believe it provides reason to be hopeful," Tyrdis said. "Once they have a healer of their own who can perform acceptably, they should release Adelle." She clamped her mouth shut to avoid revealing her own worries about what may happen when they didn't need Adelle's skills any longer. That would still be weeks—if not months—away. "Bruna, will you be staying here?" Tyrdis asked. "Would you be more comfortable in your home in town?"

"I will be where Svanhild is, and she insists upon being where you are," she answered. "My house is cozy, and there's room for the three of us, so we can divide the time between both places. Which do you think is safest?"

Tyrdis considered the question while Svanhild spooned fish soup into her mouth. "Although the hospice should be forbidden to attackers, we have discovered some ignore the rule. Your house lies within the town walls, which provide some protection, and it is near Jarl Niklaus's great hall and his band of warriors; however, it is more likely to fall under attack. It is difficult to predict which is the more secure location."

"We're safest wherever you are, Tyrdis," Svanhild chirped. Tyrdis wished that was the case, but, after only one day of normal activity, her limbs felt as though they were iron and her torso like it had been assaulted with boulders.

"When Jarl Niklaus leads the warriors on their attack, we will inquire with Lady Lynnea if we may stay in their great hall," Tyrdis suggested. "I am to coordinate the town's defenses, but I shan't leave you again."

Bruna smiled. "Lynnea will be glad to have us, I'm certain. Now, I have things to do, but I'll check on you later."

"I'll collect herbs from the garden," Joren said, and they both wandered off. Svanhild stayed, feeding Tyrdis.

"Will you come with me to pick berries today?" the little girl asked. "We need more berries, and you need gentle exercise."

Tyrdis couldn't hide her smile at the bossy tone in Svanhild's voice that reminded her of Adelle. The thought also made her recall their conversation and how Adelle had mentioned they don't really know each other. Tyrdis determined to use this time to get to know Adelle, even if she wasn't here.

"Acceptable, providing you answer questions for me in return."

"What kind of questions?"

The sleek, gray-striped feline caught her gaze as she leisurely strolled across the floor, hopped onto a vacant bed, and began kneading a spot in the blanket. Tyrdis wondered about the cat, how much Adelle liked or tolerated it, and a flood of questions raced into her awareness at once.

"I want to learn all of your mother's favorite things," she said. "We could surprise her with them when she comes home. Would that be satisfactory?"

Svanhild grinned, her eyes lighting up. "What a great idea!" She shoveled another spoonful into Tyrdis's mouth, spilling a few drops in her excitement. Her enthusiasm swelled Tyrdis's heart, causing her to realize how strange—and yet pleasant—it made her feel.

Tyrdis listened with eagerness while Svanhild spouted off Adelle's favorite things. "Mama's favorite color is pink—we have to get her something pink, like a batch of her favorite flowers, fiell azaleas. Then you could sing her favorite song, *When the Chaffinches Sing in the Trees.*"

A momentary panic flew over Tyrdis at the suggestion. She hadn't thought she'd need to sing. Svanhild must have noticed her look of dread and asked, "What's wrong?"

"Isn't that song a child's lullaby?"

"Maybe, but Mama must love it," Svanhild explained. "She used to sing it to me all the time—still does if I'm not feeling well. Then Amma can help us make her favorite food: fluffy cakes topped with honey, berries, and cream."

Tyrdis would have thought Adelle would prefer something more healthy and less sweet, but she had expounded on the virtues of berries before.

"And we can play her favorite game—spinning tops!" Setting the almost empty bowl aside, Svanhild sprang across the room, opened a chest, rummaged through it, and pulled out a set of wooden tops painted bright colors. "See?" She rushed back and dumped them on the bed beside Tyrdis. "We each have one and you have to set it on the pointy end and give it a twist, like this." Using the relative flat of the upended crate end table, the little girl demonstrated. The yellow top spun vigorously until it wobbled off the edge and crashed to the floor. Svanhild grabbed it up. "We'll have to use the table or the floor. There's not enough room on here. Whoever's top spins the longest before falling over wins. We count the wins to see the overall winner. Usually, Mama, Amma, and me take turns winning. Oh, and Mama's most favorite is puppet shows! You and I must create a puppet show for her. See?"

Another mad sprint, this one to her bed and back, and Svanhild retrieved an armload of dolls. "We hide behind a sheet and hold up the dolls and talk for them. They say funny things and it makes Mama laugh. Could you help me make up a funny puppet show?"

All the dolls and toys were new to Tyrdis, and she couldn't recall a single humorous story. The thought shot a fresh wave of terror through her. She hadn't known she'd be called upon to entertain Adelle. The healer had seemed so much more serious to her during their few interactions. Yet she wished more than anything to please Adelle and to know her well enough to be considered her friend. If it meant singing and performing puppet shows, she'd humble herself and do them.

Hearing a muffled giggle, Tyrdis glanced across the room at Bruna, who busied herself rolling dry bandages she had pulled down from the rafters where they had been hung. "Do you have something to add?" Tyrdis asked in curiosity.

Bruna's playful eyes darted her way, then back to their task. "Oh, no. I believe Svanhild has given you quite a bit to go on." The woman's smirk gave Tyrdis pause.

"You think I cannot learn something new, is that it?" she asked in challenge. "I do not accept the word impossible; therefore, I shall allow you and Svanhild to instruct me on how to play these games, pick these flowers, and cook the fluffy cakes. I want to make Adelle happy after all she has done for me. Is that so unreasonable?"

Bruna set the rolled bandages on a shelf and turned a broad, beaming smile to Tyrdis. "No, dear shieldmaiden, it isn't unreasonable. In fact, it delights my soul to see how determined you are to make my girls happy."

"Come on." Svanhild tugged on Tyrdis's arm. "Let's go pick berries. I'll show you where to find the azaleas too. Then we can start planning the puppet show and I'll teach you the song. Don't worry, Tyrdis. I know exactly what Mama likes."

Tyrdis's body protested, but she got up, still wearing her clothes from yesterday. A sniff informed her that another bath and a change of tunics and trousers were in order, as hers reeked with the odors of horse, dirt, leaves, and perspiration. Because of Svanhild's urgency and apparent obliviousness to the distasteful smells, she decided it could wait until after they collected berries and flowers. However, she took time to lace up her boots and secure her belt with an ax and knife Sweyn had provided her, along with a staff that leaned outside the back door. It would come in handy for fending off a bear or human she didn't wish to kill, not to mention something to lean on if her strength waned.

Svanhild snatched up a basket and skipped ahead. "This way," she sang out as she danced and twirled in the sun. Tyrdis noted the intensity of the rays and figured it would be a hot day. They should return to the longhouse before Svanhild's fair skin burned. They could improvise a puppet story sitting in the shade of the back lean-to and enjoy whatever breeze blew their way.

"You are still too sore to skip, so don't try it." Svanhild spun around and faced her with a commanding expression.

"I will comply with your wishes."

Tyrdis must have skipped and danced about as a small child—they all do—only she couldn't remember how it was done. At Svanhild's age, she had served as a mother to Erik and a servant to their father; she couldn't recall frolicking or laughing or crying or any of the vast array of emotions that seemed to continually explode from this little girl. *"Waste no energy on mirth or tears,"* her father had drilled into her repeatedly. *"Such are only for the weak. Be of a serious mind and never talk too much."* The lessons had formed the woman she had become.

And wasn't Svanhild's exuberance exhausting? Yet her radiant energy kindled a dormant desire locked away in some dark chest buried beneath the shackles of discipline and restraint Tyrdis had practiced so faithfully all her life. Inwardly, she yearned to have fun.

You may amuse yourself with frivolous behavior after Adelle is home safely, she reminded herself. So she kept a watchful eye for any sign of danger while they gathered berries and picked flowers. She paid close attention while Svanhild taught her to play tops and Bruna showed her how to make fluffy cakes from a type of liquid batter consisting of milk, eggs, flour, and butter. The batter, when grilled in a pan over the fire, puffed up with air pockets into round, flexible edibles enhanced by the additions of honey, fruit, and thick cream. She had experienced nothing like them before.

Tyrdis made time to check in with Sweyn, who still seemed distressed, and spent a while drilling the six new warriors-in-training she had been working with. She didn't reference the king's deception or the war, but Sweyn mentioned Jarls Bjarke and Raknar were coming with more troops in a few days. By the time she returned to the hospice, Svanhild had fallen asleep on her bed surrounded by a host of dolls and a stuffed bear. She helped Bruna and Joren with a difficult patient and then vowed to stand watch while Bruna went down the road to visit Karl at the mead hall.

With all quiet, Tyrdis slipped out to the lean-to with the washtubs and some soap to clean herself. She borrowed a too-short underdress of Adelle's while she scrubbed the tunic and trousers she had been wearing, along with her socks and undergarments. The linen of Adelle's clothing smelled like her and added to Tyrdis's longing to grow close to her.

After drying herself and hanging her clothes on a line in the yard, Tyrdis quietly slipped into bed beside Svanhild, needing to rearrange the dolls to make room for herself. The little girl nestled beside her and draped an arm over her without ever opening her eyes. The arrangement felt odd to Tyrdis, but not unpleasant. In fact, she could probably grow accustomed to it—if she had to.

CHAPTER 23

Firdafylke camp, same day

"Pass me the jar of leeches," Adelle requested as she leaned over a man with a festering shoulder wound. He grimaced at her with a disgusted expression.

"Just make it better fast," he grumbled. "It's on fire and stabs me with pain every time I move my arm."

"Then don't move your arm." Adelle arched a brow at him and took the jar from Karyna.

"How do you know when to use leeches and when not to?" her new apprentice asked. "Or which poultice to employ or herbs to prescribe?"

Adelle assumed an aspect of patience as she instructed Karyna. She had in a few short days become an able assistant, and Adelle was pleased with her eagerness to learn.

"There are some grædari who overuse leeches, in my opinion. When they can't think of any more appropriate treatment, they prescribe leeches. But for warriors wounded in battle or any patient who has already lost blood, I believe they do more harm than good."

She pointed at the patient's foul-smelling, flame-red shoulder gash oozing with a yellowish secretion. "We do not want to see this puss. It is a sign something isn't healing correctly and if left untreated could delay or even prevent the sore from ever improving. However, leeches when applied, devour the puss and clean the wound site."

Reaching slender fingers into the jar, Adelle pulled out a slimy, black, parasitic worm and placed it on the affected region of the man's shoulder. Then she added a second one. "For an area this size, I'd recommend two. We'll leave them for today and check back on their progress later. They may need to stay overnight."

"Are festering wounds the only reason to use leeches?" Karyna asked in curiosity as she eyed the creatures.

"I sometimes use them for patients suffering from specific symptoms of dizziness, headaches, and shortness of breath," she answered and handed the jar back to Karyna. "They can prove beneficial as a regular regimen for people who are overweight and have suffered a heart attack — as they suck out the bad blood—but they aren't especially effective for anything else. Diet, herbs, and adding or restricting strenuous activity, along with fresh air and flushing fevers with much water and cold packs, are much more effective than leeches for most illnesses."

Karyna set the jar aside and peered at the patient's shoulder.

"What else should I prescribe?" Adelle asked.

"Something for the pain," griped the injured man.

"Willow bark tea!" Karyna announced in triumph, glee shining on her face.

"Will that alone be strong enough?" Adelle queried.

Karyna glanced at the trunk of herbs. "Before, you had me add ground hemp seeds."

Adelle smiled in satisfaction. "Good. Glad you remembered that. Yes, add some ground hemp seeds and let it steep for a few minutes. Myrdan," she said, calling her patient by name. He peered up at her with a hopeful look. "If the leeches have cleaned the puss by tomorrow, I'll reapply the salve and poultice. It's important to clear out this infection before you return to normal activities."

"I suppose," he muttered. "You aren't trying to poison me, are you?"

Irritation flashed across Adelle's face. "No. If I wanted to do that, I'd fill you with cowbane or hemlock."

Karyna leaned in close to Adelle and laid her hand on Myrdan's. "Adelle is a trusted servant of Eir, dedicated to relieving pain, not causing it. Do not fear, Myrdan; she is acting in your best interests and teaching me to do the same."

Relief washed through Adelle at Karyna's reassuring words, and she sensed the sincerity in the younger woman's voice. Turning an expression of concern to Adelle, she asked in a subdued tone, "What about Renrick's fever?"

"Let's check on him," Adelle responded in a friendly manner and followed Karyna to the big man's cot. She checked the temperature of his forehead and cheeks, noting both heat and perspiration along with a flush in his skin. "Drench a few rags in the coldest water you can find," she instructed. "At other times of the year, you could gain a quicker response with some snow or ice. It's important to bring the fever down by cooling off the patient. Then we need to get nutritious liquids into him, like the leftover bone broth from last night."

"The water in the rain barrel isn't cold, but it's cool," Karyna responded.

"Then it will have to do. If you could bring in a pail, I'll scoop him a cup of broth."

WITH RENRICK COOLED DOWN and all the patients resting, Adelle and Karyna took a moment to sit outside the healing tent to relax in the fresh air. A guard remained posted at the tent entrance, but most people in the camp went about their business, paying the women no attention.

"I'm pleased with your progress, Karyna," Adelle praised. She considered her student as a breeze caught her loose, fawn hair a shade lighter than her own.

"Thank you," she answered. Karyna sounded tired, which was understandable. She had been on her feet all morning and had been up with Adelle several times during the night, checking on patients.

"I take it you know Sweyn," Adelle mentioned, hoping to engage in conversation about something other than work.

The young woman pushed her hair back from her face and let out a breath. "Yes. We met as children and have interacted on several occasions since. Be honest, please: what do you think of him? Is he a spoiled, rich man's son accustomed to getting what he wants? Is he a brutish warrior who celebrates chopping off the heads of his enemies? Does he have a different woman every night, or does he prefer men?"

Adelle raised her brows, giving Karyna an incredulous expression. "You really don't know Sweyn at all if you think any of those things. He's quite a decent young man. Everyone in Sæladalr likes him—except a few fellows who are envious of him, I imagine."

"So, he really is who he seems to be?" Karyna's gaze seemed sad and hopeful at the same time.

"When my husband died, my son, Runar, was angry and depressed." Adelle clasped her hands around her crossed knee and tilted her head toward Karyna. "Sweyn didn't owe us anything; we were simply members of his community, and yet he went out of his way to make time for Runar. He took him hunting and fishing and made sure he was prepared for the winter games, like a father would do for his son. That was not a singular occasion. Sweyn pays attention to others and takes time to be a friend to them when there is no advantage in it for him. I've met plenty of politically-minded men and scheming women, but he is honest and noble in his virtues."

Karyna listened intently, distress seeming to grow in her manner as if she had hoped he was a louse. Adelle smiled and added, "Now, I can tell you plenty of embarrassing stories about him, like the time he came to me with a sprained ankle after falling off a friend's roof. When Sweyn was a gangly youth, he wished to play a prank by stuffing a bag of rotten eggs in his friend's smoke pipe, only he misstepped, fell off the roof, and the rotten eggs broke all over him. Except for him being laid up nursing his injured ankle and wounded pride for a week, it was quite funny."

The story drew a light giggle from Karyna, encouraging Adelle to relay more humiliating incidents. By the time her apprentice was squirting tears of laughter, Adelle reined in the tales. "But to address your concerns, Sweyn doesn't drink too much or chase every skirt in town. He doesn't hide ulterior motives and, while he has a healthy opinion of himself, he's quick to praise others and admit his mistakes. He really is who he appears to be."

Slumping, Karyna propped her elbow on her knee and rested her chin in her hand. "I've liked him since the first time we met." A laugh escaped her lips. "I was such a brat bossing him around, and he never complained. I acted like his winning the games didn't impress me at all, when in fact I admired him for it. My father has tried a few times to find me a husband, but I didn't like any of the prospects. I behaved horribly toward them so they wouldn't want me, so Papa wouldn't think I just rejected all his candidates. I'd love to spend more time with Sweyn so we could get to know each other as adults, only there's this stupid war, and who knows how it will turn out?"

Her sharing made Adelle think of Tyrdis, and how she would have liked to get to know her better if the war hadn't gotten in the way. Then again, without the war, Tyrdis may have never come to Sæladalr, and they might have never met at all.

"He hasn't chosen a wife and Jarl Niklaus isn't pressuring him to do so," Adelle said. "I could see the hurt on his face when you passed by him in the tent without a word the other day and he chased after you. Did you talk to him then?"

"I did." Karyna sat up and smoothed back her hair again. "Seeing him caught me off guard and I fussed at him like I was angry, and I am—only not at him. We had a few minutes, and I could have said something meaningful, but all we did was argue. Oh, Adelle, he's only gotten more handsome! And he wasn't opposed to me becoming a healer; he thought it was admirable. Most men want their wives to do nothing but focus all their attention on them and their children. How did you do it? What did your husband think of you pursuing your calling?"

A snicker jarred Adelle's belly, and she smiled. "I was already training when he asked me to marry him. I told him if he wanted me, he would get the grædari too. He said, 'Fine,' I said, 'Fine,' and that was that. He was gone adventuring a lot, anyway."

"And you haven't remarried?"

Adelle shook her head. "I don't need to. Fortunate is the woman who marries for love. In my experience, most do it because they can't survive on their own—or they want children and a traditional home."

"I suppose." Karyna hesitated, considering Adelle with a curious expression. "Did you love your husband?" When Adelle didn't answer, her apprentice turned away. "I'm sorry. It's not my business, and I didn't mean to pry. It's just … my mother is very formal and distant, and I can't talk to her about personal things. She isn't like you, so open and—"

"You don't need to apologize or explain," Adelle said. "My mother is always in my business, which is annoying in a different way. Sometimes I think people only want what they don't have. I cared for him a great deal, but I married because it was expected, because I wanted children, not because the sun rose and set in his eyes. We had a better-than-average marriage, I think. I have no complaints or regrets. And I have half my life before me, so who knows what the future will hold?"

Karyna smiled. "What a wonderful attitude. No wonder you are such a gifted healer. I don't want to sit about doing nothing but menial chores, waiting for my husband to come home every day. I want to matter too—

beyond the political ambitions every jarl has for his children. I want to do something meaningful, and, though I tried a few failed endeavors, I believe this one will stick. I started assisting Freyvoldr because he needed help and I needed to contribute. Father forbade me from taking up a sword or even a bow, but he approved of healing work. Since then, I've found it interesting, challenging, and rewarding. One part is really hard, though."

Adelle peered at her, trying to guess what she'd say. "And that is?"

Karyna glanced around the camp at the men and women coming and going, most with purpose and serious faces. Others sat in small gatherings in the shade, partaking of their midday meal and engaging in light conversation. "How do you deal with it when a patient dies?"

She understood the dilemma, one that took her years to come to terms with. "By realizing that ultimately, such matters are out of my hands. I lost a child once, a baby girl. She made it through her first few weeks with no noticeable signs of trouble, and I was encouraged she'd be just as strong and healthy as my son. Sunevar, my husband, was pleased with her, saying now he had a son and a daughter, that we had replaced ourselves in the world and could pass on in that knowledge. But the Norn or the gods had other designs. She died in her sleep in her crib for no apparent reason. She hadn't been sick or dropped or had a loss of appetite; Aldith just stopped breathing."

"Oh, Adelle, that is so horrible." Karyna reached a hand to her arm, exuding empathy so palpable Adelle could sense the vibration. "I am so sorry. It's every mother's worst nightmare to lose a child, especially a baby. But there's nothing you could have done. I'm sure you took every precaution and did everything right."

Adelle met her eyes with appreciation. "I knew that in my head, but my heart was sick and second-guessed everything I had done. I was stunned, angry, grief-stricken, despondent, all the emotions. Weeks later, our völva paid a visit and said the gods had made a mistake, that Aldith's soul essence was intended for an elf mother in Álfheim and had been accidentally deposited into my womb instead. She said the Norn promised me another baby girl to replace her, declaring she would be just as beautiful as the elf girl. I didn't believe her for the longest time, and then Svanhild was born, and she was perfect."

"Your experience is both sad and beautiful," Karyna said as she stroked her arm in comfort. "Now you have the right daughter and so does the elf mother, but I'm certain it was a very painful time in your life."

"It was, but I learned an important lesson that has helped me to be a better healer. I strive to be the best at my art, to never stop learning, and to care for each patient with dedication, but, at the end of the day, whether they get better or die isn't up to me. The gods have their own agenda. Some believe the Norn set the day of a person's death when they are born and regardless of anything we do, they will not die until that day nor live past it. But whether that's true or not, I am convinced our lives do not end with our last breath in Miðgarðr—there's more. Whether it is fighting and feasting in Valhalla, dining with Freyja in Fólkvangr, enjoying a peaceful existence in Helgafell, the holy mountain, or some- where else, perhaps among the stars. Or maybe, like little Aldith, we get reborn in one of the other worlds. All I can tell you is to do the best you can and never accept blame when a patient passes on. Such things are beyond our control."

"I suppose you're right," Karyna answered thoughtfully. "But it sounds like something I'll have to experience and work out within myself the way you did. I'm sorry my father had you kidnapped and forcibly removed from your home, but I'm also really glad you're here to teach me."

"Me too." Adelle laid her hand atop her pupil's with a warm smile. As much as she missed her family, something about teaching Karyna felt very right in her spirit. The war would end, and she'd be sent home ... eventually.

CHAPTER 24

Sæladalr, three days later

"Tyrdis!" Sweyn called with urgency from Bruna's doorway.

Tyrdis had spent the previous day and night in town with Bruna and Svanhild and divided her time between watching over them and training her new warriors. She had fully recovered from the ride to and from the Firdafylke camp but had not regained her full strength and stamina. She still was forced to spend much of her time sitting down or engaging in light activities, but she had handled her weapons and demonstrated grips, stances, and footwork with her students. While impatient with her progress, Tyrdis reminded herself it had only been about a moon since she had been run through, and regaining her power would take time.

She glanced up from her spot by the hearth where she was helping Bruna chop vegetables to go in the iron pot of water heating over the fire. Bruna had said that in the heat of summer, meals should be cooked early in the morning while some coolness still hung in the air, so they could dampen the fire as the temperature in the house rose. Some residents took to only cooking outdoors at this time of year, but Bruna didn't have ample yard space, and what she had was taken up by a small garden.

"Yes?" She stood while Svanhild rushed up to the door to meet him.

"Is Mama back?" Her chestnut eyes glimmered with anticipation.

Sweyn, looking more nervous than celebratory, stroked her hair with tenderness. "No, honeybee, not yet." He raised his gaze to Tyrdis. "Jarl Raknar and his warriors are approaching the town, and Garold is riding at his side."

Tyrdis's jaw tightened, and she pulled back her shoulders. "Allow me a moment to put on the new armor you have provided me, and I will join you to meet them."

With a nod, Sweyn replied, "My father has asked me to assemble an escort. He wishes to meet Jarl Raknar personally. Come join us as soon as you're ready but make it quick."

Sweyn stepped out, and Tyrdis opened the chest Sweyn had delivered. "Let me help you with that," Bruna said as she appeared by Tyrdis's side. "And no stubborn arguments."

"Very well." Tyrdis was surprised by the contents of the wooden box and may have gasped if she ever gasped, which she did not. She lifted out a blue gambeson and black trousers, the official Raumsdal colors. Jarl Raknar had expected each warrior to provide their own clothing and protection and only handed out spears to fighters, as they were frequently lost or broken during combat. The leather belt with loops for hand axes and a sheath for a seax was also dyed black, as were a brand-new pair of boots her size. But what lay beneath them truly took her breath away—a chainmail shirt. Her eyes widened at the rows of silver ringlets that took some craftsman days to complete. She knew it to be heavier than leather yet lighter than scale armor, and it would provide significantly more protection than what she had always worn in the past.

"What pretty armor," Svanhild cooed as she pressed in over Tyrdis's shoulder to peer at it.

"Appearance is irrelevant," Tyrdis stated. "However, this is far superior quality to any I've worn before."

Bruna smirked. "You think it's beautiful; you don't fool anyone."

A slight blush rose in Tyrdis's cheeks, and she wrapped the gambeson around her undertunic, tying it with its cord.

"Why did Sweyn provide such expensive equipment for me?" she asked in confusion while stepping into the new trousers. "I am not even bound to him."

"Perhaps not by oath," Bruna supposed, "but by an even stronger cord. You are friends, comrades, and he trusts and admires you."

"I trust and admire him as well." Tyrdis sat on the bed to secure her boots, still trying to fathom the young man's generosity. She thought about their conversation on the road, the secret he tried not to reveal, and the fact she had mentioned it to no one. Such wasn't her place. She didn't make decisions, except those on the battlefield relating to combat. Instinctively knowing whether to dodge left or lunge right, to raise her weapon or swing a low strike, to duck or jump, estimating her opponent's skill, using the landscape and environment to her advantage, and employing decisive movements—these were her strengths, not determining matters of state.

Bruna lifted the chainmail from the trunk. "This is heavy," she commented. "I will help you put it on, so you don't strain your mending side. Adelle will be angrier than a disturbed nest of hornets if she comes home to find you've reopened the hole."

Rather than argue and chastise Bruna for her help, Tyrdis humbled herself and allowed the woman to assist her in pulling the armor over her head. Standing, Tyrdis inspected the fit. The mail was tunic size, hitting her upper thighs with three-quarter length sleeves.

Svanhild took on a look of strain as she lifted the belt to her. Tyrdis buckled it on.

"Thank you both for your aid," she said.

"Wow, Tyrdis!" Svanhild exclaimed. "You look fearsome in that."

Tyrdis slid her weapons into the holders on her belt and granted Svanhild a smile. "And it makes me feel fearsome too. Do not worry. I am only accompanying Sweyn and Jarl Niklaus to greet Jarl Raknar and my fellow warriors. I'll be in no danger and will return to you soon."

Bruna stepped behind Svanhild and laid her hands on the girl's shoulders. "It's not too heavy?"

"I will adapt," Tyrdis replied.

Bruna seemed amused. "You look fabulous in the new armor. Remember: avoid the pointy ends of weapons."

Raising a brow, Tyrdis answered in a droll tone, "Very funny. Be sure to rush Svanhild to the jarl's great hall at the first sign of danger."

"I've been avoiding danger long before you were born," Bruna said. "We'll see you later."

Tyrdis rode beside Trygve, along with a small contingent of warriors, behind his father, uncle, and older brothers to meet Jarl Raknar and her fellow Heilagrfjord warriors. As they neared, she recognized many familiar faces, including her brother Erik's friend, Sigbjorn. Roar and Thorgil had rejoined the unit, but Myrbrandr, with his one arm, wasn't to be seen, and most likely would never return to combat duty.

Jarl Raknar the Cunning rode a dark Nordic fjord pony, the breed of small horse common to the region. He displayed a regal bearing in fur-lined leather spaulders and cross straps over a blue-gray gambeson studded with steel bits the size of coins. A long, blond mane flowed over his shoulders, and his sandy beard fell in ringlets from a firm chin. He donned a serious expression, while his relative youth and vigor were apparent in his toned physique. Older than Bjarke and younger than Niklaus, he was a man in his prime, a fact he appeared to be aware of.

However, his cousin riding the dun pony beside him was an entirely contrasting specimen. Sure, he might seem a member of a noble family with no swords pointed at him, but Tyrdis knew differently. Her jaw hardened and her fists clenched as she narrowed her eyes at the incompetent fool. Was Jarl Raknar allowing him to keep his position? Had he not heard of the fiasco a month ago? Or had he reprimanded Garold in private to avoid bringing shame to his whole family?

Detecting the smug look on his face, she vowed in barely contained fury, *I'll ask to serve Sweyn's father before I'll take orders from that níðingr again.* Tyrdis was glad Niklaus had assigned her to safeguard Sæladalr rather than take part in the coming attack; otherwise, she might be tempted to turn her weapons on Garold. *One day.*

"Greetings, Jarl Raknar," called Niklaus. His robust tone was welcoming; however, no smile graced his lips.

"Thank you, Niklaus," Raknar replied and inclined his head. "I wish it were under better circumstances. We are ready and willing to answer King Gustav's call, although I'd like to hear more about your plan."

"Indeed. Njal will lead your warriors to the campsite," he said, motioning toward his younger son, who resituated himself in his saddle. "Come and enjoy the hospitality of my great hall and I'll impart all the details."

The welcome group split, half accompanying the warriors and half escorting the jarls. Tyrdis and her student, Trygve, plodded along with the latter group. Displeasure writhed in her gut to see Garold accompanying his cousin to be Niklaus's guest and be part of the planning.

"I won't be included in any strategy meetings," Trygve assumed in a disheartened tone. "Papa won't even let Njal sit in. Second and third sons." He huffed out a dry laugh. "Never important until someone dies."

"Your reasoning and conclusion are faulty," Tyrdis replied as they ambled behind the leaders. "They do not consult you because of your youth and inexperience, not because you lack value. I thought you understood this already. My brother was second born, but, by the time he became an adult, my father put more stock in him than in me. Each member of a unit has a place and serves a purpose based on many factors besides order of birth, such as their skill set and interests. Do you recall Gunnvaldr?"

"The ancient man who led us to find Adelle?"

"Yes. One would be foolish to employ him to head a charge with spear and shield, yet he is the best tracker in Raumsdal," Tyrdis explained. "He was not born with such knowledge and instincts but rather honed them after many years of practice. You are a sprig. Enjoy being a sprig, for once you become a tree you'll never be a sapling again."

Trygve sighed and turned a satisfied look to her. "You're right. I'm sure I'll find something I'm better at than Sweyn and Njal, and I have the rest of my life to be an adult. Maybe I'll find my friends and play a game or two before dinner."

"Or perhaps we'll gather the others and spend the afternoon training," Tyrdis corrected with a raised brow and superior expression on her commanding face.

"You aren't going to the meeting?" Trygve seemed surprised.

Tyrdis stared daggers at Garold's back ahead of them as he laughed at something. "It would not be advisable."

* * *

SWEYN ITCHED with nervous energy as the company gathered around his father's table in the great hall. Everyone not invited was sent away, including the servants, after they brought the refreshments. Lynnea took the youngsters outside to help her in the garden, despite the heat of the day being the wrong time to engage in gardening, and Niklaus set Edan and Karvir to guard the entrance. Sweyn sat on his father's right, his uncle Horik on his left, and Jarl Raknar, Garold, a gothi advisor, and another first warrior rounded the table.

"King Gustav is sold on your plan," Raknar began after sampling a meat pie and mead. "However, he is blinded by grief and revenge and willing to entertain any wild proposal. I, on the other hand, possess a level head in the matter."

"As do I," Niklaus replied. "But there is another urgent concern we must discuss with you before we can finalize plans for the attack, mainly if there will be an attack at all, and whom it should be against. I prefer to await Jarl Bjarke's arrival before discussing either."

An angry scowl consumed Raknar's face. "What do you mean *if* there will be an attack? I brought the bulk of my army all this way, expended energy and resources, and for what? They are driven with battle-lust, ready to fight."

Niklaus held up a hand to calm him. "Don't get riled up, Raknar. I'll explain."

Just then, the door burst open. A burly man with untamed brown hair and a bristly beard strode in, his armor splattered with blood and a cut over his eye. He beamed excitedly at the gathering. "Am I late?"

CHAPTER 25

Firdafylke camp, morning of the same day

"*L*ars has made a mess of his wound," Karyna complained to Adelle in an irritated hush. They stood across the room at the table Adelle had her supplies laid out on. The brash young man had just returned, bleeding all over the place.

Adelle handed her apprentice a roll of clean bandages and picked up a needle and thread. "Lars, what did you do? We had your wound closed and looking good yesterday."

"Yes, and I felt better. I have to train, don't I? There could be an attack any minute," he explained innocently. "Garrick and I were sparring to stay sharp, and, I don't know, the stitches just tore open and it started bleeding again."

"Of course, it did, you silly goose!" Karyna reprimanded. "Didn't we order you to rest and allow the injury to heal? But you knew better—had to disobey. I have half a mind to send you back to your tent."

"Easy, Karyna," Adelle soothed in a calm voice. "Lars is a young man and a warrior; we can't get too angry at him for acting according to his nature. Sit down, Lars, and I'll see if there's any good skin to stitch."

With the expression of a scolded puppy, he complied. "I didn't do it on purpose. I thought it would hold if I wasn't too vigorous."

"You used a heavy iron weapon?" Adelle interrogated as she inspected the gash. He nodded. "And swung it around practice fighting with your friend?" Another nod, his chin bunched up and brows pulled down. "And you hopped and twisted like a frolicking goat kid?"

"We weren't frolicking," he pouted. "We were sparring, more like virile rams."

Karyna rolled her eyes, and Adelle suppressed a laugh. "We can repair the damage this time, but I can't say what will happen if you do this again."

Setting the bandages on the bed beside Lars, Karyna said, "I'll go prepare a new poultice for him, and, yes, I remember how."

"I wasn't going to ask this time," Adelle replied in her defense. It felt good to have established such an easy rapport with Karyna despite the complication of their two kingdoms being at war. She enjoyed the young woman's company, appreciated her grit and sharp mind, and was pleased with her progress. Adelle even wondered if she and Svanhild would get along so well when she was grown; of course, they would. Svanhild was the most wonderful child ever—even if she had adopted a soldier as a friend.

Tyrdis—now there was a paradox. *Why do I still think about her day and night, wonder what she's doing, if she is less of a fool than Lars? I know she is, but ... why do I miss her company when I have a fellow healer with me? I swore to never become attached to another warrior. Is my resolve so easily swayed by an attractive face ... a perfect body, stunning eyes that make me want to dive into them and swim until all my energy is spent? She's so different from anyone I've ever met. I would like to get to know her better, to be her friend, and ... maybe more. Am I crazy?*

They had just finished repairing the damage Lars had done to himself when a commotion started outside the tent. People were shouting, running about, along with the sounds of equipment clanking, horses squealing out fearful cries and stomping their hooves. The tent flap flew open, and a man holding a spear called to them, "Stay inside. The camp is under attack." Then he disappeared, the flap falling back in place after him.

Lars leaped off the bed. "I'm sorry, but I can't sit here and wait for stitches to heal." Off he raced, following the man with the spear.

Adelle exchanged an anxious glance with Karyna. "We should prepare to be inundated with casualties," she advised. "I hope ..." What could she say? She bit her lower lip and turned to her supplies.

Karyna's hand caught her arm, and her intense eyes recaptured her gaze. "It is not your fault. No one here blames you for your king's actions. I guess this will be a real test for me."

"You're ready for it, Karyna," Adelle assured her. "And thank you."

With the sounds of battle near enough to make Adelle nervous, she and Karyna addressed the wounded as they arrived, first in a trickle, then a dozen at once. Adelle assessed the severity of each person's injuries to determine who could wait, who could not, and those they couldn't save. It was a gut-wrenching job, though necessary to preserve as many lives as possible.

A fear haunted Adelle: were they here to rescue her? She had made it clear to Sweyn and Tyrdis that she was safe and did not require any military action on her behalf. *Surely, they would understand this is the last thing I would want.* No. There had to be another explanation. She wasn't certain she could live with the guilt if men and women were killing each other over her. The burden would be too crippling to imagine.

When the din of combat grew louder and nearer, Karyna's hands shook as she bandaged her patient. The men's fear cast a dark aura inside the tent, as they had been caught completely off guard.

"Grimolf is dead," one stated in a shocked tone. "And Erfynn. Why didn't the scouts warn us? Was no one standing guard?"

"The attack came from the east, not the north," answered another patient who sat with a bandage around his head. "Everyone was watching the approach from the north."

Probably not Jarl Niklaus's troops then, Adelle thought with a small measure of relief.

She and Karyna were working on a fellow with a serious gash across his back when a pair of brawny warriors carried in a man and laid him on the only open cot. "Karyna, over here," called one with urgency. "It's Jarl Stefnir, and he's in bad shape."

Adelle's heart catapulted into her throat. "Lie still," she instructed her patient as she turned to rush to the jarl's aid.

"Papa!" Karyna fell to her knees beside him, pushed a strand of hair behind her ear, and grasped his hands in distress. Adelle leaned in from Stefnir's other side. When a soldier grabbed her shoulder, Karyna yelled at him. "No! Let her help." She tore her eyes away from her father's face, pale from loss of blood, to lock gazes with Adelle. "What do we do?"

Adelle pulled back his torn garments soaked in blood to reveal a gaping chest wound. She returned a sorrowful glance to Karyna, and swallowed. "Fetch me a compress and let's try to stop the bleeding. He's lost a lot of blood already."

She rushed back with a stack of thick rags and pressed them against the hole in his chest.

"Karyna." Stefnir's voice was weak. He stopped talking to cough, spraying the air with tiny droplets of blood.

"Don't try to say anything, Papa," she instructed.

Adelle grabbed the yarrow powder from the worktable. "Here," she said to Karyna. "Lift the cloth and I'll pour on some of this to help clot the blood." A chest wound like his was beyond her ability to correct. Some nasty implement of war had struck too near his heart, possibly perforating a lung as evidenced by coughing up blood, and likely opened one of the large arteries, thereby producing such a crimson river. She couldn't save him, and she knew it. "Call for your gothi," Adelle added. She took the compress from Karyna's hands and pressed it to the wound, lifting her own silent prayers. If he died under her care …

"Where is Olavi?" Karyna's frantic glance flitted from face to face.

"I'll find him," vowed a woman from the camp who had followed her father in. She ducked out, and Karyna returned her focus to Stefnir.

"Stay with me, Papa," she pleaded. "Olavi will be here soon."

"Even his prayers can't save me now," he uttered with labored breath. His lids fluttered closed, and his breathing came raspy and shallow. "My sword."

While Adelle tried to slow his issue of blood, Karyna took the sword from one of the warriors who had brought him in.

"Thank you, Brandt." The jarl's daughter gently wrapped Stefnir's fingers around the hilt of his sword, and he gave it a feeble squeeze.

"I see the light of Valhalla," he breathed with a smile spreading across his lips. His body shuddered with his next breath, and it was his last.

"I love you, Papa." There was a cry in her voice and tears streaming down her face as Karyna said goodbye.

The blood flow from the crater in his chest slowed as his heart no longer pumped it out, but Adelle did not give up her efforts. She began rhythmic chest compressions, attempting to restart Stefnir's heart, even though she realized they were futile.

"Olavi, you're too late," Brandt let out with sorrow. "This Raumsdal grædari has killed Jarl Stefnir."

"She did no such thing," Karyna growled and mopped at her eyes. "Do not belittle my father with such a preposterous lie. He was killed in combat like a true warrior, not the victim of poor medical care."

"Then she let him die when she could have saved him," shouted an angry voice from the crowd that had gathered in the healing tent.

Adelle's nerves grew shaky and tense, but she no longer noticed battle sounds coming from the camp.

"The invaders have fled," Olavi said as he walked calmly up to where Jarl Stefnir's body lay on the blood-soaked cot. "Tyr has taken our side. I saw five others dead, two tents on fire, and the bearers chasing down a dozen ponies that ran off into the meadow. The rest of our casualties are here. Karyna, may I examine your father?"

The dark-haired man of average size who appeared to be around Adelle's age shot her a commanding look through deep blue eyes. She and Karyna both stepped back. The clean-shaven gothi lifted the bloody rags, peered at Stefnir's chest wound, then ran a finger through the bloody powder and raised it to his lips. "Yarrow."

"I tried it to stop his bleeding," Adelle explained, "but the offending weapon sliced through a major artery. He had lost too much blood before he arrived and—"

Olavi raised a smooth palm displaying long, delicate fingers with clean, trim nails. He wore a purple and gold silk tunic, bracelets, and rings, as if he was a nobleman. Some völvas, gothis, and grædari were granted noble status in Norvegr, depending on the wishes of their king, because of their special expertise and close relationship with the gods. "I can see you did everything possible. There was no time for me to perform rites and sacrifices. It was indeed a mortal wound. Today, Jarl Stefnir takes his rightful place in Odin's Hall. And, while we are grieved because he has left us behind to toil here in Miðgarðr, we celebrate with him as he receives his reward. Let us observe a moment of silence followed by a hearty cheer he can hear as he travels to Ásgarðr."

Adelle could have heard a feather fall. After a count of ten, everyone let out a victory shout—except for Karyna, who couldn't quite muster a strong enough voice. Adelle was disillusioned to find even gothi perpetuated the cult of violence, this worship of warriors, but it was no different in her kingdom. People holding similar beliefs comprised a small minority of elder women, healers, and the occasional völva. She could never convince them that lethal combat was a vice, not a virtue.

"The enemy is gone for now," Brandt, a fighting man with dusty brown hair and arms like lodgepoles noted in a warning tone, "but they could return. Jarl Stefnir was a worthy man and a steadfast leader, but his son has only seen twelve summers and is too young to take his place. We cannot be without a leader in a time of war, waiting to call a Thing and allow the citizens to consider various candidates. Likewise, we would be left vulnerable waiting for King Tortryggr to appoint a new overseer of our fylke. The reasonable thing to do would be to accept my leadership, and I say we punish the witch." Narrowing menacing brows, he pointed at Adelle.

"Aye," echoed a few others as they crossed their arms, nodding their frowns to each other.

Adelle's blood pumped fiercely through her veins at their animosity. *This is what Tyrdis meant when she said things could change on a dime. Eir, please let them assign me a swift death instead of torture.* Instantly, her mind was flooded with memories of their last conversation and of the affectionate embrace they had shared. *Tyrdis will be wracked with guilt over not being here to protect me. She promised to watch over Mother and Svanhild, but for how long? If I never return, will she still stay with them? Oh, my precious honeybee! I long to hold you one more time before I die.*

"Reasonable in whose eyes?" Olavi questioned. He raised his chin and took a step in the warrior's direction. "I was Stefnir's closest advisor who possesses knowledge of the sacred runes. It requires more than a strong arm to keep our people safe but a cool head and keen intellect. You would make a servant of Eir your scapegoat, while I would devise a plan of retaliation and punish the true villains—the Raumsdal warriors who attacked us."

"You are both forgetting an important detail." When Karyna spoke, all eyes turned to her. Gone was the weeping daughter; in her place stood a formidable woman. "I am Jarl Stefnir's firstborn. I have received a noble's education, can also read runes, and now possess the knowledge of a grædari. My father believed he had many more years to live, and Styfialdr would be ready to assume his position. While my brother is still too young and inexperienced, I am not. I inspected my father's wound where he took a battle ax to the chest. Brandt, both of your hands could fit in the hole it tore through his ribs into his vitals, and we all know in our hearts this woman only tried to save his life. No one will touch her, and that is my command. I will stand for jarl until such time as the king or the voice of the people call for another leader."

Brandt laughed, shook his head, and ran his fingers through his hair. "I see you still have a love of playing larks." Several of the other men joined his laughter and disregard, while others seemed to give her serious consideration. Hope sprang into Adelle's soul that all may not be lost.

Lars, who had slipped into the tent at some point, bleeding from his torn wound site again, spoke up. "I can tell you Adelle is an honest and compassionate healer, and I have long admired Karyna for her sense of duty. She is quick to learn new things and always considers the greater good. I support her claim to her father's seat."

"Now, wait a minute," Brandt let out in a patronizing tone. "You can't be serious. She's a woman—a young, unmarried woman. Men would coerce her into a quick marriage to gain her position of power if we were to allow such a thing."

Karyna stared at him with such intensity he was forced to divert his gaze. "And who shall intimidate me so?" she quipped. "Certainly not you, Brandt." That gained her a few laughs.

Adelle took a glance at the gothi, detecting his calculating expression. He would bow out and support whichever of the two he thought would win.

Brandt inhaled and let out a long breath. "I'll admit you have singular qualities, but we need a warrior leading us in a time of war, pure and simple. I was Jarl Stefnir's first warrior, the leader of our fighting force. The men will rally around me as I lead them to victory. What will you do —sit on your horse and bark orders from the rear? We all know your father never allowed you to practice with weapons. I have to admire your determination, but you need to leave this to me, Karyna."

Adelle had not left Karyna's side, thankful for her support, but Brandt was winning the room. Dread flooded back over her like a rolling tide.

Karyna raised her chin, stepped forward, and called out in a robust voice, "Then I challenge you, First Warrior Brandt, to a feat of martial skill. If you win, I'll concede my claim, but, if I win, you must honor my right to rule. In fairness, I only ask that I be given the choice of weapons."

Murmurs arose amid worried expressions and shaking heads.

"Karyna." Lars, his hand pressed to the bleeding slice in his side, pleaded her name as he took a step nearer. "No one wants to see you hurt. Who will take care of us?"

Adelle laid a hand on her upper arm and whispered into her ear, "I am so grateful to you for trying to save me, but I agree with Lars. I'd rather die than see harm come to you; you mean too much to me now. If you propose a swift execution—"

"There'll be no execution," she snapped with fire in her eyes. "Trust me. I know what I'm doing."

"Karyna, I can't fight you," Brandt said with outstretched palms. "It would be humiliating for both of us."

"Oh," she responded in a bold tone, raising her brows in question. "So, you would lead our troops to victory over our enemies, but you are afraid of a challenge posed by a woman?"

"I'm not afraid to fight you," he moaned in aggravation. "I'm afraid of hurting you. Look, I know you are grieving, and your father just died. Maybe you've become attached to this Raumsdal woman who's been teaching you—I understand. What if I promise not to execute her?"

Karyna crossed her arms firmly over her chest, staring him down like he was a pesky mosquito. "Too late for compromise. I have issued a challenge in the presence of these witnesses. Will you allow me to choose the weapons?"

Olavi seemed to be on to her scheme and rejoined the debate. "Yes, Brandt. What will you do? If you step down, I'll accept the lady's challenge. Why not let the gods decide? Isn't that how it's done?"

Brandt hemmed and hawed and shifted his weight from one foot to the other while the crowded tent hummed with excitement.

"When this is done, we will carry my father back to Oskholm and hold a proper funeral," Karyna announced to the group. "We will bury him with his fathers and honor him with a feast. But first, I must secure my place as jarl. What shall it be, Brandt?"

His frown morphed into a miserable scowl. "Oh, all right! Choose the weapons, but I will set the conditions. The first one of us to be disarmed loses. There should be no blood spilled at all in the contest. Do you agree?"

A sly grin tugged at the corners of Karyna's mouth. "I agree."

She turned and walked to a chest across the room, opened it, and retrieved a board with dark and light squares painted on it and a box. Moving to the table, she brushed the healing supplies to one side, laid the board face up, and opened the box.

"I choose a game of Hnefatafl," she decreed with an air of satisfaction.

Clever girl. Adelle beamed at her in appreciation. *Now that woman deserves to be jarl.*

"Hold on a minute!" Brandt's features took on a look of panic. "Game pieces are not weapons. You can't call this a challenge!"

"If you will all recall my words," Karyna said, lifting her voice to the whole tent. "I said I challenge Brandt to a feat of martial skill. I said nothing about physical combat. In what arena can one display more martial skill than the noble strategy game of Hnefatafl? Brandt, would you prefer to attack or defend?"

"I—I," he stuttered, stunned embarrassment swallowing him.

"He doesn't know the difference!" hollered someone from the back. Laughter ensued.

"This is serious," Olavi reminded everyone. "Karyna offered a challenge, Brandt accepted. Now, they must play the game, and the winner will act as jarl until further notice."

"Aye," voiced several men and women in agreement.

Brandt shuffled up to the table with the frightened look of a lost fawn. "You pick."

Adelle beamed with joy while Karyna made short order of capturing all Brandt's pieces. The camp cheered her for her ingenuity, and even burly, old warriors shone with admiration. One grizzled elder patted Karyna on the shoulder, proclaiming, "You are your father's daughter, every bit. I'd follow you to Helheim and back."

Now pardoned from any suspicion of murder, Adelle shooed all the bystanders out of the hospice tent. Olavi stayed to help, conducting prayers and a Blót for the wounded. Karyna returned to her father's body, considering him with a mixed expression.

"It is hard to be happy for him when I must go on alone," she admitted.

Adelle stepped over and rested her hand atop Karyna's. "Yes, but you showed genuine strength today—cunning and courage in the face of overwhelming opposition. Jarl Stefnir is so proud of you at this moment."

Karyna turned a questioning expression to her. "Do you think he knows? Do you believe he can see?"

"I am convinced this world is not the end, not all there is," Adelle replied honestly. "You heard him say he saw the brilliant light of Valhalla just before he died. I know he is proud of you … because I am."

Karyna leaned into Adelle, accepted her embrace, and sobbed on her shoulder.

CHAPTER 26

Sæladalr

"J arl Bjarke, what happened?" Jarl Niklaus jumped to his feet in astonishment, and Sweyn rushed over to offer him a towel and see if he was all right.

"Are you injured?" Sweyn asked with concern.

The jovial man waved a hand at him. "No, no, but you should see the other guys."

Taking the towel, Bjarke wiped his face and beard, not removing all the blood, and tossed it onto a nearby sleeping bench. He swaggered forward with a triumphant gleam. "We trounced them!"

"Who?" Jarl Raknar asked. He appeared just as unsettled as Niklaus.

"Our enemies, of course!" Jarl Bjarke plopped into Sweyn's seat at the table. He wasn't happy about it, but Bjarke was a guest, so he squeezed in between his uncle and one of Raknar's attendants.

"I don't understand," Niklaus confessed as he retook his seat. "We are planning to attack their unsuspecting port to the south—maybe," he added with reservation.

In an animated fashion, the youngest of the three jarls relayed his tale. "You see, as we were traveling over the mountain from Austrihóll, we spotted a Firdafylke camp sitting all laid out pretty as a meadow of wildflowers. They were daftly unsuspecting, too, I'll tell you." He winked and elbowed Niklaus in the ribs.

Niklaus was not amused, and realization struck Sweyn with a wave of alarm. "Why did you attack them?" he shouted in a surreal accusation.

Bjarke sat back and shot Sweyn a confused expression. "Because they were there. It wasn't far out of our way, and my warriors were itching for a fight. I thought it would be good practice for them to, you know, get their blood pumping before the big invasion. Don't worry; none of my men were killed and only a handful sustained serious injuries. They're up at your hospice with a nice young fellow looking after them."

"Father ... Adelle," Sweyn began in disbelief.

Niklaus's expression had hardened to granite, and he ground his jaw. "Our healer was being held captive in that camp. You fool! You've probably gotten her killed, and for what? Target practice? Man, you were told to meet us here with your army, not gallivant all over the valley slaughtering our neighbors like flies."

Leaning forward on an elbow, Bjarke pointed at Niklaus as his face reddened with anger. "I am not your errand boy, Niklaus. I am your equal, and don't you forget it. No one declared I wasn't to attack the camp. How was I to know you had people there? Am I supposed to be a diviner as well as a warrior and commander?"

"Now, settle down, friends," Raknar coaxed in a tone that sounded anything but friendly.

Fear spread through Sweyn like a raging plague. Not only was Adelle in that camp, but Karyna too. "Tell me you spared the healing tent," he begged.

Bjarke leaned back with a smirk and flailed his hand. "It was hardly a battle—just a skirmish, really. We were in and out in no time. We lit a few tents before moving on; can't say if one was full of healers."

Sweyn stood, anxiety not allowing him to remain still. "Father, let me go—"

"Sit down." It was a command, not a request. "If you go back there now, they'll kill you. We'll check on Adelle, but this is not the time. Bjarke, you said your injured are at the hospice; where are the rest of your warriors?"

With a frustrated glare, Sweyn complied, though everyone must have known it was against his will to do so.

A smile returned to Bjarke's blood-freckled face. "I suspect most of them are enjoying your mead hall—and any willing wenches." He flashed his grin around, only to be met by grave expressions of displeasure.

Horik rolled his eyes and pulled at his hair. "They'll wreck our town," he groaned.

"Bah," Bjarke dismissed and helped himself to the drink in the bowl. "Where's your sense of hospitality?"

"Horik, would you please take a sizable escort and show our guests to the campground? And be sure to secure enough barrels of ale and mead to keep them satisfied."

"I'll take care of it," Horik avowed, and left to carry out his orders.

Sweyn's anger toward Bjarke was about to burst, and he felt like ants crawled under his skin. How did his father expect him to sit there and be cordial after that brutish idiot ruined everything? His reasoning concluded Niklaus was right about the timing. The warriors in the camp would be standing watch, ready to kill anyone from Raumsdal who dared approach. What about Adelle? If she was spared during the fighting, would Jarl Stefnir take out his anger on her? And what about Karyna? Had she been harmed, killed? He shuddered to think about these very real possibilities, but his hands were tied. If he tried to do anything, he would only make the situation worse.

I hope Tyrdis doesn't find out, he thought. While not devoting much time or energy to deciphering their relationship, he knew the shieldmaiden cared for Adelle. But Tyrdis was too disciplined to rush in, especially against the leader's command. *"Bridle your emotions," she would say. "Wait for the ideal moment to make your move. This is not it."* And, like his father, she would be right. *Odin, I'm not one for praying, but, if you're listening, keep them safe.*

"Now, back to the business at hand," Raknar said, steering the attention at the table his way. "Niklaus was about to reveal some vital bit of information that has a bearing on whether we will go through with the attack on Griðlundr." He set down his cup, and the room went silent.

"Indeed," Niklaus said. Sweyn could feel the weight on his father's shoulders and would not have wished to carry it for all the gold in the world. "King Gustav has lied to us all."

Sweyn's mind wandered while his father relayed the story and all the clues that supported its validity. *We've got to put an end to this war, make peace with Firdafylke. Then, maybe, after a little time has passed, I can go see Karyna. Maybe she won't still hate me. Maybe her father will find me suitable. In fact,* he pondered, a fresh idea sparking in his imagination. *Maybe a wedding between a jarl's son from Raumsdal and a jarl's daughter from Firdafylke will be just the thing to seal the peace—if Karyna will have me.*

"I've never been content with the way Gustav operates, anyway," Bjarke growled, drawing Sweyn's attention back to the discussion. "He charges taxes from our fylkes, but it seems we don't get anything in return."

"In my opinion, he should never have gained the title," Raknar brooded and reflexively clenched a fist on the table. "When old King Grith Longbeard died with no son, each of us jarls stood in line to assume the crown. Bjarke, you weren't jarl of the Austrihóll fylke yet."

"No, but my father was, and I recall his complaints. The three of you traveled to Skeggen for a kingdom-wide Thing where the freemen would vote on Grith's successor—his eldest daughter or one of you. Gustav was a fierce fighter who had been on raids and foreign exploits, bringing back enough spoils to gain him wealth."

"He tricked Grith's oldest daughter into a quick marriage, then supported her claim to leadership," Raknar added. "Somehow—probably through bribery—he gained enough support for her to receive the most votes."

"I never remember seeing her smile," Niklaus commented in a contemplative manner. "And now I'm suspicious of her untimely death."

"He brings whores to his great hall to sleep with him while his sons occupy the next room," Sweyn growled in disgust. "I don't understand it. Why didn't he just announce to the kingdom that Ivar and Jarivald got into a heated fight and Jarivald was killed? Why would that tarnish the character he clearly lacks?"

"I think we all know why," Niklaus answered.

"He wishes to extend his power," Raknar declared with an icy glare. "The only question is, what are we going to do about it?"

"Kill the bastard," Bjarke proposed.

Sweyn shook his head. "Consider my father's proposal."

Niklaus gave him a nod. "While my brother and I concocted a foolproof plan of attack against the port for the day after tomorrow, I fear we will lose valuable warriors we need to take back our kingdom from an unworthy, dishonorable liar. Instead, we should march our combined forces to Skeggen and confront him. The fifty warriors he promised to provide haven't arrived yet. If we meet them on the way, we'll deal with it.

Anyway, we will outnumber him so badly, he'll be forced to abdicate. Then we can assemble the Thing and call for a new vote."

"What do we do with Gustav?" Raknar asked.

"A beheading is too honorable a death for him," Bjarke replied. "A slow disembowelment, perhaps? Or we could perform the blood eagle."

Niklaus sighed. "I was thinking banishment would be a fitting punishment. For a king to live many more years as a pauper in a foreign land would be a far greater penalty than death. Let everyone he meets ridicule him."

"What about his sons?" Bjarke followed up. "Do we banish them too?"

"Surely you aren't considering letting Ivar become a candidate before the Thing," Raknar declared.

Niklaus fidgeted in his seat and hesitated to answer.

"Hallfrid swore Ivar and Kerstav wanted to tell the truth, but the king forbade them," Sweyn said in the young men's defense. "They don't deserve as cruel a sentence as Gustav, but I can see how allowing Ivar a chance at the crown may not be well accepted."

"Not well accepted," Bjarke repeated under his breath with a laugh. He downed the rest of his cup and slapped it on the table. "So, it's the three of us, like it was fifteen years ago, eh?"

"I can live with that," Raknar agreed. "But, if Gustav won't go quietly, are you prepared for a civil war?"

Niklaus issued a grave nod. "It wouldn't be much of a war, just a little skirmish," he added with a sarcastic glance at Bjarke, who cackled in laughter. "I have served Gustav faithfully, believing he was at least tolerable, if not completely honorable, all these years, but he has crossed a line. Yes, I'm willing to go to war to remove him from power."

"Let's take an oath then," Raknar suggested, "to remain allies in our venture to rid the kingdom of Gustav. Once that has been accomplished, we'll consider the next steps and perhaps agree to support whichever of us is selected as the next king."

"Here, here!" shouted Bjarke exuberantly. The three men shook hands, and Raknar's gothi sealed the agreement by sacrificing a ram and sprinkling them all with its blood. But Sweyn's heart remained tortured as he worried about three very different women he cared for greatly.

CHAPTER 27

Sæladalr late that night

After getting Bruna and Svanhild settled on the only empty bed left, Tyrdis lay down on a blanket on the floor beside them. She found it cooler, and a breeze occasionally whisked in from under the back door.

When Jarl Bjarke showed up earlier in the day, the three of them moved back to the hospice to help Joren handle the influx of injured warriors. Tyrdis didn't know an herb from a weed, but she could wash bloody rags and bandages, carry water and blankets, and follow general instructions. When she reprimanded a patient for excessive displays of emotion and expressions of pain unbecoming a warrior, Svanhild shooed her away and apologized to the wounded man. Then she informed Tyrdis that she lacked bedside manner, whatever that was supposed to mean, and it would be best if she didn't say anything. Irritated over her inability to perform her hospice duty properly, she refrained from speaking to Bjarke's soldiers again.

By the time they had finished bandaging and soothing the injured, Bruna had prepared a meal to share with her, Svanhild, and Joren and some kind of meat broth for the patients. Svanhild had rehearsed the puppet show with Tyrdis—again—except the child kept changing the lines and story. Now she had concocted a distressingly inaccurate portrayal of a bunny who became king after defeating a fearsome bear.

The three princess dolls all proclaimed their love for the bunny and ended up fighting each other over the right to marry him. Still, Tyrdis adored Svanhild so much that she didn't complain or point out the story's obvious flaws.

Tyrdis expressed concern that Adelle wouldn't like the play since it contained so much fighting, but Svanhild insisted it would be fine because no one died. Then she changed the ending—again—so that the three princesses agreed to all share the bunny king, which Tyrdis knew would never happen in real life.

Tired from the labors of the day and her body's constant need to suck energy for healing, Tyrdis had fallen into a light sleep when a noise outside caused her to react with alarm. She lurched to her feet, grabbed her axe and long-bladed knife, and slipped quietly to the front door from which the sounds emanated. A horse ... no, two, and two riders. One climbed down. More wounded? Sweyn coming to get her—or danger? In naught but a brown, linen sleeping tunic, she eased a crack open and peeked out.

At once, her spirits soared, the elation overwhelming her dispassionate façade. Dropping her weapons, Tyrdis rushed out to greet Adelle with an enthusiastic expression of relief. "Adelle, you are back!"

Adelle glanced up at a man on the other horse whose presence Tyrdis barely registered. "Thank you, Lars. Send word if Karyna needs me again." Then she turned to Tyrdis with a jubilant smile. "I'm back."

Tyrdis froze just before throwing her arms around Adelle in wild abandonment. What should she do? All this planning and she hadn't thought about how she should behave the moment she first saw her. What if she would consider such an embrace too much? But gazing at Adelle, seeing she hadn't been harmed and had been sent back sooner than expected, Tyrdis couldn't hide the well of emotion that threatened to erupt.

Adelle laughed, despite how exhausted she looked. "Breathe, Tyrdis. It's all right to breathe."

Though she hadn't realized it, Tyrdis *had* been holding her breath. When she complied, Adelle wrapped her arms around her and drew her into a sweet hug.

Tyrdis closed her eyes in blissful contentment as she held Adelle close, reveling in her presence. She recognized the moss-green apron and cream underdress Adelle had worn often, but noted it was clean and void of damage. "We are so glad to have you back safely."

They stayed like that for a moment, Tyrdis feeling Adelle's heartbeat against her chest, registering the fact it wasn't a dream. Though the hour was late, the sun behind a mountain to the north still illuminated the summer sky.

"Svanhild? Mother?"

"They are in satisfactory condition and sleeping comfortably," Tyrdis answered and slowly loosened her grip. "Your hospice is full of Jarl Bjarke's warriors, but Joren performed adequately. Bruna, Svanhild, and I assisted."

Adelle took a step back, her hand lingering on Tyrdis's shoulder. "Yes, well, they attacked the camp you visited. Jarl Stefnir was killed, and Karyna has assumed his authority."

Tyrdis's jaw gaped as she stared at Adelle. The news was more than distressing. A thousand concerns flooded her consciousness, and she tried to lasso one to have a place to begin. "They could have harmed you in retaliation." She grabbed Adelle's hand and squeezed. "Wait, Karyna is now jarl in her father's place? The waif you were training, the one Sweyn is smitten with?"

"Yes," Adelle beamed. "And she would not let them hurt me, though I experienced a few fearful moments. Come, and I'll tell you what happened."

They had just turned toward the door when it flew open. Svanhild and Bruna rushed out to hug Adelle.

"Mama, you're home! We missed you so much, but Tyrdis stayed with us and kept us safe."

"My little elf," Bruna cooed and kissed Adelle's cheeks. "I knew you would return no worse for wear. Come in and sit down. It's a bit crowded and everyone is sleeping."

"I don't want to disturb—"

"Nonsense." Bruna took her by a hand, and Svanhild clung to her other one as they led her inside. Tyrdis followed as if she walked on a cloud of joy.

"Tyrdis wanted to know all your favorite things so she could plan a celebration when you got back," Svanhild relayed in a loud whisper.

"Is that so?" Adelle cast a demure glance over her shoulder at Tyrdis, whose cheeks reddened despite her attempts to remain unmoved.

"I'll be right back." Tyrdis rushed out and collected the flowers she and Svanhild had been keeping fresh in a pail of water. When she returned, she wrapped a pink silk scarf around their stems and brought them to the bed where Adelle sat between her mother and daughter. Holding them out, she knelt in front of the trio and began to sing.

"When the chaffinches sing in the trees, and the heather blooms on the hill, Freya rides on the breeze, and I will love you still. Sleep, sleep now, my little one; dream of beauty and charms. Jörmungandr holds back the seas, and I hold you safe in my arms."

Adelle pressed her lips together, as it appeared a laugh pounded behind them to escape. She passed an amused glance from Bruna to Svanhild before fixing her eyes on Tyrdis, who was feeling very self-conscious and uneasy at her response.

"You have a lovely voice, Tyrdis," she complimented. "Why didn't you ever mention you could sing?"

Feeling a bit like an ill-prepared suitor, Tyrdis sat all the way down on the floor and caught her arms around her updrawn knees. "I have never sung before, so I did not know if I was accomplished at it. Svanhild taught me the song. I heard it before, but Father discouraged my brother and me from engaging in any artistic activities. They are frivolous and irrelevant."

"Silly nonsense," Bruna replied, rolling her eyes. "Music, art, and storytelling are extremely relevant. How does he think our heroes and the gods are praised? How does he think our histories are preserved? Art, music, poetry, and storytelling are the foundation of our culture, not swords and axes. You warriors are called to preserve and protect our culture, not disregard it. And besides, it is an affront to the gods for one with as beautiful a voice as yours to refuse to share it with others."

Tyrdis's eyes widened, and her mind opened at Bruna's rebuke. "I didn't know."

"And pink azaleas wrapped in a pink scarf," Adelle commented as she held the bouquet to her nose. Then she pushed it away, giving the scarf a scrutinizing frown.

Suddenly Tyrdis wondered if she had done everything wrong, and a trickle of dread twisted in her gut. "The fluffy cakes!" she exclaimed in a hush, though by now half the longhouse was awake and watching them.

"And the puppet show!" Svanhild beamed. "Amma, can you make the fluffy cakes while Tyrdis and I perform the play? We need a sheet to hide behind."

Desperately hoping to get something right, Tyrdis quickly strung a cord about four feet off the floor and draped a sheet over it while Svanhild gathered the dolls, carvings, and stuffed animals. To Tyrdis's dismay, the story had more changes and Svanhild kept whispering new lines to her. Relief poured over her like a raging waterfall when Svanhild finally pronounced, "The end."

Adelle and the warrior patients all laughed, clapped, and cheered. Bruna walked over with a plate of the light, pan-seared bread smothered in honey, berries, and thick cream. "Just for you, sweetheart," she said with a wink as she handed Adelle the dish.

The two women exchanged a glance that informed Tyrdis they must share a secret. Was it an amusing story about the fluffy cakes? Something to do with the puppet show's preposterous, ever-morphing story, or something else that amused them?

"Come sit with me," Adelle bade, and Svanhild bounded onto the bed at her left. When Adelle looked at Tyrdis and patted the bed on her other side, she stepped over and took the seat. "Have you ever eaten these?" she asked.

Before Tyrdis could answer, Svanhild piped up. "We fed them to her for the first time when Amma was teaching her to make them. I told her it was your favorite food, and she wanted to make them for you, but I needed her to help with the show. I told her how much you love to be entertained by my puppet shows, and Tyrdis wanted everything to be just right." Svanhild pressed into her mother's side, beaming up at her with a big grin.

Adelle kissed the top of her head, then pivoted to Tyrdis, who couldn't decide if she was about to burst out laughing or lean in and kiss her. She hoped it was the latter.

"Open your mouth," she instructed. Tyrdis complied, and Adelle poked in a bite of the culinary delight. "Sweet, isn't it?"

Tyrdis chewed and swallowed, enjoying every forbidden flavor. "I have never been offered indulgent foods like this," she said. "I feel guilty even having a bite."

Adelle raised a brow with a look that beckoned, *I'll give you a bite of something to feel guilty about.* Something in Tyrdis's loins tightened, and she felt a rush ripple through her. Swallowing, she lowered her gaze and began silently reciting the Rules of Warfare in her head as a distraction. Was Adelle teasing or tormenting her?

"You have all been so thoughtful," Adelle said as she gave Svanhild the last bite of loaded fluffy cake. "This is the best homecoming ever." She hugged and kissed Svanhild. "I missed you so much, honeybee," she cooed. "But you must go back to sleep now."

Tyrdis stood so Adelle could tuck Svanhild into bed. The girl let out a big yawn. "Tyrdis has been singing me the song to go to sleep to," she said. "Tyrdis, can you sing it one more time?"

With Adelle's smile and nod of approval, Tyrdis repeated the simple, comforting song while Svanhild's eyes closed.

"Thank you, Mother," Adelle said, and hugged her again. "Fluffy cakes —really?" She handed Bruna the empty plate and rolled her eyes.

Her reaction puzzled Tyrdis, whose former elation was quickly baking into trepidation.

"I'm going home now, darling," Bruna said. "There isn't enough room here. And don't worry about the hour; it's still light out. Besides, Karl will be closing the mead hall about now."

With a flirtatious flash of teeth, Bruna spun and strolled out the door. Adelle shook her head with a little laugh, then took Tyrdis by the hand. "Would you come out back with me?"

Still more than a bit terrified, Tyrdis nodded and walked out with Adelle. "I hope everything was acceptable," she said in a small voice. "I wanted to do like you said and get to know you better. So, I asked Svanhild to tell me all your favorite things, so I could have them ready to greet you upon your return. So why do I feel like I have failed?"

Adelle rubbed Tyrdis's fingers between hers fondly and leaned against the wall near enough to brush Tyrdis's shoulder with hers. "You didn't fail, Tyrdis. It's just that Svanhild didn't tell you my favorite things—she told you hers."

The light that flashed in Tyrdis's awareness was reflected in her eyes. "I should have guessed. I was suspicious about the lullaby."

With a laugh, Adelle expounded. "I used to sing it to her all the time, so maybe she thought I did so because I love the song. While you sang it far better than I ever did, my favorite song is *Fólkvangr*."

"I'll learn it," Tyrdis vowed eagerly.

"She always brings me those flowers, and I say, 'How beautiful! Thank you so much.' I don't have the heart to tell her I prefer bluebells."

"And your preferred color is not pink," Tyrdis surmised.

"Purple."

Tyrdis let out a breath and relaxed enough to smile. "Good. I like purple better than pink."

"And your favorite color?" Adelle pried.

"Blue," Tyrdis answered in a tone that implied, *What other color is there?* Adelle laughed and stroked Tyrdis's face with her fingertips. The sensation sent ripples of delight flowing over her skin. "And I doubted you preferred a sweet treat to the healthy food you always espouse."

"You would be correct." Adelle edged closer and peered at her. "What are your favorite foods?"

The corners of Tyrdis's mouth fell into a straight line. "I never thought to choose a favorite. I've always just eaten what was put in front of me. Taste is a luxury."

"Oh, get over it!" Adelle wrapped an arm around her waist, and Tyrdis responded in kind. It felt so good to hold Adelle again, to experience this closeness. She couldn't recall ever sharing a moment like it with anyone.

"If you could choose any food you wanted to eat simply for the pleasure of tasting it, savoring every bite like golden apples from Ásgarðr, what would it be?" Adelle swayed with her—or Tyrdis was spinning, and Adelle held her upright; she wasn't sure which.

"Roasted reindeer with garlic and herb gravy over fresh bread with white goat cheese and ..." Tyrdis hesitated, and her eyes turned dreamy as she concluded, "fresh berries with thick cream, like my mother used to give me as a treat."

Adelle smiled and nodded. "Reindeer is tender, succulent, flavorful, and nutritious. I'd share that meal with you, only we need to add some greens and root vegetables."

Tyrdis felt her breath quicken and her pulse raced like a hare being chased by a fox. This was really happening—and to her. "The vegetables would be acceptable," she squeaked out.

"That you did all this, tried to plan things I would like, get to know me, even that ridiculous puppet show," Adelle said in an adoring manner, "means so much to me. You have pleased me, Tyrdis, very much so."

The fingers which had explored Tyrdis's face slid behind her neck and drew her head down. Offering no resistance, Tyrdis brought her lips to meet Adelle's. Thor must have struck his hammer because a jolt like lightning quickened through her senses. Adelle's kiss was tender, inviting, and sweet like berries and cream. Tyrdis craved more.

When Adelle slowly backed out of the kiss, Tyrdis was overcome with twenty-eight years' worth of pent-up desire. Sucking in a deep breath, she took Adelle's cheeks between her palms and dove deeper, exploring her mouth like a starving woman scavenging for a life-saving morsel. For a while, she lost herself in the kiss, delirious with pleasure, intoxicated with emotion, giving no thought to restraint. Coming to her senses, she immediately broke off and stepped back with a horrified expression.

"Adelle, I'm sorry. I overstepped. I don't know what came over me. I've never done anything like that—"

"It's all right," Adelle assured her as she wrapped her arms around Tyrdis's neck. "You don't have to apologize for feeling or for acting on your feelings. By all the gods, woman—I've never been kissed like that. If I wasn't certain before, I am now. This is what I was missing," she crooned.

Tyrdis's befuddled brain was trying to put two sensible words together when Sweyn rushed around the corner of the hospice.

"Tyrdis, it's time," he announced in a commanding tone. Then his face brightened. "Adelle, you're back!"

CHAPTER 28

$\mathcal{A}$delle jumped and spun around to face Sweyn. She had been so deeply engrossed with Tyrdis that he had startled her. In fact, her head was still spinning from that glorious, reality-altering kiss. Was it always supposed to have been like that? Had the boyfriend of her youth and her husband both been so inadequate, or had she merely needed a woman? Then again, it could just be Tyrdis.

The shieldmaiden was so powerful and vulnerable, decisive and hesitant, ruthless and loving, honorable and duty-bound, while infuriatingly stubborn with a penchant for disobeying her medical advice. She had snapped a man's neck with her bare hands—and who knows how many others she had slain in the course of her occupation—the same hands that had just presented her with an offering of flowers and seared her flesh with tantalizing pleasure. Here was a woman who seemed to have missed out on her own childhood yet was eager to share Svanhild's. Though rigidly disciplined in every aspect of her life, when she let go … imagining the heights Tyrdis could drive her to wasn't something she could do with Sweyn staring at them.

"Yes, I'm back," she answered, trying to will the blush out of her cheeks. She smoothed the apron over her dress to have something for her hands to do.

"Karyna?" he asked, as if balanced on the tip of a sword.

"She is remarkable," Adelle answered. She gave him a friendly hug of greeting.

"Is Jarl Niklaus embarking in the middle of the night?" Tyrdis inquired in a business-like tone, so different from the intimate sounds she had been purring moments ago. She stood at attention, like a stone statue erected to memorialize an ancestor.

"There have been some changes," Sweyn said as he moved between the women. "We have to hurry; I'll explain on the way, but Adelle." He turned an imploring gaze to her. "What happened?"

She related a summary of her work with Karyna, the attack, Jarl Stefnir's death, and how his daughter secured his seat of authority. Sweyn was spellbound, hanging on her every word. Then his expression of awe fell into anxiety.

"This changes much. It was Bjarke, that oaf!" His face displayed his disgust, and he brushed his fingers down his trim beard. "I'm sorrowed by the loss of Jarl Stefnir; he was a good neighbor, and I know Karyna's heart is heavy with grief. We must put an end to this, and that is precisely what we are going to do," he declared boldly. "Tyrdis, we still need you at my father's compound to oversee the defenses in case Firdafylke launches a counterattack, but we aren't going to Griðlundr as previously planned."

"You are going to Skeggen," Tyrdis replied as though she had read his mind. "Are the other jarls in agreement as to how to proceed?"

Sweyn's eyes rounded. "You know?" he questioned.

"I pieced it together from things you shared on the road a few days ago," Tyrdis said.

"What?" Adelle glanced from one of her friends to the other. "What's going on?"

Sweyn answered her in a gruff voice she seldom heard him use. "Gustav lied, started the war under false pretenses, and we have decided to remove him from power."

While Adelle stood with her mouth agape, trying to process the new information, Tyrdis asked, "Who will take his place?"

"That hasn't been decided yet," he answered. "The plan is to hold a Thing and let the people vote."

"Raknar is a fit leader, cunning, a skilled warrior, competent administrator," Tyrdis said, enumerating his qualities. "He is also ambitious. When he would have too much to drink at festivals and the conversation turned to matters of state, he would snarl about how he should have been king instead of Gustav. I have fought under his banner for ten years, and my only grievance concerns that rat bastard cousin of his, Garold. But Sweyn, your safety means more to me than my oath to him. Beware. He will not lie to your face, but mark his words carefully. He desires the crown."

Sweyn gave her arm a squeeze and nodded as he held her gaze. "Thank you, Tyrdis. I care about you too, and we all trust you. You will keep Sæladalr safe while we are away."

"Depend on it," she affirmed.

"Come now, we must hurry. Father wants to load the ships during the short dark. Those traveling by horseback have already left. Horik, Bjarke, and half of our fighters are with them. Raknar, Njal, and I will join Niklaus on the ships. Adelle, if you talk with Karyna again ... if something goes wrong and I don't make it back ..."

Adelle wrapped her arms around his neck and gave him a firm hug. After brushing his cheek with a kiss, she stepped back. "She also cares for you, Sweyn, and is torn over her feelings. She wishes to visit you when the war is over and tell you these things herself, so make sure nothing happens to you—grædari's orders," she added with a subdued grin.

Tyrdis twisted to face her with a bittersweet expression of regret. "Adelle."

"I know." She passed her an understanding look and an approving nod. "I'll come by to check on your wound when I get a chance." And then the two were off. Warriors. But the role they played could be necessary at times. *Our king did that? Wasted countless lives, took the lives of others, all because he thirsted for more profits? I never thought I would concede a military action could be the high road, but Sweyn's right; that man cannot rule as king, and if it costs a fight ... maybe it won't come to that. Perhaps he'll see reason and step aside.* But who was she kidding? Adelle knew—as surely as summer and winter—Gustav would not go quietly.

And Tyrdis would need to focus on matters of security. She didn't need Adelle distracting her by exploring erotic sensualities together. Hopefully, it would all be over soon because she really wanted to pursue those newfound pleasures.

* * *

SWEYN STOOD at the bow of one of four longboats his father had launched to convey a hundred and twenty warriors to Skeggen while a similar number traveled by horseback. They divided the force, not because of an attack strategy, but because Niklaus didn't own enough dragon ships to convey over two-hundred people to their destination; however, sea travel was more efficient, and he liked to have options if things went wrong.

The wind whipped his blond hair back as the crew pulled on the oars. The clinker-style, shallow-draft vessel bore a sail, but the wind was not ideal for their route. Normally, Sweyn enjoyed being out on the water with the salty air, the gulls gliding by, watching for dolphins and whales, but this was a solemn occasion. It was not every day that a band of jarls set out to overthrow their king.

Jarl Niklaus waved to him from the ship cutting through the waves to their port, and Sweyn returned the greeting. They had made plans to meet Horik and the overland half of the army at a narrow inlet to the southwest of Skeggen so they could combine the fighting forces. To avoid creating alarm, a small party of the leaders and an armed escort would ride in to confront King Gustav. If he insisted on a fight, they would call in their warriors.

Everyone had agreed to spare civilians, as these were the citizens one of them would soon govern, and whoever it was would need the support of the masses. Every soldier had been forbidden to loot, burn, rape, steal from or kill anyone who did not offer armed resistance. He hoped they would remember and obey the directive in the heat of battle.

The sun reflecting off the gentle waves looked like a thousand tiny mirrors flashing at him, and he had to use his hand to shade his eyes lest the brilliance blind him.

"What do you think will happen?" asked Njal, who appeared behind him.

"I fear Gustav will fight to keep his power," Sweyn answered candidly. He was glad his younger brother was taking this seriously and was a little surprised their father allowed him to come. But he was eighteen, and Sweyn had been engaging in true combat already by that age.

"You have to do exactly whatever I or whoever is in charge of you directs." Sweyn turned from the expansive ocean to meet Njal's gaze. "You are good with your weapons in practice but everything changes when your opponent is trying to kill you. Battles get messy."

"I know," his taller brother with the scant beard answered. "What if Father is chosen to be king?" he asked with hesitant excitement in his voice. "We would be princes. Talk about being able to get whatever woman we want." His face morphed into a silly smile.

"It's possible he'll become king and just as likely he won't," Sweyn answered. "We need to be ready to accept either outcome with equal grace. Father doesn't need to be embarrassed by bitter sons who can't control their emotions."

"I know how to control myself," he snapped in haste, then fudged. "I'm learning to, anyway. Were you afraid—you know, your first time in a battle?"

Sweyn smiled and patted a hand on Njal's shoulder. "Brother, I'm always a little afraid in battle. Anyone who says differently is either lying, or they're Tyrdis," he added with a hint of humor. "The key is to focus on one thing at a time and not let the enormity of the situation distract you. Concentrate on one foe and remember your training. Some movements should be second nature to you by now, but you can't worry about the man who screams on your right or the one who falls to your left nor arrows or spears that might be racing toward you. Keep your eyes moving, but your heart steady. It is not bloodshed Odin values, but courage. Courage isn't the absence of fear—it's the determination to work through your fears to accomplish the goal."

"So does that mean Tyrdis is fearless instead of courageous?"

Considering his response, Sweyn answered, "Some experienced warriors build up a resistance to fear. They are victorious so many times they come to expect it. They have mastered a level of confidence that expels doubt. Others simply look forward to entering Valhalla, preferring its promise to whatever life they have in this realm. Those are the ones you don't want to fight. Steer clear of them in favor of the normal variety, especially for your first few battles."

"How will I know which ones they are?" Njal asked.

"You'll know. You'll see it in their bearing, the look in their eyes, the precision and speed with which they dispose of all in their path. I'm not advising you to run; you can't ever do that," he emphasized. "Flee one fight and you'll forever be branded a coward. Just try to engage fighters your own age or who don't exhibit such prowess."

"How do you know all this?" Njal asked. "I've been training for two years, and no one has taught me these things."

Sweyn smiled. "Three and a half years ago, the first time I competed in the winter games as an adult, I ended up matched against Tyrdis in the second round—the round I was eliminated in. She went on to place second overall in the kingdom while I was too far down the line to be worth mentioning, but she took me aside and mentored me. I could handle a sword, bow, axe, spear, and shield as well as anyone; however, I hadn't developed any instincts. She taught me to read my opponents, to quickly assess their strengths and weaknesses, and to do the unexpected. Instead of hacking and jabbing in hopes of knocking the weapon out of my adversary's hand, she taught me the art of combat. It's better to avoid a blow than to take one, use your foe's weight against him, brush off a charge rather than meet it head-on, and so many nuances that make her the invincible shieldmaiden she is. If her enemy hadn't thrust his spear through her back, he'd have never touched her with it at all."

Njal shook his head. "As much as I hate you telling me what to do, Sweyn, I'd be a fool not to learn from you. So why is it everyone loves you and they only tolerate me? It isn't fair. Is it because you are more handsome or witty, or do they just lick your boots because you stand in line as Father's heir, and they may need a favor of you one day?"

Sweyn glanced at the longboat full of underlings. Some were mature warriors who had earned their mettle, while others were young adventurers striving to win their father's approval. All were sweating as they strained at their oars, propelling the ship through the waves. Behind them followed the craft Bjornolf commanded. Sweyn observed him also standing by the dragonhead carving at his bow, surveying the shoreline, and glancing out to sea, a short cloak billowing around his broad shoulders.

"Come, I'll show you." He took Njal's elbow and led him down the center along the keel between the trunks the oarsmen sat on. A hearty shieldmaiden didn't even seem winded, but an older, heavyset man and a youth appeared to be struggling. Nudging his brother, he motioned toward the youth. Then he addressed the older warrior. "Sigil, it's my turn to row. I need you to move to the stern and check on our navigator. You've made this journey many times, and he may require your advice."

The hefty fellow Niklaus's age offered an appreciative nod. "If you insist," he huffed out between forced breaths. "I'll make sure he's watching for the proper signs."

Exchanging a glance with Njal, he spied his brother rolling his eyes.

"What's the point of being in charge then," he whispered, "if we have to put blisters on our hands too?"

"Leadership." Sweyn left him with the single word as he sat and took up Sigil's oar. When Njal shook his head and lumbered over to relieve the struggling youthful soldier, Sweyn grinned. Maybe there was hope for his little brother after all.

CHAPTER 29

Skeggen, after their arrival

Sweyn had to be civil to Garold, even though he wanted to pummel him into a sniveling heap. Jarl Raknar's cousin rode beside him as they, along with Jarl Bjarke's first warrior, kept pace behind the three jarls along the path to King Gustav's great hall. Uncle Horik had been left in charge of the army, and Sweyn prayed he didn't do something foolish and unpredictable with his authority. He seemed to be onboard with everything; he seemed to be loyal to Niklaus, just like Njal seemed to be loyal to him, but who knew? Sweyn was glad he didn't have to worry about such lofty matters yet. All he had to do was refrain from knocking Garold on his arse.

Six more warriors, two from each of the three fylkes, followed, holding their spears aloft. While they garnered a few puzzled expressions, the folks in the market and most in town ignored them. Seeing a little girl trying to sell flowers reminded him of Hallfrid's pleading expression before he left her behind with his mother and younger siblings. "Please don't get hurt," she had begged, a single tear rolling down her face. "I didn't know you would go off to fight him. I shouldn't have told you."

"Then I'd still be going off to fight," Sweyn had answered, "only it would be more likely I'd be hurt in Firdafylke than in Skeggen. All will be well; you'll see." He had patted her head and strode out with a few last words to Tyrdis and a hug and kiss from his mother.

When they trailed through the king's palisade entrance, the party dismounted and looped their reins over a split rail. A towering hulk of muscles with a shaved head marched up to them wearing a frown deep enough to consume a whole hog. "What are you doing here?" he demanded and crossed his log-sized arms over his heaving chest. "You are supposed to be invading Firdafylke."

"We require an audience with King Gustav first," Raknar said. "A few details we need to get settled."

The mountainous guard hmphed and stomped off toward the great hall. "Come on then," he grumbled.

Niklaus asked their escort to stay with the horses while the six of them stepped up into the king's hall. Sweyn was suddenly aware he had now made more trips here this summer than he had in the past three years put together. Ivar and Kerstav came in from the back door in worn armor, sweaty from a practice bout, and eyed them warily.

"We weren't expecting you," Ivar said.

"Well, we're here," Bjarke bellowed and plopped his fists on the sides of his belt. "Where's your father?"

"I'll see if he's available," Kerstav replied in an irritated voice.

"Would you like to have a seat?" Ivar offered as his younger brother disappeared into the private wing of the longhouse.

"No, thank you," Niklaus answered.

The atmosphere in the chamber was tense, and Sweyn did not envy Ivar's position. Would he confess the truth or keep his vow of silence?

Out of the corner of his eye, Sweyn spied Garold ogling the women working at a loom at the far end of the hall. *One day*, he thought. *But not today.*

Kerstav returned followed by Gustav in a green silk robe barely pulled around his protruding belly. His hair was tousled, and his beard wet with what smelled like strong wine. Nonetheless, he jutted up his chin and curled his lip at them.

"What are you three doing here?" he demanded.

The king's appearance sickened Sweyn. He recalled hearing the man dispense a fair and wise judgment in his court and had admired him. Had that day been a fluke? *Everyone is a mix of their best and worst,* he reminded himself. *But we hold rulers to a higher standard. We must.*

"We know what really happened to Jarivald," Niklaus stated in an even tone. "You deceived everyone, covered up what wasn't a crime with lies for your own gain."

Fury flashed in Gustav's face, his eyes narrowing to beady pinpoints. "My son's murder was indeed a crime."

"Only he wasn't murdered, was he?" Raknar's words were more of a statement than a question.

"He was—"

"Come on, Gustav!" Bjarke took a step forward and gestured toward Ivar. "Your boy here bested him in a fair fight. Why not admit it? We've heard from a witness."

"A witness!" Gustav passed an incredulous glance at his two sons. "Impossible!"

"I did not kill my brother," Ivar proclaimed with an angry edge to his voice. "Those assassins did. I'm the witness."

"And Kerstav?" Raknar turned his assessing gaze on Ivar's younger brother. "What did you see?"

"I didn't see anything," he replied innocently with shrugged shoulders.

"What is this?" Gustav barked. "Why are you accusing us—"

Niklaus stepped forward and jabbed a finger in his direction. "Because you sent our warriors to kill and die for you out of greed. It's no secret you covet the fruitful Firdafylke land along our southern border. So you concocted this story as an excuse to appear honorable in declaring war on them. But where are *you*? My town, my subjects are bearing the brunt of this and where are *you*? If you are so outraged, why are *you* not on the front lines leading the charge?"

"Now see here," Ivar burst in. "Our father has been sick with grief."

"Bull skitr!" Bjarke laughed and waved a broad hand up and down at the king. "So grief-stricken he has taken to drinking and whoring in the middle of the day, safe in the assumption we will gladly die for him."

"Watch your tongue, Bjarke!" shouted Gustav. "I am king, and you will show me respect, or I'll snatch your fylke from you faster than you can take a piss."

"I don't think so," Raknar countered smoothly. "Tell the truth, Gustav, and maybe we'll spare your life."

The king's face turned so red it looked almost purple. He pounded his fists on the table and bellowed, "Guards!"

Eight warriors rushed in, weapons drawn, while Ivar and Kerstav eyed each other fearfully and backed away.

Then Niklaus spoke with authority ringing from his lips. "Your dishonorable king has lied to you, to us, to all of Norvegr. Are you certain you wish to die for him? We have an army three times the size of the troops you could muster from Skeggen sitting right outside the walls. Do not deceive yourselves, thinking this is a battle you could win."

"Throw them out!" Gustav wrapped his gown tighter and glowered at his soldiers. They hesitated.

"Just tell us the truth," Raknar implored. "Ivar killed Jarivald in a fair fight; there is no shame in it. You blamed Firdafylke assassins because you wanted to expand our borders."

"But I didn't kill him!" Ivar insisted. "Jarivald was an accomplished swordsman. I'm not foolish enough to engage him in a duel."

"All right!" Gustav let out a tremendous sigh and ran stubby fingers through his graying strands. "Maybe I let this all go to my head. You know I was once a formidable warrior, gaining the name of Ironside. I admit I've become too comfortable in my luxury and have lost my way since my wife died. I drink too much and consort with women; I enjoy myself. You think, skim a little off the top of every merchant's sale, collect my share of each adventurer's haul, it's my right. I'm king. I have to make the hard decisions. I've supported each of you in your times of need."

"When?" Raknar raised a brow along with the question. "You collect taxes from my lands—"

"Reasonable taxes," Gustav broke in.

Raknar continued, as if he hadn't interrupted. "Yet you have never sent financial or military support to Heilagrfjord."

"I," Gustav began with a raised hand. Then he faltered, letting his hand and his countenance drop.

"You didn't even attend my father's funeral when he died," Bjarke added in an offended tone. "Neither did you send a gift."

"I'll do better," he vowed in contrition. "But which of you has lost a son? I am still torn with grief and—"

"And you wish to comfort yourself with an acquisition of land we must fight and bleed for," Niklaus concluded.

"There were assassins," Gustav insisted. Then, lowering his chin, he muttered, "Can't be sure they were from Firdafylke, but they could have been."

"So now you wish to change your version of events to another lie." Raknar's patience was reaching its limit.

Ivar dared to speak up. "There was only one, not three or four. I didn't want to appear so weak and helpless. He wore black, not blue, and I didn't see his face. Father said he must have been sent from King Tortryggr because they had been arguing for some time. He said I must swear there was a group of them, and I did really get cut with his sword. The killer was swift and powerful, in and out in a flash. I tried to chase after him, then couldn't find him, and I had to get back to Jarivald."

"So now it's a lone assassin who vanishes like a specter!" Bjarke threw up his hands. "The bottom line is you lied to us, our warriors have died for you for no reason, and you're a terrible king. Step down or we will force you to."

"What?" Gustav's face took on an incredulous look. "I am the rightful king. The people chose me." Fire burned in his eyes as he thrust a thumb at his sagging chest.

"The people chose the princess," Niklaus reminded him. "The one you hastily wed, then assumed her authority. How did she die again?"

"That's my mother you're talking about!" Kerstav burst in angrily.

"Indeed, boy," Bjarke agreed. "Curious how she died when she was so young."

"There was an illness being passed around the town that winter," the king alleged. "She caught it and died of a fever."

"Or poisoning," Raknar added in a low hiss. Raising his voice, he asserted, "You will step down, or we will force you to. Either way, this is your last day to occupy this hall."

In a fit of rage, Gustav cried, "Kill them! Kill them all!"

Sweyn drew his sword and assumed a stance to protect his father's back. Following his lead, Garold and Bjarke's man did the same. The jarls drew their swords, and the guards closed in. They clinked blades, pushed, shoved, threw punches, but the guards didn't seem inspired to follow Gustav's orders. Within seconds, the six of them had shuffled out the door and made haste to their horses.

"We're leaving," Niklaus called to the six who waited with their mounts near the gate. Before anyone thought to bar the exit, the twelve were galloping out of town toward their waiting army.

CHAPTER 30

Same day in Sæladalr

ithin the ramparts of Jarl Niklaus's estate, Tyrdis stood erect with her feet planted shoulder-width apart, clasping her hands behind her back, while Trygve scrambled up the lookout tower. Her other fully-armed trainees were positioned behind her, while the small contingent of capable guards Niklaus left under her authority manned their posts. Taking a metal bar, Trygve banged vigorously on the hollow copper pipe that hung from a rope.

Ever since the night before last, when she and Adelle shared that amazing kiss, Tyrdis hadn't been able to concentrate on anything. Memories of the sensations, emotions, and revelations born from the experience had infiltrated her thoughts every waking moment and consumed her dreams during sleep. She hungered to do it again. It had awakened something in her that had been missing, something she wanted. Tyrdis craved having the magic of Adelle's hand on her body, her mouth on hers, and fulfilling every desire she had denied herself all these years.

I must focus on the task at hand!

Lynnea, the jarl's younger children, and Hallfrid, along with other servants, already occupied the great hall. Tyrdis had thought about sending for Adelle, Bruna, and Svanhild before carrying out the surprise drill but decided she wished to see how long it took them—as well as the other townspeople—to respond.

199

Some rushed through the gates, clinging small children to their breasts, displaying signs of panic while others wandered about, peering toward the docks, checking for the arrival of a merchant ship, perhaps.

By the time most of the citizens had gathered inside Niklaus's palisade, Tyrdis signaled Trygve to stop ringing. "You may have realized by now this was a drill," she proclaimed in a forceful voice drenched in authority. "Had this warning preceded an actual attack, half of you would be dead now. This was the most inefficient emergency practice I have ever witnessed. I had time to recite the poem *Song of the Sibyl* three times in its entirety while you wandered, meandered, and tarried in your response to the warning alarm."

To her left, Trygve slid down a pole from the platform rather than descend the ladder. His feet hit the ground with a thud, and he jogged over to fall in beside her.

"Listen to Tyrdis," he called to the crowd. "She is trying to save your lives."

"The army is away," she continued, "and Jarl Niklaus charged me with protecting you all." Scanning the gathering, she spotted Bruna stroll in, holding Svanhild's hand. She frowned at them in deep discontent. "We are still at war with Firdafylke, and Jarl Bjarke's soldiers recently attacked them, so we must be prepared in case they retaliate. Likewise, another emergency could arise for which you are woefully unprepared."

"You mean you disrupted our day for nothing?" a craftsman complained.

"I should have stayed with my boat," dismissed a fisherman, who turned to walk away.

"You, Fynnvaldr, stop!" Trygve employed his most demanding tone, his voice cracking in his excitement. "Practice and training are vital. Don't you test your nets before throwing them out for a catch? You don't want to lose a grand haul because you were too slothful to repair worn fibers. When this alarm sounds, you must run with haste as if your life depends on it, because—when it isn't a drill—it will."

"Thank you, Trygve," Tyrdis said with a nod to her pupil. Turning back to the population, she announced, "I understand such procedures may disrupt your normal activities, but only for a few minutes—minutes that can save your lives. Repetition is the key to learning and the road to perfection. While I am in charge in Jarl Niklaus's absence, we will repeat this training until each one of you responds promptly. This small guard cannot protect you when you are in the fields, at the seashore, or in your dwellings. However, these fortifications are sturdy, and, from their ramparts, we can repel invaders."

"Then who will protect our property?" a man asked. "They will loot and burn without opposition."

"Houses can be rebuilt, gardens replanted, and material goods replaced," Tyrdis declared. "But even Adelle's skill or your völva's seiðr cannot raise the dead. We will hold another drill before time for sleeping, and you can expect more tomorrow until you master this exercise. I do not wish you to be afraid but prepared and diligent. Lady Lynnea has issued a generous invitation, opening the great hall to anyone who wishes to remain here temporarily. I encourage all who are elderly or infirmed, those who cannot walk quickly or who are hard of hearing, mothers who are nursing infants, and residents who stay on the outskirts of town to move into this longhouse until Niklaus returns and the threat has been neutralized. No one will think you inferior, for such is a rational course of action."

Murmurs arose from the crowd as neighbors quietly discussed the offer with each other. Then an impatient man called out, "Can we go back to work now?"

Tyrdis eyed him with disapproval and exhaled an irritated breath. "You are dismissed."

Abandoning her stately stance and releasing the people from her energetic hold, Tyrdis eased her way to Bruna and Svanhild. "Where is Adelle?"

"Mama's still up at the hospice," Svanhild chirped. "She told Amma and me to come stay in town close to the safe place but that she must still take care of her patients."

Irritation dug its claws into Tyrdis's gut, and she had to muster all her control to avoid a display of emotion. Naturally, her professional veneer didn't fool Bruna.

Laying a hand on her arm, Bruna offered her a shy smile. "You know Adelle. She won't run from danger and is compelled to put the well-being of her patients first. If there was an actual attack, she'd do what was necessary."

"Doesn't it infuriate you?" Tyrdis asked through tight lips, her nostrils flaring with the question.

Bruna nodded and patted Tyrdis's arm. "It took some getting used to," she admitted. "More than anything, I wish my children and grandchildren to be safe, healthy, and happy. However, I must also understand Adelle is a grown woman with a calling from the gods. You, of all people, should understand."

Tyrdis started at her words, offering her a curious gaze.

A mischievous look blossomed on Bruna's face. "Where do you run when danger presents itself?"

"Toward it," Tyrdis declared. "But that's different. I am an experienced, trained warrior, and defending the people is my duty and privilege. However, I can't protect them effectively if they refuse to heed my instructions."

"While Adelle will never pick up a weapon, safeguarding others is also her duty and privilege," Bruna explained. "She won't run to safety if it means leaving a vulnerable person behind. You must accept her for who she is, Tyrdis, or let her go. This aspect of her character will not change for me or you."

"Or even me," Svanhild added in a meek voice.

Tyrdis exhaled and lowered her gaze to meet Svanhild's innocent eyes. "Then you and I will have to be strong," she concluded.

Svanhild reached out and took her hand. "We can be strong together."

When Tyrdis looked up again, a spindly, older man stood with his arm around Bruna. "You think you have it bad?" he asked in a humorous tone. "My son isn't content unless he's racing headlong into the jaws of danger. At least yours doesn't go looking for it."

Bruna snaked a hand around his waist. "Tyrdis, this is Karl, who I am to wed. Karl, meet Tyrdis."

"Yes, well, I've heard plenty about you," he chuckled. "And I must say, Bjornolf is more jealous of you than he lets on. It's just his competitive streak."

Not knowing how to respond, Tyrdis just nodded.

"I'd better get back to the mead hall now and make sure patrons aren't just helping themselves." He wiggled his brows and winked. "You know these Norsemen—can't say no to a free drink."

"I'll be by later," Bruna assured him. "I want to finish the cloth I'm weaving, then check in with Adelle. And someone has to keep track of this little rascal," she added, mussing her hand over Svanhild's hair.

"I'm not a rascal." She thrust up her chin and slapped her hands to her hips like a tiny woman in charge. "I'm a storyteller. One day, I'll be the greatest skald in all the land. People will flock and give me silver to tell them the most fantastic tales."

Bruna laughed, and Karl kissed her cheek. "I certainly believe that, honeybee!" her Amma affirmed.

* * *

ADELLE HAD BEEN KEEPING herself busy, caring for Bjarke's injured warriors, only now most of them were on the mend. Several had already left to join the town guards at Jarl Niklaus's great hall. Joren hadn't been as confident or quick a learner as Karyna, but he was a kind-hearted young man who could finally put her teaching into practice. She had praised him for how well he carried on in her absence, which made him buoyant with cheer.

Even though she'd purposely stayed away from Tyrdis these two days —and last night, which was even harder—she couldn't stop thinking about her. Her toe-curling kiss played on a loop in her mind over and over, sending her heart racing and her soul singing. Every step felt like she walked on air. Every chore seemed effortless, and no amount of belly-aching or talk of hacking off enemies' arms, legs, and heads by her patients could dampen her cheerful radiance.

Joren had noticed and inquired about her dreamy mood; she had merely acted as if she hadn't noticed and changed the subject. She had spared a few thoughts for Karyna and prayed she was well, but imaginings of making love with Tyrdis clouded her brain like a thick fog and caused her skin to vibrate like a tight drumhead.

"There's the alarm clanging again," Joren said as he looked out the open doorway toward town. "Do you think it's a real attack this time?"

Adelle crossed to him and shook her head. "Tyrdis is running drills. You should dash to the great hall and count how long it takes you," she suggested. "Then come back and let me know. Soon all our injured will be able to walk without aid, and we can join in the exercises."

"All right," he agreed and trotted off toward town.

Adelle stood gazing out, rubbing a hand down the smooth wood of the doorpost, pretending it was Tyrdis's thigh. When a markedly grumpy and disagreeable patient called for her, she shook the image away and went back to work.

A short while later, Joren returned with stories about the drill, how long it took him to arrive, who was slower, what Tyrdis had said, and a host of gossip from town.

"The price of eggs rose since Jarl Niklaus left," he noted with concern. "I keep telling you we should keep our own chickens up here."

"And I keep telling you birds spread disease. They splash excrement everywhere, and too many people depend on trading us eggs or fowl meat for healing services," she answered. "Jarl Bjarke left us a pouch of silver coins to compensate for treating his soldiers. We won't starve anytime soon."

"I know," he muttered. "Oh, and Trina left her brute of a husband and is now living with Bragfeil. If you ask me, it took her too long to make the move, but I'm happy for her."

"What about you, Joren? Any interest in securing a mate?"

He flashed her a nervous grin that showed way too many teeth and shook his head. "Not me. I'd rather wrestle Fenrir. I'm content to assist you and try to draw nearer to the gods. Maybe one day I'll develop the courage required."

She smiled at him and thought about whom *she'd* like to be wrestling with about now.

"Tyrdis looked strong and well but very stern and disgruntled," he added. "She looked at me like I had committed some unpardonable offense or something. Maybe you should check on her. All the stress could be causing her physical pain."

Adelle suspected the reason for Tyrdis's mood; she hadn't been to see her. Adelle understood Tyrdis couldn't leave her post to come to visit her, and Adelle didn't wish to distract her, but ... A horrible thought struck her. *What if Tyrdis construes my absence to mean I regret what we did, that I don't want her that way? I can't have her thinking she's been rejected.*

"You could be right," Adelle said. "Take care of things here while I go check on her. I'll just take an assortment of remedies in case she needs something."

Joren smiled and looked relieved. "Good, because one place I do not wish to be is on her bad side."

Adelle tossed a few assorted herbs and salves into a small basket and glided out the door, allowing anticipation to replace trepidation in her heart.

· · ·

ADELLE FOUND Tyrdis marching the interior perimeter of the compound, prodding a row of pointed tree trunks driven into the ground. When one gave an inch under the pressure of her might, she called to the nearest sentry. "This portion is not secure. I want it reinforced with a brace, all along here," she instructed as she pointed to the minimally-loose area. "If I can push it to waver, think what a shield wall of warriors twice my size can do."

"Aye, right away," the guard replied.

When Tyrdis glanced her way, Adelle smiled innocently and sashayed over to her. "I came to check on you." She made sure her invitingly playful expression conveyed the intended sentiment.

Tyrdis's enchanting blue-green eyes lit with seductive pleasure, and the shieldmaiden smirked. "About bloody time. Even Joren attended one of my emergency drills."

They fell in step together and strolled along the wall side by side.

"Tyrdis," Adelle began in an apologetic tone.

Tyrdis held up a hand as she continued to survey the barricade. "I have come to terms with our positions," she said. "You and I are much more alike than we first imagined. You will not leave your patients defenseless even when you refuse to take up arms to protect them. Instead, you utilize divine fortitude and your connection to higher powers to cover them with your shielding aura. I do the same for the people under my charge, only I employ weapons I am skilled with to defend them. If you can accept the fact that I must sometimes kill our enemies in order to save the lives of our friends, then I will try not to balk at your leaving yourself open to danger when I am not present to protect you. It is exceedingly difficult because I feel if you were to be harmed or killed—"

"Trust me," Adelle broke in. "For I trust you absolutely. Neither of us can swear we will live to a ripe old age. In the course of my work, I see those who have never been in harm's way die from a sudden or chronic illness despite being young. A fire breaks out, a bitter freeze descends, a wild animal attacks, a tree falls on their house. It pricks my soul like a thousand needles to think of you risking your life in combat, even though I am aware of your extraordinary expertise. Anything can happen to anyone at any time. That's life."

Tyrdis nodded as if she understood. Then she motioned toward a shed under a large shade tree. "This granary is half empty, and Lynnea has already commissioned today's bread to be baked. We could step in here to gain some privacy while you check on my wound's healing progress."

A little thrill leaped inside Adelle like a frolicking lamb. "That would be perfect."

She let Tyrdis open the door and usher her in. It smelled of barley, rye, and oats. When the door fell shut, light and air still filtered through the cracks in the plank walls. A startled mouse squeaked and dashed away. "Jarl Niklaus requires a cat," Tyrdis commented with upturned lips, and she took Adelle in her arms.

Unwilling and unable to wait any longer, Adelle dropped her basket and pressed her lips to Tyrdis's with searing desire. She was rewarded with the woman's hum of pleasure and the easing of her tense muscles. A tingle pulsed through Adelle, urging her into a sea of unabashed delight that almost distracted her from her primary purpose.

Easing back, Adelle lowered her hands to grip the hem of Tyrdis's mail shirt. "I need to examine your side," she uttered in a much lower, huskier voice than intended.

Tyrdis's gaze flashed at her. "You are free to examine all of me if you desire."

The look in her eyes and the tone of her voice were enough to throw Adelle into a whirlpool of orgasmic delirium. Struggling to maintain some sense of self-control, she responded, "Let's start with your abdomen, shall we?"

Gathering both the chainmail and gambeson beneath it, Adelle pulled the armor upward until she could raise it no further. "This is ridiculously heavy!"

Her lips curving in an adorable smile, Tyrdis lifted it the rest of the way, revealing her firm muscles and bleak scar. Adelle glided her fingertips gently over the burn mark, noting the healthy color of the skin and lack of any seepage.

"It looks good. How do you feel?"

"Satisfactory," Tyrdis replied. But when Adelle pinned her with a disbelieving expression, to her surprise the ever-serious shieldmaiden rolled her eyes. "It doesn't hurt just being there, but, when I strain certain muscles when holding up weight like this or swinging my weapons, it pulls, presenting some discomfort. The worst part is the continuing weakness on my right side."

"Your strength will return in time and let down your arms," Adelle instructed. "I don't want to cause you pain."

Tyrdis's voice turned seductive. "A better solution would be to remove my armor. Isn't that what you would prescribe?"

"Oh, yes," Adelle purred, wishing she had thought of it first. She unfastened the belt and helped Tyrdis pull the chainmail over her head. With it safely lowered to the dusty floor of the granary, Tyrdis untied the strings of her blue gambeson, allowing it to fall loosely over her torso.

Adelle slid her hands through the slit in the garment over Tyrdis's bare belly, in awe of her exceptional, hard muscles coated with tempting, silky flesh. Their lips met again in an enticing taste that only whetted Adelle's appetite more.

"When did you learn to kiss like this?" she sang in delirium.

"Two nights ago."

Adelle took a step back, blinked, and stared at her. "Are you serious?"

Tyrdis took on the unfamiliar look of a lost child. "I ... there was never ..." She swallowed and diverted her eyes.

Gently catching her face between her palms, Adelle steered her gaze to hers. "But you are so ... beautiful. And smart, and funny, and kind. Never?"

"I had to focus on my training and duty," she explained. "Men were intimidated by me and women ... well, I don't know, but none ever seemed interested. Besides, my father instilled in me the notion that physical pleasures and emotional attachments were distractions I was better off without. Although I'm uncertain it applies anymore."

"I should hope not," Adelle allowed, still marveling at the woman she touched. She pondered the incredible realization that she had been the one to sneak past the warrior's defenses, to put a smile on her serious face, to turn her formidable body into putty in her hands. Not only a virgin, but she was her first kiss? It was unfathomable and yet filled Adelle with a joy she could have never expected. *How is it she finds me so special when she is the remarkable one? Out of all the people in Raumsdal, she chose me to let down her guard with, to share her first intimate moment.* Then an amusing thought struck her. *No, it was Svanhild. She's the one who broke the ice; I just get to drink the cool water.*

Adelle brushed her lips over Tyrdis's and beamed at her in wonder. "Then you must possess legendary talent and mythical instincts because your kisses send me reeling." Since Tyrdis's hair was down, Adelle took advantage, running her fingers through sunny, silky strands, reveling in the sensation, and praying no one came calling for Tyrdis.

"If that is so, you are my Kvasir, the one to evoke such passion from me as I never imagined possible," Tyrdis confessed. "I can't stop thinking about you, about us. You have set my ordered world spinning like a top. Please don't let me fall."

Gripping Tyrdis's shoulders, Adelle caught her in an intense gaze. "Don't be afraid, Tyrdis. If you fall, I'll be here to catch you."

Adelle felt the moment Tyrdis relinquished the last of her resistance and smashed the walls that had held her heart captive for her whole life. She flew on her kisses and rode the waves of ecstasy with her as they explored secret places of both their bodies and souls. Adelle came to learn as much about herself as she did about Tyrdis, who left her both completely satisfied and longing for more. Most of all, she thanked the gods they were not in mid-climax but lay recovering in each other's arms when Trygve came looking for Tyrdis.

CHAPTER 31

Skeggen, the same night

Sweyn sat on the ground in a circle with his father and uncle, Jarls Raknar and Bjarke, and their first warriors. He was extremely happy Raknar hadn't brought his cousin Garold to take part in the strategy session. The last thing they needed was stupid ideas or blatant cowardice in the mix.

He gnawed on a goose leg, listening carefully to everything that was discussed. A narrow ribbon of smoke rose from the small fire while its crackle interrupted the silence. With most of the leaders having finished their meal, Bjarke spoke first.

"So, are we going to kill him now?"

"Only if he dies in battle," Niklaus answered in a most serious tone. "He was our king for fifteen years and deserves at least that much."

"I agree," Raknar seconded. "But our primary goal now is to devise a plan of attack that will assure our victory with minimal losses."

"Did you notice how Gustav's guards reacted in his great hall today?" Sweyn pointed out. "His soldiers may not be enthusiastic about fighting us to keep him in power."

Recognizing him with a look and a nod, his father elaborated. "Enthusiastic or not, they will offer stiff resistance. Not only do they have oaths to honor but families to protect. They don't know we have no intention of harming women and children."

"I say we get a battering ram and storm his gate," Bjarke suggested and bit into the loaf of bread in his hand.

"How subtle," Niklaus muttered and rolled his eyes.

"No, wait." Raknar's energy spiked as his expression revealed a plan springing to life. "There are three of us, three armies. What if we strike the compound at three different points simultaneously?"

"Then their warriors would be spread too thin to be effective on all the fronts," Niklaus replied in inspired realization.

"The walls give them an advantage, but we could neutralize it if we play it right," Raknar pointed out. "All right, Bjarke. Why don't you build a battering ram and storm the front gate? Use a turtle formation with shield barriers to protect your soldiers from arrows and stones hurled from above. Meanwhile, my archers will assault the rear wall with a raining fire. We may get lucky and set some roofs ablaze."

"While Gustav's warriors are busy with all that, I could send some men with grappling hooks in on horseback to catch a portion of the wall and pull it down," Niklaus suggested. "We'll use horns to signal each other and all inundate the fortress through whichever point is breached first."

Bjarke's first warrior chimed in. "We should use our archers as support, shooting at anyone atop their walls to keep them pinned down."

"We could keep a second wave in place to intercept anyone who tries to flee," Sweyn proposed.

Raknar smirked. "I wouldn't be surprised if Gustav and his sons tried to sneak out during the fighting. Sweyn, could you be in charge of scooping up any who try to run?"

With a glance at his father for approval, he nodded. While he would much rather be in the thick of the fighting, he also didn't wish the king's family to be massacred. As the one in charge of apprehending runaways, he could ensure that didn't happen.

"I want to send scouts," Niklaus said, "to evaluate the palisade, look for back doors and weak spots, and map out the terrain. If I recall, there is a rise above the eastern wall which would make a perfect place to position your archers."

"And Gunnar," Bjarke said to his man, "I need you to oversee the building of the battering ram. We need a large, solid tree trunk to be cut and fitted with hand poles."

"I'll get on it right away," he replied, stood up, and trotted off.

"Let's all get a good rest tonight," Raknar recommended. "Tomorrow, we make history."

Tossing the bare bone of his goose leg into the fire, Sweyn pushed up. "Do you need me for anything else tonight?" he asked his father.

"No, son. Go make sure Njal isn't getting into trouble. You can assemble your team in the morning."

He headed out to find his brother, far too wired to sleep. Sweyn had been in battles before—even led troops—but nothing on this scale or importance. A voice in his head wanted to second-guess their decision. *Are we doing the right thing?*

Another voice replied, *Indeed. Wasn't this your plan from the beginning? And see how everyone has fallen in line to execute it.*

Only because King Gustav proved himself dishonorable, he answered himself. *I had never even entertained the possibility of being a prince until it came up later. It's about what's right for Raumsdal, not personal gain.*

Then you have your answer, the other aspect of his mind replied. *Stop worrying and relax. All will turn out as it should.*

Sweyn found Njal lounging with a group of young warriors, drinking, laughing, and shooting dice. "Did you all decide our fate so soon?" His eyes met Sweyn's with irritation, and there was an edge to his tone.

"It's an excellent plan," Sweyn answered. "We are dividing into various spearheads. Would you rather go with me or Father?"

"Oh?" Njal sat a little straighter, a hard expression on his face. "Do I get a choice?"

It was clear he was irritated and jealous again over being excluded from the council. Sweyn sighed and rubbed the back of his neck. "I don't know. As far as I'm concerned, you may choose, but, as usual, I can't speak for our father. Will you be angry if he places you under my command?"

Njal slumped against the large stone at his back and took a sip of his ale. "I suppose there are more careless and inept fellows I could take orders from."

"Yeah, like this one!" One of his friends laughed, jerking a thumb toward the wiry guy sitting beside him.

With a laugh, Sweyn added, "If it's any consolation, he's given me the least exciting, safest task."

At once, Sweyn recalled old Revna's prophecy: "*The man who should be king, would be king, but he would not wish to pay the price.*" Catching Njal's gaze, he added, "I think he just wants to protect us."

"I suppose I should be thankful he let me come at all," Njal concluded with a shake of his head. "Oh, come join us for a harmless diversion. We aren't wagering money on the dice, but whoever loses has to relate an embarrassing fact about himself."

Sweyn held up his hands and backed away. "Then I am definitely not playing," he laughed. "See you in the morning."

As he walked to his tent, an uncomfortable twinge crawled up his spine. Just what did that prophecy mean? Who would be king, and what would the price be?

SWEYN WORE his bright chainmail over his blue colors as he sat in his saddle watching and waiting to send his reserve troops into action. The sounds of battle ringing in his ears beckoned him to come join.

"Sweyn, maybe we should," urged Njal, who sat on his pony beside him.

"No." Sweyn cut him off with a slice of his hand. "A commander has a reason to hold warriors in reserve. If we disobey, seduced by the call of combat, we could ruin the plan and snatch defeat from the jaws of victory. We will do as we were told, and that's an order."

Njal glowered and tightened his hands on his reins.

Sweyn's group of twenty warriors—most of whom were old or youths lacking experience—were positioned between the edge of town and the king's citadel. Mainly, residents either crouched in their houses behind locked doors or fled to the seashore to distance themselves from the fighting; however, a few stayed behind to heckle the rebels, throwing rotten produce and manure at them. Sweyn ordered his squad to stand firm and ignore the insults, reminding them these were their countrymen, citizens they were sworn to protect.

He watched Bjarke's army batter at the tall gate, shielded by pinwheel-colored rönds forming a shell over them. They heaved and pounded with songs and battle shouts while arrows and rocks fell, sticking in or rolling off the shields. A cry cut through as a lone shaft found its way into a crack in the defense and struck a warrior.

The smell of smoke and the emergence of a black cloud informed Sweyn that Jarl Raknar's archers had caught something on fire. He didn't think this would take long.

Then, from the south side of the battlements, a horn sounded.

"Niklaus has pulled down a wall," he called out with excitement. "Hold your positions!"

The urge to gallop over and storm the compound with the others seized Sweyn as powerfully as it did his warriors. It required practiced discipline for him to remain firm. Fifty yards ahead of him, Jarl Bjarke yelled to his soldiers. They dropped the battering ram and dashed toward the gap in the perimeter. If anyone was going to try to escape, this gate is where they would most likely come. It faced the relative safety of the town and had just been abandoned by the attackers. Sweyn had a scout watching a back exit just in case, but, gauging from the origin of the smoke cloud, he suspected it was inaccessible.

"Steady now," he instructed them. "We are to capture, not slaughter, any who flee. Is that understood?"

A few of the young warriors responded, but most merely strained their necks to glimpse the fighting. Leaving horses behind, Niklaus's forces had poured inside and now Bjarke's followed them. Sweyn clenched and unclenched his fists, sweat beading at his hairline, as he listened to the music of battle coming from behind the barrier that blocked his view. Was his father all right? How strong was the resistance? Had any of his friends been slain? The unknown nibbled at his gut like a pack of rats threatening to shatter his nerves. Focusing on his training, Sweyn held them at bay with his will.

After a period that seemed like an eternity, the gate pushed open, and seven individuals concealed by cloaks and hoods rushed out. Sweyn spotted them at once. "Surround them and bar their escape," he commanded and led the charge.

Njal stayed at his side as his band encircled the small party. Sweyn slid from his saddle, and the others followed his lead. "Stop!" he demanded and drew his sword. "Who are you?"

Warriors under his authority raised shields and spears to form an impenetrable ring around the fugitives, who whirled about with uncoordinated movements, seeking an escape.

"Lower your hoods," Sweyn barked. "I shan't murder you."

With nowhere to go, the seven slowed their frantic movements. First a man, and then four women, lowered their hoods. The brown-haired man was neither old nor young, with fine clothing, a lack of musculature, and a flowing beard that may never have been trimmed. Sweyn recognized him as the king's gothi who had attended one of their meetings.

"You, gothi." He pointed the tip of his sword toward the quaking fellow, whose eyes displayed desperation. "Speak."

"I am Heimdall," he answered with timidity. "You know me. The king has fallen in combat and our troops are surrendering. Fearing a massacre, King Gustav charged me to flee with his household. These are his concubine and her servants," he explained, motioning to the women who clung to each other, encompassed in shrouds of fear. "I beg you, Sweyn Niklausson, to show mercy, as I know you are wise and just."

"You other two," Sweyn ordered. "Show yourselves."

Ivar ripped off his cloak and thrust it to the ground with a scowl, while Kerstav dragged the cloth away and lowered his head in shame.

"I desired to stay and fight, to die with honor like my father, but they dragged me away," he snapped. Ivar yanked out his sword and brandished it as he stepped away from the others. "I beg you, Sweyn, do not slaughter me like a hog with my hands bound behind my back. You are too honorable for that. Slay me with a weapon in my grip, so Odin will see and know I am not a coward."

Though his voice was robust, Sweyn spotted the quiver in his sword arm. "We are not here to execute you and your brother," he stated in an even tone. "But neither can we let you go to sow discontent and rally resisters to your side. The jarls decided to banish you. You and Kerstav are to be sent away to a foreign land together with your belongings and servants, so you may start a new life where no one knows you. However, should you return without invitation, you will be killed on sight."

"I can't accept that," Ivar countered and edged closer to Sweyn. "The humiliation is too great. First the incident with my brother, then my father's mistakes. I challenge you, Sweyn Niklausson, to a fair fight to the death in the presence of these witnesses. I beg you to spare me the shame of banishment!"

Though they were approximately the same size and age, Ivar was far less skilled than Sweyn, and he didn't want to kill him because of an impulsive challenge. None of this was Ivar's fault, and he didn't deserve to pay for his father's crimes. Likewise, he could not be allowed to remain and pose a threat to whomever the next king would be.

"You have seen me compete in the games." Sweyn stepped away from Njal and the circle of shields, assuming a preparatory stance as he locked eyes with Ivar. "You haven't seen me in actual combat. You won't win, and, even if you do, Njal will not release you."

"I know your reputation," Ivar admitted as he sidestepped into position. "And I also know those of the jarls. Bjarke is an oaf who couldn't think his way out of a fisherman's net, while Raknar is like a son of Loki, cunning and self-serving. Your father probably thinks there will be a vote, as was held when we were children, but think—would Raknar risk losing again? You need me as an ally."

"I'm under orders," Sweyn declared. "You can take it up with my father before he packs you onto a longboat."

"Then do your worst!" Ivar lunged at Sweyn, who batted his sword to the side, throwing his impetuous opponent off balance. Neither held shields as they clinked their blades together again. While training for the shield wall had taught Sweyn to bash, batter, and cover up with a rönd, Tyrdis had taught him finesse. His weapon had been forged from the finest steel, and Sweyn wasted no time demonstrating exactly what he could do with it. The difficulty was to disarm the banished prince without dealing him serious damage. The objective took five more strikes to accomplish.

Whipping around behind Ivar, whose sword lay in the dirt where the marketplace usually set up, Sweyn caught his right arm behind his back and brought his blade to the prince's throat. "Yield. I will not execute you."

Ivar slumped in his grasp and sighed in anguish. "Why couldn't you kill me during the duel?"

Sweyn nodded to Njal, who jogged over to collect Ivar's sword. No longer detecting sounds of battle coming from within, Sweyn concluded the fighting had ceased. Then he answered Ivar with confidence. "It is not your day to die."

Raising his voice, Sweyn instructed, "Come, all of you. Bring the prisoners into the compound, and let's see for ourselves what has transpired."

"You know I hate you for this," Ivar seethed between clenched teeth.

Sweyn tied his wrists with leather cords and poked the tip of his sword in his back to prod him forward. "You do today," he acknowledged. "One day, when you are content with a pretty wife and healthy children, you'll thank me."

"Never," he snarled and jerked his shoulders.

Surrounding the captives, all their hands bound to prevent unforeseen resistance, Sweyn and his team of reserve warriors marched through the rampart gates.

CHAPTER 32

*T*he copper scent of blood hung in the air, along with smoke, sweat, jubilance, and anguish. Bodies lay wounded or dead from everyone's camp. Sweyn called out to Edan when he saw him leaning against a silver birch, bleeding from a head wound. His instinct was to run to him, except he held Ivar at sword point.

"Edan, how badly are you injured?" He called, catching his friend's attention.

He turned a pained expression toward him. "I'll live."

"I'm healthy as a horse and strong as an ox, thank you very much for asking," announced Bjornolf as he strutted over to Sweyn and his crew. The victors were busy identifying and lining up the losers when, to Sweyn's relief, he spied his father shaking hands with Raknar amid the activity. Bjarke's bellowing laugh let him know the third jarl was also unscathed.

The corners of his mouth turned up at the sight and he replied, "Yes, Bjornolf. I never doubted such would be the case. I suspect you will be the sole survivor of Ragnarök. Now, who's seen Karvir?"

"Over here!" Sweyn spun to spot Karvir propping himself up with a spear, while a field healer's assistant bandaged his leg. "That little trouble-maker you're holding your blade on thought I needed a memento."

"See!" Ivar turned a scornful look at Sweyn. "I told you I am no coward."

In a tone filled with enough compassion to surprise Sweyn, he answered the ex-prince, "I never said you were one."

He took Ivar by the arm and led him toward the jarls, passing King Gustav's body along the way.

"You can't leave him to lie there!" Kerstav cried as he tugged against Njal's firm grip.

"Oh, let him rot," Bjarke allowed, then turned to bump chests with a grinning warrior whose axe dripped with blood.

"The boy's right," Niklaus said. He and Raknar veered around Bjarke to stand over the slain king.

"He put up a good fight, considering how out of shape he had let himself become," Raknar commended. "I'm sorry it was necessary."

Ivar stared down at where his father lay in a puddle of blood with a pale, stone face. Sweyn wondered if he would be welcome in Odin's Hall. He died in battle with a weapon in his hand, but he had not acted honorably in the time leading up to his death. What would that mean for his spirit? What really happened when someone left their body and traveled on? Were they truly judged according to their deeds, or did everyone end up in the same place, after all? Since no one ever returned from the lands of the dead, the Norse depended on the poems, tales, and traditions handed down to them from their forefathers, the lessons from the gods, and the foresight of seers.

"Olaf, Jenvaldr," Niklaus directed to nearby warriors. "Carry Gustav's body into the hall. We will allow his family to make preparations to bury him in the mound with the former kings before they leave. Gothi, you may perform a ritual for him this evening. Njal, Floki, and Gunnar, go with them and watch that young Kerstav and Ivar don't behave foolishly."

Hearing the name of Bjarke's first warrior made Sweyn think about Garold. When he glanced about at the warriors, celebrating or licking their wounds, he didn't see him anywhere. *Probably ran off and hasn't realized the fight is over yet.*

Ivar took one more opportunity to glare at Sweyn before he went with the others to see to his father's body.

"Too generous, I'd say," Bjarke complained. "Allowing him to be buried with the past kings? Really?"

"Let the dead bury the dead," Raknar replied. "We have a more pressing matter."

"Indeed," Niklaus agreed. "Sweyn, organize our warriors to build a pyre for the dead and to assist the injured. Now I wish we had brought Adelle, or at least Joren, along. I really didn't think he'd put up so bold a fight when he had no chance of victory."

"Aye, right away." Sweyn turned and began issuing orders. He took the task of seeing to the wounded upon himself, sending them all into the stable. Spotting a familiar face among the residents of Skeggen, who now curiously trickled into the king's estate, he charged him with finding the local grædari. "Your Gustav's guards require aid, the same as our warriors," he explained. "We are all countrymen here. There will be a new king, a fairer king, and no harm will come to you or your family. Now, bring the grædari at once."

With a tentative nod, the man wandered off. By the time Sweyn had all the wounded sitting or lying comfortably on the hay, the townsman returned with a clean-shaven man in a colorful embroidered tunic and a purple cap carrying an enormous bag of supplies.

"I'm Henrik," he said with a nervous bow to Sweyn.

"Are you dedicated to the goddess Eir and have taken the oath of a healer?" Sweyn towered over the slight man, who nodded and then glanced around at the injured. "Good. Tend their wounds. Treat my friend Edan first, and he will serve as your assistant."

"As you say, my lord." Then Henrik set about his work.

Satisfied he was no longer needed here, Sweyn left to find his father and the other jarls. What he discovered was immediately upsetting.

"That's not what we agreed to," Niklaus ardently insisted. His expression was as granite, his shoulders tense, and his fingers circled into fists.

"If that's what you want, Raknar, I'm game," Bjarke countered in an arrogant tone. "But I insist on witnesses."

"Niklaus, you are free to bow out, to give up your claim," Raknar said with superiority ringing in his words. "No one will hold it against you. I even vow you may keep your fylke."

"I'll not bow out," he snapped back. "I have as much right as you do."

The strained exchange plunged Sweyn into a sea of anxiety, and he quickened his pace to reach them. The three jarls stood about six feet apart right where he had left them, eyes shooting darts at each other.

Bjornolf stopped his march, planted his feet, and crossed his arms. "What's going on here? I thought we were celebrating our victory."

"Here's a witness," Raknar declared in derision. "Niklaus, order your son to stand down."

Niklaus glanced over his shoulder at Sweyn's approach. "What's wrong, Father?"

His father held up a hand. "Halt, son. You and Bjornolf keep the people back. I don't want any bystanders harmed."

"Bystanders?" Horik asked as he walked up and joined the discussion. "What's going to happen?" His manner became wary and his face hardened as he planted himself next to Sweyn.

Sweyn gritted his teeth as he tried to vanquish the monster determined to devour him. He had been warned, by both Tyrdis and Ivar, but he had thought Raknar would remain true to his word. This was a distressing and unexpected nightmare.

"They plan to contend for the crown," Sweyn uttered, half in disbelief.

Bjornolf dropped his arms and his jaw as his appearance reddened. "I'll round up our warriors."

"No, you won't!" Niklaus shouted. "We can't afford to deplete our numbers any further. Firdafylke still believes we are at war with them. Once he discovers Gustav's deception, King Tortryggr may invade with his entire army, supported by allies from Svithjod. If there is to be a contest, it must remain between the three of us."

"But, Raknar, you said," Sweyn began, his heart pounding vigorously in his heaving chest.

"I said we would decide which of us took up the crown later," he reminded them, "and that might entail a vote by the people. I swore an oath to be your ally until the king was deposed and no longer. Therefore, I have in no way broken my word."

Sweyn thought back over Raknar's choice of words and how he cleverly linked them together. While he made it appear he was agreeable to a vote by the Thing, he never pledged an oath to it.

"I say when, where, and what constitutes a win?" Bjarke bellowed, far too jovially. Sweyn's stomach felt sick, and his hand wrapped around the hilt of his sword.

"Be patient, men," Horik implored. "Haven't enough leaders died today?"

This couldn't be happening. Bjarke was younger than the others, brash, fearless, and abounding with muscles; however, he was by far the heaviest of the three, and no one credited him as a superior tactician. Raknar was older and slimmer but wily and ruthless. Sweyn gathered this three-way duel had been his proposition, as Bjarke couldn't spot a bright idea on a starless night.

That left his father. While still fit and practiced, he was the oldest of the jarls and the least likely to relish killing the others. Sweyn knew he possessed a strategic mind, but would his hand falter in the fray? Would he be an instant too slow?

"Here, now, to the death," Raknar pronounced. "Any objections?"

"I object!" Sweyn shouted. Blood raced through him like a raging fire. "Allow me to stand in my father's stead, or do you fear a superior warrior?"

"Pay no attention to the boy," Niklaus said. "I forbid any such foolishness. Sweyn, swear an oath on Thor's hammer you will not interfere."

Sweyn hesitated. He was young, agile, and powerful—perhaps not as powerful as Bjarke, but certainly smarter. Confidence soared in him at his chances of victory. "Father, I implore you, let me do this."

"The fight is not yours, son, but your father's," Raknar said. "We three claim the throne; you must wait in line."

"He's right, Sweyn," Niklaus echoed. "Give me your oath or leave this hallowed ground at once. You, too, Horik."

Though a war raged within him, Sweyn was left with no choice. He pulled his hair and squeezed his fists before dropping his chin, unable to look his father in the eyes. "I'll not interfere."

"Nor I," his uncle grumbled.

"That goes for everyone!" yelled Bjarke. "My warriors must kneel and vow an oath to not strike either of these men and to accept the outcome of our contest."

"Also for my fighters," Raknar seconded. "This is a field of honor, a duel between three equals. The gods are watching and will tolerate no deceitfulness."

Sweyn raised his gaze to witness the oaths from the growing crowd of spectators, his anxiety mounting exponentially. Glancing around, he still didn't see Garold, which worried him even more. Was Raknar using him to cheat in some way? Had he devised a trap Garold was to spring at the planned-upon moment?

"Where is Garold?" Sweyn demanded.

"I sent him home to inform my family of our victory," Raknar answered in an even tone. Sweyn didn't believe him, yet he possessed no knowledge to the contrary. It was just a gnawing in his gut that screamed something was very, very wrong.

"What are we waiting for?" Bjarke asked with his arms stretched wide toward the other two jarls.

He wore red beneath his scale armor, Raknar black, and Niklaus blue. The men looked as different as their personalities as they inched apart, spreading the width of their circle to about ten yards. Each man slowly drew their axes and knives, weapons they could throw at an opponent while leaving their swords sheathed.

Scenes of experiences shared with his father flashed through Sweyn's mind as the tension in the air thickened to an oppressive, hideous cloud of dread. His gaze flitted from Niklaus to Raknar to Bjarke. Each man's muscles tightened as they deliberately placed their feet, each assuming a secure stance from which he could strike at either foe. Expressions were grim, eyes darted, fingers twitched, and a breeze ruffled their hair. The crowd had become so breathlessly silent, all Sweyn could hear was the throbbing of the pulse in his ears.

The three jarls were assessing, calculating, anticipating, watching for a foot to shift, a gaze to set, a grip to tighten on a weapon handle. Niklaus clutched an axe in his right hand, a dagger in his left, as did Raknar, while Bjarke grasped two axes. The minutes were as an eternity, the pressure building like that in a white-domed mountain, the kind that shoots fire when it's had enough. Which one would make the first throw?

In a flash, both Niklaus and Raknar hurled their axes at Bjarke, burying their sharp blades in his chest. The stunned expression was forever etched on his face as he sank to his knees and fell over to the hard ground. Before he landed, Raknar and Niklaus had flung their short blades at each other, and both had evaded them.

With a determined jaw, Niklaus grabbed his hilt and whipped his sword from its scabbard. He and Raknar clashed blades from side-on stances, which offered less body for their foe to strike. As they dueled, each landed incidental slices that slid off armor or nicked the skin in superficial cuts. But the weapons were heavy, and Sweyn noticed his father wasn't holding his weapon as high as when they first began. He offered a silent prayer to Odin, yet the knots in his chest only squeezed tighter.

"Yield," Raknar advised. "Give me the throne and swear your allegiance. Don't let yourself end up like Bjarke."

"You yield, and I'll hold naught against you." A chop from Niklaus's steel emphasized his determination. "I have the same right as you to wear the crown."

Raknar executed a feint followed by a twirling advance from the opposite side, but Niklaus deflected his attack and spun to face him as he passed. To Sweyn's horror, both men drew back in preparation, then thrust their swords forward at the same time, their battle cries filling the air. Blood sprayed and groans fell from their lips. Sweyn couldn't breathe. He started to rush forward, but a broad hand on his shoulder held him back. A scornful glance revealed Bjornolf as the offender preventing him from rushing to his father's aid. With a grim visage, the adventurer shook his head at Sweyn; he was following Niklaus's command.

Whipping his attention back to the battle, Sweyn watched his father step back, pulling his sword from Raknar's chest. As he retreated, Raknar's blade slipped out of his abdomen, and he pressed his left hand to the bleeding wound.

Raknar stared at Niklaus in stunned disbelief before collapsing in an ineffectual heap at his father's feet. He took his final breath with his sword still clutched in his right hand.

Bjornolf released Sweyn's shoulder, and he ran to his father's side. "Let's get you to the healer," he said.

Niklaus sheathed his weapon and draped an arm around Sweyn's shoulders.

"Long live King Niklaus the Wise!" shouted Horik.

"King Niklaus," seconded Gunnar, Bjarke's first warrior, who knelt beside his fallen jarl. The affirmation was repeated by Raknar's first warrior and then by all present.

Niklaus waved to the crowd. "I accept the title and responsibility that goes with it," he declared in a powerful voice. "I vow to serve you in more ways than I will ask you to serve me."

"We will install Niklaus as king tonight after Gustav's funeral," Horik proclaimed.

"Now, let's please get this wound tended," Sweyn urged.

Niklaus nodded. "I'd laugh, but it would hurt too much."

Behind them lay the hopes, dreams, and bleeding bodies of two men who would be king and were too impatient to await a vote by the people. While Sweyn considered it a momentous waste, relief poured through him that his father had come out alive and on top. This was a cause for celebration indeed. He supported Niklaus as they walked to the stable, unable to wipe the ear-to-ear grin from his face. What a day it had been— one if he lived until the end of the age he'd never forget.

CHAPTER 33

Sæladalr, earlier that morning

$\mathcal{T}$yrdis lay on the sleeping bench assigned to her in Niklaus's great hall, vibrating like a harp strummed by Adelle's talented fingers. She had been sleeping blissfully on a cloud among the stars, reliving every divine sensation of being with the woman who had healed her—in more ways than one.

So, this is how it feels to be in love, she pondered in triumphant pleasure. *I don't want it to ever end.* It was exhilarating, fulfilling, and terrifying, driven along by eager anticipation, the curiosity of what would come next, and a deep desire to share all she had, all she was with Adelle. It was empowering, while leaving her weak in the knees, satisfying, yet she craved more. She felt as if she had been reborn, with new eyes and a fresh understanding of life. Not that her dedication to duty didn't matter, but Tyrdis realized life had more to offer and she wanted it all. She had always had a purpose to die for; now she had a reason to live.

The aroma of fresh bread baking somewhere enticed her to take deep breaths, which brought her body back to wakefulness. She should get up, dress for the day, make her rounds, and check in with all the relevant people —Adelle being the most relevant of all. An automatic smile had formed on her lips before her lids rose just thinking of her. Yes. Wash up, dress, and—.

The longhouse door burst open, and Helga, the young shieldmaiden

Tyrdis had been training, rushed in. "They're coming!" she yelled between frantic breaths. "We're under attack!"

Bolting up, Tyrdis pulled on trousers under her gray tunic. "Firdafylke?" she asked. "Can you tell if it's Jarl Stefnir's army?"

"No." Shock radiated from Helga's innocent face. "They're wearing Raumsdal colors."

"What?" Tyrdis shoved her sock-feet into boots. "Trygve, Grolier, wake up!" Returning her gaze to her lanky student, she asked, "Are you certain they are attacking? Maybe a portion of Niklaus's army has returned early."

"Then why would they set barns on fire and pull down fences?"

This was surreal. Something was wrong, and Tyrdis needed to get to the bottom of it. "Where are they?"

"Marching along the coastline from up the fjord. They must have beached their boats rather than invade our harbor," she reported.

Trygve, the other recruits, and the other warriors of the great hall gathered around half dressed. "What's happening?" Trygve asked with a yawn.

"Get up in the tower and sound the alarm bell," she snapped. "And I want the name of the man who's supposed to be on post up there. We're under attack."

With a crisp nod, Trygve lit out barefoot and without his trousers to skitter up the ladder and ring out the warning.

"Grolier, you and Ermundr finish dressing and secure the compound gate," Tyrdis ordered. "Let the people in, but once the hostile forces arrive, close and bar the entrance. Helga, get the archers in their nests and you join them. You are good with a bow."

They sped out to execute their instructions. "The rest of you, grab your weapons. Battle stations!"

Despite some lingering pain, Tyrdis pulled on her mail shirt and buckled her belt. Lynnea and the children poured into the hall with fearful expressions.

"What's happening?" Hallfrid asked.

"You all stay put," Tyrdis charged as she slid her axe and seax into their slots. "And get ready for an influx of townspeople. Someone is attacking us."

Lynnea hugged the young ones close. "Be careful. Tell Trygve—"

Tyrdis cut her off before she could finish. "Be proud, Lynnea. Today, Trygve becomes a man."

The bell was clanging urgently by the time Tyrdis snatched up a spear and sword and rushed out into the yard.

The day was overcast with a hint of moisture in the air. *Rain would be acceptable,* she thought. *It will help quench any fires.* Without wasting energy trying to figure out why warriors from Raumsdal would attack Sæladalr, Tyrdis stepped into her role of protector in chief, directing arriving townspeople where to go and ensuring her guards were all at their stations with their weapons at the ready.

Adelle, you better not ignore this warning signal. Heated ire jolted through her at the thought. She knew they had discussed this, but weren't her patients all better by now? The notion to send two soldiers up to the hospice to escort them here flew through her mind except she didn't have two to spare, and they wouldn't make it there and back before the attackers arrived.

While Trygve banged on the pipe, Tyrdis set her shield and spear aside and sped up the ladder into the tower to gain a better view. Marching up the beach was a squad of around twenty-five fighting men with blue and black shields, wearing their kingdom gambesons, and carrying iron-tipped spears. They strode with purpose, fishermen fleeing before them as they knocked over a yardhouse, tossed a torch onto a thatched roof, and caused general mayhem. Her features hardened, brows narrowed, and Tyrdis sensed rage rising from her gut. They were too far away for her to make out faces, so she still didn't know who the attackers were or why they were here.

Bruna dashed through the gate, holding tight to Svanhild's hand. "Inside the great hall," Tyrdis called down. "Trygve, keep ringing the alarm." With his nod of consent, she slid down the pole to land in front of Bruna and Svanhild.

"Tyrdis, what's happening?"

The fear and confusion on Svanhild's freckled face touched Tyrdis, and she longed to grab her up in her arms and shelter her until the danger had passed, only she couldn't. Emotions were no good to her now. Tyrdis must focus with her mind and her might to secure the safety of all.

She addressed them in a stiff, impersonal way, pointing at the enormous longhouse. "Go inside and do not come out until I say."

"Come on, honeybee." Bruna tugged her toward the jarl's hall. "Let Tyrdis do her job."

"But what about Mama?" Tears welled in the corners of her eyes and Tyrdis had to look away.

"She'll come if she can," Bruna assured her and Tyrdis before moving on.

"They're getting closer!" a scout positioned outside the gate called. "Hurry, people!"

Most residents must have understood this was not a drill, for even the complaining fisher and craftsman tore past her in nothing but their sleeping tunics.

"Should we close the gates now?" Grolier asked with a distressed look plastered on his oblong face.

Adelle wasn't there yet. Was she even coming? The jarl's compound lay between the invaders and the hospice. Tyrdis would have to stop them here. Despite the foes' numbers surpassing that of her guards, they would have the advantage of the stronghold … unless they simply started burning and looting the town and ignored the protective walls.

"The gates?" Ermundr repeated with a plea in his deep voice.

"Wait!" cried the scout standing on the path to town. "It's Adelle, Joren, and Bjarke's warriors. Hurry!" he yelled to them. "RUN!"

Tyrdis bolted through the opening. She first glanced toward the invasion force, then in the other direction to Adelle. "Now, now!" she urged, waving them on.

Joren broke into a sprint and was still passed by several of the recovering wounded. Adelle picked up her pace but refused to move faster than her slowest patient. Frustrated and anxious, Tyrdis whipped her head back to the hostile warriors. She blinked, and her jaw fell open at whom she beheld. With his golden hair brushing his burnished beard, Garold marched at the head of the band, a steely, determined stare in his shifty eyes.

Adelle and the man who quickly limped ahead of her arrived just in time. "Shut the gates!" Grolier and Ermundr shoved hard, and two more guards secured the timber bar in its place.

As much as Tyrdis wished to grab Adelle in a fierce hug, there was no time for that. The important thing was, she was safe.

"Set up the great hall to receive wounded," Tyrdis directed toward Adelle. "And thank you for coming this time."

"I knew this one was real," Adelle admitted, "because you aren't such an early riser. We'll be ready."

With a nod, Tyrdis returned to the task at hand—discovering what in Helheim Garold was doing here. She raced up a ladder to the small platform occupied by two archers to the right side of the gate and peered down at the menace, her hatred building toward him by the minute.

"What, in Odin's name, are your intentions, Garold? Why raid our town? Do you think Jarl Raknar will not find out?" Her grip on the pointed timber tops beneath her hands was tight enough to drive in splinters.

He peered up at her with a wicked gleam and replied, "Who do you think sent us?"

The revelation nearly knocked her senseless. "You lie!" she accused as she tried to process the new information.

"At this very moment, Jarl Raknar and the others are mounting an assault against Gustav, who refused to abdicate. What the others don't know is that Jarl Raknar will challenge them to a three-way duel, which he will win, laying both Bjarke and Niklaus in their graves. He promised if I could take this fylke from you, he would appoint me Jarl of Sæladalr. These will be my lands, and these peasants, my subjects."

"You will rot in Náströnd, in the land of darkness, where the dragon Nidhogg will suck your blood in unrelenting torment for all time," Tyrdis snarled.

Garold laughed. "I see how you hide behind your doomed jarl's walls. Come out with your ragged band and fight us, or we will slay every head of livestock, burn every home to the ground, take your ships, and carry off with what remains in your storehouses. Your people will then be without food or shelter and will have to come to me for subsistence or perish."

Tyrdis didn't answer immediately. Her brain was busy calculating the odds of their success versus the results of his threats. If she ordered her archers to fire now, they could knock out a third of his troops, only to do so while still negotiating the terms of combat would be dishonorable. Command was hard and took more than being the best fighter; it meant making tough choices.

"Oh, I forgot for a moment," Garold taunted with a smirk. "You're only a woman. What in all the nine worlds was that foolish Niklaus thinking? And you people believed he could be king?"

Suddenly, all of Garold's warriors were laughing, causing Tyrdis a flood of fury. She could feel she was not alone in the sentiment as the archers next to her glared at him.

"We can take them, Tyrdis," Trygve called. He must have overheard what Garold was spouting and would be fueled with blinding emotions over Raknar's plot against Niklaus.

"That cowardly trickster shouldn't be allowed to breathe!" shouted one of Bjarke's warriors. His jarl was in danger as well. With the aid of Bjarke's men who were well enough to fight, they may stand a chance.

"Don't let them destroy our whole town!" cried the discontented fisherman. "If I can handle a harpoon, I can certainly wield a spear."

"Let us defend our homes!" yelled another.

Tyrdis's icy glare bore down on Garold, all her muscles tense. She sensed the flow of energy that always washed over her before a battle—the tingling anticipation, the cloak of confidence, the unyielding resolve. There had been times in her past when fear figured into the mix—more a fear of an inferior performance than of death. Tyrdis had never had that much to live for before; now she did, except a desire to smite Garold from the face of the earth overpowered any chance fear may have of creeping up on her this day.

"As you wish," she bit off bitterly and descended the ladder.

Every fighting man and woman in the compound save Grolier lined up behind her. "Shield wall!" she commanded. Once the formation was in place, with Trygve pressed to her left shoulder, Tyrdis roared, "Open the gates." Grolier, a brawny man exhibiting considerable strength, lifted the barrier, tossed it aside, and pulled the gates inward. In a flash, he snatched up a spear and rönd and was enveloped by the group.

Across from them stood a mirror image of shields stacked against shields, spear points projecting through tiny gaps, all in the same colors. It felt wrong, so wrong, and yet this conflict was not of Tyrdis's making. Her heart hardened toward the jarl she had served for so many years. Sure, he wanted to be king, but this was beyond the pale. Promising that despicable Garold a jarldom if he crushed a small great hall guard? He would end here, and she would be the one to finish him.

CHAPTER 34

*T*yrdis's boots ground into the soil beneath her as she pushed with the shield strapped to her left arm. She was aware of Trygve, shorter and leaner than she was, at her side in naught but his tunic. She had sent him up the tower to sound the warning and he hadn't wasted the time to dress. Vowing to protect him at all costs, the shield-maiden pressed forward another inch. About half of her band were vigorous men familiar with fighting, while the other half consisted of her trainees and civilians. She recalled even they probably had experience, whether from fending off wild animals or raiders. Some Norse may choose not to take up weapons, but all were taught their use from childhood.

The rows of combatants grappled for inches at the line, jabbing, evading, forcing their weight and muscle against that of the other side. Tyrdis refused to give, continuing to make exploratory thrusts with her spear despite the pain it ignited in her right side. They didn't know if Niklaus was dead or alive and neither did the rat bastard Garold. Raknar's plan could have fallen apart for all they knew. Regardless of plots and duels, Tyrdis would prove her word true by protecting all those in Jarl Niklaus's longhouse. Adelle was in there and her mother. *Svanhild.*

Just thinking of the sweet girl with the honey hair and outlandish imagination caused her fortitude to swell. She couldn't love the child more if she had been born of her own body. Before, Tyrdis thought she had lost her family. Now she realized these were her family, and she would move the heavens and the earth to defend them.

Using her sturdy thighs as leverage, Tyrdis surged forward again, lunging with her spear. This time, it hit its mark. The hulking warrior across from her fell. Together with Ermundr on her right, they forced a crack in Garold's shield wall. In the blink of an eye, her entire squad had powered their way through the enemy ranks, splitting them in two. That's when the free-for-all broke out.

Tyrdis blocked her first foe's strike, spun around his weapon arm, and lodged her spear into the chest of the next. Snatching the axe from her belt, she pivoted to her first opponent, feigned high, drawing his shield up, then hacked a deep slice above his knees. Tyrdis didn't wish to waste time with these underlings. She wanted Garold.

She batted away a strike and cocked her right arm for the return when she realized she was eye to eye with Thorgil, the fellow warrior she had stayed to help when the Firdafylker impaled her from behind. They had shared weeks together in Adelle's hospice before he was released to return home.

"Why are you here?" she demanded, shock registering in her features. She held her blow, and he took a step back.

"Jarl Raknar ordered me to go with Garold. I didn't know he was planning to attack you," Thorgil affirmed.

"You would put your life on the line for him a second time?" Incredulity rang through her voice. Instinctively, she blocked an attack from her other side and dispatched the stranger with a whirl of her axe blade.

"I don't like it, but I fight where they tell me," he barked in an irritated, offended tone, raising his rönd against a blow. "Why didn't you return to us? You should be on our side."

Tyrdis waved her warrior off. "No," she snapped. "You should be with me. I cannot contend with you. I must stop this at once."

She spun and darted away, spotting Garold fighting Trygve. Fury surged through her veins as she charged him. With his shield facing Trygve, he drew his sword back and up for a return blow when his head snapped around to see her coming. He was too late, as she plowed into him, knocking him off his feet. Unfortunately, in her blind ambition to annihilate her enemy, Tyrdis tripped over him, and they both crashed to the ground.

Scrambling up, Tyrdis shook out her shoulders and loosened the tension in her arms. Garold was also back on his feet, repositioning his sword and rönd. "You are arrogant and impudent," he sneered. "I can't wait to put you in your place."

"I do not engage in idle conversations with dung beetles," Tyrdis spat with derision.

They circled and exchanged blows. Tyrdis was half surprised he hadn't run away; his ambition must have outweighed his cowardice. They danced, each striking the other with incidental cuts and inflicting bruises that one of them would feel the next day. It took Tyrdis a moment to calm her temper and gain her wits about herself. Hatred would not win this battle; only her unhampered training and skill could do that.

He kept poking at her right side, smashing his shield to her axe arm, because he knew she had sustained a serious injury to that side. She let him think it was weak. With a grimace of pain, she fell to a knee, throwing up her shield at his next blow. His sword split the wooden rönd asunder. She tossed aside the pieces and thrust her axe up just in time to block his next attack.

Tyrdis spied the look of glee in his eyes as she made herself appear frightened and weak. When he drew his sword back to set up his killing strike, she ripped the seax from her belt and, with the speed of a viper, sprang up, driving the blade into his ribs up to its hilt. While he stared at her—awestruck with horror—she pushed off of him, yanked out the knife, and sliced it across his throat.

Garold's shield clamored to the ground, followed by his sword and then his lifeless body.

"Garold is dead!" Trygve shouted. In his excitement, his voice skipped a register.

"Garold is dead!" Grolier bellowed, loud enough for all to hear. "Tyrdis has slain him. Throw down your weapons and live."

Tyrdis heaved in and out a breath, reestablished a ready stance, and glanced around the field of combat. Personal engagements slowed or stopped as the warriors and citizens looked and listened. Seeing Thorgil throw down his axe first, she smiled, feeling the triumph of the moment.

"You heard him," Thorgil shouted. "We've no reason to kill our countrymen."

"This conflict is ended." Tyrdis stood tall with her shoulders back and her head held high. "Let us lend each other a hand of comradery. We will carry our wounded into the great hall and share in a meal to celebrate the peace."

"Here, here!" cheered one of Bjarke's warriors as he clasped arms with Thorgil.

Satisfied the danger had passed, Tyrdis sent Helga and her farmer students to go put out fires and assess damages. Turning to Trygve, she instructed, "Will you go—wait." She took his arm and inspected it. "You have a deep cut that continues to bleed." Glancing down, she directed, "Look at your feet! You have been battling with no shoes, and they require immediate attention. I order you to Adelle to be repaired."

"But Tyrdis, we won!" he exclaimed, ignoring his wounds. "This is a time to celebrate. My first real battle. Did I perform satisfactorily?"

Tyrdis smirked at him and crossed her arms. Then she tsked with a stern expression. "If you had performed any better, I would not have needed to dispense with Garold. You held your own with excellence, young man. I will present your father with a favorable report—*if* you go straight to Adelle to be treated and bandaged. Then you may celebrate with your friends."

Beaming with delight, he answered, "I would hug you, except I'm afraid you would have me flogged. Thank you, Tyrdis. Not only are you an excellent teacher but a superior commander. I doubt Sweyn could have done a better job. Now, before I incur your wrath, I'll just go get bandaged up."

The young man started to trot away but had to slow to an aching trudge once he noticed the condition of his feet. Tyrdis smiled fondly at him and prayed his father and Sweyn were safe.

* * *

ADELLE AND JOREN were ready for the wounded to arrive with water heating over the fire, benches cleared, and bandage rolls laid out on the table. Lynnea and Bruna offered to help, as did several of the townspeople. When the battle noise began, the fear and tension levels inside rose. Adelle had not only been afraid for Tyrdis but also for her son, Runar. Sweyn had taken him to Skeggen to train with the king's guard so he would be far from the front lines, only the jarls had sailed to the capital to confront Gustav. From inside the longhouse, she couldn't hear any of the verbal exchanges, only incomprehensible shouts and clanks of iron and steel. How had things gone in Skeggen, and why was Garold attacking here? The illogic of it worried her the most.

Then the din of combat morphed into cheers of joy, and she gained a small sense of relief. Still, she was on edge wondering, and needing answers. The doors flew open, and wounded poured in.

"We won," announced a bright-faced youth bleeding from various lacerations. "Tyrdis killed their leader, and everyone stopped fighting. I got a few blows in first, though."

That means she must be all right! The news gave her nerves a reprieve, and Adelle relaxed, focusing on her work. Bearers laid one of Bjarke's warriors she had just nursed back to health on a bench with a mortal wound. He gripped his axe in both hands so tightly a whole troop would prove unable to pry it free.

"Our fathers, our mothers," he recited. "I set sail to the west to find my reward. See, even now, the Valkyries approach on winged horses to carry me home. I have fought the good fight."

She pressed fingers to his neck, detecting a weak pulse, and blood poured from his chest like a crimson river. He peered up at her with a victorious smile and a strange glow about him. "I will give Eir your regards," were the last words he uttered.

Two more guards and a farmer who joined the fight suffered serious injuries requiring immediate attention, but most would recover quickly and without lasting consequences. Leaving the farmer under her mother's care to get more supplies from the table, Adelle bumped into Trygve. "You're injured," she said.

The lad of fifteen grinned at her while pressing a rag to his arm. "Indeed." He lifted the cloth to show her his gash. "Do you think it will leave a scar?" His tone sounded much too eager.

Noticing he wasn't completely dressed, she glanced down at his feet. "Have a seat, Trygve, and don't be so impatient to collect scars. Wouldn't receiving fewer of them be evidence of superior skill? Hallfrid?" she called, peering around Trygve to spot the jarl's new servant. Svanhild had mentioned the new girl, who was older than both she and Solfrig. She appeared wearing a helpful expression.

"Yes, grædari?"

"Fetch a bucket of warm water large enough for Trygve's feet to fit in and pour in a scoop of salt."

"Ouch." Trygve pulled back with a fearful look. "Is that really necessary?"

"It is," Adelle promised. "Keep that rag on your arm and your feet in the bucket until I get to you."

He hemmed and hawed and poked out his lip. "All right," he groaned, glancing around for an unoccupied place to sit. "But you should have seen Tyrdis take that horse's arse down. She was astounding!"

"I'm sure. Now, sit." Adelle returned to the more seriously injured patients, supposing Tyrdis had indeed been amazing, and yet glad she hadn't been there to watch. It was hard to get used to the idea of being with a warrior, but Adelle was ready to make the leap. Tyrdis was worth it, not only because of what she meant to Svanhild, or Sweyn, or all the people she knew, not only because she was a woman of integrity and valor who stood up for what was right and never allowed her own desires to interfere with her duty, but also because of the way she made Adelle feel. When she was with Tyrdis, she wasn't just the town's healer or a servant of Eir; she could be at ease to reveal the woman under the title. She felt loved.

Adelle had known love and affection her whole life, unlike Tyrdis who had been deprived of such normal expressions. Yet, in the shieldmaiden's arms, they took on a whole new meaning.

Some wounded warriors spoke in whispers with solemn concern in their appearances, and she tuned her ears to overhear.

"Garold said Gustav was dead and Bjarke and Niklaus, too," a man she didn't know said.

"Garold is a liar," the other retorted in a hush. "He just wanted to seize this fylke."

The door opened, and a cheer arose. Shifting her attention to the front of the hall, Adelle spied Tyrdis entering with her unique bearing and grace. She held up a hand, her face a vision void of emotion. "We accomplished this together, as comrades in arms. Now, I implore you to make peace with Garold's warriors. They never wished to attack Sæladalr but were only doing as their jarl commanded. All who wish shall share a meal with them tonight while we wait for Jarl Niklaus to return."

"What is the word from Skeggen?" Lynnea dared to ask, her fingers twisted tightly in a spare bandage.

"Only hearsay," Tyrdis replied. "Any words you heard fall from the traitor Garold's lips could be lies. Now, everyone, as you were."

She walked a gauntlet of congratulations, pats on the back, and handshakes until Svanhild raced into her arms. Cracking her first smile, Tyrdis hoisted her up and hugged her to her shoulder, kissing her cheek.

"I knew you would win," Svanhild proclaimed with a grin.

Gazing over Svanhild's shoulder, Tyrdis locked eyes with Adelle, giving her heart a little leap. The silent exchange simmered with seduction, an unspoken proposition for a private audience later.

Adelle thought she would melt into a puddle right there as she beamed in return. Then Tyrdis set Svanhild down and took her by the hand.

"Are you prepared to entertain our guests with a story tonight?" she asked, weaving through the crowded hall.

"Can I?" Svanhild returned in amazement.

Tyrdis shrugged. "Ask Lady Lynnea. I'm certain she would appreciate your help."

Adelle laughed and shook her head. She detected the sound of her mother whispering in her ear. "Do you have another parent for Svanhild there, or have you acquired a third child?"

Shooting Bruna a sarcastic expression, she replied, "I'm not sure yet."

"At least I can now marry Karl without leaving you lacking for company," she quipped and walked off.

Taking a glance across the hall at Tyrdis standing with Svanhild and Lynnea, Adelle sighed to herself. *Gods help me, but I love that woman!*

CHAPTER 35

Skeggen, after the duel

Sweyn and his uncle Horik escorted Niklaus into the stable where the wounded were being treated. "Henrik!" he called out. "We need you over here."

They eased Niklaus onto an upturned trough while he pressed his hand to his left side. "I'll be all right," he hissed between clenched teeth, pain riding his features. "It's not my first wound in battle. Horik, go over to the king's hall and let Njal know what happened. Keep an eye on Ivar, too."

"If you're sure you don't need me to stay."

It pleasantly surprised Sweyn to detect genuine concern on his uncle's face and in his voice. "I'll stay with him," he said.

Horik nodded and left them with the other injured.

By then, Henrik had made it to them. "Let me see," he instructed.

When he noticed his father struggling with his armor, Sweyn pulled the leather and metal ringlet shielding over his head and laid it aside. Niklaus winced and raised the torn, padded gambeson he had worn underneath, revealing a deep puncture wound just to the left of his center mass.

"I've had a compress on it," he said and opened his hand, bearing the blood-soaked rag.

"This is a serious wound," Henrik noted with concern. "On that haystack," he pointed. "Lie down."

Sweyn made to help him, but Niklaus growled and shooed him away. "I can walk four steps," he huffed.

The wound reminded him of the one Tyrdis had been dealt by the spear. He couldn't see light pouring in from the other side and it wasn't as massive as hers had been, though it struck a little lower on his torso and the opposite side. Since his father had a wider girth, it made it difficult for Sweyn to predict what internal organs might be harmed.

The spear that tore through Tyrdis missed her liver and intestines, but were his vitals damaged?

Henrik mopped away blood and peered into the chasm. "Our first priority is to stop the bleeding. You must lie still and relax. I will treat it with yarrow powder and apply a fresh compress. Then you sip the tea and take calm breaths. Think pleasant thoughts to slow your heart pumping so hard. We can tell more when there isn't such an issue of blood."

"I'll make sure he follows your orders," Sweyn said and gave his father a stern expression. "Did you hear that?"

"Aye. I'm sure this healer is adequate, but I wish I was under Adelle's care. I know I can trust her, and she's gifted."

"I'll send for her," Sweyn suggested. "That will be faster than waiting for you to be healed enough to sail home. We need to send for the whole family unless you wish to travel back and get them yourself when you're better."

Sweyn noticed how pale the exsanguination made Niklaus's face and he didn't like it. Henrik returned to treat the bleeding with yarrow and applied the clean rags. He handed Niklaus a cup. "Drink this."

As he glanced around the stables with all the injured soldiers from four different units, he caught sight of a familiar face. "Runar, is that you?"

Sweyn approached a young warrior who was propped against a pile of hay with a cut across his forehead and a compress on his elevated leg. The fellow glanced at him, and an aspect of recognition brightened his countenance. "Sweyn."

"Looks like you saw some action today," Sweyn commented. "Does it hurt much?"

"No," Runar replied with tough pride. "I'm all right."

"Your mother will be very glad to hear that."

The young man's self-regard deflated, and he turned away. "I don't want her to know."

"What?" Sweyn asked in a friendly manner. "That you got a couple of cuts?"

"That I fought against you all," he confessed in shame. "But I had to. The king ordered everyone to stand and fight. He really lost his senses toward the end before he got skewered. He was shouting nonsensical things and swinging his sword at shadows. It was sad. But she'll be glad to know I didn't kill anyone."

"Then you fulfilled your oath to the king and to my father," Sweyn acknowledged, causing Runar to glance up at him with a hopeful expression. "You fought for Gustav like you had to, but you didn't kill any of your countrymen."

"That's right." He appeared struck by the realization for the first time. "I'm not a traitor. I'm not a bad guy." A slow curve inched across his lips.

Sweyn laid a hand on his shoulder with assurance. "No, Runar, you're not a bad fellow at all." He could see Adelle in him—his hair, the shape of his face, his desire to do good—while his blue eyes and broad shoulders favored his father. While on the lean side still, he must have grown two inches since the last time Sweyn had seen him. Runar was at that age and was too young to have been pressed into combat.

"You'd better learn to brush your hair and wash your hands, though, because I think your mother will be coming here tomorrow."

With a slightly terrified expression, Runar sat up straight. "Coming here?"

Sweyn laughed. "She'll be overjoyed to see you." Leaving Runar, Sweyn returned to see if his father had arrived at a decision.

Having finished his tea, Niklaus consented. "Go ahead and send Njal with one longboat and a minimal crew. Tell him to bring back Adelle, Lynnea, and your brothers and sister. But I don't wish to wait for the swearing-in ceremony to become king. The situation is too volatile. I need to assume authority now. We'll hold funerals for Gustav, Bjarke, and Raknar, then get the crown, the king's sword, and ..."

He paused to catch his breath, clearly experiencing excruciating pain.

"That's enough talking for now. Rest. I'll send them on their way, and Adelle should be here by this time tomorrow," Sweyn said.

When he closed his eyes, Henrik came back and put pressure on his bleeding side. "This is ready to be stitched closed. Now skitter off somewhere and let him rest," he instructed. "I'll not allow the future king to die under my watch. Do you think I wish to be devoured by worms for eternity?"

* * *

Sæladalr in the middle of the night

TYRDIS LAY on her bench in Niklaus's great hall with her arms wrapped around Adelle while everyone else slept. There had been no opportunity for privacy—not that there ever was much in a jarl's hall or a small town where everyone assumed their neighbor's business to be their own. Still, just holding her, cradling her in her protective arms, felt wonderful to Tyrdis.

Bruna and Svanhild slept in the spot at their heads with their feet pointing toward the door. Karl had to return to reopen the mead hall, as many citizens preferred to do their celebrating with friends instead of strangers.

While thoughts spun aimlessly through her brain, Tyrdis was aware of Adelle's slow, steady breathing as she snuggled behind her and took comfort in her nearness. In the past, she never understood why couples would press their bodies together and stay that way for hours. She had thought it would be hot and sticky and serve no purpose. Now, as she synched the rhythm of her breath to Adelle's, touching her at almost every point, Tyrdis enjoyed an inexplicable connection that made her feel happy.

Happy is good, she mused, still too restless from the day's events to drift off. *I've known several notable warriors who laughed, smiled, and engaged in amorous relationships. Their fighting skills were not diminished by being happy. I can experience delirious delight and remain competent in my duties. I think maybe that's how it's supposed to be.*

As Tyrdis lay pondering her feelings and her future, the door to the hall flew open, and Njal and an escort of four warriors burst inside. "What happened?" he questioned in a thunderous voice.

Tyrdis lifted her head, and people in the chamber began to stir.

Rushing into the midst of the hall, Njal continued to babble anxiously. "It looks like a battle happened here. There were some burned-out build-ings, those pyres. Where are Mother and my brothers and sister?" Light streamed in through the open doorway, for the midnight sun had arrived in its fullness.

"All is well, Njal," Tyrdis replied, awakening Adelle as she sat up. "Garold attacked us, spreading disturbing news. What happened in Skeggen? How fare Jarl Niklaus and Sweyn?"

"Garold?" The young man halted and fixed her with a confused frown. Then he shook his head. "We defeated Gustav, but then Jarls Bjarke and Raknar insisted on fighting a three-way duel—right then and there—for the crown. Can you believe it?"

She could, actually. In fact, it was predictable, as she had warned Sweyn. "Who—" a warrior in the hall started, then held his tongue.

"Father won but is badly injured. He sent me to fetch the family and Adelle," Njal explained, turning his troubled gaze to the woman who leaned against Tyrdis.

Adelle pushed back her hair and dropped her feet onto the floor. "Let me get my medicines, and I'll be ready to go. What news of my son, Runar?"

"I saw him up and around after the battle," Njal confirmed.

Relief swept through Tyrdis on Adelle's account. She hadn't met Runar, but she cared about him all the same.

"Njal, what happened?" Lynnea, wrapped in a woolen night robe, entered with sleepy Braggi and Solfrig on her heels.

"Father was crowned king tonight," Njal answered excitedly. He greeted them with hugs. "At least that was the plan. I had to leave to come get you and Adelle."

While Njal relayed the story to his mother, Adelle pulled on her shoes and overdress. "All this upheaval," she muttered. "Gustav defeated might as well mean Gustav's dead. And Bjarke and Raknar? And how many others? Probably dozens of warriors over what? Who gets to be the sorry guy who's burdened with the responsibility of running the kingdom?"

"Shhh," Tyrdis cautioned. "Some of Bjarke's warriors occupy the hall. We should not voice assumptions. I do not like this strife any more than you, but I do judge Jarl Niklaus is more fit to rule than the others. I still can't understand why Raknar would send Garold to attack us."

"Hearing this news, I do now," Adelle confirmed and headed toward the exit.

Tyrdis followed, having slipped on trousers and boots with her tunic. "Here, I shall accompany you and help you carry your supplies back." She followed Adelle outside to a landscape cast in a pale, golden hue, and the smell of smoke from smoldering pyres hanging in the air. No one else in the town stirred. "Why is that?"

"Because." Adelle's tone was sharp and irritated as she strode along the path, setting a brisk pace for Tyrdis to keep up with. "If he was planning to challenge the other jarls rather than wait on a vote, he would wish to crush any opposition from their home fylkes. Their warriors in Skeggen would be sworn to honor the outcome of the duel but he knew some must remain behind, and he needed to crush any opposition. Raknar might have thought you would join ranks with Garold if you were well enough to fight. He assumed he would win or had a plan to ensure victory but something went wrong, and Niklaus defeated him—which must mean he killed him because I don't see Raknar yielding."

"Neither do I."

Adelle shot her a concerned glance. "How does that make you feel?"

Tyrdis shrugged. "Normally, I would respond with, 'My feelings are irrelevant.' However, you believe I should acknowledge them. I have known Raknar my whole life and Niklaus not so long. But I consider Sweyn a close friend and have gotten to know Trygve now. They are worthy young men. I can be sad Raknar chose this path and is no longer with us and also be glad Niklaus prevailed. Therefore, I process the news with conflicting sentiments."

"Quite understandable. Now, was it so difficult to express how you feel about something? Do you see that how events affect you is relevant?"

Tyrdis opened the hospice door and motioned for Adelle to enter first. "Perhaps. But whether I accept events with joy, anger, or sorrow, it will not change the outcome. What occurred will remain unaltered despite how I feel. Therefore, in truth, my feelings are irrelevant."

Adelle stopped her hurried march, turned to Tyrdis, and draped her arms around her neck, gazing at her with ardent honesty. "They matter to me." Her lips pressed tenderly to Tyrdis's, and she returned the kiss with pure affection.

"You matter to me, Adelle. I want to travel with you and Jarl Niklaus's family to Skeggen to ensure your safety." Tyrdis peered into her eyes with bittersweet hesitation.

"But you have to stay here to oversee the well-being of the fylke until you are officially relieved of that duty." Adelle slid out of her arms to gather herbs, salves, bandages, and other necessities into a basket.

Tyrdis's heart sank. Adelle knew her so well. For the first time she could remember, the shieldmaiden felt torn between her duty and her own desires. Would it be like this from now on?

"And you still want me?" asked Tyrdis tentatively. "You wish me to be here waiting for you when you return?"

Adelle dropped the honey jar into her basket and glanced up at Tyrdis with a questioning look. "Certainly I do. Do you wish to wait for me?"

"On my oath."

"I must go, and you must stay—this time," Adelle qualified with a coy smile. "Sometimes you will leave me behind for a short while. We both have responsibilities and obligations to perform, Tyrdis. They don't mean I'll stop loving you."

Tyrdis's breath caught, and her heart pounded against her chest. For a moment, she worried she might pass out right there. Words she had hoped for, words she had never heard, save from her mother's lips so long ago, touched her ears like a fairy's wings, engulfing her in brilliant delight.

"You … you love me?" She reached out and pressed her hand to a support post to ensure she didn't fall.

Adelle beamed at her, tossed a few small pouches tied with colored cords into her tote, and crossed to her. "I love you, Tyrdis. And you have a home with Svanhild and me if you want it."

Enraptured beyond her wildest imaginings, Tyrdis enveloped Adelle in her arms—basket and all. "I love you so much that at times, I think I will burst. I did not comprehend such emotions were even possible until I met you. My only question is, will you stay here or move to Skeggen with Jarl Niklaus? It doesn't matter," she answered her own question and brushed kisses across Adelle's face. "Wherever you go, I will go. Whomever you serve, I will serve. And Svanhild will never lack for any good thing. I will guard her with my life while you're gone, and Bruna too."

Adelle captured her mouth in a searing kiss of affirmation. "Let's see where we'll be most needed. I can follow you to an assignment too, you know. After Niklaus hears of your triumph over Garold, he may wish to appoint you to an important post. Now, I must make haste. Njal said his injury was severe."

"Yes, assuredly." Tyrdis, steadier on her feet now with emotions still soaring, stepped back and ushered Adelle out. "We don't want to keep the new king waiting."

CHAPTER 36

Skeggen, the day after the battle

Sweyn fell asleep in the king's chamber on a cot near his father's bedside. Henrik, the healer, had been in and out several times to check on him, making peaceful slumber impossible. After everything that had happened, Sweyn didn't think he'd sleep at all.

After Njal left, he and his uncle Horik observed the funerals for Gustav, Raknar, and Bjarke. Then Heimdall, Skeggen's gothi, pronounced Niklaus king and performed a sacrifice to secure the gods' blessings. His father had bound extra bandages around his midsection and borrowed a clean tunic from Gustav's household to have something to wear. Sweyn had helped him wash up and stood beside him, but Niklaus had forbidden any assistance.

"Wounded or not, I will stand on my own two feet to accept the crown," he had declared. And, naturally, he had to give a speech, howbeit a brief one. Sweyn had been on the edge of a knife, praying his father didn't stumble or faint. Thankfully, he got through it, recognized everyone for their service, and named men of station and integrity as replacements for the slain jarls. He gave his fylke to Horik and dared him to become a capable leader. For the other two fylkes, Niklaus had resisted the common practice of appointing his friends and chose Bjarke's first warrior and one of Raknar's advisors on the condition they swear oaths of loyalty to him. Sweyn understood this was to preserve unity in the kingdom and considered it wise; he'd still be keeping a close eye on those two.

Afterward, he walked beside his father until they cleared the crowded great hall into private quarters. Then Niklaus leaned heavily on him and admitted his discomfort.

"Help me to bed, son, and get more of the tea that's supposed to relieve pain. I feel sick in addition to being stuck like a pig."

Sweyn did so, but, when he returned with Henrik and the tea, his father had fallen asleep. Henrik left the tea and said rest was what he needed, not to worry; Sweyn worried anyway.

He awoke to the sounds of an argument in the hall, accompanied by what sounded like furniture smashing. *I'd better go out there before someone gets hurt.* Who knew what time it was? During mid-summer and mid-winter, it was near impossible to know if it was time to wake up or go to sleep, but he deduced he'd slept later than whoever was causing the commotion.

Strapping on his sword belt, he strode out in an irritated mood. "What's all this?" he demanded. "Stop it at once!"

One of Bjarke's warriors punched one of Raknar's who then pulled a knife. "Take it back!" the seasoned soldier with wild red hair demanded.

The brawnier combatant's brown tresses whirled around his furious broad face as he ducked and spun, missing the swipe of the other man's blade.

"I said stop!" Sweyn seized Raknar's follower's knife arm and twisted it behind his back, forcing the handle from his fingers. It fell with an innocuous clatter to the plank floor.

Everyone in the hall was awake by then, and the two men Niklaus had appointed as jarls rushed forward to reprimand their warriors.

"You forget yourself," Bjarke's former first warrior barked at the bigger fellow.

"This is not the time or place for violent arguments," scolded the new jarl of Heilagrfjord to the angry ginger-haired warrior who squirmed in Sweyn's grasp.

"That *fifl* accused me of being a lying traitor like Raknar."

"Because you are!" thundered the other man. When he lunged, the new jarl of Austrihóll arrested him in a forceful grip.

"Cease this pointless name-calling!" he commanded.

Sweyn released the red-haired soldier to his new jarl's authority and stepped between the angry men, pinning each with his intrepid gaze one after the other. "I understand this is a tense situation."

"Brought about by Jarl Raknar's ambition!"

Sweyn slapped a hand on the dark-haired fellow's shoulder and stared him down. "What's done is done. My father lies wounded by Raknar's hand, yet I would not blame this man," he said, pointing at his opponent, "or you or anyone else. I don't even blame Raknar. He wanted to be king, and he sought to win the title in a fair fight. We Norsemen are no strangers to the spear, sword, or axe. See how you contend with him? Let us put blame behind us now. Only united can we prosper. King Niklaus the Wise will lead us to much success. Next summer's raids will bring chests of silver, and our harvests will overflow our granaries, but only if we unite behind him. Listen to your new jarls," he stressed. "This is not the time or place to lash out because of potent emotions. Change is hard, but change is inevitable. Give our new leaders a chance."

When the man's tension eased, Sweyn turned to the one he had disarmed. "The same goes for you. You have conflict within you over Raknar's actions and the fact we buried him last night. You want to defend him but are also angry with him for putting you in this position. Let it go. It is foolish to kill or be killed over an argument that is but a spark of powder, over in a flash."

Relaxing his shoulders, Raknar's former warrior nodded and lowered his chin. Sweyn exchanged knowing glances with the two new jarls before taking a step back. "And by the way," he added lightly. "If you two decide you must kill each other for no good reason, do it far from my father's new hall."

Sweyn took this opportunity to visit the yardhouse. When he returned, hunger twisted in his belly, yet was greeted by neither the aromas of food cooking nor bread baking. Ivar sat across the room with his brother under Edan's and Karvir's watch. Sweyn joined them. "I know this is difficult for everyone. Did you sleep?" He didn't add the "well" part because he understood such would be impossible.

"A little," Kerstav muttered.

"Where are your servants? Why is no one preparing food?" Sweyn asked.

Ivar shrugged. "Our thralls don't work for you."

"Yeah," Kerstav added with a scowl. "Get your own."

Sweyn sighed and nodded. "I just thought the two of you might wish some traveling rations for your voyage, but I'm sure you can manage without. So, who will accompany you to Gotland?"

"You're sending us *there*?" Ivar leaped up, balling his hands into fists.

"It is a civilized place," Sweyn replied. "A fine land for new beginnings."

"But it's so far away," Kerstav complained.

"Which I believe is the point." Sweyn studied the brothers with a mixture of compassion and distrust. "Your ship will be ready to depart at noon. Suit yourself about the food."

Leaving the sound of their complaints behind, Sweyn returned to check on his father. He didn't like the way he looked, neither the pallor of his face nor the heat radiating from it. Sweyn laid his palm on Niklaus's forehead, then said with alarm, "You have a fever."

Henrik stepped in behind him, carrying ingredients to change his poultice. "That often happens with wounds. I have herbs to calm the fever, and Heimdall included prayers for his recovery when he performed the blót last night."

The grædari's words did not ease Sweyn's anxiety. He sat on the side of the bed and took his father's hand. "Adelle and our family are on their way, Father. Someone needs to go to Firdafylke under a banner of truce and negotiate a peace. We must tell them what has happened here and that we are no longer at war."

Niklaus gave his hand a squeeze. "You should go," he directed and pried open his eyelids. "You said your friend, Karyna, is jarl of Oskholm now?" He nodded and swallowed, understanding the trip would take two days, both ways. He didn't want to leave his father, yet he longed to tell Karyna the war was over. Would she forgive him? "She will trust you and arrange a peace treaty with King Tortryggr."

"I'll depart once Adelle and Mother arrive and I have sent Gustav's sons on their way," Sweyn promised. "But who will speak for you? Who will ensure your safety?"

"I will."

Sweyn glanced over his shoulder to where his uncle leaned in the doorway, munching on an apple. "And my first order of business will be to secure a cook."

A chuckle spilled from Sweyn's mouth. "Then get to it. I'm starved!"

With a familiar grin and nonchalance Sweyn expected from his uncle, Horik disappeared back into the main hall.

"I'll be all right." Niklaus tried to sound convincing, but his normally robust voice was weak, and he seemed so small confined to the enormous bed. "Select a crew to take Ivar and Kerstav to Gotland. You need an experienced navigator, some strong backs for rowing, and a trustworthy commander who will not take a bribe from the boys."

"Bjornolf has sailed everywhere," Sweyn suggested, "and no one is more trustworthy than Karvir. Edan can go with me. If Adelle arrives in time, it would be expedient for the longboat to drop us off at Sæladalr, and we can ride from there to Oskholm."

Niklaus nodded in satisfaction while his heavy lids slid shut. "Karyna is a formidable woman," he commented. "It is rare for a woman to gain power, whether through might or diplomacy. Take her a gift, something special, something ..." And he drifted back to sleep.

"Make your preparations and let him rest," advised Henrik.

Sweyn nodded and left the bedchamber, feeling a weight on his shoulders. He could easily arrange travel for Ivar and his brother but choosing the right gift to make peace with Karyna seemed like an insurmountable task.

* * *

ADELLE WAS tired and anxious when she entered the king's chambers in Skeggen along with Lynnea and the children. She hadn't been rowing, but choppy seas battered by an unrelenting west wind had made getting any rest impossible. Besides, she didn't know what Niklaus's condition would be.

"Sweetheart," Lynnea crooned as she gently settled onto the bed beside her husband.

"How do you feel, Father?" Njal asked.

"Are you really king?" Braggi's voice was bright and excited.

"We missed you," added little Solfrig as she climbed into bed beside her parents.

Then Trygve boasted, "Tyrdis said I performed satisfactorily in combat. I might even have a scar. See?" He pointed to the cut.

Hallfrid stood with two adult maidservants against the wall, all wearing expressions of concern.

Niklaus smiled, cheered by the loving attention of his family. "I am so glad to have you all here. Sorry I couldn't hold off on the ceremony. It was too risky with all the factions hot from battle and stunned by the turn of events. Raumsdal needed a king. But you are here now."

Though he smiled, Adelle could spot the underlying grimace of agony and itched to inspect his wound. "Has Henrik been treating you well?" she inquired.

Niklaus nodded. "I got stabbed with a sword, so it hurts, but Henrik hasn't tried to do me in."

"Where?" Adelle asked. "I don't wish to cut the reunion short, but I need to see it."

He motioned for her to approach, and Lynnea moved the children away from the bed to give her space. Adelle pulled down the covers to see bandages wrapped around his bare belly. "I need to remove your bandages," she said and Niklaus pushed himself up to a sitting position. This time, the grimace erupted over his face, but he refrained from groaning. She gently unwound the strips of cloth to reveal an angry, red, oozing puncture closed by four stitches under the compress of salve and healing leaves.

"Thank you. You may lie back down now." Noting the location of the injury, she leaned down and sniffed. *Inconclusive.* "Is there any onion or leek soup?" she asked. "Something with a potent aroma?"

"I can make some," Hallfrid offered.

"And take this." Adelle held out a small pouch to a maidservant. "Brew a tea of it for him, please."

The woman and girl left, and Lynnea gathered the younger children. "Let's go take a tour of our new longhouse while Adelle checks on Papa's injury."

"But I want to stay," Solfrig pleaded.

Lynnea took her by the hand and sent a worried glance at Niklaus. "We'll come back later."

She ushered them out, followed by the other maidservant, while Njal and Trygve stayed to keep vigil.

Heat from Niklaus's body radiated through Adelle's hands as she touched him. The fever was not a good sign. Still, it could be conquered as long as his bowels weren't compromised. *It's been two days,* she considered. *If Henrik stitched the skin closed with bile leaking inside his body, it could be too late.* A patient could recover from a gut wound more readily than one to the neck, head, or chest—only if the viscera remained intact.

Adelle prepared cool, moist rags in the absence of ice or snow and laid them on his face, head, neck, and chest. Presently, Hallfrid returned with the tea, and Adelle insisted he drink it all. She paced, waiting on the soup, while he slept. She didn't want to rip out his stitches and attempt surgery if it wasn't necessary. Trying to maintain a hopeful attitude despite bleak circumstances was a struggle, and Adelle turned to prayer.

Eir, Niklaus is a good man and will make a fine king. Why steer him through all this to gain the crown, only to take his life now? Guide my hands. Stream your healing touch through them so that he might live.

At last, the servant returned with steaming leek soup. Adelle took the bowl and lifted the spoon to Niklaus's lips. "Here. You must drink this," she instructed.

Offering no resistance, he opened his mouth and let her pour it in. She had half the bowl in him when a feeble hand reached up and took her arm. "Enough. I don't feel well."

Adelle set the remainder aside, leaned in, and sniffed the puncture site. The pungent odor of the soup permeated his gut so powerfully it hit her with the unavoidable truth—there was nothing anyone could do to save his life. He hadn't suffered a nick of the intestines, causing slow seepage; for the smell to be so pervasive, it must have been sliced in two. Poisonous bile had been pouring into his gut for two days. No wonder he suffered a raging fever, excruciating pain, and felt sick to his stomach. And Henrik had stitched it closed rather than suction the seepage and try to repair the bowel.

Fury flashed through her for an instant. Was the man secretly trying to kill the new king? Was he enacting retribution for the rebellion against Gustav? If so, Henrik had broken his vow as a healer and would incur Eir's wrath. With a stiff jaw, she swallowed her ire and took a calming breath. Even if she had been here and performed her most skilled surgery, it was doubtful he would have lived. This type of gut wound was always fatal. No matter what Henrik may have tried, Niklaus would have only had a few days of agony to live.

"Well?" Trygve questioned. "What is your prognosis?"

"Can I begin preparations for a feast?" Njal suggested with cheer in his tone. "We'll wait a week or two for Father to gain his strength back."

Niklaus must have discerned the reality from Adelle's expression. "Come here, sons," he instructed with solemn acceptance in his voice. Trygve and Njal joined him on the opposite side of the bed, sending Adelle nervous glances. Then he nodded to her.

Adelle sucked in a breath and spoke with exceeding sorrow in her heart. "His bowels were sliced by Raknar's sword. I'm sure Henrik did everything he knew how, but even if I had been here …"

"Can't you fix it?" There was a frantic cry in Trygve's request, and his youthful face twisted in mortified despair.

"No, son," Niklaus replied, moving a hand to his teenager's shoulder. "There's nothing she can do. I suspected as much, which is the true reason I insisted on pushing forward with being installed as king without you. One doesn't die immediately from a gut wound; however, they seldom recover. It would seem I wasn't meant to be king after all. Now Trygve, go find your Uncle Horik and bring him here at once. I'll tell your mother shortly."

The lad mopped at his cheeks, nodded, and rushed to obey his father's wishes. Then Niklaus pinned Njal with a serious gaze. "This is the day you truly become a man. You have known a woman's company and fought courageously by my side, but now you must put old rivalries and youthful foolery behind you and swear allegiance to your brother Sweyn. I can't go to our ancestors worrying you will be like Ivar and contend with him—or worse—betray his trust."

"Father, I have always known Sweyn would be jarl one day instead of me," he answered candidly. "Our conflicts are simply those common to all brothers, and he has never given me cause for resentment or bitterness. I only ever wanted to be taken seriously and to make you proud."

"I am very proud of you, Njal, my son," Niklaus declared. He squeezed his eyes shut for an instant as a jolt of pain twisted his features. He gripped his oozing wound and Adelle tried to soothe him with fresh, damp cloths. "Serve Sweyn with honor. A leader is only as effective as those upon whom he depends."

"Yes, Papa." He reached over and gripped Niklaus's other hand in his. "I swear it."

Trygve bounded back in with Horik, whose face was clouded with the gravest expression Adelle had ever seen on it.

"Niklaus," Horik uttered, as if at a loss for words. Adelle stepped aside to make room for him.

"Brother." Niklaus opened his eyes and tried to force a smile. "Are you content with jarl? You aren't going to stab me too, are you?"

"You offend me," Horik uttered. He took on the appearance of a child being reprimanded for a foolish prank. "I'm doubtful I can carry out the responsibilities of a jarl, let alone those of a king."

"I need you to swear a blood oath on Odin's head to be loyal to Sweyn and support him faithfully as King of Raumsdal." Authority radiated from Niklaus's gaze as he fixed it on Horik.

"Adelle will quell your fever and you'll pull through," Horik stated as he lowered himself to the open side of his brother's bed.

Niklaus rocked his head from side to side. "I haven't much time. Will you swear the oath?"

"Niklaus, do you think so little of me?" The hurt was apparent in Horik's voice and the slump of his shoulders. "Can you still not trust me, after all this time?"

"It isn't my opinion nor my faith in you," Niklaus replied. "For the sake of the kingdom, you must fulfill your oath. Power tempts. It seduces, corrupts, and destroys. We've seen that up close. Even when I took the crown, I suspected the poison at work in my body, but it was imperative to secure Sweyn's position. You know I am right."

Horik inhaled deeply and released a sigh. With a nod, he pulled out his knife and carved cuts on his palm and Niklaus's. Then he clasped hands with his brother, forcing their blood to mingle. "I do hearby swear on the Allfather's head to be faithful and loyal to my brother, Niklaus, and my nephew, Sweyn. Never will I conspire for the throne nor seek evil against my kin." Releasing his hand, Horik's expression took on one of misery, and a tear glistened in his eye.

"I know we butt heads, don't see eye to eye," Horik admitted. "We are dissimilar men who find pleasure in different pools. But you should never worry about me coveting rulership. I'll take the responsibility of the fylke because it's thrust upon me but, believe my words. I will remain loyal to Sweyn not because he's kin or because you forced me to take a vow or because I fear Odin's wrath and the punishment of an oath-breaker. I'm no fool. In my heart, I know he's a better man than me … and so are you."

"Thank you, Horik," Niklaus said with a wistful smile. "Now I can rest. I love you, you know, always have. You're my brother, and today I need you most of all. I'll not hang on until Sweyn returns from Raumsdal. I trust you with his crown."

Adelle's heart ached. She wished there was something she could do more than merely keep him as comfortable as possible. The gods could still come through unless it was indeed his time to die.

Sensing a presence at the door, Adelle glanced up to see Lynnea return with Hallfrid and her younger children. She perceived the recognition in her eyes, the burden of grief as it struck, and the tears as they shimmered. Horik moved, offering her his spot beside Niklaus as he shook his head and glanced away.

"Here, sweetheart," Niklaus beckoned with as much cheer as he could muster. He patted the side of the bed. "Come and let's reminisce on happy times."

Adelle slipped out quietly to give the family their privacy.

CHAPTER 37

Oskholm, Firdafylke, two days later

Though the solstice had come, and with it entire cycles of daylight, Sweyn felt very much in the dark as he and Edan rode into Oskholm. He didn't know how his father was doing or if the guards of the enemy town would kill them on sight. To ensure they didn't, he and Edan had removed their swords, tunics, saddles, and even their boots in an obvious demonstration they were hiding no weapons. They rode up to the village gates in nothing but their trousers. No Norse warrior would dare disgrace himself by killing an unarmed man—in theory.

Sweyn carried a birch branch with a white flag tied to it in one hand and a fist full of flowers in the other. It was ridiculous, and not the gift he had decided upon but at the last minute he was overcome with sentiment and hoped a bouquet of wildflowers would make an appropriate peace offering. Observing the curious expressions he garnered from the guards at their posts and the snickers from nearby townspeople, he doubted the wisdom of his impulse.

"Halt!" demanded a burly warrior with dusty-brown hair bound in a tail and arms as thick as cordwood. "What are you doing here?"

"Who is it, Brandt?" asked a second warrior holding a spear and shield, who narrowed suspicious brows at Sweyn.

"Jarl Niklaus's son—again," Brandt growled. "Here to surrender?"

"As a matter of fact, yes, but only to Jarl Karyna," he declared with as much dignity as he could barefooted, clinging to a bunch of posies.

The second warrior laughed while Brandt rolled his eyes with a groan. "Your people have already done enough damage. Why shouldn't I kill you first and ask questions later?"

Sweyn shrugged, displaying more confidence than he felt. "Oh, I don't know—because you don't wish to incur your new jarl's wrath? I know from experience that she can exercise a fierce temper."

"How do we know this isn't a trap?" a tall gate guard added with a scowl.

Edan answered amiably, "Because if it was a trap, we would have worn shoes." His response garnered laughs from them all.

"Very well, you may consult with Jarl Karyna," Brandt relented, "if she agrees to meet with you."

Sweyn and Edan dismounted their ponies and allowed the two warriors to escort them to the jarl's longhouse. His heart lurched when he spied Karyna sitting at a long table across the room, engaged in a serious discussion with two important-looking men in civilian attire. When she stopped and glanced up at him, his breath caught. In her elegant green gown, her soft, medium-brown silky strands arranged in various braids held in place by a gold circlet, and her expression of effortless authority, she had never looked more beautiful.

At once, Sweyn grew self-conscious about his appearance. He may have had a chiseled chest and a well-maintained beard, but surrendering nearly naked must have appeared ridiculous to her. And the clutch of wildflowers, to boot.

Then he detected a change in expression, a tender longing that drew him in and strengthened his soul with hope.

"If you would excuse me," Karyna said to the men in her conference. "I need to receive Sweyn Niklausson and hear his proposal."

The fellows, who might have been merchants, left the table, giving Sweyn and Edan a wide berth. Brandt led them in, and Karyna extended her arm toward the bench across from her.

"I must stay as a witness to these proceedings," Brandt insisted as they took their seats.

"Sweyn." Her voice sounded formal on the exterior, while he sensed the vulnerability beneath its veneer.

"First, I was so saddened to hear of your father's death. It came as a grave blow to both my father and I as we had been good neighbors before all this started." Unsure what to do with the flowers, he laid them on the table between them.

"I appreciate your condolences," she responded. "But about all this preposterous war, I assume you have something relevant to share?"

Sweyn took a deep breath, propped the stick bearing the white flag against the table, and relayed the complete story. Karyna listened, asking the occasional question, and, by the time he was done, even Brandt had been convinced he told the truth.

"My father lies recovering from a grave wound, but he requests a meeting with King Tortryggr to present gifts and a formal apology when he has recovered," Sweyn went on. "For now, the armies of Raumsdal will no longer engage in any hostilities with your people. Karyna, we didn't know we were being manipulated, and I ..." Sweyn leaned on his elbows with his head bowed. "I feel ..." Daring another glance at her, he summoned all his personal fortitude. "How can I make this right?"

"Your father is now king of Raumsdal," she answered pleasantly. "I'm sure we can forge a solution." Raising her chin and her voice, Karyna ordered the hall, "Leave us."

"But Jarl—" Brandt protested.

Karyna held up a hand and stared him down. "Leave us."

The Firdafylke warriors, servants, and Edan all exited the room, leaving the two of them alone.

Sweyn didn't know how to express himself, not with her anyway. It wasn't like talking to anyone else. He got befuddled, and words came out wrong. This was his one chance, and he couldn't blow it. From inside his trousers, Sweyn produced a uniquely-crafted silver and ivory hairpin formed in the shape of a dragon with pearl eyes and garnet scales and laid it on the table.

Karyna's eyes rounded, and her jaw dropped. She snatched it up and scrutinized it. "This is mine! I lost it years ago. Wherever did you find it?" A hint of glee shone through the astonishment in her voice.

"I think I was twelve," he answered shyly. "We were here for some feast or other, and you had been so sassy and embarrassed me in front of my brothers. They wouldn't stop laughing at me, so I determined to get back at you. I took it when you weren't looking. I knew it was wrong," he admitted. "There's nothing worse than stealing something and keeping it a secret, and I had decided to give it back to you before we left."

She cocked her head at him in curiosity as she rubbed the fine piece of jewelry between slender fingers. "Why didn't you?"

Catching her gaze, he replied, "Because I wanted something to remember you by. Even then, I liked you, thought you were the apple of Freya's eye and a challenge. I had it with me the other times we came to Oskholm but couldn't quite bring myself to part with it."

Karyna stiffened and drew in a deep breath. "But now you can part with it because I no longer affect you the same way. You are the prince of Raumsdal, and we no longer find ourselves on equal footing."

"On the contrary." Sweyn extended his upturned palm across the table and Karyna peered at it. "As prince of Raumsdal, I was hoping for more than a stolen token."

"Oh, Sweyn." Karyna sighed, laid down the hairpin, and made her way around the table to sit beside him. Then she took the hand he offered. "Things are complicated now."

"I suspected you may not want to give up your jarldom," he admitted in a resigned tone. His gaze shifted to their joined hands. This felt so right; why did it never work out in his favor? "And you deserve it. Father called you a formidable woman, and he was right. You are smart and fierce yet compassionate and fun. I heard you once chased off a bear with nothing but a broom, and I knew ..."

Sweyn shook his head and boldly raised his gaze to meet hers. "Couldn't we give it a try, at least, you and me? There could be no better way to secure peace between our kingdoms than with a marriage."

Karyna snatched her hand from his with a resentful scowl and leaped to her feet. "Do you think I'm a bargaining tool in your king's diplomatic scheme?"

"No, no!" Sweyn jumped up to follow her angry pacing. "He doesn't even know I was planning to ask you this. I just thought—"

"You thought *what?*" She threw her hands in the air. "That the poor little feminine jarl who's in over her head, bereaved at the loss of her father, weary of war, would just give herself into your hands to become your wife because it might secure a peace treaty? And I thought you were different!"

"Karyna, I *am* different."

She waved a dismissive hand at him, turned her back, and stormed away. Before leaving the hall, she spun to face him, hurt and frustration tearing through the fury. "You don't care about me, you never did. You just want what you can't have."

"That's not true!" Sweyn was losing her, and he knew it. He had to completely bare his soul along with his chest or all the humiliation was for nothing. "I love you, Karyna. Call me a fool, laugh in my face, I don't care. My father could be joining yours anytime now, so what else have I to lose? I love you, and that's the truth of the matter."

She stopped and stared at him, her features softening. "How can you know that? All put together, we've maybe spent two or three weeks of our lives in the same place at the same time."

"I know," he admitted, feeling foolish and deflated. "It's just that somehow you got lodged in my brain and in my heart. I've looked at other women, tried to feel the same way, but every time my wheels spun back around to you. It's easy to find women who want me, and that's not bragging," he added softly. "You're the only one I've found who is my match. Tell me you never thought of me, and I'll leave you alone forever."

Slowly, she glided in his direction, a bit like a butterfly that hadn't made up its mind. "Maybe I thought about you," she said. "Maybe I liked you too." As she neared him, she admitted with regret, "I suspect I won't be allowed to remain jarl of Oskholm very long. King Tortryggr will call a Thing, and the men will vote. I doubt they will choose to keep a woman in charge."

"Then they are a bunch of foolish men," Sweyn stated with certainty. "There is no one more capable than you."

When she was close enough for him to inhale her scent, to feel her breath on his face, Sweyn slid his hands to her trim waist. In turn, she latched her arms around his neck and gazed up at him with wonder twinkling across her eyes. "You love me?"

"I do. But you aren't so sure about me."

"I'm not convinced you are so sure about me," she replied in a teasing manner. "You may become irritated at me or regret being stuck with such an opinionated wife."

"Then I will sleep in the bed I made for myself," he quipped, feeling much relieved he hadn't made a total mess of his confession.

"Maybe we could start with dinner and work our way up to a discussion of marriage down the road, provided it doesn't become too bumpy," Karyna suggested as she pressed her body against his.

"I'm agreeable to your proposition, my lady." When Sweyn kissed her, she didn't swoon or lean into him with delicate fingers that explored the hard-earned muscles of his torso. Instead she held her place, met the pressure of his lips with her own, neither giving nor taking ground or extra liberties. In that moment, he was sure of two things: he had met his equal, and if Karyna would have him, he would make her his wife.

CHAPTER 38

Skeggen, two days later

Sweyn figured Edan had endured enough of his constant chatter about Karyna all the way home, but he just couldn't resist one last story.

"Then, after the most amazing dinner she cooked herself, she challenged me to a game of Hnefatafl. You know that's how she won her jarldom, right?" Sweyn's grin stretched from ear to ear. It was as if he floated over the mountain and now soared aboard a magic ship with nothing but his energy propelling it.

"I think you mentioned that already."

"You're a good friend, Edan, and I listened to your stories about Gislaug," Sweyn reminded him. The sea was calm under a cloudless sky. The sun beat so hot on his face that he was sure his nose and cheeks would be as red as strawberries by the time they pulled up to the docks.

Sweyn had volunteered for Edan and himself to help row in hopes of better speed, but the oar was like a feather in his hands. "Of course, I couldn't refuse. If so, I would look scared of losing; yet, if I played and lost, I could claim I was too mesmerized by Karyna's beauty to focus on the game."

"Oh, please!" Edan groaned.

"We're approaching the pier," called the longboat's navigator from the bow. He waved to the fishers and dock workers. "Tell the king Sweyn has returned!" he hollered out.

Fishermen left their nets, workers set down their crates, and citizens from the town ran out and lined up to meet them.

Sweaty from rowing and sunbaked, Sweyn quickly ran his fingers through his hair and straightened his tunic to appear more presentable. He was eager to find out how his father was doing and tell him about the successful secession of hostilities. They would arrange a formal meeting between the kings once Niklaus was better.

They pulled in the oars, drifting to the helmsman's rudder, and the vessel glided up to the dock. A fellow threw a loop around a post near the bow, and another repeated the action at the stern. Sweyn hopped out with an expectant smile but, when he saw the looks on people's faces, his heart sank.

"All hail King Sweyn," a man called out.

The cry was echoed by all the men and women who gathered there. Sweyn dropped onto an overturned barrel, buried his face in his hands, and wept.

SWEYN MET his family with dry eyes and a spirit of leadership wrapped around him like a mantle, taking on the responsibility of guiding them and the entire kingdom. Adelle hugged him with the assurance everything possible had been done for Niklaus. He believed her. His mother cried on his shoulder while Njal and Trygve kept offering to do everything imaginable.

"Thank you, Horik," he said and clasped forearms with his uncle. "I only ask two things of you as jarl of Sæladalr."

"Which would be?" He granted Sweyn a speculative gaze.

"Don't let the place go to seed, and I need Tyrdis."

"Hey!" he stepped back with feigned insult. "I can be responsible … some of the time … and I want to keep Tyrdis. You know she'll wish to stay with Adelle and that little girl."

"Oh, I'm keeping Adelle right here in Skeggen," Sweyn answered with confident ease. "Her son is here training, and she's eager to be near him. You get to have Bjornolf, and besides." Sweyn shifted into a more personal intonation. "I need her more than you do. She's training Trygve, and she'll keep me grounded. Having true friends nearby is more important than ever now."

Horik sighed and nodded. "And what about Karyna?"

"She's planning a visit next week. She doesn't know about Father and the king thing, though."

With a snort and a pat on the shoulder, Horik said, "I'd love to be here to witness that, but sadly, I'll be back home running the farm. The funeral is tonight and then your ceremony. My brother was king for more than a day; few men in the world can say as much. He believed in you, Sweyn, and so do I."

THE FUNERAL and crowning were solemn, well-attended events, and, afterward, the crowd moved into the king's great hall—Sweyn's great hall, now—for the expected celebration. Mead poured, musicians played, people danced, skalds recited tales of the gods and heroes, and the aroma of pork roasting over the central firepit filled the air. Although Sweyn wanted to celebrate his father's life and this incredible promotion, he found producing a cheerful spirit difficult. *How am I supposed to do this alone? I'm not ready.*

After a time of milling about the great hall, having people he knew and those he didn't shake his hand, tell him how sorry they were for his loss and then congratulate him on his ascension, Sweyn had to get away and have some quiet to think. It was too much for one day—for one week, really. He was caught in a whirlwind and half wondered if he'd wake to find it had all been a dream.

Sweyn snuck out the back and found a bench under a tree near a little garden. There he sat to breathe the fresh air and contemplate life. A couple of birds occupying the tree seemed to be fussing at each other with their sharp chatter.

"My mama would have said they are an old married couple," Hallfrid said.

Surprised, Sweyn swung a glance over his shoulder at the girl who had snuck up on him. "Is that how old married people sound?"

"Sometimes," she answered. "You know what else she used to say?"

Sweyn shook his head, thinking how much luckier he was than this child. His mother was still with him to give guidance and affection, and he had his father for twenty-one years. Hallfrid was an orphan at what, ten? Twelve?

He patted the bench for her to sit beside him. "No. What did she say?"

She was still twiggy, all arms and legs, but she had nice, clean clothes, and her hair was combed and fixed with a shiny blue ribbon. He recalled how this chain of events began with her telling him she had a secret—no, when that rat bastard Garold tried to run her down in the street. His whole world had changed so much in such a short time. All the rulers in Raumsdal from that day were dead, he was king, and he stood a chance with Karyna.

Plopping down beside him, she declared, "Mama said that things always worked out the way they were supposed to in the end, so there wasn't a reason to worry. I guess I still worry sometimes because—you know—I'm just a little girl alone in a great big world, and, well, Mama died."

"Hey, you aren't alone." Sweyn draped an arm around her shoulders and gave them a slight squeeze. "You're with my family now, serving in the king's great hall, not his stable. If anyone dares lay an unwanted hand on you, just come tell me, and I'll cut it off. Then, when you're grown up, you will be free to do exactly as you desire, whether it's marrying a nice man, taking up a trade, or remaining in our household. The choice will be yours."

She beamed at him. "You saw me," she said, and batted her lashes. "You protected me, believed me, and welcomed me into your home. You're an insightful defender who practices hospitality, and that's why you were supposed to be king."

Sweyn smiled and slid his arm away, pondering such words from a child. "But my father was a great man. I hope I can fill his shoes."

Hallfrid hopped up laughing, and grinned at him. "Of course, you can, silly. You have big feet! I'm going to the yardhouse now."

"Which I didn't need to know," Sweyn answered humorously.

As he watched her cross the yard, he recalled something she had said when they first met. *"I wish you would be king one day. You see everyone—even me."* It struck him as uncanny she would wish for such a thing and, in little over a month, her wish was manifested. Did Hallfrid possess the gift of sight? Would she grow up to be a völva?

Thinking of that reminded him of what the ancient seer Revna had predicted to Niklaus. *"The man who should be king would be king, but he would not wish to pay the price."*

"Could she have been talking about me?" Sweyn absently said aloud, though no one was around to hear. *I suppose anyone who would become king would have to pay some price, but I indeed would happily return this crown to Gustav to prevent my father's death. What potential could the gods possibly see in me that Niklaus hadn't already achieved?*

He shook his head. Such reasoning was inconceivable. There had to be another explanation. Horik said his father had been gripping his ancestral sword when he took his last breath and he had died of a battle wound, even if it was days later. He was buried with honors in the grand mound of kings, but what did that mean for his afterlife? What did any of it mean?

When Hallfrid didn't exit the yardhouse, Sweyn's curiosity turned to concern. He walked over and knocked on the door. "Hallfrid. Are you ill?" No one answered. He pounded louder. "Hallfrid!" No reply. Peeking through a crack, Sweyn saw no one. In alarm, he threw open the door to find the odorous outbuilding empty.

Could I have missed her? I must have been so deep in thought, she walked right past me unnoticed.

Sweyn plodded around the nearly vacant yard in bewilderment, hearing music and voices from the merrymaking inside. Then he caught sight of a tall man walking away toward the gate. Gray hair flowed from beneath his hat, and he was wrapped in a long cloak, despite the warm temperature.

"Hey, you!" Sweyn called after him. "Did you see a little girl out here?"

Using a staff for balance, he kept walking as if he hadn't heard.

How rude to ignore me, Sweyn thought, and chased after the old man. "Excuse me," he called again. Two ravens swooped overhead, almost catching in Sweyn's hair. Then both they and the stranger disappeared around the corner of the longhouse. By the time Sweyn caught up, there was nothing to be seen—no gray-haired man, no birds, just two gate guards stationed fifty yards away.

This was too baffling, and Sweyn had to discover what was going on. He sped around to the front entrance of the great hall to see if the stranger or Hallfrid had gone inside. The festive atmosphere of the hall almost swept him off his feet as he peered around and through the crowd, seeking either the man or the child. Then he spied Revna sitting alone on a bench, knitting.

Rushing over, he blurted out, "Did you see an old man in a hat and cloak carrying a staff come in here?"

Eyes alive with mischief peered up at him from hollow sockets encased in wrinkles set beneath thin brows. "You've seen Gangari, the Wanderer," she answered. The corners of her ancient mouth curved upward. "Did he have his ravens with him?"

Sweyn's mouth dropped as he took on an astonished expression. "How did you know?"

Just then, one of the gate guards rushed in. "King Sweyn," he addressed with a sharp salute, striking his fist to his chest. "You need to see this."

Sweyn swore he heard the völva's cackle as he dashed out. At the entrance, two men dressed in Firdafylke colors and carrying a white flag held between them a third man with bound wrists.

"King Sweyn," one foreign soldier acknowledged with a bow. "We thought we would be meeting King Gustav and were unaware of recent events here. King Tortryggr sent us in hopes of ending the conflict that has plagued our kingdoms. We caught the man who murdered Prince Jarivald."

Stunned, Sweyn shook his head. "We discovered Gustav's subterfuge. There is no need to bring us a scapegoat. I have sent a proposal of peace to King Tortryggr by way of Jarl Karyna, which he should receive any day now. We have much for which to make amends, and I swear things will be different in the future. I intend to keep an open line of communication with your king and to never make assumptions or act aggressively without first exploring every diplomatic channel."

"Well." His expression brightened. "King Tortryggr will be most pleased to hear this. However, we still want this criminal to be punished and your kingdom to be satisfied with the process."

"I don't understand." Sweyn frowned and stared at the bound man.

"Tell him," the second Firdafylke warrior prodded.

"It was me," the bound man muttered bitterly. "I killed the prince, and I'd do it again." He glared up at Sweyn with a shark's eyes, void of remorse or humanity. He was a small man, certainly no match for Jarivald in a fair fight.

A sick feeling swirled in Sweyn's gut. "Why? How? Tell me every detail if you wish to avoid excruciating torture."

"The last time that rake was in Gimelfjord, he seduced Yrsa, enjoyed her company, then left her behind, spoiled. I wanted her—*me*! A prince can have any woman he desires, but I had very few choices. When I complained, he laughed at me, said I could challenge him in public if I dared."

"Are you testifying that Jarivald raped this woman Yrsa?"

The little man shuffled his feet, glancing down at them with a frown. "Not exactly." Returning a piercing look from his hollow eyes, he accused, "He persuaded her to want him."

"King Sweyn," the first Firdafylke soldier said. "Rognvald is well known and avoided in Gimelfjord because he imagines things. Yrsa was not his girlfriend as he pretends but a tavern wench who enjoys pleasures with many men. Jarivald committed no offense except in this fellow's twisted mind. Someone overheard him boasting when he was drunk earlier this week and turned him in to the king. To think—if we had found him sooner, this whole conflict could have been avoided. King Tortryggr sends his deepest apologies."

This couldn't be. Hallfrid saw Ivar kill Jarivald. The whole family had acted strangely, and everyone knew Gustav couldn't wait to seize that fertile plot of land from their neighbors. Then again, neither Ivar nor Kerstav ever admitted to it, even after their father was dead.

"Tell me how, when, and where you killed him," Sweyn demanded.

"Last winter, a half moon after the solstice," he related. "When it was still dark all the time. It was easy to sneak over the palisade walls and hide in the hay of the stables. I waited days for an opportunity, but I had to, you see. He couldn't be allowed to get away with it. Yrsa was so my woman. She only worked at that tavern because she needed lodging. She would look at me differently when she found out I had slain the mighty Jarivald. Everyone would respect me then, only I couldn't tell anyone without facing a noose."

"So you waited in the hay." Sweyn tried to get the confessor back on track.

"And one night—day—night, who knows? There he was, coming to get a horse. I jumped on him from above and stabbed, stabbed.!" The crazed man demonstrated, making stabbing motions with his tied hands. "But then, his little brother came in. I cut him once while he tried to get me off Jarivald. But I couldn't fight two of them, so I ran. Then I was scared. When I found out he was dead, I wanted to shout to the world that it was me! Little Rognvald slayed the mighty Jarivald, only I couldn't, because," he lowered his voice to a whisper. "I murdered him, and people don't praise you for that; they execute you. So, what was I to do? I couldn't use my victory to win Yrsa's affection or the admiration of my peers. Then everyone was angry and scared because of the war. I didn't know it would start a war."

Sweyn ran trembling fingers through his mane of blond hair. "Lock this man in a cell in the armory," he commanded to the guard who had gotten him from the hall. Looking at the Firdafylke soldiers, he said, "Tell King Tortryggr the war is over." Then Sweyn turned and walked away, troubled and confused in his spirit.

CHAPTER 39

Skeggen, a few days later

As soon as the side of the longboat bumped the dock, Svanhild bounded over the side. "Wait for me," Tyrdis called and climbed out after her. "This is an unfamiliar town filled with strangers. It is unsafe for you to wander about."

"I'm not wandering, Tyrdis," the girl sang back. "I'm dancing!"

In her bright, yellow dress, the little girl whirled about with her hands in the air and her face lifted into the sunshine. After a day of rain spent packing, the sun was pleasant, but Tyrdis worried about Svanhild meeting with misfortune while under her care.

"I order you to stand still," Tyrdis demanded. Svanhild's exuberance wilted into a sullen frown as she complied. "Just for a moment while I get our things unloaded and carried to wherever we'll be staying. Then you will be free to frolic." With a glance around at hooks, nets, harpoons, fish traps, and wooden vessels bobbing on the water along the narrow pier, she added, "Away from the dangers of this wharf."

Tyrdis, in a lightweight, blue tunic and brown trousers bound by a leather belt carrying her axe and seax, reached into the boat and grabbed the handle of one of four trunks they had brought. Now that she had valuable armor and Bruna had provided her with several sets of clothing, Tyrdis found she required a trunk to keep her belongings in. While more burdensome than carrying nothing but the clothes on her back, it filled

Tyrdis with a sense of pride in ownership. She hadn't ever had things before—maybe a drinking horn, blanket, and winter cloak, nothing more. Then there was a chest for Svanhild filled with toys and puzzles along with her clothes and the colorful blanket her Amma had woven for her and Adelle's trunk of personal belongings. The fourth was filled with healer supplies. Adelle had sent instructions with Horik as to everything she wished to be brought. Joren would take over running the hospice in Sæladalr, and Bruna stayed to marry Karl. She talked about helping him run the mead hall and said to tell Adelle she'd be up for a visit soon.

Sweyn wishes me to serve as a king's advisor? The notion seemed preposterous. What did Tyrdis know about running a kingdom? But she understood his desire to retain her as a tutor for Trygve and Braggi, should he change his mind about entering training. Horik also mentioned something about splitting forces between her and Njal and having each serve as first warrior for their divisions, but they could discuss it in person.

Mainly, Tyrdis couldn't wait to see Adelle again. She had even hugged a pillow at night, pretending it was her, another thing she'd never done before. It's like her finite world of black and white had been busted wide open, and she found herself off-balance in a wondrous land of colors and feelings and awakenings.

"Here, let me take that for you," offered a voice from behind. Someone dressed as a dockworker took the trunk from her.

"I can carry it," she answered, peering at a stranger.

"King Sweyn's orders," he stated. "You and the child are to report to the great hall, and we are to bring your things."

"You hear that, Svanhild?" Tyrdis took her by the hand and looked into brown eyes like her mother's. "King Sweyn wants us to join him in the great hall."

"This is so exciting!" she beamed with unbridled joy. "I'll bet it's even grander than Jarl Niklaus's hall. And just think—Sweyn is king! I can't believe it, can you? He's so nice. Do you think he'll turn mean now that he's king?"

Walking up the pathway to town, followed by bearers toting their chests, Tyrdis and Svanhild swung their joined hands. "Sweyn will not have much time to play anymore. He will have important matters to tend to," Tyrdis explained. "But I do not believe he could ever be mean."

When they arrived, Edan showed them inside. No sooner than he spied them, Sweyn hopped up from the table where he had been discussing something with a gothi, a merchant, and a landowner. Leaving the important men, he scooped Svanhild up in his arms for a hug.

"How's my honeybee?" He tickled her, making her squeal, and she kissed his cheeks before he set her down. "And Tyrdis."

She wasn't expecting to be hugged. It felt so strange, but Tyrdis decided to go with it and hug him back. "I am sorry to learn about your father. I respected him, as I respect you. I am here for you in whatever capacity you require."

He stepped back, keeping his hands on her upper arms as he gazed at her with relief in his expression. "Everything is strange and new."

"Indeed." She knew precisely how he felt.

"And you're king now," Svanhild announced in awe. "Tyrdis said you'll be busy doing important things, but you won't turn mean."

Sweyn stroked her face with a smile. "Tyrdis is right. Why don't you go play with Solfrig? She can show you all around our new longhouse."

Svanhild's face lit even brighter, and she raced across the hall to find Sweyn's little sister. Then he turned his attention back to Tyrdis. "Let me show you where you'll be staying."

She fell in to walk beside him while the important men sat waiting at the table for the new king's return. He guided her to the far end of the massive hall to a suite of private chambers. Sweyn pulled back a blue curtain to a cozy room with a small hearth, some hooks and shelves on the wall, and a double-sized bed with end tables. The room also sported an outside door.

"Sweyn, my own room?" She gazed at him in amazement.

"Well, not just your room," he answered. "Adelle has been staying here since she arrived, and I thought, well, she holds an important station, you hold an important station, and you need some privacy. Look." He crossed the room and opened the back door.

Peering out, Tyrdis watched Adelle directing a team of workers constructing a building. "I'm having them erect a new hospice here in the safety of the palisade. And see—only a few steps from this door. Adelle was delighted with the idea. Now she can closely monitor her patients without having to expose Svanhild to unpleasant diseases, and she can go back and forth as needed. I also like having her close by in case Mother or one of the children get sick."

"Sweyn, what a brilliant idea!" Tyrdis exclaimed. "I know Adelle is thrilled about this and being closer to her son. And I thank you so much for understanding our desire for privacy. This is all so considerate of you. I am ready to assume my duties, so I may repay your generosity."

"You rid Raumsdal of Garold," he stated flatly. "That is payment enough. I do have a question for you, though."

Tyrdis turned her attention away from Adelle and the construction to lock eyes with the young king.

"Do you believe the gods intervene in the affairs of men?" he asked with more urgency than mere curiosity. "I mean, we've all heard stories of Odin taking on the guise of a person or animal and coming down to observe. The stories of the wanderer who rewards those who show him hospitality and punishes those who don't? Could there be any truth to these tales? People pray to the gods, and it seems random whether they are answered or not. Please tell me what you think."

"Sweyn, I'm just a simple warrior," she replied in humility. "What I think is irrelevant."

"No, Tyrdis," he corrected. "It isn't. In your simplicity is hidden wisdom. I bid you to share your thoughts with me."

First Adelle, now Sweyn. How could anything I conceive in my consciousness matter? But she nodded. He was her king, after all, and her friend. "He's Odin. He can do whatever he wishes, I suppose. I believe that whether any gods are watching or not, whether or not they meddle in human affairs, we should strive to live up to our own ideals of honor, strength, courage, and compassion. And, if we fail, we take responsibility for our mistakes and continue to mold ourselves into the heroes we wish to become. We defend the weak and helpless, we direct the foolish and confused, we heal the sick and broken-hearted, we build up what has been torn down, we live in harmony with the sea, the forests, and the mountains, and we stand for what is true. If the gods notice, well and good; if they do not, we can still take pride in ourselves. But if Odin or Eir or any god or goddess intervened to save my life or put you on the throne, I don't think we should let them down by slacking off now."

Sweyn smiled and kissed her forehead before leaving the room. Then he threw over his shoulder, "Tonight is a meeting with all my advisors for you to attend, and tomorrow you may start your training lessons. Oh, and Karyna is coming to visit soon; please allow Adelle to dress you appropriately."

Tyrdis smirked, shook her head, and returned to gazing out the open door at Adelle. She was so animated, enjoying every minute of the new project. Seeing her like this swelled Tyrdis's heart with immeasurable joy. She envisioned more bathing rituals, more flirtations, and more nights spent enjoying passionate pleasures in each other's arms. Yes, this new life certainly agreed with her. Come to think of it, gods or no gods, getting run through with that spear was the best thing ever to happen to Tyrdis. If that wasn't irony, nothing ever was.

EPILOGUE

Skeggen, Raumsdal, 653, ten years later

"Quit running around this hall like a wolf chasing a hare this instant!" Sweyn bellowed to his two rambunctious children.

Tyrdis glanced up from the game of Hnefatafl she and Trygve were engaged in.

"We are hosting Trygve's wedding tomorrow, and I can't have you breaking anything," Sweyn continued. "And where is your mother?"

"Helping Adelle in the hospice," answered Elena, the older of the two youngsters.

"Let's go play chase outside," Sweyn's little boy Niklaus suggested. With big grins, the two tow-headed children raced out the back.

Sweyn shook his head and crossed to Tyrdis's game table. "Shouldn't you be doing something?" he asked Trygve.

"I am doing something," he answered. "I'm practicing strategy with our most cunning warrior. Mayhap I'll learn something I can use in my impending marriage."

"Impending?" Sweyn laughed. "You say that like you're doomed."

Trygve laughed and moved a piece on the board. "If I end up with unruly children and a bossy wife, then I'm doomed."

"They are not unruly," Sweyn corrected in a robust voice. "They're spirited. And Karyna isn't bossy—she excels at leadership, among many other things."

"It's all in one's perception," Tyrdis commented as she moved her next piece. "You can view a characteristic as a virtue or a vice depending on your own mindset. I suggest you practice seeing your bride as the ultimate woman to which no other could compare. It will make your life easier."

"Oh, so is that how you do it?" Trygve asked, frowning as she captured his pawn.

"I need not trouble myself with perceptions and pivoting points of view," Tyrdis answered matter-of-factly. "My woman *is* the pinnacle. Your move."

Sweyn laughed and turned to walk away when the door flew open and an excited Braggi burst in. He had definitely not followed in his older brothers' warrior footsteps, as he sported the colorful costume and felt hat of a musician. "You'll never guess who's here!"

Tyrdis and Sweyn shrugged at the same time. The now twenty-year-old animated, twiggy entertainer bounded over, sprouting enthusiasm on his face like whiskers. "Sigrid and Elyn, the famous shieldmaidens from Svithjod—well, it's Sogn now, but anyway."

"How do you know it's them?" Sweyn asked.

"They arrived in a magnificent dragonhead ship with a little girl of about eight," he described. "The flame-red hair, powerful curves, and spectacular blue and silver lamellar armor—she has to be Elyn. And the blonde one exuded such a powerful presence with her silver breastplate and shining sword. And they're coming this way!"

The young man's enthusiasm was contagious, and Tyrdis was compelled to meet them. "I'm going to get Adelle," she said, rising from the table.

"Tell Karyna to come too, will you?" Sweyn called after her as she raced out.

Adelle's hospice was impressive, ornamented with striking carvings and protective runes. Tyrdis often sat on the bench under the apple tree and admired it, studying the detail work of dozens of artisans, but not today.

"Adelle, Karyna, come quick!" she called. They glanced up from an iron kettle over the fire where they were brewing some concoction. The two had recently taken to experimenting to find better or more long-lasting cures for various ailments.

"What is it?" Adelle asked as she blinked at Tyrdis.

"Sigrid and Elyn have brought their daughter here to visit." The words shot forth as rapidly as her excited heartbeat. "They must be headed north on a grand adventure."

"Really?" Karyna set down the bottle and jar she held, and the two healers exchanged a glance before turning back to Tyrdis.

"Well, let's go meet them," Adelle suggested.

"Where's Svanhild?" Tyrdis inquired as she hurried them along to the great hall.

"I think she and Solfrig are attending their dancing lessons," Karyna said. "They want to impress all the young men at the wedding tomorrow."

It was hard to imagine little Svanhild was already a young woman who flirted with men and was even old enough to marry one if she chose to. It seemed like only yesterday when they were performing puppet shows, picking berries, and playing tops. Lately, Svanhild had been wistfully waxing poetic about Braggi—how beautifully he played the lute and lyre, what a resonating singing voice, what a fabulous dancer.

Tyrdis didn't have the heart to tell her he spent most of his time gazing at the blacksmith's bulging muscles. It could work out, she supposed, if Svanhild really loved him and was open-minded. Society was tolerant of threesomes and women in same-sex relationships, while men engaging in such relations faced harsh ridicule and vile rejection. Braggi was in a tough situation, being the king's brother, and would have to have a wife unless he joined a traveling band of performers. She just wanted Svanhild to be happy.

Tyrdis opened the door and ushered the other two women through. By the time they arrived in the great hall, the legendary shieldmaidens and their adopted daughter Ingrid were being greeted by Sweyn, Braggi, and half the town's population.

"Oh, and my wife, Queen Karyna," Sweyn said, motioning toward her.

"So pleased to meet you." Karyna shook their hands.

"Likewise," Sigrid responded.

"Mamas, do you think I might get to be queen one day?" Ingrid asked. She rather resembled Karyna with her honey hair and brown eyes.

"Anything is possible," Elyn replied with a sweet smile.

"All right, then. Queen Karyna, they are going to tell stories of battles and adventures, but I want you to tell me all about being queen," she requested. "Would you be so kind?"

Karyna let out a laugh and held out a hand to Ingrid. "I could do that, but you must promise to share at least one story. Queens like adventures too." She led the child to a cushioned bench in front of the loom where she had been creating a tapestry.

"And these are our esteemed grædari, Adelle, and my advisor, instructor, and occasional first warrior, Tyrdis, the shieldmaiden."

"Adelle, Tyrdis," Sigrid greeted, then shot a wink at Elyn.

"I suspect we'll have a lot to talk about this afternoon," Elyn proposed.

"Here, come and take seats at my table," Sweyn offered. "You will be our guests for dinner."

"I'm getting married tomorrow," Trygve announced. "Can you stay for the wedding?"

"I love weddings!" Sigrid exclaimed. "And for it to happen to such a fine young man." She took her seat and shook her head. "Unfortunately, we must be on our way after a brief respite."

"We are taking Ingrid on her first voyage of exploration," Elyn picked up. "We're headed north to see the white bears, whales, and glaciers."

"Our first stop was to show her the cave where we met." Sigrid's face warmed toward Elyn, and her blue eyes sparkled with delight. "Anyway, we must stick to our schedule. We just wished to stop by and meet King Sweyn and you wonderful neighbors."

"The skalds say you wrestled a bear, rode on a whale, and skated on a glacier," Sweyn commented, "as well as winning many battles. And Elyn, they say you stopped a war and joined two feuding kingdoms into one."

Elyn's blush matched the hue of her hair. "It was a joint effort. But I've heard a tale that your shieldmaiden, Tyrdis, was slain in battle, and the magic touch of your healer, Adelle, brought her back to life."

"An exaggeration," Tyrdis responded. Then, with an amorous glance at Adelle, she added, "However, she did bring me to life, perhaps for the first time."

Adelle's eyes sparkled at her with deep-set joy. She reached over and laid her hand atop Tyrdis's, unashamed to let all know they were connected.

"Sigrid, did you really sail to the green isle and battle men in skirts who bellowed loud noises from their strange instruments?" Trygve asked. "Tell us your tales and we'll treat you to a feast."

"Well." Sigrid leaned back in her chair, shook her long, blonde hair, appearing completely relaxed in her own skin, and held up her empty horn. "That's an invitation I can accept."

* * *

THAT NIGHT, Adelle lay bare with Tyrdis between sleek silk sheets. Svanhild had moved out of their room into one shared by several young women of the house. She was probably out throwing a party for Trygve's bride anyway. It wouldn't be long before she became a bride herself. Runar had married last year and had a baby on the way. Everyone grew up.

She slid a foot along Tyrdis's while her fingers danced lightly across her skin. "Do you ever wish we could hold a marriage ceremony? I know it hasn't ever been done. Even Sigrid and Elyn never had a wedding. I suppose it's silly of me," she added. "Everyone knows we're together anyway and no one objects."

"But we are already wed in our eyes and those of the gods," Tyrdis responded. "Don't you remember?"

Adelle propped herself up on an elbow and peered down at Tyrdis in confusion. "We did?"

"Yes. You asked, 'Do you wish to wait for me?' and I replied, 'On my oath.' Then you told me you loved me, and I declared my love. You invited me in, saying, 'You have a home with Svanhild and me if you want it.' Then I vowed, 'Wherever you go, I will go. Whomever you serve, I will serve.' There may have been no witnesses, no ritual, no bracelets or rings, but it was the same principle. And in my heart, we have been joined ever since."

Gazing into those remarkable sea-foam eyes, Adelle was lost in love, and it was love that found her there. Once she wouldn't have looked twice at a warrior, but this one saved her little girl and stole her heart. Upon honest reflection, Adelle had never been happier.

She brushed her fingers up to caress Tyrdis's face. "You're right. I'll never forget that moment. It was the most vital turning point of my life."

"Before you, I didn't know life was a series of spectacular moments padded with some unremarkable ones in between. I still believe in duty and honor, only now I comprehend what makes them essential—so that at the end of the day I can lie here with you in my arms, confident that you are safe and happy, and all is well."

"I am so very happy," Adelle purred, shifting a knee between Tyrdis's thighs. "How about I demonstrate just how happy?"

Tyrdis's lips curved in a delirious smile. "That would be acceptable."

Adelle captured her mouth, her hands claiming flesh, and her spirits soaring. She may have never sailed to faraway lands or seen extraordinary sights, but this—loving and being loved by this incredible woman—was the grand adventure of her life. She intended to pursue it for many years to come.

MORE BOOKS BY EDALE LANE

My Book

Daunting Dilemmas: The Wellington Mysteries, Vol. 3

My Book

Atlantis, Land of Dreams

My Book

Heart of Sherwood

My Book

Viking Quest

My Book

Tales from Norvegr

Sigrid and Elyn: A Tale from Norvegr

My Book

Legacy of the Valiant: A Tale from Norvegr

My Book

War and Solace: A Tale from Norvegr

My Book

Walks with Spirits

My Book

The Night Flyer Series

Merchants of Milan, book one

My Book

Secrets of Milan, book two

My Book

Chaos in Milan, book three

My Book

Missing in Milan, book four

My Book

Shadows over Milan, book five

My Book

Visit My Website:

https://www.authoredalelane.com

Follow me on Goodreads (Don't forget to leave a quick review!)

https://www.goodreads.com/author/show/15264354.Edale_Lane

Follow me on BookBub:

https://www.bookbub.com/profile/edale-lane

Newsletter sign-up link:

https://bit.ly/3qkGn95

ABOUT THE AUTHOR

Edale Lane is an Amazon Best-selling author and winner of Rainbow, Lesfic Bard, and Imaginarium Awards. Her sapphic historical fiction and mystery stories feature women leading the action and entice readers with likeable characters, engaging storytelling, and vivid world-creation.

Lane (whose legal name is Melodie Romeo) holds a bachelor's degree in Music Education, a master's in history, and taught school for 24 years before embarking on an adventure driving an 18-wheeler over-the-road. She is a mother of two, Grammy of three, and doggy mom to Australian Shepherds. A native of Vicksburg, MS, Lane now lives her dream of being a full-time author in beautiful Chilliwack, BC with her long-time life-partner.

Enjoy free e-books and other promotional offerings while staying up to date with what Edale Lane is writing next when you sign up for her newsletter. https://bit.ly/3qkGn95

Made in the USA
Monee, IL
16 November 2024

70313205R00162